Dear Reader,

It's nice to revisit these older titles again in the
Brides To Be collection. The Australian was a lot of fun
to do, and I owe a debt of thanks to a lady named Betty
from Queensland who sent me so much information
about her beautiful country—and who continues to
write to me to this day. She is a wonderful friend. Also,
I think of Australia and immediately think of my friend
Margaret Way, one of the best authors I know! This book
brings back pleasant memories of those acquaintances,
and of John and Priscilla, who had a turbulent road to
marriage.

Heart of Ice is still one of my very favorite books. I have
been all over Wyoming, and I love the country and its
history. Egan and Katriane were textbook examples of
antagonism concealing passionate attraction, and I love
the scene where he carries her off the airplane and back
to the ranch. If you see a trace of Beauty and the Beast in
this one, you're not too far off. He was an ugly man, but
he had redeeming traits—finally realizing that the heroine
was pure gold was his best one!

I hope you enjoy Brides To Be, and as always, thank you
for your letters and e-mails!

Love,

Diana Palmer

DIANA PALMER

Brides To Be

Silhouette® Books

Published by Silhouette Books
America's Publisher of Contemporary Romance

SILHOUETTE BOOKS

BRIDES TO BE

Copyright © 2002 by Harlequin Books S.A.

ISBN 0-373-48463-1

The publisher acknowledges the copyright holder of the individual works as follows:

THE AUSTRALIAN
Copyright © 1985 by Diana Palmer

HEART OF ICE
Copyright ©1984 by Diana Palmer

This edition published by arrangement with Harlequin Books S.A.

® and TM are trademarks of Harlequin Books S.A., used under license. Trademarks indicated with ® are registered in the United States Patent and Trademark Office, the Canadian Trade Marks Office and in other countries.

Visit Silhouette at www.eHarlequin.com

Printed in U.S.A.

CONTENTS

‡ Soldiers of Fortune
* Most Wanted Series
† Long, Tall Texans

THE AUSTRALIAN

To Ruth in Sydney, Australia

Chapter 1

The airport at Brisbane was crowded, just as Priscilla Johnson had expected. She'd left Australia a college girl, but her college days were now over. With graduation had come the slow, sad process of severing friendships in Honolulu and leaving Aunt Margaret's house, where she'd lived for five years. Now the future held a teaching career in Providence, a small town northwest of Brisbane across the rain forests of Queensland's Great Dividing Range.

She looked around excitedly for her father and mother, and smiled when she remembered how happy they'd been about her plans to teach in Australia. It had been touch and go, that decision. If Ronald George hadn't been coming here to teach himself, if he hadn't prodded her...

She shifted from one navy pump-clad foot to the other. Her blonde hair curled in short wisps around her delicate oval face with its wide green eyes and creamy complexion. Those eyes were quiet and confident and just a little mischievous even now as she approached her twenty-fourth birthday. She walked with a fluid, easy grace, a result of the charm school classes her aunt Margaret had paid for. And in her white linen suit and powder blue blouse and navy accessories, she was a far cry form the teenager who'd left Australia so reluctantly five years ago to go away to college in Hawaii.

Priscilla shivered a little. Here in Australia it was spring in late September, not autumn as it had been in Hawaii. Her seasons, like her senses, were turned upside down. She'd had only two years in Queensland, after all, before college began. Her parents had left their native Alabama after Adam Johnson had applied and been accepted for a teaching position in Providence. He'd liked the idea of working in a small school mainly populated by children from three large cattle and sheep stations in the fairly remote area. Renée, Priscilla's mother, had been equally enthusiastic about the move. Neither of them had close family anymore: there were no other people to consider. All three of them had an adventurous streak. So they'd packed up and moved to Australia. And so far none of them had regretted it. Except perhaps Priscilla.

She wondered how it would be to see him again. Inevitably she would. Providence and the surrounding country were sparsely inhabited, and everyone met sooner or later in the small town to buy supplies or go to church or just socialize. Her thin brows drew together in a worried frown. It had been five years.

She was a different woman now. Besides, Ronald would be settling in soon, and she'd have someone to keep her mind off Jonathan Sterling.

John. It was impossible not to remember. Her green eyes grew hard, and she clutched her purse and carry-on bag until her knuckles went white. Her memory hadn't dulled. Neither had the pain.

She was tired. It had been a long flight, and despite the fact that most of her luggage had already been shipped over and she was only carrying a small bag, she wished her parents would appear. She wanted to get back to the small cottage where they lived, on the fringe of the mammoth cattle and sheep station known as the Sterling Run.

Her eyes wandered quickly around the crowded terminal, but before they could sweep past the front entrance, she saw a broad-shouldered man standing a full head above the crowd of travelers. Her heart slammed up against her throat, and she began to tremble. Perhaps she was mistaken! But no, his hair was light brown with bleached blond streaks all through it, thick and slightly shaggy in back, and straight. He was wearing an old tweed jacket with gray slacks and dingo boots, but even so he drew women's eyes as he strode through the crowd.

His pale blue eyes swept the travelers, and he scowled. His dimpled chin jutted pugnaciously; his firm mouth was set in a thin line. There were new wrinkles in that strong craggy face. Her eyes searched him like hands, looking for breaks.

He hadn't recognized her yet. Of course not, she reminded herself. She'd left here a long-legged gangly teenager with waist-length blonde hair and ill-fitting clothing. Now she was much more poised, a sophisticated woman with confident carriage and designer clothing. No, she thought bitterly, he wouldn't recognize her.

She picked up her carryall and went toward him gracefully. He glanced at her with faint appreciation before his eyes took up their search of the crowd again. It wasn't until she stopped just in front of him that he looked at her once more, and his eyebrows shot together with the shock of recognition that flared in his pale eyes.

"Priss?" he asked uncertainly, his eyes punctuating his astonishment as they ran up and down her slender body.

"Yes, it's me," she said with a cool smile. "How are you, John?"

He didn't reply. If anything, he grew colder as he registered the new poise about her.

"I'm waiting for my parents," she continued. "Have you seen them?"

"I've come to fetch you on their behalf," he said coldly, in the familiar Australian drawl that she remembered so well. He towered over her, big and broad and sexy as he pulled a cigarette from his pocket and lit it, while his eyes followed the lift of her eyebrows. "They had to attend some sort of luncheon in Providence."

She shifted her weight slightly, hoping her parents hadn't arranged this whole thing out of misguided affection. "Oh."

"You don't have to spell it out," he said on a cold

laugn. "I'm no more anxious for your company than you are for mine, I assure you. But I could hardly refuse when I was asked. And I did have to be in town today."

"I can always ride in the trunk, if you like," she returned with an arctic smile.

He didn't even bother to reply. He picked up her carryall and turned, starting toward the front of the terminal and leaving her to follow or not as she chose.

She had to practically run to keep up with him, and that made her angry. "Still the master of the situation, I see," she threw at him. "You haven't changed at all!"

He didn't turn his head or break stride. His face only grew harder. "Well, you have," he replied. He glanced sideways, and there were angry glints in his eyes. "I didn't recognize you."

Once a remark like that would have devastated her. But over the bitter years she'd learned control. She'd learned to hide her heart. So she only smiled carelessly. "It's been five years, after all, John," she reminded him, and had to bite her tongue to keep from asking if he liked the change.

"That suit must have cost a mint," he remarked.

She laughed up at him. "It did. Surely you didn't expect a ragged urchin, John?" she chided. Her eyes wandered over his own garb. "Odd, I remember you as being more immaculate."

His eyes darkened dangerously. "I'm a working man."

Her nose wrinkled. "Yes, I remember," she said. "Sheep and cattle and dust."

"There was a time when you didn't mind," he reminded her and abruptly turned out of the terminal, his voice sharper than she ever remembered hearing it.

Yes, she thought, there had been a time when she wouldn't have minded if he was caked in dust or covered with bits of wool. Her eyes closed for an instant on a wave of pain and humiliation and grief that almost buckled her knees. But she had to be strong. She had to remember more than just the beginning. She had to remember the end.

Her head lifted, and her own eyes darkened. That would do it, she told herself. Remembering the end would do it every time.

"How's the college boy?" he queried as he unlocked the door of his late-model white Ford and put her inside.

"Ronald George, you mean?" she asked.

He went around and got in himself and stretched his long powerful legs under the dash as he started the car. "Yes, Ronald George," he replied, making an insult of the name.

"He'll be here Monday," she told him, delivering the blow with cold satisfaction.

His eyes narrowed on her face. "What?"

"He's going to teach with Dad and me in Providence," she said. "He's looking forward to the experience of small-town life."

"Why here?" he asked narrowly.

"Why not?" she said flippantly and smiled at him. "Ronald and I have a special relationship." Which was true. They were the very best of friends.

His eyes swept over her, and he turned back to ease the car out of the terminal parking lot with a low humorless laugh. "Well, I'm not all that surprised," he said. "You were ripe for an affair when you left Australia."

She flushed, turning her head out the window. She didn't like remembering how he knew that. "How's your mother?" she asked.

"She's doing very well, thanks," he replied after a minute. He put out his finished cigarette and lit another as they drove through Brisbane. "She tells me she loves California."

"California?" she asked. "Isn't she living with you anymore? I know she had a sister in California, but..."

"She lives with her sister now."

He didn't offer more conversation, so she busied herself staring around at the landscape. Brisbane seemed as foreign as it had that first day when she'd come here with her parents from Alabama. She sighed, smiling at the tall palms and golden wattle and royal poinciana trees towering over the subtropical plants that reminded her of Hawaii. Brisbane was a city of almost a million people, with gardens and parks, museums and galleries. With the Gold Coast and the Great Barrier Reef nearby, it drew constant hordes of tourists. It was a city that Priss often had wished she'd had time to tour.

She would have loved to see Early Lane, which recreated a pioneer town—including an aboriginal dwelling called a *gunyah*. John Sterling had two aboriginal stockmen, named Big Ben and Little Ben, because they were father and son. Big Ben had tried unsuccessfully for days to try to teach Priss how to throw a boomerang. She smiled a little ruefully. Another place she had always wanted to see was New Farm Park, on the Brisbane River east of the city. Over 12,000 rose bushes were in wild bloom there from September through November, and the scent and color were reputed to be breathtaking. If she'd been with her parents, she would have asked them to drive there, even though it was out of the way. But she couldn't ask John.

He headed out of Brisbane, and she settled back in her seat, watching the countryside change. Outside the city, in the Great Dividing Range, was tropical rain forest. She could see copious orchids and scores of lorikeets and parakeets and other tropical birds flying from tree to tree. There were pythons in that forbidding glory, as well as several varieties of venomous snakes, and she shuddered at the thought of the early pioneers who had had to cut away that undergrowth in order to found the first big sheep and cattle stations. It must have taken a hardy breed. Men like John's grandfather, who'd founded the Sterling Run.

She glanced at the hard lines of his craggy broad face, and her eyes lingered helplessly on his wide chiseled mouth before she could drag them back to the window. That hard expert mouth had taught hers every single thing it knew about kissing…

She moved restlessly in the seat as the car wound over the gap in the range and they began descending again. In the distance were rolling grasslands that spread out to the horizon, to the great outback in the western part of the state, which was called the Channel Country. John had cousins out there, she knew.

Southwest of Brisbane were the Darling Downs, the richest agricultural land in Queensland. But northwest were some of the largest cattle stations in Australia, and that was where Providence sat, along a river that provided irrigation for its three sheep and cattle stations. One of those was the Sterling Run.

Priss wanted to ask why John was driving a Ford. It occurred to her that he'd had a silver Mercedes when she'd left Australia. He'd driven the Mercedes when he was going to town, and a Land-Rover on the station. But then, she also wondered about his clothing. John had always worn a suit to town, and it had usually been an expensive one. She laughed bitterly to herself. Probably he didn't feel he needed to waste his time dressing up for her. Her eyes closed. If she'd been Janie Weeks, no doubt he'd have been dressed to the back teeth. She wondered whatever had happened to seductive Janie, and why John hadn't married her. Priss knew her mother would have told her if he had.

"Turn on the radio, if you like," he said shortly.

"No, thanks," she replied. "I don't mind peace and quiet. After Monday, I'll probably never know what it is again."

He glanced at her through a cloud of cigarette smoke, his blue eyes searching.

"Why is it that you're here before summer?" he asked curiously. "The new term won't start until after vacation."

"One of the school staff had to have surgery. I'll be filling in until vacation time," she returned. "Ronald is going to work as a supply teacher, too, until we both have full-time positions next year.''

He didn't reply, but he looked unapproachable. She wondered at the change in him. The John Sterling she used to know had been an easygoing, humorous man with twinkling eyes and a ready smile. What a difference there was now!

''Dad said something about Randy being at the station now; he and Latrice,'' she murmured, mentioning John's brother. ''Are the twins with them?''

''Yes, Gerry and Bobby,'' he replied. ''You'll be teaching them.''

''How nice.''

He looked sideways and laughed shortly. ''You haven't been introduced yet,'' he said enigmatically.

''What happened to Randy's own station in New South Wales?'' she continued.

''That's his business,'' he said carelessly.

She flushed. It was mortifying to be told to mind her own affairs, and she resented his whole manner. ''Excuse me,'' she replied coldly. ''I'll keep my sticky nose to myself.''

''Why did you come back?'' he asked, and there was a note in his voice that chilled her.

''Why don't you do what you just told me to and mind your own business?'' she challenged.

His head turned, and his eyes glittered at her. ''You'll never fit in here,'' he said, letting his gaze punctuate his words. ''You're too much the sophisticate now.''

''In your opinion,'' she returned with faint humor.

"Frankly, John, your opinion doesn't matter beans to me these days."

"That goes double for me," he told her.

So it was war, she thought. Good. This time she was armed, too. She ran a hand through her short hair. "Does it look like it'll be a dry year?" she asked, changing the subject.

"No. They're predicting a good bit of rain when the Wet comes. The past two years have been good to us."

"That's nice to know."

"Yes, there have been some lean times...look out!" He braked suddenly for a kangaroo. The tawny beast bounded right into the path of the car and stared at its occupants, with a tiny baby in its pouch. John had stopped only inches from it, cursing a blue streak, and the kangaroo simply blinked and then hopped off to the other side of the highway.

"I'd forgotten about the 'roos." Priss laughed, grateful that she'd been wearing her seat belt. "They're bad pedestrians."

"That one bloody near met its maker," he returned on a rough sigh. "Are you all right?" he asked with obvious reluctance.

"Of course."

He started off again, and Priss stretched lazily, unaware of his eyes watching the movement with an odd expression in their azure depths.

He seemed content to sit there smoking his cigarette, and Priss kept her own silence. She wondered at her composure. Several years ago riding alone in a car with John would have been tantamount to backing the winner in the Melbourne Cup race. Now she was so numb that only a trickle of excitement wound through her slender body. Perhaps even that would go away in time.

Eventually they came to Providence, which looked very much the same, a small oasis of buildings among the rolling grasslands with the hazy ridges of the Great Dividing Range in the distance behind them and eternity facing them. John turned off the main bitumen road onto a graveled track that led past the Sterling Run on the way to Priss's parents' home. She tried not to look, but her eyes were drawn helplessly to the big sprawling house with its wide porches and colonial architecture. The driveway was lined with oleanders and royal poinciana and eucalyptus trees, which everyone called simply gum trees. Streams crisscrossed the land. They mostly dried up in the nine months preceding the Wet, which came near Christmas, but when the Wet thundered down on the plains, it was possible to be confined to the house for days until the rains stopped. Once she and her parents had had to stay with the Sterlings or be drowned out, and their small house had suffered enormous water damage.

"The house looks as if it has just been painted," she remarked, noticing its gleaming white surface.

"It has," he said curtly.

She loved its long porches, where she had sat one spring with John's mother and watched the men herd sheep down the long road on their way to the shearing sheds. That would be coming soon, she recalled, along with dipping and vetting and the muster of the cattle that supplemented John's vast sheep herds.

Beyond the house and its grove of eucalyptus trees were the fenced paddocks where the big Merino sheep grazed. They'd just been moved, she imagined, because the paddocks looked untouched. She noticed that the fences looked different.

"There's so little wire," she remarked, frowning.

"Electrified fencing," John said. "Just one of the improvements we're making. It's less expensive than barbed wire or wooden fences."

"What if the power goes out?" she asked.

"We have backup generators," he returned. He glanced at her. "And men with shotguns..." he added with just a glimpse of his old dry humor.

But she didn't smile. The days were gone when she could do that with John. She only nodded.

Soon they were at her parents' house, deserted because Adam and Renée apparently hadn't come home yet.

"They'll be back by dark, they said," he told her.

She nodded, staring at the lovely little bungalow, with its high gabled roof and narrow long front porch and green shutters at the windows. It was set inside a white picket fence, and Priss loved the very look of it, with the gum trees towering around it. Behind it was a stretch of paddock and then another grove of gum trees where a stream ran hidden, a magic little glade where she liked to watch koala bears feed on eucalyptus leaves and wait for lorikeets and other tropical birds to alight briefly on their flights.

"It looks just the same," she remarked softly.

He got out and removed her bag from the trunk. She followed him onto the porch, and as she looked up her green eyes suddenly flashed with the memory of the last time they'd been alone together at this house.

He searched her eyes slowly. "It was a long time ago," he said quietly.

"Yes," she agreed, her face clouding. "But I haven't forgotten. I'll never forget. Or forgive," she added coldly.

He stuck his hands into his pockets, staring down at her from his formidable height. "No," he said after a minute, and his voice was deep and slow. "I could hardly expect that, could I? It's just as well that it's all behind us. You and I were worlds apart even then."

Her knees felt rubbery, but she kept her poise. "Thank you for bringing me home," she said formally.

"I won't say it was a pleasure," he returned. "For my part, I wish you'd never come back."

He turned, and she glared after him with her heart going wild in her chest. She wanted to pick up something and throw it at him! But she stood there staring after him furiously and couldn't even think of a suitable parting shot. She stood on the porch and watched him turn the car and drive away in a cloud of dust. Then she turned and read the welcoming note on the door before she turned the knob and went inside.

It took only a minute to regain her familiarity with the comfortable furnishings and warm feeling of the house. She thought she even smelled freshly baked apple pie. Her bedroom was still the same, and her eyes lingered helplessly on the bed. If only she could forget!

She dressed in a pair of designer jeans and a yellow sweater Aunt Margaret had given her as part of her graduation present, a complete new wardrobe. Then, determined to exorcise the ghosts, she walked out behind the house over the grassy deserted paddock down to the wooden fence that separated her father's property from John's.

With a long sigh, she leaned against the old gray wood. She could still see herself as a teenager, in those long-ago days when she'd haunted this spot, hoping for a glimpse of John Sterling. How carefree she'd been. How full of love and hope and happy endings. Happy endings that had never come.

Chapter 2

It was an Australian spring day when Priss went speeding across the empty paddock toward the fence that separated her father's small holding from John Sterling's enormous cattle station. She was flushed with excitement, her long silvery blonde hair fanning all around her delicate features as she ran, her green eyes sparkling.

"John!" she called. "John, I got it!"

The tall blond man on the big black gelding wheeled his mount, frowning impatiently for an instant at the sight of Priscilla risking life and limb. Barefoot, for God's sake, in a white sundress that would have raised a young man's temperature.

"Watch where you're going, girl!" he called back in his broad Australian drawl.

She kept coming, laughing, making a perfectly balletic leap onto the faded white wooden fence that separated the properties. In her slender hand, she was waving a letter.

"Keep going, mates, I'll catch up," he told his men, trying not to notice the amused looks on their faces as he rode toward the girl.

Priss watched him coming with the same adoration she'd given him freely for two years. She knew he was aware of her infatuation—he couldn't help being aware of it—but he indulged her to a point.

He was so rugged, she thought dreamily. Big and broad-shouldered, with hands almost twice the size of her own, he filled out his moleskins and chambray shirt with delicious flair. He was almost ugly. His nose was formidable, his bushy eyebrows jutted over heavy-lidded sapphire eyes that were almost transparent. His cheekbones were high, his mouth wide and sexy-looking, his chin stubborn and dimpled. His hair wasn't truly blond, either. It was light brown, with flaring blond highlights, like his eyebrows and the thick hair over his chest and brawny forearms. But despite his lack of sophisticated good looks, he suited Priss. She only wished, for the hundredth time, that she suited him. He was still a bachelor at twenty-eight, but women liked him. He had an easygoing, humorous manner that appealed to most people, although he had a formidable temper when riled.

"Barefoot again," he said curtly, glaring at Priss's pretty little feet on the fence rail. "What am I going to do with you?"

"I could make several suggestions," she murmured with a mischievous smile.

He lit a cigarette, not commenting, and leaned his

forearms over the pommel of the saddle. His sleeves were rolled up, and Priss's helpless eyes were drawn to the huge muscular hands holding the reins and the cigarette. The leather creaked protestingly as he sat forward to stare at her from under the wide brim of his Stetson. "Well, what's the news, little sheila?" he prompted.

"I got the scholarship," she told him proudly, eyes twinkling.

"Good on you!" he said.

"Mom's proud," she said. "And Dad's especially pleased because he teaches, too. I'm going to major in elementary education."

He studied her. Anyone would be less likely to become a teacher, he thought. He smiled softly. With her long hair curling like that, a silvery cloud around her delicate features, she was a vision. There wouldn't be any shortage of suitors. That disturbed him, and the smile faded. She was still a child. Just eighteen. His eyes went slowly over her slender body, to the taut thrust of her perfect breasts against the sundress's thin top, down over a small waist and slender hips and long elegant legs to her bare pretty feet.

Priss watched him, too, vaguely excited by the way he was looking at her. She couldn't remember a time before when he'd looked at her like that, as if she were a woman instead of an amusing but pesky kid.

She shifted on the fence, with the forgotten letter still clutched in one hand. "Will you miss me when I'm gone?" she asked, only half teasing.

"Oh, like the plague," he agreed, tongue in cheek. "Who'll drag me to the phone in the middle of calving to ask if I'm busy? Or go swimming in my pond just when I've stocked it with fish? Or ride me down in the woods when I'm taking a few minutes to myself?''

She dropped her eyes. ''I guess I have been a pest,'' she agreed reluctantly. She brushed her hair back. ''Sorry.''

''Don't look so lost. I will miss you,'' he added, his voice soft and slow.

She sighed, looking up into his eyes. ''I'll miss you, too,'' she confessed. Her eyes were eloquent, more revealing than she knew. ''Hawaii's so far away.''

''It was your choice,'' he reminded her.

She shrugged. ''I got carried away by the scenery when I toured the campus with Aunt Margaret. Besides, having an aunt nearby will make things easier, and you know Mom and Dad don't want me living on campus. I kind of wish I'd decided on Brisbane, though.''

''You're an American,'' he reminded her. ''Perhaps you'll fit in better in Honolulu.''

''But I've lived in Australia for two years,'' she said. ''It's home now.''

He lifted the cigarette to his mouth. ''You're young, Priss. Younger than you realize. So much can change, in so little time.''

She glared at him. ''You think I'm just a kid, too. Well, mister, I'm growing fast, so look out. When I come back home for good, you're in trouble.''

His bushy eyebrows lifted over amused eyes. ''I am?''

''I'll have learned all about being a woman by

then," she told him smugly. "I'll steal your heart right
out of that rock you've got it embedded in."

"You're welcome to give it a go," he told her with
a grin. "Fair dinkum."

She sighed. There he went again, humoring her.
Couldn't he see her heart was breaking?

"Well, I'd better get back," she sighed. "I have to
help Mom with lunch." She peeked up at him, hoping
against hope that he might offer to let her come up
behind him on his horse. It would be all of heaven to
sit close against that big body and feel its heat and
strength. She'd been close to him so rarely, and every
occasion was a precious memory. Now there wasn't a
lot of time left to store up memories. Her heart began
to race. Maybe this time...

"Mind your feet," he said, nodding toward them.
"And look out for Joe Blakes."

She frowned, then remembered the rhyming slang
he liked to tease her with. "Snakes!" she produced.
"You Bananabender!"

He threw back his blond head and laughed, deeply
and heartily. "Yes, I'm a Queenslander, that's the
truth. Now on with you, little sheila, I've got work to
do, even if you haven't."

"Yes, Your Worship," she mocked, and jumped
down from the fence to give him a sweeping curtsy.
Her eyes twinkled as he made a face. "That's called
cutting tall poppies down to size!"

"I'm keeping score," he warned softly.

"How exciting," she replied tartly.

He laughed to himself and turned his mount. "Mind
your feet!" he called again, amusement deepening his

voice, and with a tip of his hat, he rode off as if he hadn't a care in the world. Priss watched him until he was out of sight among the gum trees, and sighed wistfully. Oh, well, there was still a week before she left for Hawaii. If only he'd kiss her. She flushed, biting her lower lip as the intensity of emotion washed over her. He never had touched her, except to hold her hand occasionally to help her up and down from perilous places. And once, only once, he'd lifted her and carried her like a child over a huge mud puddle when it was raining. She'd clung to him, as if drowning in his sensuous strength. But those episodes were few and far between, and mostly she survived on memory. She had a snapshot of him that she'd begged from his mother, on the excuse of painting him from it. The painting had gone lacking, but she had the photograph tucked in her wallet, and she wove exquisite daydreams around it.

With a world-weary look on her face, she got down from the fence and began to walk slowly back across the paddock. Maybe a snake would bite her, and she'd be at death's door, and John would rush to her bedside to weep bitter tears over her body. She shook herself. More likely, he'd pat the snake on the head and make a pet of it.

She wandered lazily back to the house and walked slowly up the steps to the cool front porch where she liked to sit and hope that John would ride by. In the distance were the softly rolling paddocks where John's Hereford cattle and big Merino sheep grazed peacefully.

Her eyes grew sad as she realized that she would

soon be far away from this dear, familiar scene. College. Several years of college in Hawaii—out of sight and sound and touch of John Sterling. And he didn't even seem to mind. Not one bit.

Renée Johnson looked up as her daughter came into the house. She smiled a little as she bent her silver head again to her embroidery. She was in her late forties, but traces of beauty were still evident in her patrician face.

"Hello, darling; back already?" she teased.

"John was busy," Priss sighed. She plopped down into a chair with a rueful smile. "He's glad I'm leaving, you know."

"Oh, I don't think he is, really," Renée said carelessly. "Friendship can survive a few absences, dear."

Friendship. Priss almost wailed. She was dying of love for him!

"Dad should be back now, shouldn't he?" she asked.

"He had to stop in Providence to pick up his new suit on the way back from Brisbane," she reminded her daughter. "And Brisbane is a good drive from here."

"All for a student he hardly knows," Priss remarked. "Just because he needed a way to the airport. Dad's all heart, isn't he?"

"Yes, he is," her mother agreed warmly. "That's why I married him, you know."

Priss got up and paced the room. "I wonder if I'm doing the right thing. Hawaii's so far away…"

"The university there is one of the best," she was

reminded. "And your aunt will love having you close by. She's your father's favorite sister, you know."

"Yes." Priss stared out the window at the distant white cloud of moving sheep. John had cattle, too, but his primary interest was his big Merino sheep. She loved watching the jackeroos move them from paddock to paddock. She loved the sheepdogs, so deft and quick. But most of all she loved John. John!

"Set the table, dear, would you?" Renée asked. "I'll be dishing up supper any minute."

Chapter 3

Adam Johnson glanced curiously at his daughter over the dinner table. It wasn't like Priscilla to pick at her food.

"Aren't you hungry, darling?" he asked.

She lifted her face with a plaintive smile. "I'm just homesick already," she confessed.

"Homesick? Don't be silly, Hawaii's not that far away," he chuckled. "You can come home on holidays and vacation."

She pushed her fork into her potatoes and stared at them. "I suppose so."

Adam turned his head toward Renée, who was shaking her head.

"It's just...well, do you suppose John really will miss me?" she asked her father, all eyes.

He laughed, misreading the situation. "Now, darling, I doubt that,'' he chuckled as he concentrated on his food. ''You do wear him out, you know.''

Priss got up from the table in tears and ran for her room. Her mother glared at her father.

''You animal,'' she accused. ''How could you do that to her? Don't you realize she's horribly infatuated with John?''

His eyebrows arched. ''With John? But, my God, he's ten years older than she is. And she's just a child!''

''She's eighteen,'' she reminded him. ''Not a child at all.''

''Well, John's too experienced for her by far,'' he said firmly. ''Don't get me wrong—I think the world of him. But she needs boys her own age. And you know how relentlessly she chases the poor man, Renée. I wonder that he tolerates it. You can see he isn't interested in kids like Priss.''

''Yes, I know. But she's so young, darling,'' Renée said softly. ''Don't you remember how we felt at her age?''

His dark eyes softened. ''Yes,'' he said reluctantly, and sighed. ''With everybody around telling us how young we were...poor Priss.''

''She'll get over him,'' Renée promised. ''Once she's with boys her own age, she'll get over him.''

Priss, standing frozen in the hall, heard every word. It all came rushing at her like a tidal wave. Had she hounded John? Did *he* realize how desperately infatuated she was?

Her face flamed. She leaned back against the cool wall, almost shaking. Of course he did. Ten years, her father had said. John wouldn't want a child like herself. She closed her eyes. It was far worse than she'd realized. And the worst thing of all was that she hadn't realized how very noticeable her infatuation was. But it didn't feel like infatuation. She loved John!

She turned and went back into her room, closing the door quietly. She felt more alone than she ever had in her life. Poor John. Poor her. Her father had said John was too experienced to want a teenager, and he was surely right. If John had felt anything for her, he wouldn't have been able to hide it. She would have known. People always said you knew when love happened.

She tumbled onto her bed and slowly pulled out the crumpled photo of him that she kept in her wallet. She stared at it for a long time, at the rugged face, the bushy blond and brown eyebrows and hair, at the sensuous mouth and dimpled chin, at the pastel blue eyes. No, he wouldn't miss her, she thought miserably.

"Well, you don't know what you're losing, John Sterling," she told the photograph. "I'm going to be a force to behold in a few years, and you'll be sorry you didn't want me. I'll show you!" She put the photograph in her trash can in a temper and flounced over to the window, glaring out at the big gum tree casting its shade over the ground. She leaned her face on her hands and sighed. "I'll come back as finished as a princess," she told the gum tree. "I'll be wearing an elegant gown, with my hairdo impeccable, and I'll be poised and ever so serene. And every man will want to dance with me, and John will be wild to, and I'll just brush past him and ignore him completely."

She smiled as she pictured it. What a proper revenge it would be! But then she realized how impossible it was going to be, living through those years without him. And where would she get the money for an elegant gown and hairdo? And what if John got married in her absence?

She felt sick. With a scowl, she fished his photo out of the trash can and put it carefully back into her wallet. She had too much time to think, that was her trouble. So she went to the kitchen and began clearing the table for her mother, trying to ignore the curious looks her parents were giving her.

"Could we all go into Providence Saturday and have lunch together?" she asked with a forced smile. "I have to leave for Hawaii Monday, you know."

Her father gave a relieved sigh. "Yes, of course we can. That's a date."

"I'll enjoy it, too, dear." Her mother smiled. "Now, suppose I help you with the dishes and then we'll go sit on the porch."

"Fine," Priss said brightly. Perhaps the pretense of being happy would lighten her spirits, she thought. Perhaps it would dull her hurt. Why, oh, why did she have to pick a man like John Sterling to fall in love with, and at such a youthful age? He was going to be a ghost, hanging over every relationship she tried to have with other men. She knew that no one would be able to match or top him in her loving eyes.

She avoided him during the next few days. For once she didn't phone him to ask unnecessary questions at night. She didn't walk along the paddock fence hoping for a glance of him. She didn't find an excuse to ride her bicycle over the distance that separated her father's land from John's, or invite herself to lunch with his mother, Diane. She kept to herself, and her parents seemed delighted by the sudden maturity in their daughter.

They couldn't know that it was killing her not to see John, to think of being thousands of miles away from him. But she was deliberately trying to put him out of her life, so that the parting wouldn't be so rough.

The hours and days dragged, but at last Monday came, and she packed for the long drive to Brisbane, where she'd catch her flight to Hawaii. It was the most miserable morning of her entire life.

"Aren't you even going to tell John Sterling goodbye?" Renée asked, her face concerned and full of love.

Priss's back stiffened a little, but her face was smiling when she glanced at her mother. "I thought it might be better not to," she said.

"Why?"

Priss shrugged. Her eyes went to her folded blouses. She fit them carefully into her carry-on bag. "I don't think I could stand having him shout for joy," she said with a nervous laugh.

Renée went close and put her arms around her daughter. "Not John. John wouldn't do that to you. He's fond of you, Priss; you know that."

"Yes, but fond isn't enough," Priss ground out, fighting tears. She lifted a tortured face to her mother. "I love him," she whispered.

Renée hugged her. "Yes, I know. I'm so sorry, darling,'' she murmured, rocking Priss as she had years ago, when her daughter was little and hurt. "I'm so sorry."

Priss hugged her mother again and smiled wanly. "You're a terrific mother, did I ever tell you?" she asked. She wiped away the tears. "I'm okay now."

"You're a terrific daughter," Renée said with a smile. "I'll leave you to pack. Your father and I are going into Providence for a little while. He's got to get something or other done to the car."

"Okay. Be careful."

"We will." Renée kissed her daughter on the forehead. "It gets better, if that helps," she added gently. And then she was gone, and Priss stared helplessly at the suitcase, hating it for its very purpose.

She finished putting in the blouses and went into the kitchen to check the dryer for spare articles. She found a lacy slip and was just pulling it out when she heard a car pull up. Surely it wasn't her parents, she puzzled; they'd hardly been gone ten minutes.

She went to the back door, opened it, and looked out. Her heart shot up into her throat at the sight of John Sterling climbing out of his Land-Rover.

He was wearing khaki trousers with a short-sleeve tan bush shirt, and under the wide brim of his hat, he looked even more formidable than usual. Priss, with her hair loose around her shoulders, in her pretty blue shirtwaist dress and white pumps, felt suddenly vulnerable.

He looked up as he reached the steps and stopped there, just gazing at her.

"You've been avoiding me," he said without pre-amble.

She twisted the slip absently in her fingers and studied the soft pattern in the lace. "Yes." She glanced up with a forced grin. "Aren't you relieved? I'll be gone by afternoon."

He hesitated for an instant before he came up the steps. "Got something cool to drink?" he asked, sweeping off his hat. "It's damned hot."

"I think there's some iced tea in the fridge," she said. She tossed the slip onto the dryer and filled a glass for him.

He took it from her, standing much too close. He was scowling, as if his mind was working on some problem. He took a sip of the tea, and her eyes were drawn to his brawny hair-roughened forearms. He was so sexy, and some lucky woman was going to grab him up before she was old enough to.

She felt more miserable than ever. She'd promised herself she wasn't going to cry, even if he did manage to get over to say good-bye. But now it was the eleventh hour, and he'd be rushing off any minute. He was probably here to see her father, anyway.

"Did you want to see Dad?" she asked, turning the knife in her own heart.

"I wanted to see you," he corrected curtly. "To say good-bye. Weren't you even going to bother?"

She shrugged, staring down at his dusty boots. "I...I don't like good-byes," she managed in a voice that was already starting to break. The thought of not seeing him for months was killing her, and this was making it worse. She didn't know how she was going to live in a world without him.

"What's this?" he asked softly. His big hands, cool from holding the tea glass, caught her arms and turned her, forcing her to look at him.

Her full lips wobbled no matter how she tried to control their trembling, and her big emerald eyes were misty with tears. Silvery blonde hair curled around her oval face, and her cheeks were flushed with emotion. The picture she made held his attention for a long minute. His eyes wandered down to the top buttons of the blue shirtwaist dress, and he studied her body as if he'd only just realized she had one.

His hands smoothed up and down her arms, slowly, making wild tremors of pleasure shoot through her.

"Homesick already?" he asked quietly.

She drew in a sharp breath and tried to smile at him, but he blurred in her vision.

He was a blur of brown hair with blond streaks through it, sky blue eyes staring curiously at her from that weathered face that she loved so dearly. It was a long way to look up, even though she was wearing high heels. He towered over her like a sunburned giant.

"You're so big," she whispered.

"To a runt like you, I probably seem that way," he agreed pleasantly, but his eyes weren't laughing. They were dark and quiet and oddly watchful.

She fidgeted under the arousing touch of his hands. "I should finish packing," she mumbled.

His thumbs pressed hard into her arms. He moved

his callused hands up to enclose her face, and the look in his eyes made her knees weak.

"Don't look so tragic, darling," he murmured, bending his head. "I'll wait for you."

That hurt most of all. He was teasing her, playing with her, because he knew how she felt and was indulging her. Her eyes closed. "John…" she tried to protest.

He brushed his lips across her forehead, and she wanted to wail. He was trying not to hurt her….

"Do you want my mouth, little sheila?" he whispered suddenly, unexpectedly, and her heart shot up like a balloon.

Her eyes opened, full of dreams and hurt pride and aching hunger, and his nostrils flared.

"Yes, you do, don't you?" he asked under his breath, and his face was solemn, intent, making her feel years older. He bent his head, letting her feel his warm breath on her parted lips.

Her body tautened, demanding to feel his against it; her mouth lifted. All her dreams were coming true at once, and the look in his eyes made her heart run wild. Her body pressed against his tentatively, shyly. She loved his warm strength, the powerful muscles tensing where her breasts were flattened slightly against him. He smelled of the outdoors, and cologne and tobacco, and her senses reeled.

"I've only been kissed once," she whispered nervously, her eyes wide. "Playing…playing spin the bottle. And his mouth was wet and I didn't like it."

His fingers traced soft patterns on her flushed cheek, and they seemed to be the only two people in the world. "Stop dithering, little one," he said quietly. "I don't mind kissing you good-bye, if you want it."

"If," she whispered shakily. Tears were stinging her eyes. "Don't you know that I'd walk across blazing coals to get to you...?"

His eyes flashed. "You don't even know what it's all about," he said sharply. "One kiss, from a clumsy boy..."

"But you aren't a boy," she reminded him, her voice trembling.

"No," he said, "I'm not." He bent slowly, holding her eyes. "Such a taut little body," he breathed, his hard lips parting on a faint smile as they brushed deliciously over hers. "Why don't you let it relax against mine?"

She tried, but she was trembling with excitement and new discoveries. "I can't," she moaned against the soft persistent brushing of his mouth.

His fingers splayed over her throat, tilting her head against his shoulder. "I'm hungry, too," he whispered roughly. There was a glitter in his eyes as they searched hers. "Don't let me frighten you. Trust me."

"I want to kiss you so much," she managed in a broken tone, so desperate for him that she was beyond pride.

"Yes," he said, parting his lips. "Yes, I can feel how much. Priss, you go to my head..." His voice trailed off into a deep slow moan as he kissed her for the first time, tenderly, coaxingly, letting her feel the very texture of his lips before he showed her that he needed more than this.

His breath seemed shaky as his mouth bit at hers.

She kept her eyes tightly closed, hoping that if it was a dream, she could die before she woke. The silence around them was deafening, and she felt afire with awakening emotions.

Her hands suddenly clawed into the thick muscles of his upper arms, and she stiffened even more as his mouth began to invade hers. She hoped he wasn't going to waste her last few minutes with him by being gentle.

His head lifted then and his mouth waited, poised over hers. His breath sighed out against her moist lips. "I can make you hungrier than this," he said huskily. "I can burn you up."

His eyes frightened her a little, but she was too consumed by longing to care. She pressed closer against his tight hard body and stood on tiptoe.

"Oh, John, kiss me hard!" she pleaded, clinging. "Kiss me hard and slow and pretend you want me!"

"Pretend!" he bit off. His mouth swooped down. He could feel the hunger building in her young body, feel the first faint stirring of response in the tender lips accepting his. Ravenously he opened his mouth and bit at hers, not wanting to frighten her, but needing more than the trembling uncertainty of her closed mouth. After a minute, she seemed to like the tender probing of his tongue. Involuntarily her lips relaxed and began to part shyly.

"Yes," he prodded roughly. "Yes, that's what I want. Open your mouth slowly; let me taste it with my tongue…"

It was wildly erotic. Priss had seen men and women kiss that way in movies, with their mouths open, their bodies crushed together, but she'd never known how wildly arousing it was. She moaned against John's demanding mouth, because the sensations he was making her feel were new and overwhelming.

"Frightened?" he whispered.

Her eyes drifted open, wide and drowsy and dazed. "No," she moaned. "Oh, no, not of you; not ever of you," she whispered shakily. "No matter what you do to me!"

"You don't know what I could do to you," he warned gruffly. He studied her face for a long moment. His hands smoothed down her back, bringing her closer to his shuddering chest. One of them edged between their bodies and traced a line between her waist and the soft underside of one breast. She trembled again, her fingers digging into him.

"Steady on," he breathed gently, watching her face as his fingers began to trace her breast, watching her eyes widen with pleasure.

She made a wild sweet sound and buried her face against his chest, clinging to him.

"I need this," he said, sounding shaken. "God help me, I have to!"

She felt his mouth searching for hers, and she turned her head a fraction of an inch to meet it.

"Keep your eyes open," he breathed as he took it, ardently, roughly, and his eyes stared into hers. His hand moved at the same time, and he saw her pupils dilate until her eyes were black as he cupped her soft breast in his big hand and felt the nipple go hard in his palm.

She moaned, feeling her body move helplessly

against his, feeling her body provoke him, beg for his touch.

He lifted his mouth. "It's passion," he whispered. "Don't be ashamed of it. I need you as much as you need me. I won't compromise you—not in any way."

As he spoke, he bent, lifting her clear off the floor, his eyes glazed with emotion. "Where are your parents?" he asked softly as he carried her into her bedroom.

"In...in town, to have...to have the car...fixed," she told him. Her voice was so shaky, it was hard to talk. "John," she moaned.

"Shhh," he whispered. His lips brushed her eyelids closed. "It's going to be exquisitely tender. I just want a taste of you."

"I've never..." she began.

"I know."

He laid her down beside the open suitcase on the bed and slid alongside her. His mouth touched her face softly, lovingly, brushing every flushed inch of it, teasing her mouth. She felt his knuckles on her soft flesh as they slid beneath the bodice of her dress, and her eyes opened, because what he was teaching her was so beautiful, she wanted to remember him like this all her life. Even if it was only pity he felt for her, she'd live on these few minutes until she died.

"I'm only going to touch you," he said gently. "Here," he whispered, tracing the slope of her breast where it was covered by the lacy wisp of her bra. "And here." They moved under the lace, to the hard pulsing tip that screamed her helpless reaction to him.

"Oh," she moaned, shocked, arching to his hand.

"New sensations?" he responded, savoring the feel of her, bursting with the triumphant knowledge that no other man had touched her. "I feel new sensations, too, Priss. You're a virgin, and all your first times are happening with me. I feel humble knowing that."

She stared into his eyes. "I wanted you...so much," she confessed brokenly.

His eyes smiled. "Did you? And now that you have me?"

Her lips parted. "I don't know what to do," she said simply.

"Do you want me to teach you?" His voice was all dark velvet, seducing her, and he smiled as his big hands found the buttons of her dress and lazily eased them open down the front.

"Yes," she entreated. "But..." Her courage failed as the last button came undone, and the full force of what she was letting him do washed over her in waves.

He shook his head, pressing a gentle finger against her protesting lips. "No," he said. "I don't want this to happen with some college boy, out of curiosity. Let me be the first."

Her body trembled. But she loved him almost beyond bearing, and she wanted his eyes on her. Only his. No other man's, ever.

His hands moved again, unfastening the bra. There was a second when she almost jerked away from him, but he controlled the instinctive withdrawal, pulling her face into his throat, making her close her eyes while he eased the garments down to her waist. She felt the cool air on her skin and his warm rough hands against her bare back, and her heart went crazy in her body.

"Now," he breathed, with his open mouth against her forehead. "Now let me look at you. Lie down, Priscilla, and let me see what you've shown no other man."

With breathless tenderness, he eased her back onto the coverlet and slowly his eyes feasted on her soft pink breasts with their hardened, uptilted tips. She flushed.

But after the first few agonizing seconds of embarrassment, she began to relax, to take pleasure from the appreciation she read in his intent gaze. Her body seemed to like it even more. It began to move in jerky sensuous motions on the mattress and lifted toward him without her consent.

"Do you want my hands?" he asked, lifting his eyes to hers.

She tingled all over, her breath catching in her throat at the deep, fervent note in his voice. His sophistication made her innocence more obvious than ever.

He sat up and one big hand smoothed across her flat stomach, across the bulge of the clothing at her waist. Lightly, slowly, holding her eyes, he touched the hard peaks of her breasts and watched her shudder.

"Your breasts are like honey," he said. "You're like honey. So sweet, you make me drunk." He bent, with his eyes on her bareness. "I want to take you in my mouth," he breathed. "Are you going to let me?"

She groaned helplessly, and her body arched again, inviting him.

"Priss," he whispered, sliding his hands slowly under her back. "Priss, come here."

He lifted her to his parted lips. She stiffened and cried out with the shock of pleasure as his mouth took her, and the excited little cry aroused him instantly. He took the hardness into his mouth and eased closer, feeling her reactions, glorying in her headlong response. Her hands tangled in his hair, frantic. Those wild little cries were pushing him right over the edge, making him shudder with a kind of desire he'd never experienced.

"Oh, God," he whispered with reverence, because she was so deliciously innocent, so trusting. She was giving him free license to do what he liked to her smooth young body, and he was going crazy with the freedom.

His mouth moved down her body, to her waist, her hips, the flatness of her stomach, as he eased the dress farther down to bare her body to his greedy lips. She tasted of delicate soap and powder, and he wanted to taste all of her....

"Do you want me now?" he whispered roughly. His mouth ran back up her body, over her creamy breasts to her face, and he cupped her breast as his lips made nonsense of any protest she might have made. "Do you want to lie with me and touch me the way I'm touching you with nothing between us except air?"

"I...ache," she said through parched lips, clinging, trembling.

"So do I," he said unsteadily. "You've taken my

mind from me. Lie still, darling. Let me touch you, let me have you.''

His face moved, touching, brushing. His mouth loved her, cherished her. She was shuddering under its tenderness, and he knew she'd make no further protest if he undressed her completely and took her. But even as he was drowning in the anguished pleasure of the knowledge, he began to think about consequences. She was a virgin. The first time for her was probably not going to be as good as it would be for him. He was more aroused than he'd ever been in his life—too aroused to take his time, to give her patience. And worst of all, she'd be unprotected. He could make her pregnant. It was that thought that brought him suddenly to his senses. She was hardly more than a child herself.

He dragged his mouth from her soft belly and managed to pull his tormented body into a sitting position, breathing roughly, running his hands through his damp hair. She was breathing roughly herself, and her body was trembling wildly.

With a harsh mutter, he brought her up into his arms and rocked her damp body against his. ''Hold me hard, darling,'' he whispered into her ear, feeling the heat of her breasts through the cotton of his shirt. Her back under his hands was like silk. ''Hold me. It will stop. Hold me hard.''

She clung to him, vaguely embarrassed at the intensity of her response, wildly frustratcd, wanting something he hadn't given her but not realizing exactly what.

''Oh, gosh,'' she whispered, awed.

"Now you know," he said gently.

Her nails bit into his shoulders, and she nuzzled her head into his neck, shuddering a little as her heartbeat calmed and her breath steadied. "You...weren't going to stop...at first. Why...did you?" It was a statement, not a question.

His big hand smoothed her hair slowly. "I could have made you pregnant."

Thrills of pleasure wafted through her. She might have liked that, being pregnant with his child. It wasn't at all frightening. But it would be a poor way of getting him, a mean trick. She sighed.

"I'd have let you," she answered.

He laughed softly. "Yes, I know. Delicious, delightful little virgin." He bit her shoulder, quite hard, and she shuddered with unexpected pleasure and laughed.

He half threw her back on the pillows and sat looking down at her seminudity with possessive, glittering blue eyes. "I've never wanted anyone so much," he said huskily. "I was on fire for you. I still am."

It was plain speaking, and a little embarrassing— like her wanton behavior. He seemed to sense those uncertainties, because he smiled tenderly when she sat up and began to tug her dress back in place.

"Don't be embarrassed," he said gently. "Only the two of us will ever know what happened here today." He touched her mouth with a long finger. "And I won't tell if you won't."

That was the John she loved so much, teasing, mischievous. She couldn't help smiling at him. He smiled back and bent, kissing her softly, amorously, as his hands drew the bodice down again. "I'll never see anything else so beautiful as long as I live,'' he ground out, staring at her pink skin where his mouth had pressed and pulled and tasted it, with something like reverence on his hard face.

She flushed wildly and blushed even there, and he bent and kissed the shyness from her eyes, her mouth.

His fingers moved the damp hair away from her face, and he looked at her as if she were a sunrise he was committing to memory. ''You belong to me now,'' he said quietly. ''Keep your body for me, and no other man. I'll wait for you.''

''It belonged to you long before now,'' she said in a choked tone, her eyes searching his. ''John, I…!''

He put his fingers over her lips. ''Don't say it.'' His mouth replaced his fingers, and he kissed her with an expertise that left her moaning, in tears, when he lifted his head. ''You're very young,'' he said, as if it bothered him. ''There's plenty of time.''

''Plenty?'' she queried. ''When I'm leaving today?''

''Darling,'' he breathed, staring down at her, ''if you weren't leaving today, you might damned well find yourself in my bed by nightfall.''

He got to his feet, stretching lazily and indulgently watched her efforts to rearrange her dress. There was possession in his eyes, and quiet pride, but she wasn't looking.

''See what happens when you avoid me?'' he asked as she got to her feet, smoothing back her disheveled hair. ''Frustration can push a man to the very limits.''

She smiled shakily. ''Was that what it was?''

He caught her waist and pulled her to him. "What do you think it was?" he asked.

She stared at his shirt, curious about how he looked without it. She'd only seen him that way from a distance, when he was working on fences with the men or digging a new bore.

"It's too late now," he said deeply, his voice amused. "If you wanted to go on safari, you should have indulged yourself while we were lying together on the bed."

She flushed, and he laughed.

"The months will pass," he said lightly, giving her a last careless kiss. "Write to me."

"Could I?" she asked, breathless.

"Of course."

"Will you write back?"

He shifted from one foot to the other. "I'm not much good at letters, honey," he confessed. "I'll get Mother to write for me."

His words hurt her. They wouldn't be love letters— he was saying as much. Perhaps he'd meant what they had just shared as a going-away present, a fond farewell. Something to make up for the times when he'd ignored her, crumbs from his table.

She felt sick all over, but she was too proud to let it show. How could she have forgotten what her father had said, about John being glad to let her go, about his being too old to be interested in her?

"I'll see you at the Easter holidays," he said. "You'll be home then?"

"Of course," she said woodenly. "'Bye, John."

He traced her cheek lightly with his finger, and his

eyes met hers in a long hot exchange, but he didn't touch her again. "'Bye, Priss. Keep well.''

"You, too."

And he was gone, leaving her with the memory of a few wild minutes in his arms. It might have been kinder, she thought, if he'd spared her that. Coming from heaven back to earth was painful. She went to the window and watched him drive away. He waved from the end of the driveway, and she knew that he was aware of her watchful eyes. He knew how she felt. It had all been a pacifier, a consolation prize. Give the girl a few kisses to thrill her.

She went back to her suitcase and stared at it, denying her eyes the tears they wanted to shed. Well, she didn't need John's crumbs, thank you, she told herself. She'd go away and forget him. She'd forget him completely.

Sure, she would. She sat down on the bed and wailed. The coverlet still smelled of the spicy cologne he wore. Her lips touched it with aching passion, and it was a long time before she could force herself to get up and finish packing.

Hours later she said good-bye to her parents in Brisbane and climbed aboard a plane bound for the Hawaiian Islands. Despite the fact that she had promised herself she wouldn't, her helpless eyes scanned the airport terminal for a glimpse of John. But he wasn't there. Why should he be? He'd said his good-byes. She sat back in her seat and closed her eyes. It was going to be a long day.

Chapter 4

Priss settled in at the University of Hawaii in Honolulu, on the island of Oahu, and found the diversity of cultures and races as fascinating as she'd found Australia. She lived off campus, with Aunt Margaret, and found her young-minded aunt a lively and delightful companion. When Priss wasn't attending classes, her aunt toured her around the island. Priss found breathtaking beauty in the beaches and mountains and volcanos and flowers, and day by day the hurt of leaving behind her family and the man she loved began to ease.

One of her biggest consolations was the new friend she'd found in Ronald George, a tall dark-haired Englishman with blue eyes who was studying for a degree in education, too.

Her introduction to him had come the first day of

classes, when he'd sidled up to her in the auditorium and leaned down to whisper in her ear.

"I say," he asked conspiratorially, "would you be interested in having a blazing affair with me during algebra? It is a bit crowded in here right now, but I do see a place just behind the curtains in the auditorium…"

She'd looked up at him dumbfounded. "What?"

"Just a short affair," he continued. "Until second period class? All right, then, you've talked me into marriage. But you'll have to wait until I have an hour to spare. Say, around lunchtime?" He grinned. "I'm Ronald George, by the way. You'd have seen the name on our marriage certificate, but I thought you might like to know beforehand."

"You're incredible!" she burst out. She stared up at him while she decided between running for help or laughing aloud.

"Yes, and just think, you haven't even seen me in action yet!" He leered at her playfully. "How about it? Or we could become engaged now. The thing is, old girl, I don't have a ring on me…."

She decided in favor of laughter. "Oh, stop, I'll hurt myself," she gasped after laughing until her stomach ached.

He brushed back a lock of his wavy dark hair. "I knew we'd hit it off. You're just my type. A girl."

She held out her hand. "I'm Priscilla Johnson, from Queensland, Australia."

"What an odd accent you have, if you don't mind my saying so," he commented. "Sort of southern Australian?"

"I'm from Alabama originally," she confessed. "My father teaches in Providence. That's a small town northwest of Brisbane, near several large stations."

"Ah, yes. Australia." He studied her with a warm smile. "I'd like to teach there myself, when I take my degree. Especially if that's where *you're* going to teach."

"It is." She smiled back. "Been here long?"

"Two whole nights," he said. "I miss the rain and the fog and the cold back home," he sighed.

"I left spring in Australia."

"I say, we'll probably both die in this island paradise," he predicted.

"I know a girl who's studying to be a doctor," she told him. "She'll save us once she gets through premed. You can't possibly catch pneumonia until then."

"Oh. Well, in that case, I shall put on a mustard plaster tonight. And perhaps a couple of hot dogs to keep it company."

The bell rang just as she was warming to him, but in the weeks and months that followed, they became fast friends. Both of them knew it wasn't going to be any mad romance, but they found they genuinely liked each other. And Priss needed a friend desperately. The longer she was away from John Sterling, the more she missed him. It became an actual pain to lie down at night and think about him.

By the time six months had passed and Easter rolled around, she'd had all too much time to think about how she'd hounded John for the last two years. It hadn't helped that Renée had written that John was riding around with Janie Weeks, a notorious divorcée in the district. It was probably nothing, Renée had written, but people were talking about it. Still, Priss was certain John was carrying on an affair and it hurt in an intolerable way.

She cried for hours after that, and her usually bright face was full of bitter hurt as she went to her sociology class just before school let out for Easter vacation.

"What's wrong, Priss?" Ronald asked her, his fond eyes concerned. "I say, you aren't breaking your heart over me, I hope?" He grinned. "Dying of unbridled passion…?"

"Well, maybe," she teased. Then her face became serious. "I don't want to go home at Easter," she lied.

"Good!" he chuckled. "Stay here and I'll take you to a luau at my roommate's parents' home."

"That sounds like fun," she said. "Really?"

"Really. I've talked about you so much, Danny's dying to meet you."

Her eyes searched his. "Well…"

"Come on," he chided. "I'm not trying to talk you into anything. Just friends, as we agreed."

She relaxed. "Okay. I'll stay."

"Great!" he exclaimed. "I'll tell Danny you're coming. This is going to be a gala affair, old girl; they're even roasting a suckling pig I hear." He leaned down. "Not to worry, the pig had absolutely nothing left to live for—he'd only just been jilted by his girl-friend."

She burst out laughing. "Oh, you're good for me!"

"What did I tell you in the beginning?" he asked with a smug smile.

She relaxed a little then, because she had a concrete

reason to stay in Hawaii. She didn't want to have to tell her parents the truth: that she was dying because John didn't care enough to write to her. That she couldn't bear to see him with another woman.

That night she called Renée and Adam from Margaret's house.

"Not coming home?" Renée gasped. "But, darling, we've made plans..."

"I'm sorry," she said, pretending cheerfulness, "but you remember I told you about Ronald George? Well, he's invited me to this big luau at his friend's home a couple of days from now, and he's such a nice guy...well, I said yes before I thought." She crossed her fingers against the lie.

"He's the British boy," Renée recalled. She sighed. "Priss, we've invited some people over tomorrow night, kind of a homecoming party for you. John was coming."

She closed her eyes on a wave of loneliness and love. "With his new lady, no doubt?" she grated.

There was a pause. "You don't understand," Renée began. "I need to explain—"

"Yes, I understand very well," Priscilla interrupted, sounding mature and sophisticated. "I had a wild crush on John, but being over here has cured me. I want someone younger, like Ronald, who can enjoy the things I do. I'm having such a good time, Mom. You don't really mind if I skip this one holiday, do you?"

"No, of course not," Renée said, "if it's what you really want."

"It is," Priscilla said firmly. "Is Dad there?"

"He's working late tonight, but I'll have him call you when he comes in if you like."

"No, don't. I'll call back in a day or so. Mom…?" She wanted to ask about John—if he was healthy and if he might marry that new woman—but she didn't dare, not after the fabrications she'd just put forth. "I love you," she said instead.

"I love you, too, darling," Renée said. "Priss, about John…"

"That part of my life is over, and I'm sure he's glad," Priscilla said quietly. "It must be lovely for him, not being chased by me."

"He looks rather lonely, if you want to know," came the soft reply. "He asks about you all the time. He said you were supposed to write to him."

She felt hot and cold all at once. "He…didn't really want me to, you know. It was just that he felt sorry for me."

"I don't believe that."

"Mom, you and Dad have to meet Ronald," she said enthusiastically. "He comes from a very upper-crust British family. He's wildly intelligent and full of fun, and he's going to come back to Providence with me when we graduate to teach! Isn't that great? He's super. You and Dad will like him a lot."

Renée sighed heavily. "Yes, dear, I'm sure we will. You must bring him home with you sometime."

After that the conversation became general, and John wasn't mentioned again. But when Renée said good-bye and hung up, memories of him ran around and around in Priscilla's head until she wanted to scream. He'd made all those comments about waiting for her and putting his mark on her, but he hadn't meant them. Her mother was a hopeless romantic, and she loved John. It was no wonder she was still playing matchmaker. But Priss was through mooning over John Sterling. She was going to survive, one way or another, and close him out of her life and her heart. She was going to get over him.

The luau was wonderful, very Polynesian and exciting. Ronald's roommate, Danny, was Hawaiian, an intelligent young man with liquid brown eyes and a quick wit. Priss liked him immediately. And Danny's parents were as open and friendly as he was. Besides, several of the kids from college were there. Priss enjoyed herself. Yet part of her was still mourning John, as she had been since leaving Australia.

"Priss, you've been brooding for days," Ronald remarked as they strolled along the beach together. He glanced down at her in the late evening breeze, studying her drawn face. "It's a man, isn't it?"

She glanced at him and sighed. "Yes." She'd never told him about John. She couldn't talk to anyone about John, not even Aunt Margaret.

"Bad experience?"

"Nothing like that," she laughed softly. "I was madly infatuated and chased him, that's all. I'm still a little embarrassed about it."

"How did he feel?"

"Sorry for me."

"Oh." He reached out and caught her hand. "I had the same thing happen, actually," he confided. "She doesn't know I'm alive."

"Have you considered putting a notice in the paper?" she asked, tongue in cheek.

He burst out laughing. "I don't think it would work. She doesn't read the paper." He wrinkled his eyebrows. "Confidentially, old girl, I'm not sure she can read. But, my, what a figure!"

"Poor old thing."

"I'll survive," he replied. He sighed, watching the whitecaps pound against the white sand. "People always love the wrong people."

"Yes, I know." She squeezed his hand. "But it's nice to have friends to console you."

He smiled. "Still sure you don't want to have a blazing affair with me?"

"Sorry. I'm just not one for blazing affairs. But I need all the friends I can get."

"Actually," he reflected, winking down at her, "I was going to say the same thing. It's nice having a female to talk to about other females. I wouldn't dare rock the boat!"

"You're a nice bloke," she said. "Does that sound Australian?" she added, all eyes. "I'm practicing."

"I say, jolly good!" he grinned. He frowned. "Does that sound British? I have to keep in practice, too, you know."

She laughed and tossed her hair in the breeze. The whole world smelled of salt sea air and tropical flowers, and she held on to his hand as they walked. It was lovely having him for a friend. If only she could forget about John and put him completely out of her mind. The thought of Janie Weeks wrapping her thin arms around the big Australian made Priss ill. What in the world did John see in that horrible man-eater? Priss's face fell. Probably someone as experienced as himself. He'd made a lot of remarks about Priss's age.

She stared at the gorgeous sunset with misty eyes. "Paradise," she said softly. "As much as I love it, sometimes I'd trade it all for a Queensland drought. Except for the rainy season in summer, we go dry most of the year."

"You mentioned it had been a dry summer back home," Ronald recalled.

"Yes, a lot of the station owners had setbacks. My parents told me John Sterling lost a lot of sheep and cattle. But I don't suppose it would bother him, with the numbers of animals he has."

"He'd be the man, I presume?" Ronald asked softly.

"Yes." She tossed back her hair. "The Sterling Run is enormous. But it was never the property that interested me. It was the man."

"Ever thought of telling him how you feel?"

She laughed shortly. "He knows how I feel. He's always known. He just doesn't care. He said he wasn't much good at writing letters, that he'd have his mother do it for him." She sighed bitterly. "Besides, he's been seen around the district with the local wild woman."

"So that's how it is."

"That's how it is." She tried to blot out the memory of that last day at home, but, as always, it haunted her.

"Poor kid," he comforted, and tightened his fingers.

"I'll get over him," she said. "All I need is a little time."

But as she lay in bed that night back at Aunt Margaret's house, she wondered if she was ever going to forget him. None of the boys at college, even Ronald, did a thing for her in any physical or emotional way. She was a one-man woman, and John was the one man. All the bravado in the world wasn't going to change that.

She tossed and turned, hearing over and over again her mother's voice telling her how lonely John seemed. Well, if he was lonely, why wouldn't he write?

Somewhere in the distance a phone rang, and minutes later Aunt Margaret's soft voice sounded outside the bedroom door. She opened it a crack and peeked in, all soft curling salt and pepper hair and brown eyes. She was like a feminine version of Adam Johnson, the only one of his two sisters who favored him.

"It's for you, darling," she said with a twinkle in her eyes. "Feel like talking to a man with a sexy voice?"

"I might as well," Priss said with a reluctant grin, "I'm not sleeping very well. Is it Ronald?"

"No," Margaret said. "Go ahead. Pick it up. I'll see you in the morning. Good night."

Puzzled, Priss lifted the receiver. "Hello?"

"You can't pick up a bloody pen and write me two lines?" John Sterling demanded.

Her heart went wild. "John!" she burst out, all her good resolutions forgotten, her pride in ashes immediately at just the sound of his voice. She twisted the cord in her nervous fingers. "Oh, John, I miss you so much!"

There was a brief pause while she tried to regain her lost composure.

Damn, I've done it again, she thought furiously. She composed herself. "I miss everyone at home," she amended. "But it's great here, John, lots of sunshine and things to do, and places to see—"

"Stop rambling. Are you still dressed?"

She forced humor into her voice. "Why? Are you getting kinky? Want me to describe my night attire?"

"Stop that. I'm having hell trying to straighten things out at the station and worrying myself sick over you all at once. I bought a plane ticket I couldn't afford, and it wasn't just to hear you make cute remarks. How soon can you get here?"

Her mind went blank. "Get where? To Australia, you mean?"

"To the airport in Honolulu, dammit," he ground out.

Her jaw dropped. "You're here?"

"Yes, I'm here. Tired and hungry and half out of sorts—darling, get a move on, will you? And ask Margaret if I can stay the night. I have to talk to you."

It was heaven. Dreams drifting down. The end of the rainbow. She cried huge hot tears and laughed through them. "I can be there in twenty minutes," she said. "If I have to run all the way...!"

He caught his breath. "Hurry, darling," he said. "I'll wait."

She kissed the mouthpiece tenderly and hung it up,

suspended for a moment in a world that had nothing to do with reality. Then she sprang out of bed and burst into Margaret's room.

"It's John; he's here; can he stay the night? We can put him on the sofa, and I have to get to the airport…!" It all tumbled out in a mad rush.

Margaret, who'd never married but remembered her own special season of love, smiled tolerantly. "Yes, he can stay the night. Get a cab to the airport—there's money in my pocketbook in the hall. Blankets in the closet. Now I'm going to sleep. Soundly," she added. "But don't take advantage of my complicity, dear."

Priss flushed. "No, I'd never do that," she promised. "Oh, Aunt Margaret, I love you," she said, impulsively hugging the older woman.

"I love you, too, dear. Now scoot!"

Priss was dressed in record time, in a pullover T-shirt and jeans and sneakers. She barely took time to run a brush through her hair, called a cab, and sat on the front steps of the small house waiting impatiently for it to come. Palm trees were silhouetted against the streetlights; the breeze rustled. And Priss was in agony. John was just miles away. John, here in Hawaii! The long months they'd been apart felt like years.

The cab came, at last, and she sat rigidly in the back until they got to the airport. She took just time enough to pay the driver before she went scurrying into the terminal.

Her wide soft eyes searched the crowd frantically. It wasn't until she felt the touch on her shoulder that she realized John wouldn't be wearing work clothes.

She turned, and there he was. All majesty and sophistication in a gray vested suit, his blond-streaked brown hair gleaming in the light, his face rigid, his eyes burning with blue sparks.

"Priss," he said in a tone that melted her knees.

"Oh, I thought I was dreaming," she remarked. Her lower lip trembled. "John, I'm sorry, but it hasn't changed, I haven't changed, I..."

He held out his arms, and she went into them like a homing pigeon, burying her face against his vest. His arms hurt, he was holding her so tightly, and she didn't even care.

She nestled her cheek on the soft fabric with a loud sigh. Her hands smoothed over the taut muscles of his back, under his suit coat. His heartbeat at her ear sounded heavy, rushed. She smiled, savoring it.

"No questions?" he asked quietly. "Don't you want to know why I'm here?"

"Eventually," she affirmed with a smile. Her chest rose and fell against him.

He laughed, although it sounded a little strained. "Let's go, honey."

"Didn't you bring a suitcase?" she asked as he put her gently away from him.

"I didn't have time. Not after Renée told me about that damned college kid," he said, and his eyes burned down into hers.

Her eyes widened as she read the stark jealousy in his expression. "You mean Ronald?" she asked, dazed.

He stared pointedly at her slender body. "Have you slept with him yet?"

Her lips parted. "No!" she gasped. "Of course not!"

"Why, of course not?" he demanded.

Her eyes softened as they searched his rugged face. "Because I belong to you, of course," she said with quiet pride. "I don't want another man's hands on me, ever."

He seemed to freeze in place. The breath he took was ragged. He touched her face with slow unsteady fingers. "I want you," he said huskily.

She managed a smile of her own. "I want you, too."

"Is Margaret asleep?" he asked.

She nodded.

He looked around. "Let's get out of here. I want to be alone with you."

She slid her hand into his big callused one, and let him lead her out of the terminal.

Minutes later they were in Margaret's plush living room, staring at each other in a momentary daze.

"I wanted to wait," he said. "I wanted to give you time, to let you see something of the world."

"Why?"

He shrugged his broad shoulders and glowered at her. "You're only eighteen."

She grinned. "Just the right age," she replied. "You can teach me."

"God, the thought of it makes me go weak in the knees." He laughed, staring at her. "Come here, you little torment, and let me love you."

She ran to him, glorying in his strength as he lifted her completely off the floor and laid her down on Margaret's green upholstered sofa. She sank into it, stretching with delicious anticipation while he shed his jacket and vest and slowly, sinuously, unbuttoned his shirt.

She'd seen him without it before, but that was a lifetime ago. The expanse of rippling bronze muscles excited her.

"Hurry up," she whispered impishly.

He grinned, his teeth white in his dark face. "Patience, darling."

She arched delicately, letting him see the thrust of her breasts through the thin material. He reached down and jerked the T-shirt up, baring her body to him. She hadn't bothered with a bra.

Her lips parted. "Yes, I like that," she whispered as he stared blatantly at her. "I like you looking at me."

"I'm going to do more than look."

"Be still, my throbbing heart," she teased, although her heartbeat *was* going wild.

He bent his head, and she lifted herself to meet his lips, gasping as his mouth found soft mounds and hard peaks and devoured them. Her nails dug into his upper arms and a tiny moan escaped her throat.

"Shhh," he silenced. "You'll have to be quiet, darling, or we'll wake Margaret."

"It's so sweet," she tried to explain through trembling lips as she stared up at him with her heart in her eyes. "Oh, so sweet, I can hardly bear it..."

"I know." He slid down beside her and let his hand run down her yielding body as his lips touched her eyelids. She whimpered as his mouth moved softly on

hers, relishing every tender line of it. "Priss," he
breathed. His mouth moved over her flushed face,
brushing, exploring, in a rhapsody of taut silence. And
all the while his hand roamed over her body, finding
the slimness of her legs, the softness of her flat stomach.

· Her hands tangled in his thick hair. Her thrusting
breasts encountered the hairy roughness of his chest,
and she froze. Her eyes opened, wide and soft and full
of discovery at the intensity of pleasure the contact
gave her.

"Does that please you, little sheila?" he asked
softly. He moved, easing his big body over hers.
"Don't fight me, all right? I'm only going to let you
feel me."

Her lips parted on a rush of breath as he let his
weight distribute itself over hers, and she learned
something shocking about the differences between
men and women. And when his chest melted into hers,
she shuddered helplessly, grinding her teeth together
and burying her forehead in his throat.

"Delicious," he whispered shakily. "Feeling
you…this way."

She moved a little, and he groaned.

"Now who's noisy?" she teased with a nervous
laugh.

"We'll have to make love in a soundproof room,"
he retorted. "Kiss me now. Kiss me hard and slow,
and let's get drunk on each other."

His large hands slid under her head and held it while
his mouth moved in and took absolute possession of

hers. It was like that hot kiss they'd shared back in Australia, and she felt his tongue exploring her mouth.

His body began to move against her, and she let his leg part her own, let him bring their bodies into a shocking kind of intimacy, and cried wildly into his mouth.

"Hush, darling," he whispered. His voice was shaking, and his mouth was insistent. His hands went down to her jeans and began to tug at them.

"Oh, John," she moaned, staring up at him.

"Do you want to?" he asked huskily. His blue eyes were dark and bright and wild-looking. "Do you want me?"

"H...h...here?" she managed.

He lay there, his body pulsating against hers, his muscles rigid, as he stared into her eyes. "Here?" He blinked and looked down at her and groaned. He forced his body to relax, although the feel of her softness under him wasn't doing his self-control a bit of good. He nuzzled his face against her hair. "I forgot where we were," he said raggedly. "See what you do to me?"

She was learning a lot about that, in a very elemental way. But oddly enough it wasn't embarrassing. It fascinated her to know that he was vulnerable with her.

Her hands moved under his shirt, against the hard muscles of his back, and felt them ripple, as if they liked her hesitant searching. She smiled with pleasure. "I never realized men were so heavy. No...!" she protested when he began to lift himself away. "No, I like it, I like feeling you over me."

"God!" he ground out, and shuddered. He rolled over onto his side, taking her with him. He wrapped her against his firm body, holding her there with a heavy leg thrown across hers.

"Sorry," she admitted dryly. "I've got a lot to learn."

"So have I," he confessed. He drew in a steadying breath and brought her small hands to his chest, letting her feel its dampness and rough heartbeat. "I've never had a woman affect me like this."

"I don't believe you."

"No, really," he said, looking into her eyes. He tugged a throw pillow under his head and smiled at her. His fingers brushed her face as they lay together in perfect accord, in a new intimacy. "I've never wanted anyone so much."

She looked down at her fingers against the broad expanse of his chest. Her fingers tugged at his dark body hair. "You're dark here," she noted. "Not blond like on your head."

"Sun doesn't get to my chest often," he reminded her. His eyes studied her pert young breasts pressed into that thickness, and he smiled. His thumbs edged toward the hard peaks and rubbed at them, feeling her shudder. "See how vulnerable we are to each other? You can't be expected to know how rare this kind of thing is. I've lain awake nights ever since you left Providence, aching for you."

Her eyes shot up to his. "But…"

"But what?" He brushed the disheveled hair away from her face, and his eyes darkened. "You said you'd write me."

Her eyes fell to his firm mouth. "And you said you'd have your mother write me for you."

He hesitated for a minute. "And you thought...yes, I understand now." He rolled onto his back and lifted her over him to study her. "I had this crazy idea that I could keep you at arm's length for another year or two—let this thing between us cool off a bit. Just until you could grow up." He smiled ruefully at her quick frown. "And then when you left, the world went dark for me. I couldn't work for missing you. And you wouldn't even write, you little horror. I looked forward to Easter vacation—I was planning all sorts of reunions. Then you called Renée and said there was a boy...!"

She put her fingers over his mouth. "I chased you unmercifully," she told him. "Everybody remarked about it. I kind of thought you came to see me that last day out of pity. I thought you felt sorry for me and then regretted what had happened and just wanted to forget it."

"I did want to forget," he confessed. "But I couldn't, Priss." His darkening eyes searched down her body to where she was pressed so closely against him, and they clouded perceptibly. "Sit up," he breathed huskily. "Let me look at you, for God's sake!"

Hypnotized, she drew away from him and watched his eyes blaze as they riveted to her.

"You...you've been going around...with Janie Weeks," she accused softly. The way he was looking at her made her feel faint.

"Janie has nothing at all to do with you and me,"

he said vaguely. He caught her around the rib cage and brought her breasts down to his mouth. "I kiss you here and taste rose petals," he whispered hungrily, while his mouth nibbled and brushed until she gasped and began to moan helplessly.

He laid her back on the sofa, crushing her mouth under his. One skilled hand cupped, molded, and caressed her, and she wanted him suddenly as she'd wanted nothing else in her life.

He drew away to look at her, and what he saw in her face made him want to throw back his head and scream his frustration. The situation was impossible. He couldn't do it, not on a sofa in someone else's house, not in a flaming rush like this.

Priss watched John deliberate for a long moment and searched his eyes curiously. "John?"

"Marry me," he said.

She trembled all over. Her hands lifted to his face and held it, caressed it. "What?"

"Marry me." He bent and kissed her mouth, softly, tenderly. "Say yes, Priss. Come on. Just one word…"

"Yes!" she ground out. Her hands tightened, trying to hold his wandering mouth to hers.

"Not right away," he explained. "I've got…a few problems to solve at the station. But by Christmas. Okay?"

"Can I come home with you?" she asked.

"No, darling."

"Why?" she complained.

"Because distance is the only thing that will save your virginity," he said bluntly. "I want you with a disgraceful lust; haven't you noticed?"

"I want you, too."

"Yes. But it has to be done properly," he said heavily. He sat up and tugged her T-shirt back into place. "Once I've had you, Priss, I won't be able to stop; don't you know that?"

"It must be like eating potato chips." She laughed wickedly.

"Much worse," he told her. He smiled slowly. "And once you've had me, you'll want me again. After the first time, anyway."

She felt drunk on pleasure. "I wish we could do it on the beach the first time."

"Pagan," he teased, but his blood was running hot in his veins as he looked down at her slender young body and realized that she wanted him just as much as he wanted her. He could almost picture them, her tanned body writhing under him, her soft young voice moaning with the intensity of pleasure he could arouse...

"You can imagine it, can't you?" she asked perceptively. "So can I. Every second of it."

"You don't even know what to expect," he chided.

"Yes, I do." She sat up, too, staring into his eyes. "I'm not that naive. I know exactly what you'll do to me, and how. And I'll bite you, and wrap my legs around you, and move my body..."

His mouth hit hers with the force of a tidal wave. He crushed her down into the sofa, his body moving roughly on hers, and she reacted like any woman in love. Her body ached for his, to know it. Her eyes misted with tears as she struggled to make him lose control, to give her what her body was starving for.

But he wasn't a boy, and he could see all too clearly what the consequences would be. Despite the raging desire that consumed him, he tore his body away from hers and rolled onto his back, dragging in air.

"John," she moaned.

He pulled her close against his side and smoothed her long unruly hair. "Close your eyes. It passes. Remember?" he added roguishly.

She blushed, smiling back. "That was my fault. I liked having my way with you," she recalled.

"Someday soon, I'll enjoy letting you. But not," he added with mock anger, "when my hands are tied. It's all or nothing with me, Priss, as you should damned well know by now."

She stared up at his face lovingly. "I guess I can wait, if you can."

"We'll struggle through together," he said with a grin. "Now, get up. God knows what Margaret would say if she walked in."

"As a matter of fact, she did say something about not betraying her trust," Priss confessed.

"What an interesting time to tell me," he returned. He pulled her to her feet, putting her wrists behind her back so he could study her young beauty with eyes that couldn't seem to get enough of it. "Lovely Priscilla," he said finally. "I'll never tire of looking at you. You're beaut."

The deep slow drawl made her tingle. She smiled at him, a woman so completely in love that happiness radiated from every pore of her skin. "So are you."

He breathed deliberately, forcing his heart to behave. "Go to bed," he ordered, bending to kiss her delicately on the mouth. "We'll talk some more in the morning, when it's safer."

Her eyes searched his. "Can't I sleep with you?"

His jaw tensed. "No."

"Just sleep," she pleaded.

He put her away from him with a curt laugh. "I can see that. Sleeping, with you in my arms."

Her eyebrows rose. "Couldn't you?"

He glanced down at her with impatient amusement. "You are a green one, aren't you? No, darling, I couldn't. I want you." At her confused stare, he drew her against his powerful body and deliberately moved her hips against his. "Want," he emphasized even as her mind made the connection between the changed contours of his body and the words.

"Oh," she exclaimed softly.

His shadowy eyes surveyed hers. "Didn't you understand?" he asked gently. "It's uncomfortable for a man."

Her face flushed with color as she met his gaze. "I'm sorry. I really do have a lot to learn."

"It will be fascinating," he murmured, watching her draw discreetly away.

"What will?"

"Shocking you speechless on our wedding night," he said with a wicked grin. "I'll live on the very thought for the next few months."

"John Sterling! And I thought you were a gentleman."

"Remind me, after we're married, to give you the real definition of that word: it's an eye-opener."

"Do I have to go?" she protested.

His bright eyes twinkled. "Unless you want to be attacked."

She sidestepped his playful grab, laughing, bubbling with joy, gloriously beautiful with her pale blonde hair curling around her shoulders in a cloud, and her emerald eyes challenging him from the perfect oval of her lovely face.

"I'll go," she said. "It must be the tropical air getting to your brain."

"It's more a case of you getting to my body," he taunted, his eyes sparkling.

She forced her legs to carry her to the door, and turned back to stare at him, at the thick blond-streaked brown hair her fingers had mussed, at the sensuous look of him with his shirt unbuttoned, his mouth faintly swollen, his eyes glittering with desire.

"I'll be the best wife you ever imagined," she said softly. "I'll love you and give you children, and never even complain when you track mud onto my clean carpets." She grinned. "And in bed, once you teach me how, I'll just blow your mind, Jonathan Sterling."

He smiled slowly. "I can hardly wait."

"Sweet dreams...darling," she added, feeling wildly adult and passionate and loved. He hadn't said the words, but he must feel them. She was sure that he did. Otherwise why would he want to marry her when he'd always clung to his freedom? When he smiled back at her, all the tiny doubts rushed away in a surge of wonder, and she danced out the door and into bed, humming a love song under her breath.

The next morning he was sitting at the breakfast table with Margaret when Priscilla got downstairs.

She'd overslept and it was midmorning, and she looked as flustered as she felt.

"It's about time," John said with a grimace. "Some way for a newly engaged woman to behave, I'll tell you."

Margaret was grinning from ear to ear. "I'll leave you two to discuss your future alone, while I call Renée and Adam and just burst with pride."

John and Priss laughed as she retreated in a bustle.

"Mom will have it all over the valley before you get back," Priss warned him. "Perhaps you'd better call your mother…"

"I told Mother before I left Australia," he said softly. "She was thrilled at my excellent taste in women. Come here, for God's sake!"

She settled down in his lap and smiled into his amused eyes. "I like this a lot," she told him, teasing his mouth with hers. "And I am going to love," she kissed him again, "getting my hands," she bit at his lower lip, "on your body…!"

He was kissing her hard, and her head went back under the pressure. She clung to him, trying to be what he wanted, trying to meet his passion with her own.

"When will you learn," he murmured breathlessly, "that I like your mouth open when we kiss?"

"Oh," she whispered back, shaken. She parted her lips and touched them to his. "Like this?"

"Yes…"

She felt the penetrating warmth of his tongue, deeply searching, arousing, and she began to ache in the oddest places. Her nails clawed into the big muscles of his upper arms as he held her tight against him.

"Why do you wear these things?" he groaned, searching under her T-shirt and finding a lacy little wisp of fabric in his way.

"Take it off if you don't like it." She laughed.

"With Margaret a few steps away?" He chuckled, but his voice was unsteady. He lifted his shaggy head and stared into her eyes warmly. "I'd much prefer your breasts to scrambled eggs, if you want to know."

She blushed from her cheeks down to her throat, and he watched with unholy amusement. "How old did you say you were?" he provoked.

"Almost nineteen," she returned with a flash of spirit. "And just be conceited, while you can. Someday I'll be shocking you!"

"I don't doubt it a bit," he agreed, smiling as he kissed her again, but softly this time. His hand pressed over her breast, and it was warm and strong even through the fabric. "I like stroking you here," he whispered, moving his fingers slowly, erotically.

Her lips opened as she struggled for breath. She looked into his dark hard face with awe. "I like it, too. Your hands...are so big."

"You're not big at all," he said gently. "You're delicate and soft and you always smell of gardenias. I don't think I'll ever tire of making love to you."

"I can just see you doing that while you herd cattle." She laughed unsteadily.

"Mustering," he corrected. "In Australia, we muster mobs of cattle."

"In America, we have laws against the mob, and

we punch cattle. And we have ranches, not stations. And—''

''And you talk a lot.'' He stoped her banter with his lips. ''Slide that little hand inside my shirt, and touch me the way I'm touching you. I like being stroked, too.''

''Really?'' she breathed, all eyes.

''Really.''

She'd gotten the first two buttons undone when footsteps sounded in the hall and she groaned. ''Oh, damn, just when I'm getting the hang of it...''

''Not my fault.'' He laughed softly, letting her get to her feet. ''You should have hurried.''

''Just you wait,'' she threatened as she straightened her T-shirt.

''I'll try,'' he sighed, studying her slender lovely body. ''But I'll ache in the damndest places until then.''

She turned away, blushing wildly, as Margaret came back into the room, beaming, full of news from home, the biggest part of it being how thrilled Renée and Adam were about the engagement. And once she started, John and Priss didn't have a chance for further conversation.

Before she knew it, it was time to go with John to the airport. He seemed as reluctant as she felt, and he clung warmly to her hand in the cab and through the terminal. She stopped when he reached Customs and Immigration, and her eyes blurred with tears as she looked up into the rough, broad face she loved so much.

''Don't look like that, or I won't be able to leave

you," he breathed. "God, Priss, I'd give anything to take you with me!"

"Would I fit in your pocket?"

"Not quite, I'm afraid." He pulled her against him. "Although without your high heels, you barely come to my chin."

"John," she said, scanning his face, "you meant it, didn't you? You do want to marry me?"

"Would I have asked you, if I didn't?" he mocked. "After all," he added, bending to whisper, "I haven't seduced you, and we don't have to rush to the altar before your waistline expands, do we?"

She reddened and grinned at him. "I thought about it last night," she confessed. "I thought about taking my clothes off and climbing into bed with you."

"What stopped you?" he asked.

She shrugged, staring at the gray vest of his suit. "I was afraid you might not like being seduced."

He tilted up her chin. "I find the idea wildly exciting," he confided, holding her gaze. "I'd like letting you make love to me."

"Oh, John," she wailed helplessly.

"Too late now." He chuckled.

Her lips smoothed over his, and he stopped laughing and kissed her with hungry passion. His arms crushed her, and his mouth devoured, penetrating, arousing, and she stood there and let him do what he wanted, drowning in the love she felt for him, loving his ardor. Her arms clung around his neck, and she felt her legs tremble when he lifted his head.

"Want me, Priss?" he whispered unsteadily, with blazing eyes. "I want you, too."

"Yes, I can feel...I mean..." she faltered, drawing away a little in embarrassment.

"We're going to be married," he said softly. "It's all right if we know intimate things about each other now."

She swallowed. "Yes."

He brushed his lips over her closed eyelids. "When we're together again," he whispered, "we'll undress each other and lie together and make out like crazy. I'll try to get back next month, or maybe you can come home."

Her heart was beating so wildly, it hurt her. She buried her face against him, trembling with frustrated ardor. "Could we do that," she questioned unsteadily, "and not go all the way?"

"Yes, I think so," he responded. He drew her close, holding her in a warm embrace, his face against her hair. "I want to do this right. I don't want to anticipate our wedding night, but there are other paths to fulfillment besides the obvious one, little innocent," he whispered softly. "I'll teach you some of them...."

"John," she moaned, clenching her teeth as the wanting became suddenly unbearable.

"Soon, darling," he assured her. He hugged her bruisingly close, and his mouth searched for hers. He kissed her hotly for a long time, and his face was ruddy with frustration when he finally drew away. His nostrils flared as he observed her bright eyes. "Wait for me," he said curtly. "No more dates with the college boy."

"No more," she promised. She smiled slowly. "No more dates for you, either."

"Fat chance," he chuckled. "Every woman I see looks like you these days. Be good, love."

"You, too."

He winked and turned to walk away. She lifted a hand toward him, wanting to call out, wanting to say, I love you. But she didn't. She watched his tall broad-shouldered back until he was out of sight. And then she went back to Margaret's, torn between joy and grief. The waiting was going to be horrible. She didn't know how she could survive it, now that he was going to be hers, at last.

John. Her husband. The thought would sustain her, like water to a desert survivor. She imagined them together in bed, straining against each other in the darkness, loving each other with their bodies. She imagined them with children, John carrying a little boy on his shoulders and laughing. She imagined them being together in the evenings, sitting together while he worked on the books and she graded papers. The dreams were beautiful. And the memories of how it had been between them physically were as satisfying as the dreams.

Chapter 5

Priss couldn't remember a time in her life when she'd been so happy. The hidden photograph in her wallet came out of hiding. She showed it to Ronald—to all her friends—with such radiant love and pride that she glowed like a new penny. John was hers at last. Hers!

She rushed downtown to an exclusive department store, where Margaret had an account, and searched for hours until she found just the wedding gown she wanted. It was a dream of a gown, with a keyhole neckline and yards of lace and satin and a floor-length veil. She sighed over it as the saleslady smilingly put it away in a box. Priss could just see how she'd look walking down the aisle to John in it.

She came back to Margaret's house with stars in her eyes. "You don't mind that I used your card, do you?" Priss asked belatedly when Aunt Margaret seemed hesitant.

"No, darling, of course not," Margaret said gently. "It's just that…well, don't you think it might be better to wait a bit on the gown? Just until you and John set a definite date?"

Priss felt a tension in the air. She studied the older woman quietly, intently. "Aunt Margaret, you don't think he'll back out?"

Margaret looked hunted. She sat on the edge of her elegant Chippendale chair with her dainty hands clenched in her lap, her eyes troubled. "Darling, it's been well over a week since John left."

Priss laughed, relieved. "Oh, you mean he hasn't called! I didn't really expect him to, you know. He said he had some things to iron out back home. Selling cattle again, I'll bet; you know how he likes those sales!"

But the older woman didn't laugh. She didn't want to tell Priss what she'd heard when she talked to Renée the previous night. That John had vanished from sight the past few days, and that no one had seen or heard from him. Perhaps it was nothing, but Priss was so caught up in the excitement of the hurried engagement that Margaret was worried. If anything went wrong…

"It's just not good to tempt fate," Margaret said finally. "You're so impulsive, darling."

"Stop worrying," Priss chided. She got up and kissed Margaret's wrinkled cheek. "Everything will be fine. And I'll pay you something every week out of my allowance for the dress," she added softly.

"It's not the money," Margaret denied. She touched Priss's shoulder affectionately. "I'll make you a wedding present of it. I just don't want you to get hurt.''

Cold chills worked their way down Priss's back-bone, but she hid her anxiety well. "Now stop that," she said. "John would never let me down. He wouldn't have proposed unless he meant it; unless he loved me. Now let's have some lunch. I'm starved!''

Margaret's eyes followed the graceful movement as Priss ran off toward the kitchen. Priss was such a child. She didn't realize that often men thought with their glands more than with their brains. John's hunger for Priss had been obvious, but Margaret wondered if it would fade with his absence from her. Perhaps he had just gotten caught up in Priss's infatuation and had been trapped by his own desire for her. He might even now be looking for a way out of the engagement. That could very well be why he hadn't contacted Priss. It was a disturbing thought, and Margaret was afraid for her niece if it was true.

Meanwhile the seed of suspicion had been firmly planted in Priss's mind, and it didn't go away. When the days kept passing without word from John, she began to worry even more. And finally, just to ease her own silly suspicions, she gave in and called him. She had to be sure. Her grades were falling from the devastating effect of loving him. And even if she went back to Australia to marry him, she had every inten-tion of finishing her education and getting her teaching degree.

She waited until night, when the rates would be cheaper, and let the phone ring for a long time before he finally answered.

"John?" she asked hesitantly.

"Priss!" There was a long static pause. "Priscilla?"

"Yes, it's me," she confirmed. She sat down in the chair beside the hall phone, gripping the receiver. Something was wrong—she could feel it. "John, are you okay?"

She heard a snap and a click, like a lighter firing up. "I'm okay," he said quietly. "How about you?"

"I just miss you, that's all," she said. "I thought you'd call."

"I was going to, later tonight."

She stared at the cord. "How are things going over there?"

There was another pause. "Fine," he said curtly.

"That's nice. How's your mother?"

He sighed heavily. "She's…doing very well. She's gone to stay with her sister in California."

"California? She'll enjoy visiting there."

"Yes." He sounded exhausted.

"How are you managing alone?" she teased.

There was a pause again. "I'm…not alone."

"Are Randolph and Latrice visiting? I heard they had twins a year ago. Your brother must have his hands full," she said softly. She knew Randy and Latrice quite well. They were frequent visitors at the Sterling Run.

"It isn't Randy." There was a thud, as if he'd hit something. "I've got a woman here, if you want to know."

It was like being struck between the eyes with a

hammer. The word echoed around in her head, rico-cheting wildly. "A...cleaning woman?"

He laughed coldly. "Now, you know better than that, don't you?" he asked. "You said yourself, I'm passionate. And being around you was enough to drive any red-blooded man wild. I came back here aching like a boy, and Janie invited me over for dinner..." She heard the sigh. "Well, honey, you know what a dish she is. I couldn't help myself. And afterward I asked her to move in."

Janie? Her eyes widened. Janie Weeks, the divorcée he'd been seen with before he flew to Hawaii? He'd said his seeing Janie didn't concern her, but he'd never denied it. And he hadn't spoken of love, either. Only of desire.

She stared at the wall blankly. Her life was ending. John was telling her that he didn't love her. They weren't going to get married and live happily ever after. It had all been a bad joke. It was over.

"But...I bought a wedding gown," she began slowly, uncomprehending.

"I came to my senses in time, thank God," he replied stonily. "Priss, you're eighteen years old. Eighteen! I'm twenty-eight. Those ten years, and your innocence, make it all impossible. I need someone older, more sophisticated, more experienced. I can't tie myself down to a kid."

Her body felt washed in heat. He hadn't treated her like a kid. She almost reminded him of that, but her pride wouldn't let her.

"I'm sorry, Priss," he said when she didn't answer. "Really damned sorry. But you have to understand, I went off the beam for a while. You went to my head a little, and I got some strange ideas about the future. Now I'm back in my right mind and stone sober, and I want my freedom more than I want you. It wouldn't have worked out. Priss, are you there?''

"I'm here." She sounded almost normal, despite the fact that her heart was breaking and there were tears in her eyes. "I hear you."

There was another pause. "You understand, surely," he said roughly. "If you'd been a little older or more experienced, we could have had a good time together, with no strings. But you're just too intense, Priss. And worlds too young for me. My oath, I shudder just thinking about what marriage would have been like with you."

Her lips trembled, and the tears overflowed. "I love you," she whispered brokenly. "How do I stop?"

He swallowed, and she heard a ragged breath over the phone. "Priss," he ground out. "It's just desire, nothing more," he said, but he sounded odd. "The same desire I felt for you. But I'm over mine, and you'll get over yours. For God's sake, you didn't really expect me to marry you just so I could sleep with you?''

The way he said it made her sound like a naive little idiot. She took a steadying breath. "That's me, all right," she laughed bitterly. "I'm just a kid, after all. Just a green little girl…"

"Isn't it better to find out now than after we'd married and messed up our lives?" he growled. "You're well rid of me. Just think of it that way, can't you?"

"I'll do my best; I promise you," she said, hating

him. "After all, I'm young. And Ronald won't let me pine away."

There was a pause before he spoke. "Your life is your own concern and none of mine. I've got Janie. And my God, what a contrast she is to you," he added on a cold laugh. "All woman. Sweet and wild and giving, not a child looking for rainbows. She's satisfied with plain sex, and I don't have to buy her a wedding band."

She could picture him with the woman. She could see them... She closed her eyes, aware of a tension on the other end of the line, but it didn't register. "So that's that," she said quietly. "What a good thing you didn't get me a ring. I'm only sorry you didn't come to your senses before I went out and told the whole world we were getting married."

"Gossip dies down eventually." He sounded bored.

"For men, certainly," she replied. "Not for women. Especially not here."

"Well, then, you'll just have to keep your little chin up, won't you?" he informed her. "Tell them you dropped me—I don't mind."

She drew in a deep breath while her heart seemed to go crazy. "Lie to my friends the way you lied to me? No, thanks. I still have some integrity," she said with bitter pride. "I'm glad you came to your senses, John," she added on a broken sob. "I wouldn't marry you now if you were—"

"You wouldn't be asked," he interrupted coldly. "I want a woman, not a silly little girl. At least now you won't be following me around like a pet dog anymore, will you?"

Tears burst from her eyes. She felt sick and empty and dead inside. "No," she cried. "I won't."

There was a brief silence on the other end of the line. But she hung up quietly before he had the chance to say anything else. She couldn't have borne another word.

She cried and cried, the tears silent and hot and profuse. She was still sitting there when Margaret came into the hall and stopped suddenly.

"Priscilla! What is it, dear?" she asked, concerned.

"That was John," Priss whispered, red-eyed. "He isn't going to marry me. He's decided that his divorcée is more than enough for him. He can have her without marriage, you see."

Margaret caught her breath. "Can he, now?" she said gruffly. "Here, I'll call Renée, and we'll find out what's going on."

Renée answered the phone when Margaret called, her own eyes red, her voice wobbling as she told Margaret it was all true, that John did…have a woman at his house, that he'd been to see them, to tell them about why he was ending the engagement.

"Can she talk to me, Margaret?" Renée asked Adam's sister.

"No," Margaret said. "She's gone up to her room in tears. She's just devastated. Why, Renée? Why would he do such a thing?"

Renée had to fight for control. "Priss is young, she'll…get over it. Darling, tell her to call me when she's calmer, will you? And thank you, Margaret, for taking such…such good care of her."

"Renée, are you all right? You sound odd…"

"I've got a cold," she replied. "I'm fine. Look after Priss. And yourself. 'Bye, darling."

She hung up, wiping the tears away. Adam came into the living room and took her quietly into his arms.

"Poor Priss," she muttered tearfully.

"Yes," he agreed, patting her. "But John was right. With the situation as it was, what else could he do?"

"What a burden he placed on us, though, darling," she stated despondently.

"A horrible mess, all around," Adam agreed. He smoothed her hair. "At least we can spare Priss." Adam kissed her. "Regrets aren't going to do either of them any good. Besides, Priss is young, as we keep saying. The young heal quickly."

"I hope you're right," Renée said fervently. "Oh, I do hope you are."

It was all Priss could do to lie in bed that night. She couldn't call her parents back. She couldn't bear the sympathy she knew would be in their voices. Margaret seemed to understand that because she left her niece alone after bringing her a cup of tea and two aspirin to help her sleep.

The next morning Priss slept late. It had been long past midnight when she finally dropped off to sleep the night before. She got up, dressed in jeans and a neat top and sneakers, and went downtown.

The lady who'd waited on her in the department store didn't ask any questions as she brought out the dress Priss had watched her put away so carefully. She arranged the ticket to credit Margaret's account, and all the while Priss stared blankly at the gown.

It was white satin with alençon lace and illusion lace appliqués from its keyhole neckline to the empire waist. It had puffy little sleeves and a Juliet cap with a full veil flowing from it. Priss had never seen anything so exquisite in all her life. She remembered daydreaming, just days before, about how it would feel to have John see her in it, as they stood before a minister and pledged to love each other forever.

"Here we go," the saleslady said politely, getting Priss to sign the credit slip. "I'm sorry things didn't work out."

"So am I," Priss said in a ghost of a voice.

The saleslady's polite smile faded. "Time helps," she said quietly, and her eyes hinted at a past hurt that must have been similar to Priss's. "There are kind, wonderful men in this world. I found mine on the second try. Don't give up."

Priss found a smile for her, for that tiny bit of understanding that eased her path. "Thank you," she said, and with one last lingering look at the gown, she turned and walked out of the store.

She didn't go to class that day. Instead she wandered through a tourist attraction, one of the many botanical gardens that Honolulu was famous for. Her eyes drank in orchids of every species, and oleander and birds of paradise and candle flowers. She touched the blooming fronds of the exquisite orange-blossomed flame tree, the royal poinciana, and sniffed the perfume that was much sweeter than anything in a bottle.

Eventually she sat down on a bench and let the numbness creep over her, deaden the pain. It was a matter of making it through one day at a time, she told herself. First she had to forget John. She had to forget the day she'd left Australia, and the night he'd flown to Honolulu. She had to remember that John wanted a woman, not a little girl, and that she wasn't worth a wedding ring to him.

She listened to her own self-pity and laughed out loud. No, that wasn't her thing. She wouldn't be caught in that bitter trap. She'd have to get her mind on something else, and fast.

Without really thinking about where she was going, she walked into the city hospital, to the admissions desk, and asked for the personnel office. And then she went in and volunteered some free time.

Inevitably people asked about her engagement, and she repeated again and again the pat little speech she had devised. It wasn't the lie John had suggested, but it wasn't the truth, either. She and John had decided that her education came first, she explained to save her savaged pride. It was much too soon for marriage. But there were sly smiles and knowing looks, and she knew she wasn't fooling anyone—least of all herself. Over and over she kept hearing John's deep voice telling her what a silly little girl she was. Laughing at her for following him around "like a little pet dog." Her pride was shattered. Despite the healing powers of time, the humiliation lingered. She should have realized that all he'd wanted was her body. She should have known it would never work out. If only she could stop loving him!

The nights were the roughest. Her days were full

now: When she wasn't in class, she was working in the children's ward, reading stories and straightening pillows and making little faces smile. By helping other people, she forgot her own problems and turned outward instead of inward. But at night the memories returned in full force, dark and sweet. John, holding her. John, touching her responsive young body. John, promising heaven after they were married. He haunted her like a persistent ghost, and she knew all too well that it was more than she could bear to go back to Providence anytime soon to visit.

She talked to her mother about it eventually, because it worried her so much.

"I'm not a coward, really I'm not," she told Renée. "It's just that it still hurts, and..."

"I know, darling," Renée said. She had to bite her tongue not to blurt out the whole horrible story. But Adam was right, it wouldn't help things. "Suppose Dad and I fly over and see you?"

She smiled. "That would be nice, but can you afford it?"

"Darling, Margaret browbeat your father into accepting the fare as an anniversary present. How about that?"

"I love Aunt Margaret!"

"So do we. We'll talk more about the visit later. But getting back to you, how are you, darling?"

Priss managed not to tell the truth. "I'm doing fine. I'm working in a children's ward, and I think I've got a secretarial job lined up for summer vacation. I wish I could come home, but..."

"Yes, I know. It's too soon." Renée sighed. "It would be terribly awkward if you ran into John."

"Have…have you seen him?" she asked, hating the question because it betrayed her.

Renée had to grit her teeth. Oh, yes, she'd seen the poor miserable soul, looking years past his true age, his eyes so haunted that she couldn't look into them.

"Actually, no, darling," Renée lied while tears welled up in her eyes.

"Oh." Priss sighed. "Well, I suppose it's all for the best. Ronald and I are going to see that new comedy movie tonight. It should be fun."

"You aren't still grieving?" her mother asked tentatively.

"Of course not," Priss assured her. "I'm getting along just fine. Perhaps it was infatuation after all."

Renée bit her tongue. "Perhaps it was. Take care, darling. I love you. Dad sends his love, too."

"That works both ways," Priss said softly. "Thanks for being such great parents. I'll call you again soon."

"Yes, please do. 'Bye."

Priss hung up and closed her eyes on fresh tears. Someday it would stop hurting. Someday she'd forget. Someday, somehow, the images would fade and there would be another spring, another season of love….

Chapter 6

It was almost dark by the time Renée and Adam Johnson pulled up in front of their small bungalow and caught sight of Priss.

"Darling, how lovely you look," Renée called out as her daughter ran across the paddock and into her arms. "College has made a sophisticate out of you."

"I'll say," Adam agreed, slamming the car door. He kissed Priss warmly. It had been more than four years since his daughter had been home, and trips to Hawaii had necessarily been infrequent. He was looking forward to getting to know Priss all over again. "What a lady we raised!"

"Soon to be unrecognizable as I begin teaching primary school," she bantered. "I can hardly wait. I brought back some storybooks from Honolulu for the children, just in case I couldn't get them locally."

"And I baked an apple pie, just for you, darling,"

Renée told her, putting a motherly arm around her daughter's shoulders.

"I know." Priss grinned. "I smelled it when I walked into the house. How was the luncheon?"

"Lovely," Renée said. "We went home with Betty Gaines and spent the rest of the day planning your homecoming party," she added with a smile. "That's why we couldn't meet you. Uh, John said he didn't mind giving you a ride."

Priss's face clouded. "No, he didn't."

Renée started to speak, but Adam shook his head quickly. "Betty Gaines teaches third grade now. You remember her, don't you?" Adam asked.

"Yes, of course," she replied warmly. "I liked her very much. It's so sweet of her to give me a party."

"Well, come on," Renée urged. "Let's go inside, darling. It's so good to have you home!"

"I'll miss Aunt Margaret a bit," Priss confided. "She was such fun to live with!"

"She'll miss you, I'm sure," Renée said. She led the way into the kitchen, where Priss and Adam sat down while she made coffee and thick ham sandwiches. "By the way, how about Ronald George? He's taking a position here, too, isn't he?"

Priss grinned. "He says so, for a little while, anyway, until he proves to his father that he can make his own living without waiting to inherit the family fortune. But just between us, I think he'll end up back in England eventually."

"He's a fine young man," said Adam, who had met Ronald during his visits to Hawaii. He glanced at Priss. "We thought you might marry him."

"Ronald?" Her expression made clear her feelings for the man in question. "No, he's a lot of fun and we're great friends. But we don't even think alike on the important issues."

Renée's eyes closed briefly, but she didn't say anything else.

"I'm glad you wanted to come back here to teach," Adam said with quiet pride. "I'm sure you could have made a bigger salary in Hawaii."

"But my parents aren't in Hawaii," she retorted. "I was getting sort of homesick, to tell the truth."

They all laughed, and afterward things settled down into a normal, sweetly familiar routine. By bedtime, Priss felt as if she'd never been away. Except when she started remembering John. Sleeping in her bed again was an ordeal, because it held such powerful memories. She imagined that she could still feel the weight of his body above hers, feel the hard, warm crush of his mouth. And it was hours before she finally coaxed her mind into sleep. But when she slept, it was dreamlessly for once.

The primary school in Providence was a small brick building and nothing fancy to look at, but her few students were enthusiastic and attentive, and she loved working with them. And although they missed the teacher they'd begun the year with, they quickly warmed to Priss. First-graders, she thought, were the best kind of people to be around. Except for the twins...

The twins, Bobby and Gerry, were all that John had hinted, and more. Apparently they had very little discipline or attention at home, Priss noted, because they did everything possible to attract any kind of notice from the other students. On her first day in class, they put frogs in her desk and hid the chalk and nailed her chair to the floor. She sent a note home to Randy and Latrice to be signed, but the next day the boys came back empty-handed.

"Gerry, where is the note I sent home with you?" she asked one of the twins, the one whose hair was a deeper red than his brother's.

"Uh, we lost it," he said and smirked.

"Dead right, we did," Bobby agreed. "Wind got it."

She pursed her lips. "Really?" she asked.

They grinned at her. "Fair dinkum!" they promised.

"I'll get you another one to take home this afternoon," she said, then thought better of the idea. "No, tell you what, I'm going to a party tomorrow night. Your parents will be there, so I'll give it to them myself and save you boys the trouble."

Their expressions were comical. They began protesting at once, but she held up a hand and began the lesson. It was the first of many skirmishes to come.

The brightest spot in the week was the arrival of Ronald George, who was helping out in Betty Gaines's third grade. His twinkling wit helped to pass the time, and Priss was grateful for a familiar face other than her father's among the staff. She still had lunch with Adam, though, and she noticed that Ronald got into the habit of sitting with Amanda Neal, one of the other teachers. He grinned at Priss sheepishly, and she winked back. Mandy was very pretty, petite, blonde, and blue-eyed. And very British. That, she told herself, looked like the beginning of a nice match.

Friday ended with a bang, as the twins beat up another boy, whose mother came to violently protest her son's abuse by "those ruffians!" Priss calmed her at great length and hurried home to eat her supper before it was time to dress for the party.

As she ate she tried to control the butterflies in her stomach. It was going to be a good night, she told herself. She was going to glow as she never had in the old days; she was going to bring John Sterling to his knees! Let him see what he was missing, what he'd thrown away. Her heart lifted as she contemplated her old vision of floating down an elegant staircase to watch his jaw fall, his eyes burn with wanting her. She smiled to herself. Yes, that would be sweet, to see his desire for her and show him that she felt nothing at all.

"I have to talk to Randy and Latrice about the twins," she told her parents as she finished her second cup of coffee. "They beat up Mrs. Morrison's boy today."

Adam nodded. "The boy's something of a bully, but they shouldn't have ganged up on him," he agreed. "I suppose Randy and Latrice will come to the party. If Latrice is home. She travels so much these days."

"For pleasure?" Priss asked.

"I suppose. I don't think she and Randy get along very well. And John can't be making it easy for them," he said quietly. "He's been pure hell, from what I hear. He's very bitter."

About what? Priss wondered, but only nodded. "Will John be at the party?"

"I don't know," he replied. "He's rarely seen these days. He sticks to the station like glue, except for an occasional trip to cattle sales."

That didn't sound like the old John, who had loved people and socializing. She stared at her father. "Are things bad at the station?" she probed.

"They have been," he said vaguely. "Drought, you know. But I guess they're picking up now. John just bought that new Ford."

"It's not a luxury car, but it's nice just the same," Renée interrupted. "We'd better rush, darlings."

Upstairs she put on the long white gown with its one shoulder strap and side slits and sequined bodice and studied herself in the mirror. She'd filled out in five years. She still wasn't quite voluptuous, but she wasn't thin, either. She looked good, she told herself. She put on a pearl necklace and bracelet and ear studs, and a minimum of makeup. To top it all off, she draped a blue fox boa around her neck. Yes, she thought. Yes, that would be just the thing to parade in front of John Sterling.

When she went back downstairs, her parents were waiting for her. Her father was dressed in dark evening clothes; her mother in a royal blue gown.

"Gorgeous couple." Priss beamed. "You look lovely. You, too, Dad."

"I'll box your ears," he threatened. "You're a dish yourself. Didn't we do well?" he teased Renée.

"Yes, we did, darling." Renée grinned, taking his arm. "You'll wow 'em, sweetheart," she told her daughter.

Priss fiddled with the boa. "I'd like to stop by the Sterling place on the way to the party, if you don't mind," she said quietly. "I need to speak to Randy and Latrice alone, and even if they do come to the party, I realize it would be better to see them in a quieter setting."

"No problem," Adam said. "Shall we go, ladies?"

It was a chilly night, and Priss almost wished she'd worn a jacket instead of the boa. But the car soon warmed up, and it didn't take long to wind up the oleander-lined driveway at the Sterling station to the old Colonial-style house with its graceful porches. It had been recently repainted and gleamed like a stoic ghost among the gum and wattle trees.

"I'll only be a minute," Priss promised. She got out of the car and walked slowly up the steps onto the wide porch. It looked just as it had years ago, when she used to come up here and have lunch with John's mother. She'd always loved the elegance of the old house.

She knocked on the door, fraught with nerves, wondering who would answer it. Footsteps sounded, and the door was thrown open. But it wasn't John, it was Randy.

He was shorter than his brother, with reddish-brown hair and pale blue eyes, and in his younger days he had had a frightful superiority complex. But now he seemed different as he grinned at Priss and let her into the house.

"Well, hello," he greeted deeply, his eyes clearly approving little Priscilla Johnson's new look. "Priscilla, how you've grown up!" He admired her.

"One does, inevitably," she said and smiled back. She was trembling, but she maintained her poise. Was John nearby; was he here? she wondered feverishly.

"Can I help you?" he asked, looking puzzled as to why she might be there.

"Yes. I need to speak with you and Latrice, about the twins," she said gently. "I'm sorry to bother you at home like this, but I sent a note, and it got lost. And at the party, it would be impossible. It won't take long, I promise."

"The twins," he said with a resigned sigh. "I've thought of tying them to trees, you know. They ignore me and laugh at Latrice—when she's home," he added darkly.

"What's all the commotion?" came a deep familiar drawl from the living room doorway. It was John, of course.

Tonight he was wearing close-fitting tan slacks and a brown plaid jacket with a white shirt and tie. Powerful muscles strained at the garments as if they were purchased when he was a little lighter, less mature. He looked faintly rumpled, and her eyes went over his worn garments with faint hauteur.

His cutting eyes flashed angrily as he received that insult, and they lingered on her own attire. If she'd expected to bring him to his knees, she was immediately disappointed. He eyed her indifferently, and then turned away. "I'm going on over to the Gaineses'," he told his brother. "See you there; but I'm not staying long. Parties aren't my style these days," he added with a cold smile in Priss's direction. "By the way, honey," he drawled, "we're simple folk around here. Designer gowns aren't the routine. All they accomplish is to make the other women who can't afford them feel uncomfortable."

Her eyes narrowed. "Yes, I can see the current style doesn't owe anything to fashion," she added with another meaningful glance at his own clothing. "You'll have to forgive me. I grew used to genteel company in Hawaii."

"Like that pommy you brought back?" John taunted with cold eyes and a cutting smile.

"At least," she replied carelessly, "he has excellent breeding and rather admirable taste in suits!"

John's face stiffened. He nodded toward Randy and walked out the door without a backward glance.

Randy looked as if he would have loved to say something, but he only shrugged uncomfortably.

"Latrice!" he called up the staircase. "Could you come down here, please?"

Seconds later an angry sigh came from upstairs, and Latrice descended. She was redheaded and petite, with a kewpie-doll prettiness.

"There you are," Priss said, forcing herself to forget John and his bad temper and get her mind on the present. She smiled. "It's good to see you again, Latrice. I'm afraid my visit isn't purely social, though. I want to have a word with you about the twins."

Latrice laughed huskily. "Oh, my. This sounds serious."

"Not yet. But we're headed that way," Priss said and recounted the incidents of the past two days.

Latrice gasped. "All that, in just two days?"

"I told you they're getting out of hand," Randy told his wife sharply.

She glared at him and seemed to be on the verge of making a sharp retort when Priss interrupted.

"Uh, the twins?" she prompted. They both looked at her. "I barely saved you from a day in court with the Morrison boy's mother," she added meaningfully.

Latrice sighed. "Well, we'll just take their telly away from them for a week," she said. "That should do it."

"Have you looked in their room?" Randy protested. "They've got a million damned toys. Being locked in there without the telly isn't a punishment; it's a reward!"

"Then, we'll restrict their toys as well."

Priss felt uncomfortable. It really wasn't the time to go into child psychology and the attention-getting mechanism that was overly active in the twins.

"What good will that do? They need a good beating," Randy said.

"You will not hit my sons!" Latrice fired right back.

Priss cleared her throat and Latrice looked at her with a guilty smile. "I'm sorry," she mumbled. "We'll have a talk with them, and we'll do... something," she added. She smiled politely. "Thank you for bringing it to our attention."

"I didn't like to bother you tonight," Priss replied, "but it was reaching the critical stage."

"That's all right, Priss," Randy said. "If the boys don't improve, we'll want to know about it."

"Yes, I'll see that you do. Well, I'd better run. I left Mom and Dad out in the car. Are you coming to the party?"

"Of course." Randy grinned, hugging a reluctant Latrice to his side. "We don't get invited out that often these days, do we, darling?"

She glowered at him. "No. Not that often."

Priss mumbled a quick good night and beat a path to the door.

Chapter 7

"Have any luck?" Adam Johnson asked his daughter after she'd climbed into the back seat and he was starting the car.

Priss gave him a rueful smile. "I hope so. They're being deprived of television."

Adam shook his head. "It won't work."

"Stop disillusioning me," Priss said, hitting his shoulder playfully.

"Did you see John?" Renée asked quietly.

Priss sat back. "Yes."

"I don't think he even noticed us," Adam related dryly. "He got straight into his car and drove off in a cloud of dust."

She stared out the window. "How odd," she said tensely, but she didn't say anything else and, after a quickly exchanged look, neither did her parents.

Betty Gaines was a petite woman with salt and pepper hair and a glowing personality. She made them all feel right at home, and Priss was delighted to find a few young people her age at the party.

"What fun this is," Ronald George commented in her ear. "I can hardly wait to go to sleep."

"Hush!" she scolded. "It's a lovely party!"

"Your Aussie friend doesn't seem to think so," he returned, glancing toward John, who was standing alone in the corner with a cup of punch in one hand, glaring at them.

She peeked through her lashes, hoping that John was miserable. Hoping that she'd hurt him. "No, he doesn't," she said too sweetly. "Why don't we go over and cheer him up, darling?" She laughed, and revenge glittered from her eyes. She caught his sleeve and half dragged him across the room.

"Why, hello, John," Priss said with false warmth. "I don't think you've ever met Ronald George, have you? Ronald, this is John Sterling, who owns the property adjoining ours."

"So pleased to meet you, old chap," Ronald said with his easy grin, and extended a hand.

John looked as if he were being offered a piece of moldy bacon. But after a slight hesitation, he shook the hand roughly and let it fall.

"I hear you're in cattle," Ronald nodded politely. "My father has a cow or two." He grinned. "He owns a chain of steak restaurants. You might have heard of them—The George Steak Houses?"

"Sorry," John said brusquely, staring down at the smaller man from his formidable height. He towered over everyone, Priss thought. He was powerfully built, right down to the huge hands whose gentleness she hated to remember.

"Ah, well, not to worry." Ronald began to look uncomfortable. He cleared his throat. "Nice town, Providence."

"My grandfather thought so," John returned quietly. "He founded it."

"Oh. Really?"

"Ronald doesn't know much about Australian history," Priss told John. "But he is quite an authority on financial matters." She smiled vaguely. "He and his father have made a fortune in investments."

John seemed to withdraw. His eyes were the only things alive in that searing face, and they cut into Priss's face. "Have they?"

"We've had some small successes," Ronald said, with a puzzled glance at Priss. He cleared his throat. "Uh, darling, wouldn't you like some punch?" he asked hopefully.

But Priss was enjoying herself. Revenge had a sweet taste, and she was repaying all John's taunts, all his cutting remarks as she played up to Ronald. "Yes, I would," she agreed. "Would you bring me one?"

"Delighted!" Ronald said and hurried away.

"Isn't Ronald a dream?" she sighed, viewing the teacher's thin back with adoring eyes. "I do so admire his taste in clothes. And he has the most delightfully cultured background. He's quite unique in these parts, don't you think?"

"He's a thoroughbred, all right," John said with a cold smile. He gulped down the rest of his punch and put the empty glass on a nearby table before he lit a cigarette. "Why didn't the two of you stay in Hawaii?"

"My family is here," she replied. Her eyes wandered over his hard face, and she saw new lines in it. A twinge of aching grief went darting through her, but she forced herself not to show it. There was no hope that she'd ever kiss that hard mouth again, or know the strength of those arms holding her. She might as well steel herself against lost hope.

"God, you've changed," he said, staring down at her.

"I've only grown up. Aren't you delighted?" she asked with venomous sweetness. "I won't be following you around like a pet puppy from now on."

He stared down at his cigarette and shadows deepened in his eyes. For an instant he looked odd. Strangely haunted. "Yes. I'm delighted." He put the cigarette to his lips and took a long draw from it. "I have to go. We're starting the muster tomorrow, and I'll have a mob of cattle waiting."

"Well, at least you're already wearing your work clothes, aren't you?" she asked with an empty smile. "You'll save some time that way."

His face grew stony. He smiled back, but it was a chilling smile. "There's an old saying about clothes making the man. But out here, little sheila, it's the man who counts. I may not dress to suit your newly acquired sophistication. And I may not have the cultured background of your pet pommy over there. But I'm satisfied with my life. Can you say the same of yours?"

She couldn't, but she smiled though it killed her.

''Without you in it, you mean?'' she asked coldly. ''Oddly enough, I look on the breaking of our engagement as a lucky escape. It forced me to take another look at Ronald.'' She glanced toward the punch bowl, where he was filling their cups. ''My, isn't he gorgeous?''

John smiled ironically. ''Just your style, Priscilla,'' he agreed. His eyes burned her. ''Perhaps you're able to satisfy his watered-down passions. You'd never have satisfied mine. Good night.''

She stared after him with trembling lips. Why did he continually do that to her? Why did he say cutting things and walk away before she could come up with a suitable reply? She picked up the cup he'd put on the table and was actually raising it over her head when Ronald came back.

''No!'' he burst out, grabbing it. His eyes were incredulous. ''You weren't really going to throw it at him?''

''Why not?'' she asked abruptly. ''Don't be so stuffy!''

Ronald looked toward the door where John had exited. ''Poor chap,'' he sympathized. ''You do give him the boot at every opportunity, don't you?''

''He deserves all he gets and more,'' she stated angrily. She shifted restlessly, her evening ruined. ''I wonder why Randy and Latrice haven't shown up?''

''Oh, the other Sterlings?'' he asked. ''Betty said Latrice had called and explained something about a headache.''

''More like a fight,'' Priss groaned. ''And my fault.

I had to tell them about the twins, and she and Randy went at it. Oh, what a miserable day!''

"Would you like to leave?" he asked.

"No. I'd like to try not to ruin Betty's evening after all the trouble she's gone to." She forced a smile. "Shall we circulate and pretend to be jubilant?"

He grinned. "Delighted! While we're circulating, could we perhaps circulate in the direction of the gorgeous little blonde?"

"Mandy?" She grinned back, observing the small teacher in the corner all alone. "Yes, let's!"

"How are you getting on with the Sterling twins, by the way?" he asked as they walked toward Mandy.

She sipped her punch. "I'm going to ask for a raise."

"That bad, hmmm? Listen, if we could get their father into the military, I think I could pull enough strings to have him transferred to another commonwealth country…"

"He's already served," she said.

"Drat!"

"Randy and Latrice said they'd take care of it," she added, without divulging their recipe for success.

He sighed. "I'll remember you in my prayers, old girl."

"Thanks."

After the party was over and Priss was lying in her own empty bed, she couldn't manage to get to sleep. All she saw was John. Her heart seemed to swell up at just the thought of him. And she'd thought it was over, that she could see him and not be affected. That she hated him. That she could take her revenge and not feel anything. Ha! She'd cut him tonight all right, in many ways. But as sweet as it had been at the time, her conscience hurt her now. He was so different. He looked so much older, and he dressed like someone without much money. But that was impossible: he still had the Run. He and Randy had the Run, she corrected. She frowned. That was another puzzle. Why were Randy and his family living with John? It was all so confusing. And most confusing were her own turbulent emotions. She was shocked to find how vulnerable she still was to John. That would have to be kept carefully concealed. Perhaps if she worked at it, though, she could force her heart to shut him out for good. Perhaps.

She rolled over. She'd realized tonight that she wasn't indifferent to him. And he'd proved to her that whatever he felt, it wasn't regret over the past. He'd said he was quite satisfied with his life.

After all that had happened, why did she ache so from looking at him? Why did her body tremble with desire to feel his again? Why were there tears in her eyes and a pain like rheumatism in her poor heart, if it was all over? She buried her face in the pillow. It was going to take some self-control to stay here. She wondered if she could....

She slept late the next morning and got up just in time to wave good-bye to her parents as they went into Providence to shop for groceries at the tiny store there. She put on an old pair of jeans and a black T-shirt and went out walking.

It was a glorious spring day. The whole outdoors smelled of freshness and new growth, and far away she could hear cattle bawling. It was spring, after all, she reminded herself. They'd be mustering cattle over on the Sterling Run. She stuck her hands into her pockets as she walked, wishing she could go over and watch. The muster was much like an American roundup, with calves being branded and immunized and neutered, and sweating stockmen trying to keep up with the pace set by John, who never seemed to tire. She wondered if Randy helped these days. In the old days, Randy hadn't liked getting dirty.

Her eyes went to the distant peaks of the Great Dividing Range and she smiled at their grandeur against the clear azure sky. She loved Australia; droughts, floods, and all. Summer would soon be here, and with it the Wet, the flooding that she remembered from the days before she went to college. She shuddered a little. The Warrego went out of its banks in flood, and sometimes it was impossible to get across the streams that crisscrossed the bottoms. Flash flooding back in Alabama had been nothing like it was here, where even the lightest rain could make little streams into rivers.

She'd often wished it would flood when she was at John's house in the old days, so that she could have an excuse to spend the night with him and his mother. She wondered how Mrs. Sterling was liking America, and if she ever planned to come back. Odd that she'd gone so willingly, when she loved this country as much as John did. And Randy hated station life; he was a city boy at heart. What was he doing up here so far from Sydney and his sheep property?

As she walked she caught a glimpse of John in the distance, tall in the saddle, his silver-belly Stetson catching the light as he eased his stockhorse in and out of the small mob of cattle he was driving down the long road between her father's property and the Run.

His head turned, and he seemed to see her. The aboriginal stockman with him herded the cattle along, with the help of one of the station's prize stockdogs, an Australian shepherd.

John turned his horse and rode over to the fence, waiting for Priss to come up to it.

It was like time turning back, she mused, as she walked to meet him. Once, she'd have run. But that would be undignified. Not to mention foolish. Let him think she didn't care anymore.

"Hello," she said. "Scorching cattle today?"

He tilted his hat back. "Something like that." He lifted his dimpled chin and stared at her quietly.

"Was that Little Ben?" she asked, nodding toward the lean young stockman who was riding away from them.

"Yes. You remembered."

"I do have a memory," she reminded him. "How's Big Ben?"

"He hasn't aged a day," he told her. "He's still the best stockman I've got. Billy Riggs is jackerooing for us these days."

She knew Billy from school: he'd been in her senior class. "Yes, I know him. He always wanted to work cattle."

"And you always wanted to teach school," he reminisced, studying her.

"Are you disappointed that I don't wear horn-rimmed glasses and black skirts with white blouses and have my hair in a bun?'' she inquired on a mocking laugh. ''Schoolteachers are no longer dull and droll and unappealing.''

''As I see,'' he agreed.

She searched him over, her eyes helplessly following the play of muscles under his khaki shirt as he shifted in the saddle. He was perfect physically, the most devastating man she'd ever seen.

''How are you liking the school in Providence?''

''Very much. I'm delighted that they let me take over for Miss Ross while she was having her surgery. It will give me a head start when school begins again in the fall.''

''The twins are brooding,'' he remarked. ''I suppose you know they've had their television privileges revoked. To top it all, Randy and Latrice had one hell of a fight last night and Latrice took off bag and baggage on another trip.''

''I'm sorry about that,'' she responded quietly.

''What those children need is a lot of love and attention—none of which they receive,'' he uttered regretfully. ''Randy is too involved with investments and Latrice in travel. They hardly communicate these days, and they have no time at all for the boys.''

''That's sad.''

''Yes. If I had sons, they'd be with me as much as possible,'' he said, and something in his eyes caught her attention. ''I've got the twins with me today, watching the muster. They're behaving quite well.''

''I'm sure they like being around you,'' she affirmed. ''They're outdoor kids.''

"Randy hates the outdoors," he remarked. "Flies, you know."

She smiled involuntarily. "How in the world did he wind up here with you?"

His face changed. "What are *you* doing out here?" he asked, changing the subject.

"Just walking. It's such a lovely day," she said.

He nodded. "I have to get back," he said. He hesitated, his eyes narrowing as they searched her face, and he asked suddenly, "Want to come up behind me?"

He seemed to regret the question almost immediately, but she was too shocked to notice. She remembered aching to have him ask that before she left for Hawaii. She had to admit it now: She wanted to be close to him. In spite of everything, part of her ached for it. But she knew she couldn't be that close without giving herself away completely. She couldn't risk it.

"No, thanks," she said. "I haven't been on a horse in years. It's safer on the ground."

He searched her eyes and smiled mockingly. "You aren't flattering yourself that I had ulterior motives for that invitation?" he taunted. "I was offering you a lift. Nothing more."

Her blood ran hot. She seethed at him with years of bitter hatred in her eyes. "I'd rather hitch a ride with a cobra!" she shot back. "I'm not in the market for an outback cowboy!"

"My bloody oath, you're asking for it," he bit off, and something in his eyes frightened her.

"Not from you," she said coldly. "I want nothing from you. Not ever again."

"Praise God," he returned with a cutting smile.

She whirled and dashed off across the paddock, hardly noticing where she put her feet.

John watched her go with a bleak expression, eyes narrowed in something approaching pain as he followed her lithe figure until it was out of sight. After a minute, he turned his mount with unusual roughness and urged the stockhorse into a gallop, his face as hard as stone.

Priscilla knew there was going to be trouble the minute the twins walked into her classroom Monday morning.

They glared at her horribly and did everything possible to disrupt the class. By lunch, when nothing she said or did worked, she went into the school office and phoned the Sterling Run.

Randy answered, and Priss hardly gave him time to say hello before she poured it all out.

"They have hidden my chalk, they've thrown schoolbooks out the window, they've talked and catcalled and made noise when I was trying to conduct class, and I'm at the end of my rope. Randy, I'm going to have to send them to the principal and let him deal with them, and it may mean expulsion."

"In the first grade," he sighed. "Where have Latrice and I gone wrong? Listen, Priss, I've got a meeting with some out-of-town cattlemen, and I can't get away right now. Latrice stormed out of here Friday night, bag and baggage, and went to Bermuda on another holiday—John and I are half crazy with work…"

"I'm sorry you have problems, but I do think this takes priority, Randy," she said with gentle firmness. "Expulsion on the twins' record at this early stage in their education would be devastating. You can see that, can't you?"

He muttered something. "All right, Priss, I'll be there in fifteen minutes."

She went back to the classroom, and as luck would have it, the twins had just returned early from lunch.

She stopped in the doorway and met their angry looks with one of her own.

"I've called your father," she said quietly. "He's on his way here now."

"Big bloody deal," said Gerry, pouting. "He never does anything."

"That's dinkum," returned his twin, Bobby, with a triumphant smile.

"Do you realize how serious this is?" she asked. She sat down at her desk and tried to think how to reason with them. They were so young to be so out of hand. "Listen. There are other students here who want to learn. It's my job to try to teach them. It simply isn't possible with the two of you disrupting my class all the time. I don't like sending you to the office. I don't like having to tell your parents that you're causing trouble. But I have a duty to all the other parents whose children are here to get an education."

"Education is a lot of rot," Gerry said. "We don't need to go to school. Big Ben never went, and he knows lots of things."

"Big Ben can smell rain," Bobby said. "And track a man through the rain forest."

"Fair go!" Gerry returned. "He knows important things."

She nodded. "Yes, I know. Big Ben used to try to teach me to throw a boomerang. But I never learned."

"I could show you that," Gerry told her. "It's easy."

"He's beaut," Bobby agreed.

She pursed her lips. "Suppose," she said, choosing her words, "that you wanted to show me how to throw a boomerang, Gerry, but two of your classmates kept making noise so you couldn't talk above them. And suppose they hid the boomerang."

Gerry scowled. "Why, I'd knock the bloody stuffings out of them," he said belligerently.

"Perhaps that's how Tim Reilley felt this morning," she continued quietly, "when I was trying to show him how to spell his name, and you and your brother kept scraping your chairs across the floor."

Gerry pondered that. "Well…" He looked thoughtful. Perhaps the twins would consider what she'd said.

"I hear your uncle took you out on the muster Saturday," Priss offered, changing the subject.

They brightened immediately at that. "Yes, and he showed us how the ringers cut out bullocks, and how to toss a rope!" Gerry said enthusiastically, all eyes.

"One of the cows got her head caught in the fence," Bobby interrupted, "and Uncle John said some words he told us not to repeat."

She smiled involuntarily, picturing the scene. "Yes, I imagine so."

"Uncle John can do anything," Gerry continued.

His face fell. "I wish my dad could ride a horse like that."

"But your dad is grand at figures, did you know?" Priscilla told him. "He can add columns of figures in his head, faster than a calculator. I've seen him. And he's a whiz at math."

"Our dad?" Bobby asked.

"Yes, your dad," she agreed. "He won a scholarship to college because he was so good at it."

"How about that, mate?" Gerry asked his brother.

"But he studied very hard," she continued solemnly. "He sat and paid attention in class and did his homework."

Gerry shifted restlessly in his chair. "They took away the telly," he complained, looking up at her with accusing eyes. "And Mom left again. She said it was because she couldn't stand us around her. And it's all your fault."

Oh, Latrice, how could you? she thought, aching for that small proud boy.

"Your mother was upset, and she didn't mean to hurt you. She loves you. So does your dad. You're very special to them."

"Then, why do they ignore us all the time?" Gerry persisted.

"Your dad's trying to make a living, so he can support you all," she began. "If he didn't work hard, you'd be poor."

"Like Uncle John was?" Bobby broke in, wide-eyed. "Dad said Uncle John didn't have a bean before we came to live with him, but I guess he's got some money now, because he bought me a truck."

Priss stared at the boy with a puzzled frown. She was going to explain that John wasn't poor, but before she could, Randy came into the room, looking angry and impatient and out of sorts.

"You lot are going to ruin me," he accused the boys, growling at them. "I had to pass up an offer on two young bulls I was trying to see, because of you."

"We're sorry," Gerry said, approaching his father with adoring eyes. "We didn't mean to be bad, honest we didn't."

"Dinkum, Dad," Bobby seconded. "We really didn't."

Priscilla stood up. "Why don't you boys walk down the hall a bit? It's ten minutes before we start class."

"Thanks, Miss Priscilla," Gerry said. "We'll go look at the bird nest outside Mrs. Gaines's window. Come on, mate!"

Bobby ran out behind him, and Priss folded her hands in front of her. "I'm sorry," she apologized. "Something has to be done. They seem penitent right now, but I can't go on letting them disrupt the class. You must see that."

Randy was wearing a business suit but no hat, and he seemed haggard. He sat down in the chair beside her desk and fumbled to light a cigarette.

"I'm at my rope's end," he said. "We restricted the television. We gathered up most of their toys and put them away. We even spanked them. None of it worked. Their mother ran off again to some social affair in Bermuda, and I just haven't time for them."

"Randy," she said, as gently as she could, "that's the whole problem. Nobody has time for them. Children who misbehave as often as not do it to get attention. They don't care whether it's positive attention or not, as long as they get it from someone. But I have a responsibility to the other parents to provide an atmosphere in which their children can learn. I'm not able to do that with the twins disrupting my class. And right now they're furious with me. They seem to blame me for the loss of their television *and* their mother.''

He looked oddly guilty. ''That's my fault,'' he confessed. ''I was muttering about how if you hadn't come to the house...''

''Yes, I understand. But the boys are too young to separate angry words from honest ones. They said Latrice told them she couldn't stand them. They took that literally, too.''

He smoked quietly, looking defeated. ''I love my kids, Priss. But we shouldn't have had them so soon. Latrice was used to being waited on hand and foot until she married me. I had money, of course, but not as much as she was used to. There were so many adjustments. And then having to come up here five years ago, to take over the Run...''

She felt herself going pale. Five years...? ''What?''

''Didn't anyone ever tell you?'' he asked. ''I realize that John didn't want you to know in the beginning, but now that things are improving, I thought—no matter. He lost it, you see. The whole property. Everything. I had to bail him out or he'd have gone into receivership.'' He searched her stunned face. ''Didn't you know?''

Chapter 8

If she hadn't been sitting down, her knees would have given way under her. She sat staring at Randy without even seeing him while the words repeated themselves in her numb mind. John had gone bankrupt. He'd gone bankrupt. And she'd never even known. There had been a conspiracy of silence all around; even her parents had kept it from her. But why? Why?

"I'm sorry," Randy said gently. "I didn't realize it would hit you so hard, Priss, or I'd never have said anything."

She straightened. Her heart ran wild in her chest. "Why didn't someone tell me?"

He shrugged. "I thought you knew. It was all over the district when it happened." He crushed out his cigarette in the ashtray on her desk.

She wasn't sure she could stand up. She felt as sick as she'd ever been in her life. All she could think about was her own cruelty to him since she'd been home, the way she'd ridiculed his clothing…and he was such a proud man. Oh, God, what had she done?

Her hands went into the drawer to produce a tissue. She dabbed at her eyes.

"I'm sorry if I upset you," he said.

She looked up. "You pulled the station out of the fire, I gather?"

He started to speak, ran a hand through his hair, and smiled bitterly. "I was a first-class wowser, if you want to know," he told her. "I lorded it over John and crushed what little pride he had left, and walked around with a head like a draft beer. I was going to show big John that I could run rings around him in business." He stared at his clasped hands on his knees. "And at the end of the first year, I'd fouled up everything. I almost lost my own station in New South Wales, and the Sterling Run was no better off. I was desperate enough to ask John for help. He hadn't seemed to care up until then, about anything. But after that, he and I put our heads together and came up with a plan. We're progressing slowly, but we've restocked and reinvested, and we're back on the way to prosperity. I managed to hold on to the sheep station down in New South Wales, and if everything goes well, Latrice and I can move back there in a few months. Maybe she'll settle better near her people."

She stared at the desk. "Yes, perhaps."

He stood up. "Priss, I'll promise you that Latrice and I will make the effort with the twins. I'll try to arrange my schedule so I have more time to give them. Meanwhile, if you have any more problems, let me know. If necessary, I'll cart them off to military school.''

She started to protest, but she held her tongue. A teacher could only interfere up to a point. Ultimately it would have to be Randy and Latrice's decision, not hers.

"Thanks for coming, Randy," she said, forcing a smile.

He nodded. "Are you sure you're okay?"

She averted her eyes and mumbled something. He left and the children filed back in from lunch.

Waiting for school to be over was the most difficult thing she'd ever had to do. And as the hours went by, her temper blazed up like a gasoline-soaked fire. By the time the final bell rang, she was out for blood. The first person she went after was her father. She ran him to ground outside in the parking lot and stared at him with wild, hurting eyes.

"Why didn't you tell me about John Sterling?" she asked quietly. "Why did you keep his bankruptcy from me?"

He looked uncomfortable. More than uncomfortable. He ran his hand around the back of his neck with a sigh. "By that time you'd broken up with him," he began, as if he was choosing his words very carefully. "It didn't seem necessary to tell you."

Her eyes stung with unshed tears. "Yes, but I've said some horrible things to him since I've been back. And all because I didn't know the situation. I feel horrible!"

He avoided her gaze. "I'm sorry, darling. Really sorry. But we promised..." He cleared his throat. "I mean, we promised each other we wouldn't say anything to you. We didn't realize the problems we might be creating, if that's any excuse."

She stared down at the ground, feeling betrayed and sick and ashamed, all at once. "I have to go and see him," she said.

He studied her bent head. "Yes. That might be the best way," he murmured absently. "Drive carefully. Are you all right?"

"I've just had a shock, that's all," she replied numbly. "I'll be home in a little while."

And with a forced smile, she got into the little secondhand Datsun her father had bought for her, and headed straight for the Sterling Run. She knew Randy would be picking up the twins, and luckily Latrice was away. Priss didn't really want an audience for her interview with John. It would be awkward enough as it was!

Her hands were shaking so, she had trouble keeping the little car on the road as she sped across the cattle grids and past the white fences to the Sterling Run. She was on her way to the front door when she heard voices down at the stables, a short walk away. She turned and headed resolutely down the dirt path.

John was saying something to Big Ben, the aboriginal stockman, who looked past him to spot Priss and grinned toothlessly from ear to ear. He swept off his stockhat and greeted her, his curly white hair gleaming in the sunlight.

"Hello, Missy," he called. "Plurry long time you go away, thought you deadfella. Good you come again."

"Thanks, Ben," she said. "I still haven't learned to throw a boomerang, but at least now I can spell it!"

He grinned and turned away to mount his horse, then rode off to carry out whatever instructions John had given him.

John stared at her, taking in her pale cheeks and pained expression.

"Well, what's your problem?" he growled.

She didn't even reply. She just stared at him and searched for words. Yes, she could see it all now. The khaki trousers and dingo boots, the wide-brimmed Stetson and faded khaki bush shirt half open over his brawny hair-covered chest—they were all old. But she had a feeling the best he owned now wasn't much better than what he had on. The Ford was an economy car. And there had been many bits of conversation about hard times at the Run. All of it came back to haunt her, most of all her own haughty remarks about the suit he'd worn to her homecoming party.

Tears shimmered in her wide eyes, and her lower lip trembled precariously as she looked up. "Randy told me the truth," she said unsteadily and watched his eyes blaze with sudden anger. "Can you imagine how I feel?"

He seemed to turn to stone at the question, at the pity that was plain in her eyes. He let out his breath slowly, and there was a dangerous look on his face as he studied her. "By God, I'll break his back…!"

"Why?" she cried brokenly. "Why didn't you tell me? Was that why you broke the engagement—because you went broke? John, for God's sake, I wouldn't have turned my back on you just because you weren't rich! I'd have been back here like a shot, I'd have helped…!''

His jaw tightened as he looked down. He turned away to light a cigarette. As he moved the muscles rippled in his powerful arms, and she could hardly bear to be so near him without touching him.

"I had all I could handle," he said after a minute. He stared off down the dirt road that led between the paddocks, where fat Merino sheep were grazing. "Bankruptcy and marriage are a poor combination. And," he added coldly, "there was your age."

She wrapped her arms around herself, staring at his tall form, so alien to her now, so different. "I was growing up fast."

He laughed, without amusement, and turned back. "You wanted me," he said flatly. "And I wanted you. But love wasn't part of it, despite your romantic little daydreams."

"That's not true," she protested, and tears filled her eyes. She went close to him, sympathy mingling with regret in her soft oval face as she stared up at him with the same eyes that had once adored him. "I wouldn't have cared what you had. I'd have stuck by you, no matter what."

"Don't pity me," he ground out. His eyes frightened her. "My bloody oath, I won't have that from you!"

"John," she whispered tearfully. "You did care, a little, didn't you?"

His nostrils flared. He slammed the cigarette down into the dust and made a grab for her. Without another word, he lifted her roughly in his arms and carried her into the deserted barn, shocking her speechless. There was one stall off the neat, clean aisle where hay was kept. He carried her in there and threw her into the golden softness, slinging his hat to one side as he loomed over her.

"Let me show you how much I cared," he said roughly and slid down against her prone body so quickly, she didn't have time to avoid him.

She fought with him, but he only threw a powerful leg across both of hers and held her down. His eyes gleamed with some violent emotion as he searched hers, his hands pinning her wrists to the straw-covered ground.

"I wanted you," he repeated, holding her still. He eased his body completely over hers, letting her feel what was happening to him, watching her face flush and her eyes dilate as the contact made her stiffen. "As you can feel, I still do," he added with a mocking smile. "But that's all it was, all it is, with me. I loved your body, Priss." His eyes devoured the soft form pinned beneath his body, and his heart began pounding, his breath backed up in his throat.

"I loved it…" His voice trailed off as he drew his lips suddenly over the erect peak of her breast, which was outlined against the thin fabric of the green dress. His hands released her wrists to slide under her and hold her to him.

She stiffened more and gasped. Her hands caught in his thick blond hair and tried to pry him away, but he only laughed huskily.

"You used to like this," he reminded her tauntingly. "Lie still. No one's going to disturb us here.

We can go all the way this time. You're not a shy little virgin anymore.''

She opened her mouth to correct that impression and felt his lips cover it. She meant to fight; she wanted to. But it had been five years, and the feel of his hard smoky mouth on hers was intoxicatingly close to heaven. She relaxed very slowly into the hay, feeling the warmth of his lips as they opened, parting hers at the same time. Her hands stopped tugging his hair and eased around to his rough cheeks. She stroked his face, feeling the corners of his mouth with her thumbs, feeling it kissing hers....

He moaned softly, as the tiny caress aroused him, and his hands smoothed over her breasts with tender possession. He bit at her mouth in a familiar remembered way, and she opened her lips to let his tongue probe inside.

His fingers went between them to unbutton his shirt. He took one of her hands from his face and edged it under the fabric, bunching her fingers against one hard male nipple.

"Stroke me there," he whispered gruffly.

Her rebellious fingers liked that telltale sign, and they obeyed him without protest. His mouth grew rougher, more demanding. His hands cupped her breasts and shaped them, his thumbs arousing them even through two layers of fabric. She hated the dress and the bra she wore under it, she wanted her flesh laid bare to his hands, and she gasped in protest when he removed them.

"Priss," he breathed into her mouth. He kissed her harder, with blatant possession. His big rough hands went under her dress and undergarments then, and he slid them along the silken skin of her thighs in a caress more intimate than any they'd ever shared.

She stiffened, catching his hands in her own. Her eyes were wide and a little frightened, her mouth swollen and moist from his kisses.

"No one will see us," he assured. His voice was like velvet, deep and slow. "You want me, don't you?"

"John, you don't…understand." She fought to explain before it was too late, before her weakness gave him what he wanted.

"Aren't you on the pill?" he asked. His hands gave in to her renewed protest and moved back up to shelter her head from the hay. "Is that why?"

"No, I'm not on the pill," she rejoined breathlessly. "I never have been. John, I…I haven't…nothing's changed about my body. I mean…"

His glazed eyes began to focus, as sanity came back with a rush. "Are you trying to tell me you're still a virgin?" he asked. "My oath, that's rich!" he added with a cold laugh. He searched for her mouth, but she jerked her face away.

"It's the truth!"

"Of course it is." His hands moved back under the skirt, roughly demanding, and his mouth crushed over hers fiercely. "Stop pretending, Priscilla," he bit off.

"Go ahead, then!" she said angrily, eyes searing him. "Go ahead! You'll find out for yourself, but it will be too late!"

She gritted her teeth and waited. He was strong

enough to force her and she knew it. But she hoped his integrity would be enough to save her. And it was.

He let her go and sat up. His big body was shaking with the effort it took and his eyes were savage, but he breathed deeply and slowly until his heartbeat slackened. His hands smoothed back his disheveled hair, and he stared down at her with an expression that made her blood run cold.

"I feel like a Saturday night special." she managed with a trembling, hard laugh. She avoided his eyes as she sat up and rearranged her clothing. "Like a street-walker."

He got to his feet and leaned over to sweep up his Stetson and cock it over one eye. He held out a hand with obvious reluctance, but she ignored it and scrambled to her feet alone.

"So now I know," she said, white-faced. She pulled hay out of her hair with trembling fingers. "I know exactly why you proposed. It was the only way you could get me, and you knew it, is that it? Your conscience wouldn't let you seduce your neighbor's teen-age daughter!"

He lifted his chin. "Call it a fleeting noble gesture." His eyes narrowed as he watched her body. "I wanted you until it was an obsession."

She swallowed. "So I saw."

His face went hard and cold. "It was only that. I never mentioned loving you."

"That's true," she managed huskily. "You never did." She forced a wan smile and turned away. "We both had a lucky escape, don't you think?"

She averted her eyes and wrapped her arms around

her chilled body. All the illusions were gone now. Every one. She realized she'd been living on the thought that he might have cared. On the hope that once she was all grown up he would realize what he had been missing. But now she knew the truth. That it could never be more than desire for him.

Her hands absently smoothed her arms, and John watched her with pained eyes.

She took a steadying breath and let it out.

"Well, what do they say about being cruel to be kind?" she avowed. Her eyes searched his craggy face, the dimple in his chin, the new lines in the deeply tanned flesh. "Thanks. I know exactly where I stand now."

She started back to the car, and he watched her hungrily.

His eyes closed. His fists clenched. "Priss," he whispered, his deep voice anguished.

But she didn't hear him. She climbed into her car and drove away without once looking back.

Chapter 9

It took Priscilla the rest of the day to get herself back together. She put on a good face in front of her parents, but it took all her willpower not to break down.

"Are you all right, darling?" Renée asked Priss when she came home. "Your father told me what happened. I'm sorry we had any part in hurting you. It's just—"

"It's all right," Priss lied, smiling gamely. "I'm okay now."

Renée hugged her and mumbled something grateful, and later her father accepted Priss's remark that at last she and John understood each other. She went to bed early, and finally was able to let loose the tears that had been building ever since she'd left the Sterling Run that afternoon.

She was convinced now that John felt nothing for

her, never had. What a pity, she told herself bitterly, that she'd kept holding on to old memories.

She got up bleary-eyed and managed to go through the motions of teaching. But her appearance gave her away.

"Well, I must say, you look like an accident victim," Ronald George remarked in the corridor as she hurried to class.

She stuck out her tongue at the dark-headed Englishman. "You should see that accident!"

He chuckled, waved, and went on his way.

The twins were well-behaved as they had been the day before, but they looked preoccupied. At the end of the day, Priss asked them why.

"Oh, it's Uncle John," Gerry remarked, and Priss's heart leapt wildly.

"What's wrong with him?" she asked, trying to sound casual.

"We don't know," Bobby said. "He was horrible yesterday. But he hollered real loud when we tried to wake him up this morning, and Daddy said he'd had too many stubbies and was inked."

"Dinkum," Gerry added. "He had a black eye, too."

"In a blue, I'll wager," Bobby remarked enthusiastically. "His knuckles was bleeding, too."

Priss didn't catch the slip of grammar. She was trying to unravel the tangle of Australian slang. Inked was drunk. A blue was a fight. John had been drinking stubbies—beer—and got drunk and had a fight. She blinked. Was that normal behavior, she wondered, or did it have something to do with their confrontation on Monday? Then she realized she was flattering herself. John hadn't batted an eye when she left the Run. As if he cared that he'd hurt her...!

"He was as game as Ned Kelly, though, Miss Priscilla," Gerry put in, mentioning a legendary Australian outlaw, "'cause he got up and went out to help with the sheep-shearing regardless of his head."

"I hope he's better," Priss said noncommittally.

"Who, me?" Ronald George grinned, sticking his head in the door.

She laughed. "No."

"Have a coffee with me before you go home," he invited. "I'll make it."

"You can make coffee?" she gasped.

He glowered at her and made a fist. "Know thy place, woman!"

"Watch thy step, man," she returned.

He left, and the twins watched her bright smile suspiciously. She couldn't know, of course, that they'd make so much out of her laughing repartee with Ronald. But what they did was to go home and tell everyone, including John, that Miss Priscilla was sweet on Mr. George.

"He even made her coffee," Gerry said over his rice pudding.

"Exciting, innit?" Bobby grinned, running the words together in fine Australian fashion. "Bet they'll get married!"

John, who'd been listening to this enthusiastic revelation with a grim, unsmiling face that was bruised and cut, put down his fork, ignored his coffee, and left the table. The twins soon excused themselves as well and ran out to watch the shearing.

"What's wrong with John?" Latrice asked carelessly, wondering at this odd behaviour on her first night back from Bermuda. "He barely touched his meal."

Randy grimaced. "I told Priss he went bankrupt five years ago," he sighed. "He all but knocked me about for it, too, I'll tell you. Then he went out and got drunk and beat up a couple of neighboring stockmen." He shook his head as he finished his coffee. "Poor old bloke. He thought she felt sorry for him, you see. Because he's living a deprived life," he added.

"Well, I can understand that," Latrice said with a venomous smile. "God knows it isn't easy, living in deprivation."

"Steak every night, trips around the world, a new fur every winter, you call that damned deprivation?" he roared.

"Yes, I do!" she shot back. And the subject of John was rapidly replaced by a rundown of problems ending with the twins.

"You've got to take them in hand!" Randy shouted.

"Keep bothering me about those boys, and I'll leave you!" she retorted. She slammed her napkin down and stood up. "I never wanted children in the first place! I won't be hounded about them!"

"They can't be allowed to terrorize the school!"

"Then, ship them off to boarding school, for all I care!"

"Some mother you are," he returned murderously. "Some fine mother!"

She had the grace to look ashamed. And when she turned, the twins were standing there with devastation in their young faces.

"I told you, didn't I?" Gerry asked his brother with trembling lips. "I told you she hated us!"

"You…you old cow!" Bobby shouted.

They both ran out the door at the same time, leaving their parents standing horrified in the hallway.

"Gerry, Bobby, come back, I didn't mean it!" Latrice called. She ran to the door, but they were already out of sight. She turned a white face to Randy. "What shall we do?"

Randy turned. "I'll go get John."

Priss had walked down to the creek behind her father's property and was sitting quietly under a big gum tree. She was wearing jeans and a pink T-shirt and sneakers and trying not to remember what had happened the day before.

She hadn't been able to sit still in the house. The memory of John's rough ardor was too fresh. She was toying with the idea of going back to Hawaii, of escaping even the threat of his company, when she heard a crashing noise on the other bank.

She looked up, and there were the terrible twins, rushing headlong toward the wide stream. They didn't even seem to notice her. It was obvious they'd been crying profusely.

"Gerry, Bobby! What's wrong?" she called, getting to her feet.

"We're running away from home," Gerry called back.

They kept coming, right through the stream, hardly pushing to avoid the slick rocks.

"Where will you go?" Priss asked reasonably.

"We'll go to Brisbane and get jobs delivering papers," Gerry said matter-of-factly. "And we'll get a hotel room."

"With what?"

Gerry reached in his pocket, his tearstained face very proud and mature. "I have five dollars. See?"

She could have cried. They looked so miserable, and she remembered from her own childhood how helpless it felt to be totally dependent on adults, with no rights at all.

She went down on one knee and stared Gerry in the eyes. "Tell me what happened."

"Mom doesn't want us," he whispered brokenly and collapsed in tears.

"Oh, Gerry," she said gently. She gathered the two of them into her arms and just held them while they cried, and they didn't even make an effort to pull away. Just a little love, she thought silently. That was all they needed—just a little love and consistent discipline.

A sound brought Priss's head up. John was standing on the opposite bank.

He was bareheaded for once, his blond-streaked hair shimmering in the dappled sunlight, and his face looked worn and haggard. One eye was black and blue, and there was a cut on his chin.

"We're up a gum tree," Gerry moaned as he

watched his uncle come across the stream with slow steady strides.

"He's narked, too," Bobby said resignedly.

But apparently he wasn't angry at the boys. He didn't fuss or accuse. He simply bent down, as Priss had done, and opened his arms. They ran to him.

"Your mother's sorry," he said without preamble. "She and your dad had a fight. You caught the tail end. You know, sometimes adults say things without meaning them."

"If she doesn't mean them," Gerry began, "why does she keep saying them, Uncle John?"

John sighed angrily and looked up, meeting Priss's quiet eyes. She averted hers, because she couldn't bear the sight of him. Was he thinking of the terrible things they had said to each other in the heat of anger?

"Your mom and dad are having some problems," John said finally. "They'll work them out. But until they do, you have to try not to take everything they say to heart."

"They won't bust up, will they?" Bobby interrupted, wiping his tears on a grubby sleeve. "Gee, that would be horrible!"

"They won't bust up," John said grimly. "Now let's go back. Your parents are frantic."

"Okay," Gerry mumbled reluctantly. He looked over his shoulder at Priss. "See you tomorrow, Miss Priscilla."

"Me, too," Bobby seconded. He started across the stream after his brother.

"Wait for me at the Land-Rover," John called to them, his deep voice carrying easily.

Priss started to leave, but he got between her and the path.

"I'm sorry," he said. "I didn't mean to hurt you like that. I said some things I didn't mean. Dammit, Priss, I couldn't bear your pity."

She avoided his eyes and backed away from him, a movement that brought his dark brows together.

"As you said yourself at the outset," she murmured, trying to sound calm, "it's all behind us now. Will you move out of my way, please?"

He searched for the right words, and couldn't find them. He ran his fingers through his thick sunbleached hair. "We could...start again," he suggested.

She stared at his dusty boots. "I don't want to. Not anymore," she added, and looked straight up into his eyes. "That makes twice you've pushed me away. I won't bother you again. Not ever. And when I finish out this school year, John, I'm going back to Hawaii."

His face went pale under his tan. "Hawaii?" he faltered.

She hadn't really decided that, but she liked the impact it made on him. Good, let him be upset! Why should she suffer alone?

"I loved Hawaii," she said. "I miss it."

His eyes searched hers for a long time. "We had a lot going for us," he tried again.

"What? Desire?" She laughed bitterly and saw him flinch.

"Why are you still a virgin?" he demanded, taking the direct approach. "If you really stopped caring about me, why hasn't there been a man?"

She held on to her nerve, but it took all the willpower she had. "I'm not that kind of girl, remember?" she asked and turned away.

"Five years is a long time," he said. "We could get acquainted again."

"Why bother?" she asked carelessly. "You've made it more than obvious that all you need is a body. Mine," she added venomously, "is not on the market."

"Priss," he growled.

"So why don't you get lost?" she told him. "Go get in another blue or barney or whatever else you call it, but leave me alone, John Sterling. I'm off men for life!"

She edged around him, deliberately avoiding any contact with his hard body, and stormed off toward the house.

He frowned after her. After a moment, with a grimly determined smile, he turned and strode off toward the creek and the Land-Rover beyond.

The twins announced the next day that their parents had gone off somewhere to straighten themselves out. They were quieter, but she noticed a new confidence in their eyes as they went through the school days. Perhaps they knew now that they were loved, she thought. It made all the difference to children.

She wouldn't think about the difference it would make to her. She hadn't one single shred of hope left about John Sterling. If only there were some eligible man she could start dating to show John how little she cared! She even considered Ronald George. But he was hopelessly smitten with Amanda now, and it wouldn't be fair to use him, anyway.

At the end of the day, she was gathering her things up before leaving when John walked into the classroom. Her eyes widened as he paused silently in the doorway, big and rugged-looking in his tan bush shirt and khaki pants and dingo boots. He had his hat in one hand, and the other worried his blond-streaked hair.

"Yes?" she asked icily.

One corner of his mouth curled. "Declaring war?" he mused.

"You did that for me," she returned, green eyes flashing.

His dimpled chin lifted, and he smiled softly. "In the hay, you mean?" he questioned.

She flushed and almost dropped the study guide in her hand. She recovered it just in time with a fumble.

"Did you want something in particular? I would like to go home," she said formally.

"The boys and I are going on a picnic Saturday," he said. "We'd like you to come with us."

The invitation caught her off guard. "Why me?" she hedged.

He shrugged. "They like you."

"And you'll suffer my company on their behalf, is that it?" she threw back. "I'm busy Saturday, thanks."

"Why won't you come, Priscilla?" he taunted. "Are you afraid you might not be able to keep your hands off me?"

She aimed the book at his head, but he held up a hand.

"If you throw it," he challenged, "I'll find a newer, more interesting use for that desk behind you."

His eyes told her what he meant, and she bit her lower lip, half afraid to find out if he was kidding or not. She tucked the book back in the crook of her arm.

"What a pity," he wondered. "I was looking forward to that."

"Save your line for some other woman, John Sterling. I'm immune," she shot back.

"Good. I won't have to shake you off," he said carelessly. "Come with us. The fresh air would do you good, and the twins could use a little womanly companionship."

"No." She forced herself to say it without flinching or feeling regret. Why was he doing this to her?

His blue eyes searched her green ones for a long quiet moment. "I've apologized."

"It doesn't change anything," she continued. "You want me. But I've already told you graphically that I'm not available in that way."

"Yes, I know," he said, watching her with a faint smile. "Fascinating, isn't it, how you've kept yourself chaste all these years. And there I was, thinking you felt sorry for me...."

"Well, hello," Ronald George interrupted, stopping by to lean over John's shoulder. "Nice to see you, Mr. Sterling. How about some coffee, Priscilla?"

"Thank you, that would be lovely, Ronald," she said, with a sweet smile. "I'll be there in a minute."

"I'll put it on, love. Good day, Mr. Sterling."

Ronald went off down the hall, and John's face grew stormy. His eyes glittered down at Priss.

"What do you see in that pommy?" he demanded.

"Refinement," she shot right back. "He'd never think of dragging me into a hay stall!"

"Thank God," he exhaled, putting his hat back on.

"That's exactly what I say!" she replied. "He's a gentleman!"

"You never used to fight with me," he mused. "I like you this way, Priss. You've grown into a passionate woman."

He was making her uncomfortable. She shifted her weight to the other foot. "Look, John, we can't go back..."

"I don't want to," he told her. "I want to go ahead. I want to get to know you all over again."

"Stop confusing me," she ground out. "I don't want this, I don't want to get involved with you...!"

"Are you coming, Priscilla?" Ronald George called from down the hallway.

"Buckley's chance, mate!" John called back in his deep drawl.

"Don't mind him!" Priss interrupted angrily.

"Who's Buckley?" Ronald asked. "And what chance?"

"My bloody oath, where did the education department dig him up?" John growled. He glared at Priss. "Are you coming Saturday?"

"I told you. No."

He sighed angrily. "You're enough to make a man go walkabout."

"I thought you'd already done that," she said with

a cold smile. "Your eye's much better. Only yellow-ish, now, isn't it?" she added.

He averted his face. "A man's entitled to an occa-sional difference of opinion."

"You didn't used to fight," she said.

"I didn't used to do a lot of bloody things," he grated. He studied her soft face irritatedly. "Nothing like a woman to drive a man to drink!"

"My, we are in a bad temper, aren't we?" she pro-voked.

He glared down at her through narrowed eyes. "Why won't you come picnicking?"

"Because I hate you!" she threw back.

"Oh, Priscilla...!" Ronald George called gaily.

"You're getting on my quince, parcel post!" John shouted down the hall.

"I say, old man, I never touched your quince! And what's that about a package...?" Ronald called back.

John took a deep breath. "You're annoying me, newcomer," he translated.

"One might have said so, mightn't one?" Ronald reacted as he started back up the hall.

"Oh, bloody hell!" John growled. He gave Priss one last glare and stomped off down the corridor.

"Good day, Mr. Ster...oof!"

There was a hard thud, and Priss ran out into the hall to find Ronald George sitting in the middle of the floor looking stunned.

"Whatever happened?" she gasped. She helped him up and watched him dust himself off.

"Big fellow, isn't he?" Ronald noted with a groggy

smile. "I didn't get out of the way fast enough apparently. How about that coffee?"

She escorted him into the teachers' lounge with a thoughtful stare toward the exit, where John had disappeared.

If she'd expected John to give up about the picnic, she had a surprise in store. He drove up unexpectedly after supper Friday night at her parents' home.

"John," Adam greeted him, "come in and join us. We were just watching the international news."

"Would you like some coffee, John?" Renée offered, smiling as she put aside her crocheting and got to her feet.

Priss sat nervously curled up in her big armchair, dressed in faded too-tight jeans and a shrunken red T-shirt with no bra underneath. Her feet were bare, and John glanced at her with a slow smile. She could have thrown the television at him.

"I'd love a cup, thanks, Renée. How are things, Adam?"

Her father motioned John to the armchair next to Priss's and sat down himself across the room.

"Going very well. I, uh, hear you and Ronald George had a confrontation a couple days ago," Adam remarked with a grin.

John looked irritated. "Damned fool walked out in front of me. I had things on my mind," he added, glancing toward Priss.

"Nice man, George," Adam murmured with a wry glance at Priss. "Excellent teacher. We're lucky to get him." He put down his coffee cup. "How about a game of chess?"

"Haven't time tonight; worst luck," John told him. "I came to ask Priscilla to go picnicking with the twins and me tomorrow."

Priss bit her lower lip. So that was his game. He couldn't get her to go on his own, so he was going to enlist her parents' aid!

"I told you—" she began.

"Good," Adam said firmly. "She could use some free time; she's worked like a Trojan ever since she's been back."

"But—" she continued.

"How true," Renée concurred, smiling when John took the silver tray from her and put it on the coffee table. "Here's yours, John," she said, serving him. "Priss, I brought one for you, too."

"Thanks, Mom," Priss said. "There's just—" she tried again.

"My thoughts exactly," John butted in. He crossed his long legs and grinned at Priss. "The change of scenery will do you good."

"I had planned—" she began once more.

"And she had nothing to do tomorrow, anyway," Renée added quickly. "We'll put together a picnic basket here, so you won't have to go to the trouble, John."

"Just so," Adam added, beaming at her. "She'll enjoy it."

Priss sighed wearily and gave up. But her eyes told John Sterling exactly what she thought of him.

"Darling, this might be a good time to go over the budget, since Priss is here to talk to John. You don't mind, John, do you?" Renée added, grinning. "We'll only be thirty minutes or so. Come on, Adam,'' she prodded to her husband, dragging him out of his chair by the arm. ''We'll just sit in the kitchen and work on it.''

Priss's father was trying to say something, but he was unceremoniously bundled out of the room before he could get it out.

John caught her eyes and held them as he sipped his coffee. ''Go ahead. Let it out. You look mad as hell.''

''Oh, no,'' she grumbled. ''Everything's apples!''

He smiled slowly. ''You sound like a native already.''

''And don't butter me up,'' she added. ''I don't want to go on your damned picnic!''

''The boys will be disappointed. I told them you would.''

''Why? You might have asked me first!''

''Listen.'' He set down his cup and leaned forward, his hairy forearms crossed over his knees. ''All I want is conversation. Just to talk. The twins would make anything else between us impossible, so what are you afraid of?''

''I won't get involved with you,'' she said firmly. ''Not physically or otherwise.''

He cocked an eyebrow. ''Did I ask you to?''

''What do you want from me?''

''I'm lonely,'' he said simply. ''I could use someone to talk to. A friend, if you like.''

''You want us to be friends?'' she asked incredulously. ''After what's happened...?''

"I don't want us to be enemies," he replied, and his voice was like black velvet. "Do you?"

She stared down at her curled-up legs. "No, I guess not."

"Then, suppose we try getting along for short stretches?"

She looked up with all her unvoiced fears in her eyes.

"I won't touch you, Priscilla," he assured her gently. "You've nothing to fear from me physically. I won't even try to hold hands."

"That's comforting," she reflected, dropping her eyes.

"I thought you might feel that way. As I said, the boys will protect you from me." He lifted his cup again and sat back. "If you really want to be protected," he added with a maddening smile.

She felt her face going hot and kept it down so he wouldn't see the wild color in her cheeks. "I got carried away before."

"So did I, love," he confided quietly, and his deeply tanned face was suddenly grave. "We were good together, that way, from the very first time we kissed."

"Dragging up the past won't help things," she declared stubbornly.

"I do realize that," he agreed. He sipped his coffee. "I've spent five years trying to put it all out of my mind. I haven't been quite successful." His eyes caught her. "And I don't think you have, either."

"I'm working on it," she echoed with a cool smile.

"With that pommy?" he grumbled.

"Ronald George is a nice man," she tossed back.

His nostrils flared as he tried to control his temper. He set the coffee cup down carefully and got to his feet. "I'd better go before I lose my temper again."

"Perhaps you'd better," she countered sweetly.

He glowered at her. "The boys and I will pick you up about eight."

"I'll be ready." She got up as well, finding herself all too close to him. She could feel the warmth of his large body; smell the clean scent of it mingled with his spicy cologne.

"Even in old clothes you're quite something, Priscilla Johnson," he said softly.

She looked up and noticed that he was blatantly staring at her. She crossed her arms over her breasts.

"Stop that," she grumbled.

"Does it bother you, remembering?" he quietly mocked.

The color in her cheeks blazed. She turned away toward the hall and quickly opened the front door for him.

"I'm being evicted, I see," he lamented. He paused in the doorway, grinning wickedly. "Tell your parents I said good night." His eyes dropped down again, and he chuckled softly at her irritated movement.

"That's all over," she reminded him coldly.

He studied her flushed face. "I've built my station back up from bankruptcy," he began quietly. "I've literally made something from nothing. I don't have a lot of money. Not yet. But I have one hell of a lot of drive. What I want, I get. So watch out, little sheila."

She swallowed down a lump in her throat. "Don't

try to make me into that kind of woman, John," she warned unsteadily.

He frowned slightly. "What the hell are you talking about?"

"There are plenty of women who give out—"

"I don't want you that way," he declared.

"Then...what?" she faltered.

He touched her cheek with the tips of his lean fingers, brushing it softly. "Be my friend, Priscilla."

It was all she could do not to catch that large hand and press her mouth against it. But she had to be strong: he was a past master at this game, and she wasn't adept enough.

"Friendship is all I can give you now," she responded.

His eyes dropped to her mouth, then went back up to meet her gaze. "Good night, love." He turned and walked away without another word.

Why did he have to use that endearment, she wailed silently, and bring back all the bittersweet memories along with it?

"Has John gone already?" Adam asked as he and Renée reentered the living room minutes later.

"He had things to do," Priss explained. She looked from one of her speculating parents to the other. "It's only going to be friendship," she attested firmly. "I can't take any more rejection from him."

"Of course, dear," Renée said gently. She bent and kissed her daughter on the forehead. "How about some more coffee?"

"I'd love a cup. I'll help you," Priss volunteered.

Renée scrutinized Adam, who winked. She was glowing as she followed her daughter into the kitchen.

Chapter 10

They spread the picnic cloth under a coolabah tree beside a water hole in the stream. Or, as John put it, a billabong.

"Do you know the original words to 'Waltzing Matilda'?" he queried her with a grin. "'Once a jolly swagman camped by a billabong, under the shade of a coolabah tree...'"

"I'd forgotten!" she exclaimed.

"The words were written by one of our best poets—Banjo Paterson," he continued, helping her unpack the wicker hamper.

"I have one of his books," Priss volunteered. "He was very good. I liked the poem about Clancy, too..."

"'Clancy of the Overflow.'" Gerry chuckled, nudging his brother. "Remember, Dad read it to us once."

"Didn't Clancy turn up in 'The Man from Snowy

River', too?" Priss asked John. "I saw the movie and loved it!"

"So did I. Yes, that was Clancy." He searched her eyes slowly. "Australia gets into your blood, doesn't it?"

"It's a big spectacular country," she agreed, dropping her eyes to his blue patterned shirt. "Much like America—especially in its history, its pioneer days."

"Yes, I suppose so. We had our desperadoes, too, like Ned Kelly."

"Can me and Gerry go swimming?" Bobby asked John.

"Sure, take your clothes off and help yourselves, if you aren't ready for your food yet," John told them.

"Bonzer!" Gerry grinned.

The boys stripped down to their swimming trunks and dived into the water.

"Is it safe here?" Priss asked.

"For whom, the boys or you?" he murmured dryly.

She moved restlessly, tugging up the shoulder of the pale blue peasant dress she was wearing. "The boys, of course."

"I didn't expect you to wear a dress," he stated. He was stretched out across from her in the grass, and her eyes helplessly followed the long powerful lines of his body from legs to narrow hips to broad chest straining against his partially unbuttoned shirt. She could see the darker blond hair on his chest, and she tingled with unwanted memories.

"My jeans were all in the wash," she muttered. That was true enough. Her mother had smiled gaily when she'd told Priss there weren't any clean jeans. "Thanks to my mom," she added darkly.

"Her middle name must be Cupid," he said dryly.

"She doesn't know you like I do," she returned icily.

"That's true enough." He toyed with the handle of the wicker hamper. "There aren't many women who do know me the way you do," he added, lifting his eyes to catch hers.

"Only a few hundred, I'm sure," she snapped.

He shook his head. "Only a handful, if you're interested," he said seriously. "I never had time for full-fledged affairs. The station always came first."

"Can't we talk about something else?" she asked miserably. The thought of him with other women, particularly Janie Weeks, was unbearable. Once again she wondered why he had never married the other woman.

"Why are you still a virgin?"

The question knocked her sideways. She stared at him with a mind gone blessedly blank.

"Yes, I know I keep harping on it. But it disturbs me. Did I damage you emotionally, is that it?" he persisted with narrowed, intent eyes. "Or couldn't you feel it with anyone else?"

"You said we were going to be friends!" she burst out.

He shrugged irritably. "Yes, my oath, I did. But I'd still like to know why."

"It's past history. As for my lack of experience," she added, "I never liked the idea of being promiscuous. Since most modern men have an opposite attitude, and word gets around, I didn't date very often. Does that answer your question?"

"I can see it all," he nodded, and smiled gently. "Miss Iceberg. Only you were never that with me. You were warm and soft and giving, and you aroused me as no other woman ever had."

"Only because I was innocent," she said, looking away. "Would you like some fried chicken and potato salad?"

"Because you were you," he corrected. "I'm sorry for what I did to you in the stable. Sorry that I made something distasteful out of it. I had this wild idea that you'd been around," he added slowly. "But once I started, when I realized that you still wanted me—"

"I don't—!" she began.

He reached out and caught her hand. Holding her eyes, he drew her fingers down over her own breast where the hard tip was visible against the soft fabric of her dress.

"You don't what?" he demanded quietly.

She jerked her hand from under his, horrified when, instead of falling away, his fingers landed gently on her breast. She pulled away from him, her eyes wide and accusing.

"As you yourself said," she shot at him, "it's a purely physical reaction. A residue from a dead relationship. Friendship is all I have left to give you."

He dropped his hand to the tablecloth and sifted through the box of plastic forks. "You don't want something a little more physical than that?"

"I don't want an affair," she stated calmly.

He smiled faintly. "Neither do I, oddly enough." He looked up. "Especially not with a virgin."

"Stop making me sound like a dinosaur."

"You're a lovely dinosaur," he remarked, running his eyes over her flushed face framed by its halo of softly curling blonde hair. "Does he turn you on?"

She blinked at the lightning change of subject. "He?"

"That pommy."

"You mean Ronald?" She smiled slowly. "He's very nice."

His face grew cold. "He's young."

"So am I," she reminded him.

He rolled over onto his back, with his arms under his head, and stared up at the sky. "Ten years my junior," he murmured. "It was a hell of a difference five years ago. Almost different generations, Priss."

"Yes."

He turned his head sideways and studied her bent head. "I kept up with you." He surprised her. "Through your parents."

"They knew?" she accused.

"I had to have their cooperation," he said. "I couldn't risk having them tell you the truth, so I swore them to silence." He nodded as her eyes mirrored her surprise.

"You knew me very well, didn't you?" she mocked bitterly.

"Well enough." He observed her. "Someday I'll tell you all of it. But in the meantime try to remember that I spared you some bitter times and some hard memories, will you?"

"And an empty marriage," she added.

He frowned. "What?"

"You said it was all desire on your part, didn't

you?'' she shot at him coolly. "We'd have been in divorce court as soon as the newness wore off."

He sat up. "Maybe it's time we talked about that—"

"Hey, Uncle John, there's a wombat over here! Can we have it?" Gerry called suddenly.

"No!" he shot back. And, knowing the twins, he got quickly to his feet. "I'd better have a look," he told Priss. "They'll be using it for a volleyball next."

She watched him walk away. He was the most masculine-looking man she'd ever seen. Muscular and graceful and sensuous. His fair hair caught the sun and gleamed like silver, and when he grinned at the boys, his face became young again, the face she'd loved as a teenager.

She still did love it, if the truth were known. But she couldn't be drawn into an affair with John. It would kill her.

Once the wombat was herded off and the boys had dried themselves, the four of them sat down to their picnic feast. Afterward the boys went back to swim some more, and Priss and John stretched out full-length on the picnic cloth and closed their eyes.

She was aware of him close at her side, and had to steel herself not to flinch every time he moved. She remembered so well another time when they'd lain like this, on Margaret's sofa, and he'd come close to making love to her.

He chuckled softly, and she turned her head sideways to study his relaxed features.

"What was that all about?" she asked.

"I was remembering that night at Margaret's," he reminisced, turning his head to catch her eyes. "You had me so out of my head that I was ready to take you, right there, door unlocked and all.''

She flushed, dropping her eyes to his partially unbuttoned shirt. That made her turn even redder, and he laughed more deeply.

"Does it bother you, little prude?" he whispered. "Look."

And he deliberately unbuttoned the rest of the shirt and pulled it free of his slacks, letting her see the rippling muscles of his stomach and chest with their feathering of dark hair.

"John..." she protested.

"I like the way you look at me," he avowed huskily, and he wasn't smiling anymore. "I like the feel of your eyes. I like knowing that you want to touch me." He reached out and brushed his fingers over hers, turning her hand so that he was lightly stroking the palm. "You'd like that, wouldn't you?" he asked. "You'd like to come over here and stroke my body the way I used to stroke yours, to watch me shudder and groan with desire."

Her lips parted. He was doing it again, and she was going under like a drowning swimmer.

"Know what I'd do to you, young Priss, if the boys weren't here?" he asked under his breath. "I'd roll you over on your back," he whispered tenderly. "And I'd pull that elastic bodice down to your waist. And then I'd put my mouth—"

"It's getting late," she burst out in a high-pitched little voice as she sat up quickly and then got to her feet.

John got to his own feet and watched her like a

mouse-hungry cat, all mischievous eyes and mocking smiles.

"Nothing's changed," he maintained. "Only the year."

"I've changed," she argued, eyes flashing. "I'm not a naive little teenager anymore!"

"No," he concurred. "You're all woman, and I want you now more than ever."

"You won't get me!" she promised.

"You said we could be friends, didn't you?" he mused.

"Not if you keep saying horrible things to me!"

He grinned, showing his even white teeth. "What did I say that was horrible?"

"About pulling my dress…" She swallowed. "You know what."

"That wasn't horrible. It was exciting," he contradicted with a lazy smile. "And that's exactly what I'd have done if the twins hadn't been around. And you'd have let me, Priscilla. You'd have helped me."

"I won't see you again, John," she asserted firmly. She bent to gather up the picnic things, without looking at him.

"Of course you will," he drawled lazily. He tucked his shirt back into his trousers and fastened it halfway up. "Tonight, in fact."

She straightened up and looked at him. "What?"

"Renée invited me to supper."

She'd strangle her mother, she told herself. "I'll go see a movie," she griped.

"You might as well give in," John advised. "You won't win."

She glowered at him. "Yes, I will. I've got too much sense to let myself in for any more heartache!"

He shook his head. "There won't be any heartache this time, little sheila," he softly supplied, and he smiled. "I promise."

"Because you won't get close enough to cause any," she returned.

"We'll see." He lifted his head and called the boys. They came running up, dripping wet, clothes clutched helter-skelter in their hands.

"That was bonzer." Gerry laughed. "Thanks for coming with us, Miss Priscilla; today was just like being a family!"

"Dead right," Bobby agreed.

Priss looked from one to the other. She hadn't realized just how much such an outing might mean to young boys who'd lacked parental affection. She smiled softly at them.

"You could come see us at home, too, Miss Priss," Gerry ventured.

"As a matter of fact, it's lambing and calving over at the Run," John added, watching her. "We've got a mob of babies you could look at."

"Too right!" Gerry agreed. "They're fun to pet, Miss Priscilla."

"Priss used to come over and watch us muster cattle," John volunteered, and his eyes were keen on her face. "Remember, Priss?"

She did, vividly. She'd always been around in spring. John never had seemed to mind, though. He'd take time to show her the newest additions to his herd and watch her enthusiastic response to them.

"You were very patient," she recalled with downcast eyes.

"I still am," he replied. "In every way that counts."

She turned away before he could see the wild rosiness in her cheeks.

"How about it?" he persisted as he helped the twins into the Land-Rover. "Want to come over tomorrow?"

She had to force herself not to give in to the lazy seduction in his voice.

"Not tomorrow," she answered.

He tilted his hat over one eye and smiled. "All right."

That threw her. She'd expected an argument. She faltered a minute before she got into the vehicle and let him close the door.

She was still puzzled that evening as she got ready for dinner. She stood staring at herself in the mirror, wondering why she was bothering to dress up. She wore a gauzy white skirt and pullover blouse, and looked like something out of the twenties—very frilly and feminine.

"It's more than he deserves," she told her reflection.

"Yes, I know, but he is a dish, my darling," Renée said from the door. She grinned like a young girl. "My, he is in hot pursuit these days, isn't he?"

"It won't do him any good," Priss assured her. "I won't be taken in again."

Renée leaned against the doorjamb and watched her daughter brush her short hair. "He's a proud man," she remarked.

"Yes, I know."

"It's not easy for a man like him to admit to weaknesses," she continued. "John was brought to his knees. He didn't want anyone to see him that way. Especially not you."

"He said it was only physical," Priss said quietly. "That he only wanted me."

"With a man, love often comes after physical infatuation," Renée told her.

"Mom," Priss began hesitantly, "whatever happened to Janie Weeks?"

Renée looked uncomfortable for a moment. "She married a fellow in Brisbane...shortly after you and John broke up."

Priss turned with scalding eyes to face her mother. "I'm afraid," she confessed. "I just don't want to risk being hurt again. I don't think I could bear it if I got involved with John and then he gave in to physical infatuation for another woman, the way he did with Janie."

"My darling," Renée advised gently, "you mustn't judge John too harshly. He's paid a terrible price for the decisions he made...whether they were right or wrong."

John was wearing a blue blazer, white shirt, and white trousers when he arrived for dinner. His blond head was bare, and he looked as urbane as any Brisbane businessman.

"You look nice," Priss complimented reluctantly.

He smiled at her. "So do you. Very roaring twenty-ish."

"I'm an old-fashioned girl," she reminded him.

"I know," he remarked with a devilish smile, and she dropped her eyes.

"Come on in to the living room while the women get the food on the table," Adam said, "and I'll pour you a brandy."

"That sounds fine," John said. "What do you think about this new political crisis in the States?"

They went off into a long discussion about politics in general while Priss and Renée set the bowls of steaming hot beef and rice and Brussels sprouts and biscuits on the table.

"What's your opinion, Priss?" John asked as they were seated.

"About what?" she asked, going blank as she looked at his rugged face with its dimpled chin and twinkling eyes.

"Oh, I don't know," he murmured, as if staring back at her had knocked a few words out of his head, too. He searched her soft green eyes for a long moment and watched her pupils widen, her lips part. It took all his willpower not to get up and go across the table after her.

She cleared her throat and reached for her glass of iced tea. Not until she'd taken a calming sip of it did she try to talk again, and she didn't look straight into his eyes this time.

"How are things going, John?" Renée asked as they waded through international politics and marked their way back to everyday topics. "This is your busiest time, I recall."

"Yes," he confirmed. "Lambing, calving, mustering, shearing.... It's great to get away from the station and all the complaints."

"You've hired on some new men, I hear," Adam remarked.

"Have to." John grinned. "Our own would quit if they had all that work to do alone. Besides, the shearers are a breed apart. It's an experience to watch them in the sheds."

"Indeed it is," Priss agreed. She smiled at him over her coffee cup. "I got to help once."

He cocked an eyebrow. "Yes, you did. I had the only sheep in the river basin with mohawks."

She flushed. "Well, I tried."

"You wouldn't have gotten near my Merinos if that shearer hadn't been sweet on you," he added, cupping his coffee cup in his big hands. "I watched you, too, just to make sure he didn't get fresh. You were a dish even at sixteen, little Priss."

"Big brother to the rescue," she chided, embarrassed because she'd never told her parents about that.

"Thank God you were around to look out for her," Adam gratefully acknowledged. "She's always been a handful."

"A lovely handful, my darling," Renée said with a smile. "The greatest joy of our lives."

"I was almost the undoing of John a few times," Priss admitted. She glanced at him, and for once all the animosity and bitterness fell away. "I worried you terribly, didn't I?"

"I could have stopped you any time I liked," he confessed. He searched her puzzled eyes. "Or didn't that ever occur to you?"

It hadn't. She studied his craggy face curiously. "Why didn't you?" she asked, her voice soft.

His thumb caressed the porcelain cup absently as he looked back at her. "I liked having you around," he offered quietly. "Despite the fact that we all knew you were years too young to be daydreaming over me," he added with a wicked grin.

"We trusted you," Adam chuckled.

"Of course," Priss submitted. "I was like his kid sister."

John's eyes narrowed and when she looked into them, she read graphically that in no way had she been like his kid sister.

"How about some dessert?" she asked quickly, and rose to get it.

In the kitchen, she uncovered the Southern pecan pie she'd made and began to slice it. Her heart was wildly racing, and she hoped she could calm down before she went back into the living room.

She felt him before she heard his voice, sensed his presence as if she'd been born with radar.

"Can I help?" John asked at her back.

"I'm just finishing up," she replied. Was that squeaky voice really hers? The kitchen shrank when he walked in.

"I love that pie," he said. "A southern-American specialty, isn't it?"

"Yes," she returned breathlessly. She reached for saucers, but his big hands slid around her waist and she froze, helpless, as his fingers moved, fondling her.

His breath sighed out against the top of her head, and she could feel the warmth of his big body, feel the muscles of his chest against her back. She was drowning again. She wanted to turn and let him crush her body into his; she wanted to lift her face and let him kiss her hungry mouth until she stopped aching.

"Did you bake it?" he asked quietly.

"Yes...I...I can cook, you know," she faltered.

His chest rose and fell roughly. His hands moved slowly up and down her waist. "You did the lunch today, too, didn't you?" he murmured. "The chicken and potato salad..."

She swallowed. "Yes."

He moved an inch closer, bringing his body into total contact with hers, and she caught her breath and stiffened.

"You still smell of gardenias," he whispered in her ear. His mouth touched it and then ran slowly down the side of her neck to her shoulder. "You even taste of them."

The feel of his hard warm mouth was doing crazy things to her willpower. Her head involuntarily went to one side to give him better access to her silky skin.

She felt the edge of his teeth then, and heard the ragged sigh of his breath.

"It's no good," he said roughly. "Turn around and give me your mouth."

She wanted that, too. She needed to taste him, to let him satisfy the aching hungers he'd created. Without a protest, she started to turn, but the sound of footsteps broke them quickly apart.

"Sorry, but there's a phone call for you, John," Adam interrupted, peeking through the door. "Your jackeroo."

"Damn," John muttered darkly. He glanced ruefully at Priss before he went out the door, and Adam made a regretful face before he followed suit. Priss went back to dishing up the pie, with hands that shook and a body that hurt with unsatisfied need.

By the time she had the dishes on a tray and had carried them into the dining room, John was standing in the hall with Adam.

"...Damned sorry," John was saying irritably. He glanced toward the dining room. "I have to go," he told her. "A blue down at the shearer's quarters. My jackeroo can't calm them down."

She could imagine John doing that, quite easily. She'd seen him break up fights before.

"We're glad you could come to supper," she told him in a low voice.

His eyes searched hers across the room. "Walk me out."

She went to him without a protest, a sheep going to the slaughter. She barely saw the knowing look her parents exchanged as she took the large hand John held out to her and went with him onto the darkened porch.

"Oh, God, come here, love," he groaned urgently, drawing her trembling body completely against his. "Kiss me...!"

His mouth opened as it touched hers, and she met the kiss hungrily, reaching up to hold him, to plaster her aching body to the hardness of his. She clung to the strong muscles of his back, feeling his teeth against her own with ardent pressure of his devouring mouth.

She moaned helplessly, in the throes of something

so explosive it rocked her on her feet, and his arms tightened.

"I need you," he whispered into her mouth. "I need you…"

He was trembling, and so was she, and the darkness spun around her like a Ferris wheel while she tried to get enough of his warm demanding mouth, the deep penetration of his tongue, the rough massage of his hands down her spine.

She felt him maneuver their bodies so the porch wall was behind her. Still holding her mouth in bondage, he eased himself down against her, crushing her hips and breasts and thighs under his so she could feel the very texture of his muscles.

She cried out, softly, helplessly, and he lifted his blond head and stared into her eyes in the dim light.

"I want you under me like this in a bed," he said unsteadily, his eyes glittering.

Her nails bit into his back as she tried to find a protest.

"Don't start making excuses," he commanded gruffly. "You want me, too."

"You're heavy," she moaned.

"Yes, and you love it," he breathed against her lips. He moved his hips deliberately and felt her stiffen and clutch at him. "Oh, Priss, I'd give anything to have you alone with me in a dark room for just an hour. Just one hour…!"

"I can't," she whispered tearfully. "I can't, I won't…!"

His mouth crushed down on hers, and he kissed her with a wild kind of frustration before he arched himself away from her and stood glaring down at her trembling body and wide misty eyes.

"Nothing's changed," he whispered huskily. "We cause a fever in each other so hot, ice couldn't quench it. Eventually you'll have me, Priscilla. Because the day will come when you can't bear the torture of wanting me any longer."

"But it won't last," she returned bitterly.

"Yes," he replied. "Yes, it will. You're all I see, hear, think, or need in all the world."

"It's just lust!" she threw at him. "You said so!"

He searched her wild eyes. "So I did. But it's much more than that," he said. "Much more. We must talk, and soon. I just wish I had the time now, but I don't. Good night, Priss."

He turned and walked away. It was several minutes before she could get her rubbery legs to take her back inside. And it was hours before she slept. She tossed and turned all night long, worrying about John's dogged pursuit and her own vulnerability. What was she going to do? She couldn't survive a second rejection. Could she believe John when he said the blazing passion between them would last? It was a question to which she still hadn't found an answer by morning.

She went with her parents to church and then came back home and brooded for the rest of the day. It was almost a relief when Monday morning came and she could go back to school.

She heard from the twins that John was frightfully busy, and her daydreams about having him repeat his invitation to the muster went up in smoke. Obviously he hadn't time for anything else except the station right now. And she couldn't even feel angry about it, now that she knew what a difficult time he'd had the past five years.

On Thursday the twins broke their record streak of good behavior by putting a frog into a little girl's dress. The ensuing pandemonium got Priscilla a stern lecture from the principal, and she had to keep the twins after class as punishment. They didn't seem to mind and, secretly, neither did she. She had a feeling that John would come for them.

"Poor Uncle John's been staggering tired," Gerry told her that afternoon after the other children had gone home.

"Dad offered to come home, but Uncle John said no," Bobby added. "He said that Mom and Dad needed...needed..." He frowned.

"A honeymoon," Gerry provided.

Priss laughed. "Well, I'm glad they're enjoying themselves. And I'm sure your uncle can cope."

"I say—" Ronald George stuck his head in the door— "your dad said to tell you that he and your mom are going to drive over to see the Thompsons and that they won't be home until about dark."

"Thanks, Ronald," she replied, grinning at him.

He seemed to take that as an invitation. He came into the room, shut the door, and perched his tall form on the edge of Priss's desk. His eyes went over the picture she made in her pale pink blouse and gray skirt.

"You look cool today," he remarked. "Like one of our English roses."

"Beware of my thorns," she teased mischievously.

"I'm not afraid of roses." He pursed his lips. He

folded his arms. "As a matter of fact, I'm not afraid of anything today. I have scored a point."

She frowned and cast a quick look at the twins. But they were in the back of the room peering into the class's aquarium, where two turtles lived.

"Scored?" she questioned.

He leaned toward her, so that his face was almost touching hers. "Remember Mandy? Well, she's finally agreed to go out with me!"

She laughed softly. "Lucky old you!" she exclaimed. "Ronald, that's just super!"

"I can hardly wait," he continued, searching her twinkling eyes. "It must be love," he added more audibly.

To the man standing frozen and furious in the doorway, it was an eye-opening little tableau. Ronald leaning over Priss, with his mouth just inches from hers, and her bright face turned up and laughing at him, while he made her declarations of love. John clenched his hands by his side, weary from his day's work, his drill pants and bush shirt covered with dust and bits of wool and dirt, his face stern with anger.

Priss saw him first, and her heart turned over. "Oh. Hello, John," she faltered.

Ronald George straightened up, grinning. "Hi, Mr. Sterling. Nice day. You look a bit bushed."

"Down here, bushed means lost, and I'm not that," John returned with cold formality. "Gerry, Bobby, let's go."

He opened the door and ushered them out. And then he followed them! Without a word to Priss, without a single word, he was gone.

She couldn't help the sick, empty feeling in her stomach. She stared at the closed door with a sense of disaster. Surely he hadn't been jealous? She laughed bitterly to herself even as she thought it. John, jealous of her—that was a good one.

"I say, are you all right?" Ronald asked.

She forced a smile. "Of course. It's just been a long day. Well, I'd better pack up and go home. Thanks for the message. And good luck on your date!"

He stood up, smiling. "I'll need it. Mentally she can cut me to pieces. But she's a lovely lady, and I'm hopelessly smitten. Perhaps I can convince her I'm a good risk."

"I'm sure you will." Priss smiled at him. "See you tomorrow."

"Have a nice evening," he called as she went out the door with her belongings.

After she got home and changed, she walked down by the creek and sat there for a long time, puzzled over John's utter rudeness. Was he angry at her, or the boys, or had it just been weariness? Oh, how she wished she knew!

After a while, she took off her shoes and waded across the cool creek to the other side. She wandered up the small rise through the eucalyptus trees and saw the Sterling Run Land-Rover coming across the grassy paddock at a clip. Her heart leapt wildly when she recognized the driver.

Across the horizon were storm clouds, and even as John pulled up at the edge of the wooded area, rain started pelting down

"Well, get in before you get wet," he growled, throwing open the passenger door.

She dived in, shoes in hand, and closed the door, scrutinizing him warily. He looked savage. His blue eyes glimmered under his heavy dark brows, and his lips made a thin line as he glared at her. He hadn't changed his clothing since she'd seen him at school, and he smelled of sheep and dust and the outdoors.

"Am I distasteful?" he asked curtly. "I'd forgotten how long it's been since you've seen me straight from the shearing sheds."

He wouldn't be distasteful to her if he were covered in tar and feathers, but she didn't say that. "You've been working hard, the boys said," she observed.

"Have to," he returned on a sigh as the rain came heavier, making the cab a private, cozy haven. "We're still a long way from financial security at the station."

"You'll make it eventually," she said confidently.

He took off his hat and tossed it into the back of the vehicle, which was littered with tools and rags and dusty equipment. His hair was sweaty and he looked as ragged as he probably felt.

"What's going on between you and that pommy?" he inquired bluntly, pinning her with his eyes.

Her lips parted with an indrawn breath at the unexpected attack. She lifted a hand to her hair and mussed it. "Nothing," she said.

"Don't hand me that," he growled. He threw a strong arm over the back of the seat, and she could see the muscles rippling under the darkly tanned skin. "He was making emphatic statements about being in love."

"Yes, but not with me," she burst out.

"There was no one else in the room, except the twins," he reminded her, glaring at her mouth.

Her breath caught in her throat, and she stared at his face with helpless longing. Her hands clenched in her lap, and she closed her eyes because she wanted so badly to kiss him. Outside the rain pelted the hood with a loud metallic sound.

"Oh, never mind," he said irritably. "Come here."

He held out one arm, and without really questioning her own docility, she went close to him, burrowing against his broad chest with a small contented sigh.

"I'll probably get you filthy, but I'm beyond caring," he murmured huskily as his arms contracted. "I'm starved for you, Priscilla." He nuzzled his face against hers and searched for her mouth. "Too starved."

She gave her mouth up to him, completely, letting him pierce the line of her lips with his tongue and penetrate to the soft darkness beyond. She didn't even protest when he turned her so she lay across his lap, or when he jerked open his shirt.

"Let me feel you," he whispered hungrily as his hand went to the buttons of her pink blouse. "All of you, against me, here..."

He had her mouth under his again, and her hands clung to his bare arms as he got the fabric out of the way and suddenly crushed her softness into the hard warm muscle and thick hair over his chest.

"Oh, God," he groaned huskily, folding her even closer. "Oh, God, how sweet, how sweet...!" He began to move her body so her breasts dragged against his skin, intensifying the need they were both feeling to such a degree that she cried out.

He lifted his shaggy head and looked into her eyes. His own were gleaming and wild. "Did I hurt you?" he asked shakily.

"No," she moaned. "Do it…do it again," she whispered.

He obliged, but this time he watched her face, watched the pleasure she was feeling as it was betrayed by her parted lips, her wide misty eyes.

His gaze dropped down to where their bodies met, and he watched the hard nipples disappear into the thick hair over his muscular chest.

"You are so beautiful," he breathed reverently. "Watching you…this way…drives me wild." He brought one hand from behind her and brushed his fingers lightly against the side of her breast. "Silk," he whispered as his fingers found the exquisite contours and then eased between their bodies to mold the peak.

His eyes shot back up to hers, and she lay helpless against him, trapped by the sensuality of his hands, his gaze. She was completely at his mercy, and he had to know it.

"I'll teach you to trust me somehow," he whispered, bending to her mouth. "Open your mouth, little virgin. All this…is only love-play. How could I take you in this damned dirty vehicle…?"

That relaxed her a little. She didn't fight the possession of his mouth as he took her own again, a little more fervently this time.

"Honey, touch me," he coaxed. "Stroke me."

Her hands obeyed him. She liked the feel of his muscles, especially the ones just above his belt buckle. She touched him there, and he groaned, and the muscles clenched like coiled wire.

"Oh!" She stilled her fingers and looked up at him.

His lips were parted, swollen like her own, and he was having trouble breathing. His blond-streaked hair had fallen onto his brow, and he looked like a lover. Really like a lover.

"Do you feel adventurous?" he asked unsteadily. "Because if you do, I'll teach you some shocking things about a man's body."

Part of her was caught in the trap and wanted desperately to be taught. The saner part knew where all this was leading, and it was to a dead end. He only wanted her.

She leaned her forehead against him and pressed her hand flat over his heart. "No," she said in a defeated tone. "No, I can't; I can't go through it again," she murmured weakly. "I can't live through it twice. John, please, don't do this to me!"

His hands went to her back, and he held her close, feeling her breasts like satin against him, loving the bareness of her back, the scent of her.

He kissed her closed eyes, her forehead, in a breathlessly tender way and then eased her away from him.

His eyes went helplessly to her nakedness. She was bigger now, fuller, firmer, and the sight of her was glorious. It made his heart soar.

He reached out and ran a gentle finger over the swollen-tipped contours. "You were made for children," he breathed, thinking of how she'd look holding his.

Her whole body shook at the words, at the mental

picture of a little blond baby suckling heartily at the place he was touching, and she stopped breathing as she met his level gaze.

It was like a moment out of time, when they were thinking the same thought, wanting the same thing. He bent his head and kissed her. And it was like no kiss they'd ever shared before. Tender, questioning. Full of wonder and shy exploration and aching softness.

He drew away and cupped her face in his hands to search her wide misty eyes. "Come and have supper at the Run tomorrow night," he invited quietly. "I'll cook."

Her mouth gaped. "Supper?"

"Yes. Only that." He reached down and pulled her clothing up, dressing her like a doll. "No more love-making for a while. I want to get to know you. What you feel. What you think. What you want from life."

Her body tingled. "Those are deep thoughts."

"Yes, aren't they." He fastened the top button of her blouse. "And in the meantime, it would help if you'd stop letting me undress you."

"I tried," she said with a faint smile.

He sighed. "Yes. I tried, too, but the feel of you does unexpected things to my brain. I'm sorry. I didn't mean for this to happen."

"It was so beautiful," she said without meaning to.

"Oh, God, yes," he ground out. He caught one of her hands and carried the palm reverently to his lips. "You've never done that sort of thing with anyone except me, have you?"

She shook her head. "I never wanted anyone else's hands..." She bit her lip and lowered her eyes.

He tilted her face up to his. "Neither did I," he said.

She searched that weathered face pensively, curiously.

His finger brushed the line of her lips. "I haven't slept with a woman in five years."

It was like a jolt of electricity going through her body. Her eyes dilated, and she gaped at him. "Five years?"

He nodded. "So you see, there's been no one else for me, either, Priscilla."

Tears bled from her eyes. She couldn't help them. "But you're a man," she whispered.

"I didn't feel like much of a man after the way I cut you up," he confessed, handing her a clean handkerchief. "I had a mental block about sex. I even tried once." He laughed mirthlessly. "She wasn't an understanding woman, and that made it worse. She laughed."

She went into his arms and held him, burying her face in his neck. "Who was she?" she ground out. "I'll kill her!"

His arms contracted. "Jealous?"

"Furious. How could she do that to you?"

He drew in a slow breath. "You're still very innocent in some ways," he reminded her.

"I'd never do that," she said fervently.

"I know. If I were totally impotent, I imagine you'd find some way to make me feel like a man again, wouldn't you?"

She lifted her face and looked into his eyes. He understood the question there.

"No," he responded softly. "I'm not impotent. Not with you."

She smiled shyly and lowered her eyes to his chest.

"If you'd like me to prove it," he offered, "I'd be only too glad to oblige."

This was the old teasing John Sterling she remembered from her teens, the man she'd worshipped and grown to love. Not the distant stranger of past weeks and years. It must have been a barren life for him, if he'd had no one since Janie Weeks. Janie. Her eyes clouded. She wanted desperately to ask him about the divorcée, to ask if it had hurt when she deserted him. Did he still feel anything for Janie? But she was too unsure of him to ask such a personal question. Instead she forced her eyes up to his and smiled softly.

"What would you do if I said yes, go ahead?" she asked.

He chuckled softly. "I'd find some excuse to go home. I don't want to take your virginity in the front seat of a Land-Rover, if it's all the same to you. I'm too old for impatient groping."

Her eyes measured the size of the seat and the size of his body and she laughed softly. "No, I guess it would be impossible."

"Sweet innocent," he sighed, touching his mouth to hers, "we could do it sitting up, didn't you know?"

She flushed from her hairline down to her breasts, and he looked at her and laughed so delightedly, she couldn't even get angry.

"I'll drive you home, darling," he said gently. "I don't want you catching cold."

He moved her beside him but held her arm when she tried to go back to her own side of the vehicle.

"No," he protested. "Stay close."

She didn't argue. She pressed herself against his side and closed her eyes and rested her cheek on his stained shirt with a soulful sigh.

His arm contracted as he started the vehicle and put it in gear with his free hand. "I've ruined your blouse," he remarked as he pulled back onto the track.

"I don't mind," she answered.

"When we do this again, I'll make sure I've cleaned up first. I went off half cocked about your pommy friend and didn't even consider how I looked," he laughed.

"You were looking for me?" she asked.

He chuckled softly. "I thought I'd probably find you at the creek. You spend quite a lot of time brooding there, don't you?"

"I like to watch the birds."

He kissed her forehead lightly. "Yes, I know."

It took only a few short minutes to get to her parents' home, and she drew away from him with all-too-obvious reluctance.

"I meant what I said," he repeated. "No more love-making for a while. We're going to learn about each other in less physical ways."

That was promising and rather exciting. She smiled at him with a little of her old spirit. "Afraid I might seduce you, John?" she teased gently.

He caught her hand and held it to his lips. "Yes," he admitted, and he didn't smile. "And deathly afraid I might seduce you. So we'll cool it for a while. All right?"

"All right." She glanced at him one last time and

got out of the Land-Rover. He studied her warmly for a long minute.

"What was the pommy telling you?" he asked finally.

She grinned at him. "That he had a date with the girl he's dying of love for, and how happy he was."

He grimaced. "Well, as long as he's not after you, I suppose he's safe enough. I'll pick you up about six tomorrow."

"I could drive over—" she began.

"I'll pick you up about six," he returned firmly. "I don't want you on the roads alone at night."

He backed out of the driveway before she could make any remarks about being liberated and able to take care of herself. And as she went inside she couldn't help thinking how nice it felt to be cared for, protected. But what was he after now? He'd said he didn't want to seduce her. Did that mean that he was beginning to feel something for her after all? Her heart raced wildly. Her eyes closed. And if he was, did she dare take the risk a second time? That nagging thought weighed on her mind all night.

Chapter 11

It was an unexpected treat to find the twins, as well as John, dressed to the hilt when they all came to get Priscilla the next evening. She was wearing the same white gauzy creation she'd worn several nights before, and John admired it.

"I like that," he complimented.

She grinned. "I haven't gone shopping in quite a while, so it will just have to do."

"Have fun, darling," Renée said from the door.

"We'll have her home by midnight," John promised as he helped her into the Ford.

"Dinkum, we will!" Gerry called out the window.

Priss looked over the back seat at the terrible twins. Gerry was wearing a blue suit, Bobby a brown one, and they did look elegant.

"I'd never have believed it," she told them with pursed lips. "You're both very handsome."

'Uncle John is, too, isn't he?'' Gerry pressed her.

She surveyed John as he climbed in the front seat. He was dressed in a tan safari suit, his head was bare, and he looked as rugged as the country he lived in.

"Yes, he is," Priss commented absently, studying him. "Very handsome, indeed."

He lifted an eyebrow and smiled at her. "Thank you, Miss Johnson," he responded dryly. "I must say, you look lovely yourself."

She smiled back and started to settle herself on the seat, when he laid his big arm over the back of it and stared at her.

"Come here, love," he said in a voice that made her toes curl.

She eased closer without a single protest and felt the reassuring warmth and strength of his body with surging delight.

"That's more like it," he murmured as he started the Ford and eased it into gear. "Tell Priss what we're having for supper, boys," he called into the back seat.

"We're having steak and salad!" Gerry said.

"And apple pie for afters," Bobby added.

"And homemade rolls!" Gerry interrupted. "Uncle John did them all alone!"

"When I was a boy, the cook we hired on for the shearing gang used to go on benders at the damndest times," he explained as they drove toward the Run in the moonlit darkness. "I learned to pinch-hit in self-defense." He looked down at her. "Men work harder when they've been fed."

"Do they?" she questioned, smiling up at him.

His arm tightened, and she sighed. Minutes later he

pulled up in front of the Colonial-style house and the boys piled out quickly, racing for the porch.

John helped Priss get out and then stiffened at the haunting doglike howl that echoed beyond the outbuildings.

"A dingo," he growled.

"But doesn't the dingo fence keep them out?" she asked, recalling the miles and miles of fence around the sheep-raising country in the state of Queensland, along the New South Wales border and into western Australia. It was something of an international legend.

"Not entirely," he informed her. "We still have to hunt them down occasionally."

She shivered as the sound came again.

"They rarely attack people," he told her, drawing her close at his side. "Besides, love, I'd never let anything hurt you."

"Yes, I know," she murmured. She let her eyes half close as they walked. Those were the sweetest steps she'd taken in five long years.

In no time, they were seated at the long elegant dinner table Mrs. Sterling had imported from England, enjoying the succulent steak John had cooked.

"You're very good at this," Priss praised when they'd worked their way through to the apple pie.

"Necessity," he explained with a smile. "I can think of things I'd rather do than cook."

"How's your mother?" Priss asked then.

"Doing very well. She tells me she's dating a financier." He glanced up. "I expect she may marry him."

"Will you mind?"

He shook his head. "She's entitled to some happiness."

"Uncle John, can we be excused?" Gerry asked as he finished off his apple pie. "There's this dinkum movie on about the outback..."

"Go ahead," John told them. "Don't put the volume up too loud, though," he added.

"Sure!" Bobby agreed. "We'll be quiet as mice," he promised as they rushed off into the living room.

"They've changed a lot in the past week," Priss noted.

"Yes, I've seen it. I think when Randy and Latrice work out their problems, things will be better all around." He sat back with a glass of white wine he'd just poured, and sipped it casually. "Did you mean what you told me the other day—that you were planning to go back to Hawaii?"

She studied the tablecloth. "At the time, I did."

"And now? After yesterday?"

She looked up into his serene, steady gaze and felt her heart do cartwheels in her chest. "I don't know that I could leave now."

He searched her eyes for a long moment. Then he put the wineglass down. "Do you feel you could live in Australia for the rest of your life, without regretting it?"

"I planned that from the day my family came here," she said, curious about where the conversation was heading.

But he changed the subject abruptly. "How does your father like having you at the school with him?"

She laughed. "He likes it a lot. He says now he has

someone to sit with at lunch. I love my parents," she
related quietly. "They've been everything to me."

"I'm rather fond of them myself," he concurred.

"John, what was your father like?" she asked as
she sipped her own wine.

He shrugged. "I'm not sure. All I have is my
mother's memory of him. And she worshipped the
ground he walked on." He stared blankly at his wineglass. "I was only a toddler when he died. Randy was
newborn. Neither of us ever knew him. He was killed
by a brumby."

"That's a wild horse, isn't it?"

"Yes." He put the glass down. "I've often wondered how things might have gone if he'd lived. Randy
and I were never close, until this crisis came up.
Mother..." He laughed. "You know Mother. She
likes her independence. I grew up not liking ties. It's
been hard for me to change. To get used to the idea
of answering to another human being."

She supposed he meant to Randy, since his brother
had taken over the station. She put down her wineglass
and dabbed at her full lips with the napkin.

"I suppose it was the other way with me," she replied. "I was loved and indulged and protected. Oh,
my parents disciplined me along the way, but I was
never allowed to learn things by experience."

"Except with me," he mused, watching her.

She smiled slowly. "Except with you." She looked
up into his broad tanned face wonderingly. "Why did
you put up with me?"

"You were a beautiful girl," he said simply. "Like
sunshine to be around. Full of life and joy and delight-

ful warmth. I enjoyed being with you, even before I discovered what it was like to want you in any physical way.''

''Did you want me before that afternoon I left for college?'' she queried, but she couldn't manage to meet his eyes as she asked the question.

''Remember the morning you came running across the paddock barefoot?'' he asked, smiling at the memory. ''To show me the scholarship you'd won?''

''Yes,'' she said.

''That was the first time. I looked at you and had a sudden, and rather frightening, reaction to you.'' He stroked his wineglass as if it were a woman's body, but he was looking across the table at Priss. ''I was trying to decide what to do about it when you started avoiding me.'' His eyes fell to the table. ''I didn't quite know how to handle that. It disturbed me greatly.''

She felt her nerves tingle with pleasure as she studied his broad chest. He looked up then, his eyes mysterious and vividly blue in his craggy face as he viewed her.

''Then I came out to the house to ask why, to say good-bye. And I kissed you.'' His eyebrows lifted, and he smiled wickedly. ''It was meant to be just a kiss, for good-bye. But once I started, you see, I found that I couldn't stop. You never knew that it was touch and go with me, did you, Priss?'' he added meaningfully. ''All that saved you was the fear that I might make you pregnant.''

''Terrifying thought!'' she murmured, trying to make light of it.

"Not at all," he countered quietly. "I found myself considering children. And ties. And settling down. And that was when I decided to go to Hawaii and ask you to marry me." He pushed his chair back. "And then the bottom fell out."

She didn't like thinking about that. She heard him come around the table to pull her chair out.

"Let's go sit in my study," he suggested. "I could use a brandy, and the boys won't disturb us in there."

She got up, her eyes involuntarily going to his face.

"No," he breathed, looking back with equal urgency. "We can't. Sure as hell they'd walk in on us, and I don't want them asking embarrassing questions."

She flushed. "I wasn't—" she protested.

"I want it, too," he ground out. He was standing close enough that the warmth of his body warmed hers, too. He smelled of spicy cologne and soap.

She drew in a steadying breath. "I'm sorry."

"There's nothing to be sorry about. Come on." He caught her hand in his and locked his fingers into hers. Big warm fingers, very strong, very capable. She felt lighter than air as he led her along with him. "I missed you," he confided. "For five years, I didn't spend a night without thinking about where you were, what you were doing. Who you were with."

She'd done that, too, but she wasn't going to admit it. Her pride had taken a hell of a blow already.

"It must have been very hard for you, at first," she prodded. "Losing the station, I mean."

"Yes. It cut my pride to ribbons. And Randy had a bit of a superiority complex at the outset. That didn't help, either.'' He tightened his grip on her hand. ''I was devastated at first. I all but gave up. There was so little left to lose that I stopped giving a damn.'' He led her into the study, leaving the door open, and left her at the couch while he poured brandy into two snifters. ''Then Randy got in over his head and came to me for advice. A first,'' he added with a faint grin. ''I got caught up in the challenge, and we've been working well together ever since.''

She stared down at her folded hands. ''So everything worked out for the best, anyway.''

''Not quite.'' He handed her a snifter and dropped down beside her with his in hand. ''I lost you.''

''Was that so bad? You didn't seem to think so at the time.''

''Someday, at a better time, I'll tell you all about it. But not tonight.'' He slid an arm around her. ''Come close, love. Tell me about Hawaii.''

She kicked off her shoes and curled up in the curve of his arm, loving the warm contact. Her head rested on his shoulder and she nuzzled against him.

''There isn't a lot to tell. I studied hard. I had friends. I went on weekend trips to the other islands, and once I flew to California for summer vacation. I had a marvelous time, but I missed Australia.''

''You never came home, did you?'' he probed.

She smiled sadly. ''I was afraid I might see you.''

He shifted restlessly. ''But the pommy was always around, wasn't he?''

''Ronald was my best friend,'' she confirmed. ''I'm very fond of him. He was there when I needed someone to cry on. But it was only friendship.''

"I thought you loved him," he said.

She shook her head, feeling the hard muscle of his arm behind her nape. "No. Not even at first."

"Did you miss me?" he quizzed after a minute. "Or were you too bitter?"

"I was bitter at first. But I got over it," she lied. "Then I tried not to think about you."

"Successfully?"

She bit her lower lip. "Sometimes."

His fingers curved under her chin and nudged it up so he could search her wide, sad green eyes. He caressed the side of her throat with a light pressure that made her pulse go crazy.

"I'd think of you at night sometimes," he said. "And it would get so bad, I'd climb into my clothes and saddle a horse and ride for hours. And when I got back, tired to the bone and half dead from lack of sleep, I'd lie awake and remember how it felt to cherish your mouth under mine."

Her lower lip trembled, because it had been that way with her, too.

"I missed you so badly," he whispered gruffly, bending. "It was like losing part of me."

His mouth pressed down against hers, cool and moist and tasting of brandy. He kissed her tenderly, lovingly, breaking the taut line of her lips with a lazy coaxing pressure that soon became slow and deep and urgent.

She made a tiny sound in her throat and turned to get closer to him,

"Wait a minute," he whispered. He stopped long enough to get the brandy snifters out of the way, and then she was in his arms, held close, crushed against his shirt. He kissed her so deeply, that she felt her heart turn over in her breast.

He groaned deeply, forcing her head into the curve of his elbow with the urgency of his need.

She touched his cheek, ran her fingers into his hair. She moaned softly as one big hand moved under her arm and began to lightly stroke the soft flesh there.

"Yes," she murmured eagerly, moving her body to tempt his fingers onto it.

"No," he ground out, lifting his head. He was breathing roughly, and his eyes devoured her, but he put her away from him. "No more. I can't handle this."

He got to his feet, running his fingers through his blond-streaked hair, breathing heavily. His back was to her as he stared out the darkened window and stretched to ease the tension in his body.

She sat up, gnawing her lip, wondering at his self-control.

"You always could do that," she commented on a nervous laugh.

He turned, frowning. "Do what?"

"Pull away. Stop before things got out of control." Her eyes fell. "I was never able to draw back."

"You were an innocent. I wasn't." He laughed softly. "And I had plenty of practice controlling my urges when I was with you. All I had to do was hum Brahms's lullaby to myself."

"I might not have gotten pregnant," she argued.

"I'd have bet the station on it," he returned shortly.

His eyes searched hers, and he smiled. "Did you expect that I'd have stopped with one time?"

Her lips parted on a surprised breath. "Wouldn't you?" she asked in a whisper.

He shook his head from side to side. "Three or four times by morning, darling," he said quietly. "At least."

Her face flamed. "I always thought...men gave out."

"You've got a lot to learn. And someday soon," he added with an intent stare, "I'm going to teach you all of it."

She steeled herself to refuse. "I won't have an affair with you—I've already said that."

"I know." He moved back to the sofa and sat down beside her. His face was solemn as he drew a box out of the pockets of his bush jacket and pressed it into her hands. "Open that when you get home. I'll come for you first thing in the morning, and we'll talk."

She touched the gray felt of the small box lightly, her eyes conveying her puzzlement.

"Don't open it until you get home," he repeated. He bent and kissed her mouth tenderly. "And don't worry yourself to death about my motives. Think about what life will be like without me. Because I've already considered that question. And I've decided that no life at all would be better than living without you."

She hardly heard anything else he said for the rest of the evening. She was still in a daze when he took her home, and she mumbled something to the boys, forgot to say anything at all to John, and went into her

house at ten o'clock feeling as if she'd been out all
night.

It wasn't until she was in bed that she opened the
tiny box with trembling fingers and looked at its con-
tents. It was a blazing emerald, small but perfect, in a
gold setting. The engagement ring was accompanied
by a solid-gold band with the same intricate design.
She watched it blur before her eyes and only then realized that she was crying.

All the long years she'd loved John Sterling, she'd
never imagined how it might feel if he bought her a
ring. He hadn't when he'd proposed in Hawaii; he
hadn't even mentioned buying a ring. And now here
it was, without the proposal, and she didn't think she
had enough strength in her body to turn him down.

For better or for worse, for richer or for poorer…she
didn't mind that he wasn't rich. She'd work beside
him. She'd take care of him. And at night she'd sleep
in his big arms. And in time would come children.
Then perhaps he'd grow to love her. Perhaps the physical need he had of her would grow into an emotional
one and what she felt for him would be returned.

There was, though, the chance that it wouldn't. Yet
when she thought about living the rest of her life without him, it was a chance she was willing to take. She
knew there'd never be another man. She didn't want
anyone else. She hadn't in five years.

Her fingers trembled as she took the emerald out
and slid it onto her wedding finger, finding the fit perfect. Her eyes closed in a silent prayer. This time it
had to work. This time she had to make him love her.
It was already too late to run away. She was more
deeply in love than she had been at eighteen. Too
much in love to let go.

Chapter 12

Naturally Priss didn't sleep all night. She climbed out of bed at five A.M. with bloodshot eyes and tugged on a frilly long white robe over her blue pajamas before she dragged herself to the kitchen to start breakfast.

Her parents were still asleep, and she felt as if she were sleepwalking herself. She yawned as she put the biscuits she'd just rolled out into the oven and started the coffee.

A noise in the yard caught her attention. It sounded very much like a car engine, but surely John wouldn't be here at five in the morning…

She opened the door and he came up the back steps into the house. He looked as tired as she felt. He was wearing his work clothing, pale drill trousers with a khaki bush shirt and the slouch hat he wore to work cattle. He took off the hat and closed the door and stared down at her with eyes so blue and piercing, they made her heart race.

"I couldn't wait any longer," he explained softly, searching her sleepy face. "I've hardly slept."

"Me, too," she returned.

He tossed his hat onto the counter and sighed. "Well?"

She felt shy with him. Eighteen all over again and half afraid of his formidable masculinity. Instead of answering him, she held out her left hand, where the emerald ring sparkled with green fire in the kitchen light.

His breath caught. His eyes closed. "Thank God," he uttered. And he reached for her.

She held him as hard as he was holding her, overwhelmed by the pleasure of belonging to him at last.

"I've never wanted anything so much," he breathed over her head, rocking her gently in his enveloping arms. "No regrets, Priss?"

She drew in a slow breath, and all the old doubts gnawed at her for a minute. "Not...regrets, no. But..." She drew back to look up into his tanned face. "John, you're sure this time?"

His face hardened as he read the uncertainty and fear of rejection that lay naked in her pale green eyes.

"If it's any consolation, what I did to you will haunt me all my life," he replied quietly. "Yes, I'm sure this time. No, I'm not going to back out at the last minute. We're going to get married and live together and build a life for ourselves."

Her eyes misted, and she smiled wobbly at him.

"Gee, that sounds nice," she whispered. "I feel all eighteen and nervous again."

His fingers touched her disheveled hair, and his eyes ran over her with possession in their twinkling depths. "You look about that this morning," he agreed with a warm smile. "I didn't know you liked pajamas."

She smiled. "I can wear nightgowns after we're married, if you like."

"I'd like it better if you don't wear anything at all," he teased. "I don't."

Her face colored, and he seemed to like that. He bent and touched her mouth lazily with his. "You belong to me now," he whispered, and lifted her high in his arms. "That's better. You're short without shoes."

"Because you're so big."

"I'll take care of you, Priss," he promised, searching her eyes. "We won't have a lot, but I'll try to ensure you never regret marrying me."

She studied his hard face with loving eyes. At least he was willing to commit himself this far, she thought. Perhaps love would come eventually.

"I'll never regret it," she promised, meaning it. She tugged his head down to hers and kissed him softly, slowly, savoring the very texture of his hard lips. His arms contracted. She felt his chest crushing her breasts gently, felt the long powerful line of his legs against hers and moaned, clinging to his broad shoulders.

They were so lost in each other, they didn't hear the door open, or see the stunned, then delighted look that Adam and Renée exchanged.

"Ahem!" Renée grinned.

They broke apart, looking guilty, and then John started laughing.

"It isn't quite as bad as it looks," he said with a wicked glance at Priss, who was clinging to his side. "I haven't been here all night."

"I don't know about that," Adam gibed with a mischievous smile. "You both look guilty as sin to me."

"Yes, they do, don't they?" Renée added fondly.

"Actually, we've been sealing our engagement," John volunteered.

Priss held out her hand, and her eyes were the same fiery sparkling emerald as the stone. "We're going to be married," she said in a voice that was husky with feeling. She was sure her feet were floating above the floor.

After that was pandemonium. It wasn't until they were all sitting at the table eating breakfast that there was a break in the conversation.

"Well, when is the wedding?" Adam inquired.

"As soon as I can get a license," John said firmly, glancing at Priss. "I've waited five years. I won't wait any longer."

"That suits me very well," Priss added. "We can be married here, can't we, Mom?"

Renée was staring blankly at her daughter. "Here?"

"Well, yes. Just the minister and all of us and maybe Randy and Latrice…?"

Renée let her breath out. "It sounds just like us, doesn't it, darling?" she addressed Adam, laughing. "We did the same thing, you know. It's better than a large wedding, really; much less anxiety."

"Also much quicker." Adam grinned at John.

John grinned back. "We're both so old, we need all the time we can get; don't we, darling?" he added, winking at Priss.

"Speak for yourself, old fossil," she told him as she dug into her scrambled eggs. "I'm a mere child, myself."

"That's no way to talk to your future husband," John chided sternly.

"Excuse me, darling," she cooed, relishing the word as she peeked at him through her lashes. "You just give the orders, and I'll ignore them. All right?"

John sighed. "I can see that we're going to have to have a long talk about some of the finer details of marriage."

"Okay," Priss agreed. She laid down her fork. "What would you like to know?"

He threw back his head and laughed. "I've done myself in!"

She only smiled. "Yes, darling," she replied seductively, and batted her eyelashes at him. "Lucky, lucky you!"

He didn't laugh then. He just searched her face with soft intent eyes. "Luckier than you know," he responded. "I'll check on the license today," he added, dragging his eyes back to Adam and Renée.

Priss just stared at him, her gaze so full of love that Renée had to drop her eyes.

The next two weeks seemed to go by in a flurry of activity, as Priss tried to balance work and daydreaming, and being with John every evening.

He didn't press his advantage, now that they were

totally committed to each other. He was more friend than lover, and they talked to each other as never before. She learned that he liked classical music, and he learned that she was an old-motion-picture fanatic. They discovered mutual interests in ballet and opera and art. And every day she grew to love him more. All her doubts and uncertainties slowly faded as she realized that nothing was going to stop the wedding this time.

He surprised her by phoning Margaret and having a wedding dress identical to the one she'd chosen five years before flown in from Hawaii. It was a measure of the regard he felt for her, she saw, and she felt a fleeting regret that he couldn't love her as she loved him. But at least he liked her, she consoled herself, and after they had children, surely he'd grow fonder of her.

The ceremony was held at Priss's home, and Randy and Latrice were there as well as Ronald George and Betty Gaines. Even the twins were invited, and they astounded the assembled company with perfect textbook etiquette. Latrice and Randy looked like newlyweds themselves, and Latrice was actually sitting with her sons, hugging them, before the ceremony began.

Ronald George came forward to offer his congratulations, extending his hand warily to John as if he expected it would be instantly removed. But John didn't say an unkind word. He only smiled.

Minutes later the ceremony began, and Priss clutched her small wildflower bouquet in her hand as they stood before the minister and the words of the marriage service were spoken.

When the minister came to the part about speaking now or forever holding your peace, Priss froze. She darted a glance up at John, all her old fears haunting her. But he looked down at her and smiled slowly, softly, and she relaxed.

He slid the wedding band that matched her engagement ring onto her finger and repeated the appropriate words with so much feeling that Priss felt tears sting her eyes. When she added her own part, and the minister concluded the ceremony, tears were rolling unashamedly down her cheeks.

She kept her eyes open as John bent to kiss her, and so did he. She thought there had never been a more beautiful time in her entire life. For so many years she'd worshipped him, and now he was her husband. He belonged to her.

"Don't cry," he whispered, lifting his mouth. "This is only the beginning. The best is yet to come."

She tried to smile, and he kissed her wet eyelids closed. They were surrounded by well-wishers during the next few minutes, and in the excitement of cutting the cake and changing into her beige traveling suit and saying good-bye to her parents, there was no time to think.

Minutes later they drove away in John's Ford, waving good-bye. They would spend the night in Brisbane before boarding a plane to Hawaii the next morning for a brief honeymoon. A substitute teacher had been engaged to fill Priss's place for the few days that John could afford to be away from the station.

"Next year, I'll take you to the States," he promised as they drove away

"I don't mind if we never go anywhere, as long as we're together," she said quietly. She squeezed the fingers that he had imprisoned on his thigh and leaned her head against his shoulder.

"Five years," he said unexpectedly, and his eyes were stormy. His jaw was clenched, making the dimple more prominent. He looked formidable at that moment, and Priss stared at him uneasily.

"What's wrong?" she asked. "Are you sorry that we—"

"No!" He glanced at her quickly, then dragged his eyes back to the road. He lifted her hand to his mouth and kissed it softly. "I'm only sorry that we wasted so many years because of my damned black pride, that's all."

"Maybe it was for the best," she said gently. "I was very young."

"You still are, in all the ways that count. You make me feel like celebrating every time you smile at me," he said unexpectedly.

"In that case, I'll smile a lot," she promised. Her eyes searched his profile dreamily. "I used to hide and watch you when you'd ride the fence line," she mused. "I thought you were the handsomest man on earth."

"Did you?" He chuckled.

"I still do. There was never anyone who compared with you, in all those years." Her eyes dropped to his white collar and missed the look of love on his face. "Eventually I gave up looking."

"I'm glad of that," he acknowledged quietly. "I

used to have nightmares about hearing that you'd married someone in Hawaii.''

''Did you really?'' she asked. Her eyes fell. ''I had the same nightmares about you and Janie Weeks.''

There was a long poignant silence. ''We'll talk about that when we get to the hotel in Brisbane,'' he said then. ''It's time, past time, that we cleared the air about Janie. And a few other things.'' He studied her intently. ''Turn on the radio, will you, love?''

She tuned in a pop channel and snuggled close to him. All the rest of the way, not one word broke into the music. She closed her eyes, pretending he loved her.

They arrived in Brisbane about dusk and checked into an exclusive hotel on the beach. John had said that this one luxury would have to last a long time, but she didn't mind. Anywhere with John was heaven: she wouldn't have minded camping on the beach in a tent.

Once they got upstairs, she took advantage of the huge whirlpool tub to soak away the tiredness of the long day. She'd had some wild idea that her wedding night would be conventional. That John would take her out to supper, bring her back to the room, and that then their married life would begin. But knowing John, she should have expected what happened.

She was lying in the enormous bathtub, surrounded by soap bubbles, enjoying the soft gyration of the water as the whirlpool jetted currents all around her in its gentlest cycle. Her eyes were closed, and she didn't hear a sound until the bathroom door suddenly closed.

She opened her eyes, and John cocked an eyebrow

at her wild blush. She was startled to see him nude as she was, bronzed skin rippling under the dark blond hair that covered his broad chest, muscular stomach, flat hips, and long powerful legs.

"You might as well get used to me," he murmured. "I'm not going to spend our married life undressing in closets, and I sleep like this." He tossed his robe over the vanity chair. "Feel like company in there?" He nodded toward the tub.

She swallowed. It was all happening so fast. He's my husband, she told herself firmly. We're married. I have to forget all my hang-ups now; it's all right to sleep with him.

"Yes," she managed in a strangled voice. Her eyes measured him. "Is the tub going to be big enough?" she asked.

He searched her eyes. "Yes. More than adequate for what I have in mind, Mrs. Sterling."

She moved over, watching him approach, long-legged, slim-hipped, powerfully built. He was the most beautiful thing she'd ever seen—even more sensuous than the Greek statues that had fascinated her in school.

"This is kinky," she commented impishly as he eased down into the tub with her.

"Why?" he asked.

The contact with his long bare body was doing frightening things to her nerves. Her whole body tensed deliciously as she felt his powerful thigh against hers, as his arm went around her shoulders and she felt its warm weight.

"Bathing together?" She laughed.

He looked down at her with amused eyes. "Don't you like it? The government will be delighted that we're saving water."

"Yes, I suppose so." The soap bubbles hid most of her from his curious eyes, and vice versa, but she was still blushing. "Oh, John, I've got the most horrible hang-ups about sex," she blurted out, and turned to bury her face against the wet mat of hair over his chest.

He chuckled softly, holding her there. "Why?"

"I don't know anything, and I'm afraid," she answered. She looked up at his broad face with its firm lips and twinkling eyes and dimpled chin. "John, you aren't going to hurt me, are you?"

He brushed the damp hair away from her face. "I'll try not to. I don't think it's going to be so difficult. All virgins don't have a rough time." He bent and kissed her mouth tenderly. "You know I've been a long time without a woman," he reminded her. "Is that what frightens you? Are you afraid I may go wild in your arms?"

She touched his chest nervously. "You're so strong…"

"And so intent on pleasing you," he countered amusedly. "It may not be heaven the first time, but if it isn't, I'll more than make it up to you by morning. Now relax."

"We aren't going to…in here, are we?" She hesitated, wide-eyed.

His hand slid over her shoulder, against one full hard-tipped breast, down her waist and her flat stomach and the silken skin of her inner thigh. "Why not, love?'' he asked, letting his eyes hold hers as his hand moved with expert precision on her soft body.

She gasped, and he took the soft sound into his mouth as he kissed her for the first time with total possession. She stiffened a little, but seconds later she yielded to him, and he felt her fingers grasping helplessly at his arms.

He turned her, knocking the drain with his foot so that some of the water seeped out while he was kissing her senseless. He touched her lovingly with expert, seeking hands, exploring the satin of her skin, the tender innocence of her body.

''I'm glad,'' he breathed roughly as his head went to her slippery breasts. ''Oh, God, I'm so glad you kept yourself for me, that I'm your first man.''

Tears welled up in her eyes at the sharp, sweet twinges of pleasure he was causing. ''So...am I,'' she moaned. Her teeth bit at his shoulder, and she began to move, not because she wanted to, but because she couldn't help it. He was making her feel things that shocked, frightened, fascinated her. Priss's eyes opened wide as he did something new and intimate to her body.

She cried out, and he lifted his head.

''It's all right,'' he whispered, shifting so he was above her. His eyes held hers. ''Relax for me. Just relax. We'll go at your pace, so don't be frightened, darling.''

And all at once, before she had time to be afraid, he was making her a part of his own body. Her eyes dilated, and she started to stiffen, but he stroked her and smiled down at her. His own lack of urgency, his evident self-control, made it possible for her not to fight him. She let her body sink in the water with a breathless little sigh.

His large hand under her hips lifted her gently. "You see?" he soothed. "It's not going to be difficult, is it?"

"I didn't think—" She couldn't manage to tell him what she didn't think, because he moved unexpectedly, and she saw stars. Her breath caught in her throat as his hips shifted and she clung wildly to him, really frightened of the sensations that were making her shudder helplessly.

His mouth eased over hers, and just before he took total possession, he looked straight into her eyes.

"Now," he whispered shakily, as the hunger and need and newness of being with her took his control. "Now we'll make up for all the long, lost years. We'll make them up here, now, together.... God, Priss, love me!" he groaned against her mouth, and his big body shuddered with fierce need. His fingers dug into her slender hips, lifting her. And it began. She almost fainted as he brought her to the precipice and let her back down again, only to start once more, arousing her and calming her, over and over, until at last there was no coming down from the peak.

She clung and wept and shivered, hearing his rough breathing suddenly stop just before a harsh cry burst from his lips. She felt him shudder, too, and only then realized what was happening. And by that time, it was happening to her, too, and she gave her mind up to it.

They lay together in the churning water, clinging, kissing softly, tenderly, as trembling passed and their heartbeats calmed at last. He brushed back her wet hair and gave a low triumphant laugh.

"This is one memory we'll never share with our children," he murmured devilishly. "That we came together for the first time in a whirlpool bathtub filled with bubbles."

She kissed his shoulder and snuggled against him, loving the feel of his body. "I love you."

"Yes, I know. I've always known. That was what made it so very difficult to let you go."

Her fingers traced a slow pattern in the hair over his heart. "I guess I was pretty obvious," she murmured.

"That much love is hard to hide," he said tenderly. His hand smoothed her hair. "It was all that kept me going sometimes—knowing that you hadn't stopped loving me."

"How did you know that?" she asked curiously.

"Renée told me."

"My mother sold me out?" she exclaimed, lifting her head.

His eyes were solemn. "There was a time, only once, when I was ready to do something drastic. I thought of selling the station to Randy and joining the service. When Renée found out, she told me." He kissed her eyes closed. "I lived on it," he breathed huskily. "I lived on it for years! Then you came home, and it was so difficult to get close to you again. I was sure you hated me. Then when Randy told you the truth, I was terrified that it was pity you felt. When I told you I only wanted your body, it was because I was hurting. It wasn't true." He kissed her mouth slowly, passionately. "Only later, when I started asking myself why you had stayed a virgin all those years, did the pieces fall into place. That was when I decided I still had a chance. And I went after you with every weapon I could find."

Her heart pounded heavily, and he felt it, because his hand was cupping her breast.

He lifted his head and rolled over, so that her body was resting atop his. His hands smoothed up and down her back while his eyes grew drunk on her pink bareness. "Priss, it was never only physical, except maybe for that afternoon in your bedroom. After that, it was an obsession that got completely out of hand; that took over my very soul. I came to Hawaii after you because I was dying without you."

Tears sprang to her eyes. "You loved me?"

"Darling," he breathed roughly, "I still do. I always have; always will. Otherwise do you think I'd have been celibate for five damned years? Didn't that give me away?"

She stared at him blankly. "I never dreamed—"

"Greenhorn," he chided, "it's nothing short of sainthood for a man to go that long without sex!"

"Oh," she exclaimed. Her eyes searched his. "But...but there was Janie Weeks..." she began hoarsely, and the pain wrenched her.

His arms folded her gently against him in the warm water, and he sighed bitterly. "I never touched her," he said at last, feeling her stiffen with shock. "That's right, never. Oh, we went out enough times, and I'll admit that I hoped at first she would take my mind off you. But I never saw her again after I got back from Hawaii. I didn't even want to.''

"But why?" she ground out. "Why did you tell me that lie? And my parents—they told me you were seeing her, too.''

"I made them promise to back up my story,'' he said quietly. "Because I knew the fiction of another woman was the only way I could keep you from rushing back here and sacrificing yourself for me.''

"I loved you,'' she wept. "It wouldn't have been a sacrifice!"

"Inevitably it would,'' he corrected, his voice even. "You were too young to cope with it all. I couldn't risk having your feeling for me turn to hatred in the face of all the obstacles. Remember, Priss, I wasn't even sure I could salvage the station at all. My pride was in the dust. And as it was, I had to go to work for Randy. That was rough. It changed me.''

"I knew you'd changed, yes. I just didn't understand why. And I hated you for Janie." Tears ran down her cheeks onto his hairy chest. "Oh, John,'' she wailed. "Five years. Five long years, and I grieved for you so!"

His arms tightened around her. "So did I, for you,'' he confessed under his breath. "Ached for you, hungered for you! There was never another woman. My God, how could there have been? After the first time I kissed you, I couldn't have touched anyone else.''

"You said you tried,'' she reminded him.

"Yes. When I thought you and that pommy were going to make a match of it. That was before I spoke to Renée." He sighed. "I stayed drunk two days after

I tried, Priscilla. I felt as if I'd tried to commit adultery."

She smiled wobbly. Her fingers traced patterns on his chest. "John, could you say it, just once, do you think? I've waited most of my life to hear it."

There was a look of infinite tenderness in his face. His eyes searched hers reverently.

"I love you," he whispered huskily. "With my heart. With my mind. With my body and my soul. I'd do anything for you."

The tears rolled slowly down her cheeks, and she laughed with delight, triumph, shyness. "Oh, John," she moaned, pressing down hard against him. "Oh, John, I love you so much!"

"How would you like to come into the bedroom and show me how much?" he murmured dryly, but it wasn't completely a joke, because his body was already telling her that he needed more than words.

She bent and kissed his eyes, his nose, the dimple in his chin, and his hard mouth. "Will you let me?" she implored daringly.

His eyes opened, blue fires staring up into hers. "All the way?" he asked softly.

"Yes."

He searched her eyes. "I've never let a woman take me," he said quietly. "Not in all my life. But I suppose being my wife does give you a few privileges, Mrs. Sterling," he mused.

She bent and kissed him softly. "I'll be very gentle with you," she whispered, teasing, but he pulled her mouth down hard, and the kiss he gave her was anything but humorous

It was the most incredible experience of her life. He lay sprawled on the mattress like a sacrificial victim, letting her make new discoveries about his body and its responses. Letting her touch and taste and stroke him, until he groaned aloud, until his big body trembled. And all through it he smiled and laughed, and his eyes blazed like blue coals while he watched her, guided her, whispered and coaxed and gloried in her fascination, the laziness of his smile at variance with the tension that built to explosive force in him.

When he was just seconds away from losing his mind, he ended the torment himself, whipping her over and crushing her under him, dragging her down with him into a maelstrom unlike anything he'd ever experienced before. It took him a long time to be able to move without shuddering, to speak. Her own plateau had been nearly as high, and she trembled gently in the aftermath.

She smoothed his hair, kissed his flushed face, stroked his chest and arms until he calmed.

"My God," he breathed, opening his eyes at last, and they were filled with wonder as they searched her face.

"I can't believe I really did all that," she said flushing. Her eyes fell to his mouth. "I'd never even read about some of those things."

"It's called instinct," he managed. "When it's coupled with love, it goes a long way. I've never climbed that high before," he added with a slow smile. "I'm having trouble coming back down again, as you see."

She blushed again and slid down against his body, holding him. "Does this help?"

He caught her hips and moved them against his. "This helps more." He eased himself over her body and smiled at the shock in her eyes. "Yes, I know." He laughed. "The books say this is impossible, don't they? Lie still. This time," he breathed as his mouth opened over hers, "is going to blow your mind…"

She could hardly stand in the shower later while he soaped her body under the warm spray. She clung to him weakly, and he laughed.

"Worn out already?" he teased. "You'll have to take vitamins."

"You're marvelous," she whispered at his lips. "Worth waiting all my life for."

"I could return that compliment," he murmured, smiling as he kissed her. "No lingering doubts? No second thoughts?"

She shook her head, and her eyes adored him. "I'll take care of you all my life. I'll be the best wife you could ever want."

"You already are," he said. He held her against him warmly, without passion, his head bent over hers. "It won't be easy sometimes. We won't have a lot at first. But I'll work hard to give you the best life I can. And even if we don't have money, Priss, we'll have love. Of the two, that's the more important." He kissed her forehead. "I'll spend the rest of my life making up to you those five years we lost."

"I'll do the same for you," she promised. "Darling, darling, I can hardly believe it's happened! It's like a sweet dream. I'd rather die than wake up and find it isn't real at all." Tears stung her eyes. "I've lived on dreams for so long…"

"So have I," he whispered, nuzzling his face against her damp hair as he held her. "But we have each other now. Forever, Priss."

She kissed his chest affectionately. "Later on, I'll give you a son."

He trembled a little. His hands contracted. "How much later on?" he whispered.

She looked up at him quietly. "Whenever you like."

He was breathing unsteadily. "I'm thirty-three already."

"Then...we'd better not wait...too long," she whispered at his lips.

"A few months—no more," he whispered back. "I'd like a baby."

"So would I." She pressed herself completely against him, loving the freedom love gave her to be so intimate with him. She closed her eyes. "You're a nice bloke, John Sterling." She grinned. "Gone to the pack, of course, but...ooh!"

He pinched her and laughed at her expression. "Shut up and wash my back, woman. I want my tucker."

"Big, bad Australian," she teased. "I can see right off that you're going to be a horrible bully."

"Not to you, mate," he murmured and kissed her.

She smiled under his mouth, loving the feel and taste of it. The years ahead were going to be the best of her life; she already knew it. And the best part was loving this big, burly Australian who'd given her his wild heart. Dreams did come true, it seemed. Because she was holding hers in her arms.

* * * * *

HEART OF ICE

Chapter 1

"**Y**ou didn't!" Katriane wailed at her best friend. "Not at Christmas!"

Ada looked pained and visibly shrank an inch. "Now, Kati…" she began placatingly, using the nickname she'd given the taller girl years ago. "It's a huge apartment. Absolutely huge. And you and I will be going to parties all over town, and there's the charity ball at the Thomsons'… It will be all right, you'll see. You won't even notice that he's here."

"I'll notice," Kati said shortly. Her reddish gold hair blazed in the ceiling light, and her brown eyes glared.

"It's our first Christmas without Mother," Ada tried again. "He's got nobody but me."

"You could go to the ranch for Christmas," Kati suggested, hating the idea even as she said it.

"And leave you here alone? What kind of friend would I be then?"

"The kind who isn't sticking me with her horrible brother during my one holiday a year!" came the hot reply. "I worked myself to the bone, researching that last book. I was taking a rest between contractual obligations...just Christmas. How can I rest with Egan here!"

"He'll be fun to have around," Ada suggested softly.

"We'll kill each other!" Kati groaned. "Ada, why do you hate me? You know Egan and I don't get along. We've never gotten along. For heaven's sake, I can't live under the same roof with your brother until Christmas! Have you forgotten what happened last time?"

Ada cleared her throat. "Look, you planned to set that next big historical in Wyoming, didn't you, on a ranch? Who knows more about ranching in Wyoming than Egan? You could look upon it as an educational experience—research."

Kati just glared.

"Deep down," Ada observed, "you both probably really like each other. It's just that you can't...admit it."

"Deep down," her friend replied, "I hate him. Hate. As in to dislike intensely. As in to obsessively dislike."

"That's splitting an infinitive," Ada pointed out.

"You are an actress, not an educator," came the sharp retort.

Ada sighed, looking small and dark and vulnerable.

So unlike her elder brother. "I may wind up being an educator, at this rate," she said. "I am sort of between jobs."

"You'll get another one," Kati said easily. "I've never seen anyone with your talent. You got rave reviews in your last play."

"Well, maybe something will turn up. But, getting back to Egan..."

"Must we?" Kati groaned. She turned, worrying the thick waves of her long hair irritatedly. "Don't do this to me, Ada. Uninvite him."

"I can't. He's already on the way."

"Now?" Kati looked hunted. She threw up her hands. "First my royalty check gets lost in the mail when my car payment is due. Now I wind up with a sidewinder to spend Christmas with...."

"He's my brother," Ada said in a small voice. "He has no one. Not even a girl friend."

"Egan?" Two eyebrows went straight up. "Egan always has a girl friend. He's never between women."

"He is right now."

"Did he go broke?" Kati asked with a sweet smile.

"Now, Kati, he's not that bad to look at."

That was true enough. Egan had a body most men would envy. But his face was definitely not handsome. It was craggy and rough and uncompromising. Just like Egan. She could see those glittering silver eyes in her sleep sometimes, haunting her, accusing her—the way they had that last time. She hated Egan because he'd misjudged her so terribly. And because he'd never admitted it. Not then, or since.

She folded her arms over her breasts with a curt

sigh. "Well, Mary Savage used to think he was Mr. America," she conceded.

Ada eyed her closely. "He's just a poor, lonely old cattleman. He can't help it if women fall all over him."

"Egan Winthrop, poor? Lonely?" Kati pursed her lips. "The old part sounds about right, though."

"He's thirty-four," Ada reminded her. "Hardly in his dotage."

"Sounds ancient to me," Kati murmured, staring out over the jeweled night skyline of Manhattan.

"We're both twenty-five." Ada laughed. "Nine years isn't so much."

"Fudge." She leaned her head against the cold windowpane. "He hates me, Ada," she said after a minute, and felt the chill all up and down her body. "He'll start a fight as sure as there's a sun in the sky. He always starts something."

"Yes, I know," Ada confessed. She joined the taller woman at the window. "I don't understand why you set him off. He's usually the soul of chivalry with women."

"I've seen him in action," Kati said quietly. "You don't have to tell me about that silky charm. But it's all surface, Ada. Egan lets nobody close enough to wound."

"For someone who's been around him only a few times in recent years, and under the greatest pressure from me, you seem to know him awfully well," Ada mumbled.

"I know his type," she said shortly. "He's a taker, not a giver."

"Neither one of you ever gives an inch," Ada remarked. She studied her friend closely. "But I had to invite him. He's the only family I have."

Kati sighed, feeling oddly guilty. She hugged the shorter girl impulsively. "I'm sorry. I'm being ratty and I don't mean to. You're my friend. Of course you can invite your awful brother for Christmas. I'll grit my teeth and go dancing with Jack and pretend I love having him here. Okay?"

"That I'll have to see to believe."

Kati crossed her heart. "Honest."

"Well, since that's settled, how about if we go and get a Christmas tree?" Ada suggested brightly.

Kati laughed. "Super," she said and grabbed up her coat to follow Ada out the door. "And if we get one big enough," she mumbled under her breath, "maybe we can hang Egan from one of the limbs."

They trudged through four tree lots before they found just the right tree. It was a six-foot Scotch pine, full and bushy and perfect for their apartment. They stuffed it into the back of Kati's Thunderbird and carried it home, along with boxes of ornaments and new tinsel to add to their three-year supply in the closet.

Ada went out to get a pizza while Kati tied ribbon through the bright balls and hung them lovingly on the tree. She turned on some Christmas music and tried not to think about Egan. It seemed so long ago that they'd had that horrible blowup....

It had been five years since Kati first set eyes on Egan Winthrop. She and Ada had met at school, where both were majoring in education. Ada had later switched to drama, and Kati had decided to study En-

glish while she broke into the fiction market in a small
way. Three years ago, after graduation, they'd taken
this apartment together.

Egan and Kati had been at odds almost from the
first. Kati got her first glimpse of the tall rancher at
school, when she and Ada were named to the college
honors society in their junior year. Egan and Mrs.
Winthrop had both come. Kati had no relatives, and
Ada had quickly included her in family plans for an
evening out afterward. Egan hadn't liked that. From
the first meeting of eyes, it had been war. He disap-
proved vehemently of Kati's chosen profession, although he was careful not to let Ada or his mother see
just how much he disliked Kati. They'd hardly spoken
two words until that fateful summer when Kati had
flown out to the ranch with Ada for the Fourth of July.

It had been the first year she'd roomed with Ada,
almost three years ago. Ada's mother had been diag-
nosed with cancer, and the family knew that despite
the treatments, it would only be a matter of a year or
two before she wouldn't be with them. Everyone had
gone to the Wyoming ranch for the July Fourth holidays—including Kati, because Ada refused to leave
her alone in New York. Kati's parents were middle-
aged when she was born, and had died only a little
apart just before she finished high school. She had
cousins and uncles and aunts, but none of them would
miss her during the July vacation. So, dreading Egan's
company, she'd put on a happy face and gone.

She couldn't forget Egan's face when he'd seen her
getting off the plane with his sister. He hadn't even
bothered to disguise his distaste. Egan had a mistaken

view of romance writers' morals and assumed that
Kati lived the wild life of her heroines. It wasn't true,
but it seemed to suit him to believe that it was. He
gave her a chilly reception, his silvery eyes telling her
that he wished she'd stayed in New York.

But his cousin Richard's enthusiastic greeting more
than made up for Egan's rudeness. She was hugged
and hugged and enthused over, and she ate it up. Richard was just her age, a dark-haired, dark-eyed architect
with a bright future and a way with women. If he
hadn't been such a delightful flirt, the whole incident
might have been avoided. But he had been, and it
wasn't.

Richard had taken Kati to the Grand Teton National
Park for the day, while Mrs. Winthrop soaked up the
attention she was getting from her son and daughter.
She was a lot like Ada, a happy, well-adjusted person
with a loving disposition. And none of Egan's cynicism. Kati had liked her very much. But she and Richard had felt that Mrs. Winthrop needed some time
alone with her children. So they'd driven to the park
and hiked and enjoyed the beauty of the mountains
rising starkly from the valley, and afterward they'd
stopped in Jackson for steaks and a salad.

On the way home, Richard's car had had a flat tire.
Richard, being the lovable feather-brain he was, had
no spare. In that part of the country on a holiday night,
there wasn't a lot of traffic. So they walked back to
the ranch—which took until four in the morning.

Egan had been waiting up. He said nothing to Richard, who was so tired that he was hardly able to stand.

Richard went inside, leaving all the explanations to Kati.

"You live down to your reputation, don't you?" he asked with a smile that chilled even in memory. "My God, you might have had a little consideration for my mother. She worried."

Kati remembered trying to speak, but he cut her off with a rough curse.

"Don't make it worse by lying," he growled. "We both know what you are...you with your loose morals and your disgusting books. What you do with my cousin is your business, but I don't want my holidays ruined by someone like you. You're not welcome here any longer. Make some excuse to leave tomorrow."

And he walked away, leaving Kati sick and near tears. She hadn't let them show, she was too proud. And she'd managed to get to bed without waking Ada, who shared a room with her. But the next morning, cold-eyed and hating Egan more than ever, she packed her suitcase, gave some excuse about an unexpected deadline and asked Richard to take her to the airport.

They were on the porch when Egan came out the front door, looking irritated and angry and strangely haggard.

"I'd like to speak to you," he told Kati.

She remembered looking at him as if he were some form of bacteria, her back stiff, her eyes full of hatred.

"Go ahead," she told him.

He glared at Richard, who cleared his throat and mumbled something about getting the car.

"Why didn't you tell me what happened?" he asked.

"Why bother, when you already knew?" she asked in glacial tones.

"I didn't know," he ground out.

"How amazing," she replied calmly. "I thought you knew everything. You seem to have made a hobby out of my life—the fictionalized version, of course."

He looked uncomfortable, but he didn't apologize. "Richard had been drinking. It was four in the morning—"

"We had a very long walk," she told him curtly. "About fifteen or twenty miles. Richard wasn't drunk; he was tired." Her dark eyes glittered up at him. "I didn't like you much before, Mr. Winthrop, but I like you even less now. I'll make a point of keeping out of your vicinity. I wouldn't want to contaminate you."

"Miss James..." he began quietly.

"Good-bye." She brushed past him, suitcase in hand, and got into Richard's car. Ada and Mrs. Winthrop had tried to talk her into staying, but she was adamant about having an unexpected deadline and work pressure. And to this day, only she and that animal in Wyoming really knew why she'd left. Even Richard hadn't been privy to the truth.

That episode had brought the antagonism between Egan and Kati out into the open, and their relationship seemed to go from bad to worse. It was impossible for Kati to stay in the same room with Egan these days. He'd find an excuse, any excuse, to nick her temper. And she'd always retaliate. Like last year...

Egan had been in town for some kind of conference and had stopped by the apartment to see Ada. Kati had been on her way to a department store in downtown

Manhattan to autograph copies of her latest book, *Renegade Lover,* a historical set in eighteenth-century South Carolina. Egan had walked in to find her in her autographing clothes—a burgundy velvet dress cut low in front, and a matching burgundy hat crowned by white feathers. She'd looked like the heroine on the front of her book, and he immediately pounced.

"My God, Madame Pompadour," he observed, studying her from his superior height.

She bristled, glaring up at him. "Wrong country," she replied. "But I wouldn't expect you to know that."

His eyebrow jerked. "Why not? Just because I'm in oil and cattle doesn't make me an ignoramus."

"I never said a word, Mr. Winthrop, honey," she replied, batting her long eyelashes at him.

The term of endearment, on reflection, must have been what set him off. His lips curled in an unpleasant smile. "You do look the part, all right," he replied. "You could stand on the street corner and make a nice little nest egg..."

She actually slapped him—and didn't even realize she had until she felt her fingers stinging and saw the red mark along his cheek.

"Damn you!" she breathed, shaking with fury.

His nostrils flared; his eyes narrowed and became frankly dangerous. "Lift your hand to me again, ever," he said in that low, cold tone, "and you'll wish you'd never set eyes on me."

"I already do, Egan Almighty Winthrop! I already do."

"Dress like a tramp and people are going to label

you one,'' he rejoined. His eyes cut away from her with distaste. ''I wouldn't be seen in public with you.''

''Thank God!'' she threw after him, almost jumping up and down with indignation. ''I wouldn't want people to think I cared so little about who I was seen with!''

At that moment, luckily, Ada had rushed in from her bedroom to play peacemaker. Without another word, Kati had grabbed up her coat and purse and had run from the apartment, tears rolling down her cheeks. It was a miracle that she managed to get herself back together by the time she reached the department store.

That was the last time she'd seen Egan Winthrop. And she never wanted to see him again. Oh, why had Ada agreed to let him come, knowing the state of hostility that existed between Egan and her? Why!

She put the last ball on the tree, and was reaching for the little golden angel that would sit atop it when she heard the door open.

It must be Ada with the pizza, of course, and she was starved. She reached up, slender in jeans and a pullover yellow velour sweater, laughing as she put the angel in place. As she moved, she knocked into one of the balls, but caught it just in time to keep it from dropping to the carpet.

''Back already?'' she called. ''I'm starved to death! Do you want to have it in here by the tree?''

There was a pregnant pause, and she felt eyes watching her. Nervous, she turned—to find herself staring at Egan Winthrop. Her hand clenched at the sight of him—so powerful and dark in his gray vested suit—and the fragile ball shattered under the pressure.

"You little idiot," he muttered, moving forward to force open her hand.

She let him, numb, her eyes falling to the sight of his dark hands under her pale one where blood beaded from a small cut.

"I...wasn't expecting...you," she said nervously.

"Obviously. Do you have some antiseptic?"

"In the bathroom."

He marched her into it and fumbled in the medicine cabinet for antiseptic and a bandage.

"Where's Ada?" he asked as he cleaned the small cut, examined it for shards, and applied the stinging antiseptic.

"Out getting pizza," she muttered.

He glanced up. He'd never been so close to her, and those silver eyes at point-blank range were frightening. So was the warmth of his lean, powerful body and the smell of his musky cologne.

His eyes searched hers quietly, and he didn't smile. That wasn't unusual. She'd only seen him smile at Ada or his mother. He was reserved to the point of inhibition most of the time. A hard man. Cold...

Something wild and frightening dilated her eyes as she met that long, lingering look, and her heart jumped. Her lips parted as she tore her gaze down to the small hand that was visibly trembling in his big ones.

"Nervous, Katriane?" he asked.

"Yes, I'm nervous," she bit off, deciding that a lie would only amuse him. If granite could be amused.

"How long did it take Ada to talk you into this visit?" he asked.

She drew in a heavy breath. "All of a half hour," she said gruffly. "And I still think it's a horrible mistake." She looked up at him defiantly. "I don't want to spoil Christmas for her by fighting with you."

His chin lifted as he studied her. "Then you'll just have to be nice to me, won't you?" he baited. "No snide remarks, no deliberate taunts…"

"Look who's talking about snide remarks!" she returned. "You're the one who does all the attacking!"

"You give as good as you get, don't you?" he asked.

Her lower lip jutted. "It's Christmas."

"Yes, I know." He studied her. "I like presents."

"Is anyone going to give you one?" she asked incredulously.

"Ada," he reminded her.

"Poor demented soul, she loves you," she said, eyeing him.

"Women do, from time to time," he returned.

"Ah, the advantages of wealth," she muttered.

"Do you think I have to pay for it?" he asked with a cold smile. "I suppose a woman who sells it expects everyone to…"

Her hand lifted again, but he caught it this time, holding it so that she had to either stand on her tiptoes or have her shoulder dislocated.

"Let go!" she panted. "You're hurting!"

"Then stop trying to hit me. Peace on earth, remember?" he reminded her, oddly calm.

"I'd like to leave you in pieces," she mumbled, glaring up at him.

His eyes wandered from her wild, waving red-gold

hair down past her full breasts to her small waist, flaring hips and long legs. "You've gained a little weight, haven't you?" he asked. "As voluptuous as ever. I suppose that appeals to some men."

"Ooooh!" she burst out, infuriated, struggling.

He let her go all at once and pulled a cigarette from his pocket, watching her with amusement as he lit it. "What's the matter? Disappointed because you don't appeal to me?"

"God forbid!"

He shook his head. "You'll have to do better than this if you want to keep a truce with me for the next few days. I can't tolerate hysterical women."

She closed her eyes, willing him to disappear. It didn't work. When she opened them, he was still there. She put away the antiseptic and bandages and went back into the living room, walking stiffly, to clean the debris of the shattered ball from the beige carpet.

"Don't cut yourself," he cautioned, dropping lazily into an armchair with the ashtray he'd found.

"On what, the ball or you?" she asked coldly.

He only laughed, softly, menacingly; and she fumbled with pieces of the ball while he watched her in that catlike, unblinking way of his.

"I thought Ada told me you'd stopped smoking," she remarked when she was finished.

"I did. I only do it now when I'm nervous." He took another long draw, his eyes mocking. "You give me the jitters, honey, didn't you know?"

"Me and the cobalt bomb, maybe," she scoffed. She threw away the debris and ran an irritated hand through her hair. "Do you want me to show you to your room, like a good hostess?" she asked.

"You'd show me to the elevator and press the Down button," he said. "I'll wait for my sister and a warmer welcome."

It was Christmas, and he'd lost his mother, and she hated the surge of sympathy she felt. But knowing he'd toss it right back in her face kept her quiet. She went to the window and stared down at the busy street. "Ada, hurry," she wanted to scream.

"I saw your book advertised on television the other day," he remarked.

She turned around, arms folded defensively over her breasts. "Did you? Imagine, you watching television."

He didn't take her up on that. He crushed out his half-finished cigarette. "It sold out at the local bookstore."

"I'm sure you bought all the copies—to keep your good neighbors from being exposed to it," she chided.

His eyebrows arched. "In fact, I did buy one copy. To read."

She went red from head to toe. The thought of Egan Winthrop reading *Harvest of Passion* made her want to pull a blanket over her head. It was a spicy book with sensuous love scenes, and the way he was looking her over made it obvious what he thought of the book and its author.

"I like historical fiction," he remarked. "Despite having to wade through the obligatory sex to get to it."

She flushed even more and turned away, too tongue-tied to answer him.

"How do you manage to stay on your feet with all that exhaustive research you obviously do?"

She whirled, her eyes blazing. "What do you mean by that?" she burst out.

He laughed softly, predatorily. "You know damned good and well what I mean. How many men does it take?"

The door opened just in time to spare his ears. Ada walked in and her face glowed with joy as she saw her brother. She tossed the pizza onto a chair and ran to him, to be swung up in his powerful arms and warmly kissed.

"You get prettier all the time," he said, laughing, and the radiance in his face made Kati feel like mourning. She'd never bring that look to Egan's face.

"And you get handsomer. I'm so glad you could come," Ada said genuinely.

"I'm glad someone is," he murmured, glancing at Kati's flushed, furious face.

Ada looked past him, and her own expression sobered. "Ooops," she murmured.

Kati swallowed her hostility. She wouldn't ruin Christmas for Ada—she wouldn't. She pinned a smile to her lips. "It's all right. He patched me up when I cut my hand. We're friends now. Aren't we?" she asked, grinding her teeth together as she looked at Egan.

"Of course," he agreed. "Bosom pals." He stared at her breasts.

Ada grabbed him by the hand and half dragged him from the room. "Let me show you where to put your suitcase, Egan!" she said hastily.

Kati went to take the pizza into the kitchen and make coffee. And counted to ten, five times.

Chapter 2

"**H**ow have you been?" Ada asked her brother as
the three of them sat around the dining room table
munching pizza and drinking coffee.

"All right," he said, staring at the thick brown mug
that held his coffee. "You?"

Ada smiled. "Busy. It's helped me not to dwell on
Mama."

"She's better off," Egan reminded her quietly.

"I know," Ada said, her eyes misting. She shook
her head and grabbed another slice of pizza. "Anybody else for seconds? There are three slices left."

"No more for me," Kati said with a speaking
glance at Egan. "I wouldn't want to get more voluptuous than I already am."

"Nonsense," blissfully ignorant Ada said. "You're
just right. Come on, have another slice."

"Go ahead," Egan taunted.

"Why don't you?" she dared him.

"And be accused of making a pig of myself?" he asked innocently.

"Who would be so unkind as to call you a pig?" Kati asked sweetly.

"Excuse me," Ada interrupted, "but it's Christmas. Remember? Holly and mistletoe...?"

"Mistletoe?" Egan glanced at Kati. "I'd rather drink poison."

Kati glared back. "Ditto!"

"Let's watch television!" Ada suggested frantically. She dragged Kati into the living room and quickly turned on the set. "I'll clear the table, you keep Egan company."

"You're just afraid of getting caught in the line of fire," Egan accused as his sister rushed out of the room.

But Ada only grinned.

Egan eased down into the armchair he'd vacated earlier and stared at Kati. He'd taken off his coat and vest. Both sleeves of his white silk shirt were rolled up and the neck was opened. He didn't wear an undershirt, and through the thin fabric, bronzed muscles and a thick pelt of hair were visible. That bothered Kati, so she carefully avoided looking at him while the evening news blared into the room.

"How's the writing going?" Egan asked conversationally.

"Just fine, thanks," she replied tersely.

"What are you working on now?"

She swallowed. Ada had finked on her, she just knew it. "Actually, I'm doing another historical."

"On...?"

She cleared her throat. "Wyoming," she mumbled.

"Pardon?" he said.

Her lips made a thin line. "Wyoming," she said louder.

"A historical novel about Wyoming. Well, well. Have you done a lot of research?"

She glanced at him warily. "What do you mean?"

"Historical research," he clarified, watching her. "You'll have to mention cattle-ranching, I imagine?"

"Yes," she said grudgingly.

"Know a lot about it, city lady?" he mocked.

She glared at him. "I have been on a ranch before."

"Sure. Mine." He stared down his nose at her. "I don't imagine they have many big cattle ranches in Charleston?"

"We have good people," she returned. "With excellent breeding."

His eyebrows arched. "Yes, I know. My grandmother came from Charleston."

She glared at him. "Did she, really?" she asked coldly.

He smiled softly. "She used to say it was where the Cooper and Ashley Rivers meet to form the Atlantic Ocean."

She'd heard that, too, in her childhood in the South Carolina coastal city, and she had to bite her lip to keep from smiling with him.

"She was a redhead too," he continued, waiting for a reaction.

"My hair isn't red," she said, predictably.

"Honey and fox fur," he argued, studying it.

She flushed. That sounded oddly poetic, and she didn't like the tingle that ran through her.

She glanced at her watch. "Excuse me. I'd better put on a dress."

Egan glared. "Going somewhere?"

"Yes." She left him sitting there and went to find Ada. "Jack's coming for me at seven," she reminded her friend. "I've got to get dressed."

"I'll go keep Egan company. Lucky you, to have a boyfriend in town." She sighed. "Mine's out at sea again."

"Marshal will be back before you know it," she murmured. "Sorry to run out on you."

"You'll have fun." Ada grinned. "And so will I. I like Egan. He's great company, even if he is my brother."

Well, there was no accounting for taste. She couldn't imagine Egan being great company; but then, she wasn't related to him.

She put on a black cocktail dress and wore red accessories with it. Her eyes gave her a critical appraisal. She'd twirled her hair into a French twist and added a rhinestone clip to it, and she liked that elegant touch. She grinned. Jack would love it.

Jack Asher was a reporter for the *New York Times*, a political specialist who was intelligent and fun to be with. She'd known him for several months and enjoyed the occasional date. But things were still platonic between them because she didn't want any serious involvement. She was too independent.

The doorbell rang while she was putting a gloss of lipstick on her mouth, and she knew Ada would get it. Then she remembered that Egan was here, and rushed to finish her makeup and get back into the living room.

Jack was standing in the hall, talking to Ada while Egan glared at him.

He cleared his throat when Kati joined him, looking painfully relieved to see her.

"Hi, lady," he said with a forced smile. He was blond and blue-eyed and not nearly as tall or muscular as Egan. Sadly enough, in comparison he looked rather pale and dull.

But Kati grinned at him and Ada as if nothing were wrong. "Had to find my purse, but I'm ready when you are. Night, Ada. Egan," she added, glancing his way.

Egan didn't answer her. He was still glaring at Jack with those dangerous narrowed eyes glittering like new silver while he smoked a cigarette. Ada made a frantic gesture, but he ignored her too.

"Night, Ada," Jack said uncomfortably and led Kati out the door.

"Whew!" Jack exclaimed when they reached the elevator. "I felt like an insect on a mounting board for a second there! Is he always like that? So... uncommunicative?"

"Egan?" Kati's eyes flared up. "He's usually much too communicative, if you want to know. We're stuck with him for Christmas. Ada invited him because their mother died earlier this year. She felt sorry for him, being all alone."

"I should think so," Jack said gently. "Well,

maybe he talks to her.'' H̲ ̲ ̲ ̲ ̲ ̲
him, do you?''

"Not one bit. Not one ounc̲ ̲ ̲ ̲ ̲
glared at the elevator.

Jack laughed. "Poor guy!''

"Not Egan. Feel sorry for me. I'm s̲ ̲ ̲
apartment with him for the next week,' ̲ ̲ ̲ ̲

"You could always move in with me,' ̲ ̲ ̲ered.

She laughed, knowing the offer was a joke, just as
it always had been. They didn't have that kind of relationship. "Sure I could. I can just see your mother's
face.''

"Mother likes you.'' He chuckled. "She'd probably
be thrilled.''

"Only because she could pump me for my latest
plots.'' She grinned. "You know she's one of my biggest fans. Sweet lady.''

"She's sweet, all right. Well, where do you want to
go? The Rainbow Grill?''

"Let's save it for a special time. How about the
Crawdaddy Room at the Roosevelt?''

He chuckled. "You just like to go there because of
their pudding,'' he accused.

"Well, it is terribly good,'' she reminded him.

"I know, I know. Actually, I like it myself.''

She followed him into the elevator and put the confrontation with Egan right out of her mind.

A prime rib, a salad, several hard rolls and a dish
of delicious whiskey pudding later, Kati sat drinking
her coffee and looking around at the elegant surround-
ings. She saw a nice little old German waiter she knew
from other visits there and smiled at him.

yours?'' Jack asked her.

rybody's my friend.'' She laughed. "I used to nk New York was a cold place until I moved here. New Yorkers just take a little getting to know. And then they're family. I love New York,'' she sang softly, and laughed again.

"So do I. Of course, I was born here,'' he added. He looked out the window at the traffic. "I've got tickets for a modern ballet, if you'd like to use them.''

"Could we?''

"Sure. Come on.''

He led her down a side street where a group of people were just entering what looked like an old warehouse. But inside, it was a theater, complete with live orchestra and lighted stage and some of the most beautiful modern ballet she'd ever watched. The people onstage looked like living art: the women delicate and pink in their tulle and satin, the men vigorous and athletic and vibrant. Kati had been going to the ballet for years, but this was something special.

Afterward, they went to a lounge and drank piña coladas and danced to the hazy music of a combo until the wee hours.

"That was fun,'' she told Jack when he brought her home. "We'll have to do it again.''

"Indeed we will. I'm sorry I didn't think of the ballet weeks ago. I get free tickets.''

"Let's do it again even if we have to pay for them,'' she said, laughing.

"Suits me. I'll call you in a few days. Looks like I may have to fly down to Washington on that latest scandal.''

"Call me when you get back, okay?"

"Okay. Night, doll." He winked and was gone. He never tried to kiss her or make advances. With them, it was friendship instead of involvement, and she enjoyed his company very much. Jack had been married and his wife had died. He wanted involvement even less than she did and was glad to be going out with someone who wouldn't try to tie him up in wedding paper.

Dreamily, she unlocked the apartment door and stepped inside. She closed the door and leaned back against it, humming a few bars of the classical piece that had accompanied one of the pieces at the ballet.

"Do you usually stay out this late?" Egan asked from the living room. He was standing by the window with a glass of amber liquid that looked like whiskey in his hand.

She stared at him. "I'm twenty-five," she reminded him. "I stay out as late as I like."

He moved toward her slowly, gracefully, his eyes holding hers. "Do you sleep with him?" he asked.

She caught her breath. "Egan, what I do with anyone is my business."

He threw back the rest of his drink and set the glass on a small table in the hall, moving toward her until she felt like backing away.

"How is he?" he asked lazily. Then he caught her by the shoulders and held her in front of him, looking down quietly, holding her eyes.

Her lips parted as she met that intimidating stare. "Egan..."

His nostrils flared. The lean fingers that were hold-

ing her tightened. "Is he white all over?" he continued in a faintly mocking tone. "City boy."

"Well, there aren't many cattle to herd up here,"
she said tautly.

"No, but there are too damn many people. You
can't walk two steps without running into someone,"
he complained. "I couldn't survive here. Answer me.
Do you sleep with him?"

"That's non—" she began.

"Tell me anyway. Does he do all those things to
you that you write about in your books?" he asked,
studying her. "Does he 'strip you slowly,' so that you
can 'feel every brush of his fingers...'"

"Egan!" She reached up to press her fingers against
his lips, stopping the words as she flushed deeply.

He hadn't expected the touch of her fingers. He
caught them and held them as if he wasn't sure what
to do with them. His eyes held hers.

"Is that the kind of man you like, Katriane Desi-
ree?" he asked, using the full name that she didn't
know he'd ever heard.

She watched him helplessly. "I like...writers," she
managed.

"Do you?" He brought her hand to his mouth and
kissed its warm palm softly, slowly. His teeth nipped
at her slender forefinger.

"Egan," she breathed nervously.

He took the tip of her finger into his mouth and she
felt his tongue touching it. "Afraid?" he murmured.
"Don't they say that a woman is instinctively afraid
of a man she thinks can conquer her?"

She wrenched away from him like an animal at bay.

"You'd be lucky!" she whispered. Was that her voice, shaking like that?

He stared at her, sliding his hands into his pockets, and the action stretched the fabric of his trousers tight over the powerful muscles of his legs. "So would you," he returned. "But one of these days I might give you a thrill, honey. God knows, my taste never ran to virgins. And an experienced woman is... exciting."

She felt the blood rush into her face, and she whirled on her heel. If she stayed there one second longer, she'd hit him! Boy, wouldn't the joke be on him if he ever tried to take her to bed! Egan, in bed....

She went straight into the bathroom, oblivious that she might wake Ada, and ran herself a calming cool shower.

Chapter 3

Kati didn't sleep. Every time she closed her eyes, she could feel the hard grip of Egan's fingers on her shoulders, the touch of his mouth against her hand. She hated him, she thought miserably; that was why she couldn't sleep.

She dragged into the kitchen just after daylight, with her long gold and beige striped caftan flowing lovingly over the soft curves of her body. Her tousled hair fell in glorious disarray around her shoulders, and her dark eyes were even darker with drowsiness.

With a long yawn, she filled the coffee pot and started it, then she reached for the skillet and bacon and turned on the stove. She was leaning back against the refrigerator with a carton of eggs in one hand and butter in the other when the kitchen door opened and Egan came in, dressed in nothing but a pair of tan slacks.

He stopped at the sight of her and stared. She did some staring of her own. He was just as she'd imagined him without that shirt—sexy as all get-out. Bronzed muscles rippled as he closed the kitchen door; a mat of hair on his chest curled down obviously below his belt buckle. His arms looked much more powerful without a concealing shirt, as did his shoulders. She could hardly drag her eyes away.

"I thought I'd fix myself a cup of coffee," he said quietly.

"I just put some on," she said.

He cocked an eyebrow. "Does that mean I have to wait until you drink your potful before I can make mine?" he asked.

She glared at him. So much for truces. "There's a nice little coffee shop down on the corner," she suggested with a venomous smile.

"I'll tell Ada you're being unkind to me," he threatened. "Remember Ada? My sister? The one whose Christmas you said you didn't want to spoil?"

She drew in a calming breath. "Do excuse me, Mr. Winthrop," she said formally. "Wouldn't you like to sit down; I'll pour you a cup of coffee."

"Not until you tell me where you plan to pour it," he returned.

"Don't tempt me." She reached up into the cabinet for a second cup and saucer while he pulled out a chair and straddled it.

When she turned back with the filled cups, she found him watching her. It unnerved her when he did that, and she spilled coffee into one of the saucers before she could set them on the table.

"Couldn't you sleep?" he asked pleasantly.

"No," she said. "I'm not used to sleeping late. I'm at my best early in the morning."

A slow, wicked smile touched his hard mouth. "Most of us are," he commented.

It didn't necessarily mean what she thought it did, but she couldn't help the blush. And that increased her embarrassment, because he laughed.

"Will you stop!" she burst out, glaring at him. "Oh, why don't you take your coffee and go back to bed?"

"I'm hungry. Don't I smell bacon?"

"Bacon!" She jumped up and turned it just in time. It was a nice golden brown.

"Going to scramble some eggs, too?" he asked.

"No, I thought I'd let you drink yours raw," she said.

He only laughed, sipping his coffee. "I like raw oysters, but I draw the line at raw eggs. Want me to make the toast?"

"You can cook?"

"Don't get insulting." He stood up and found the bread and butter. "Get me a pan and some cinnamon and sugar."

She stared at him.

"Cinnamon," he said patiently. "It's a spice—"

"I know what it is," she grumbled, finding it. "Here. And I've lined the pan with aluminum foil. It's all yours."

"Ungrateful woman," he muttered as he mixed the cinnamon and sugar in the shaker she'd handed him. He buttered the bread and spread the mixture on top.

"Don't get conceited just because you can make cinnamon toast," she mumbled. "After all, it isn't exactly duckling *a l'orange*."

"I'd like to see you cook that," he remarked.

She cleared her throat. "Well, I could if I had a recipe."

"So could I." He turned on the oven and slid the toast in under the broiler. "Get me a pot holder."

"Who was your personal slave yesterday?" she asked, tossing him a quilted pot holder.

"I liked the old days," he murmured, glancing at her. "When men hunted and women cooked and had kids."

"Drudgery," she scoffed. "Women were little more than free labor...."

"Cosseted and protected and worried over and loved to death," he continued, staring down at her. "Now they're overbearing, pushy, impossible to get along with and wilder than bucks."

"Look who's talking about being wild!" she burst out.

He stared down his nose at her. "I'm a man."

She drew in a breath and let it out, and her eyes involuntarily ran over him.

"No argument?" he asked.

She turned away. "Your toast's burning."

He took it out—nicely browned and smelling sweet and delicate—and put it on a plate while she scrambled eggs.

"I like mine fried, honey," he commented.

"Okay. There's a frying pan; grease is in the cabinet. If you're too good to eat my scrambled eggs, you can mutilate your own any way you like.''

He chuckled softly, an odd sound that she'd never heard, and she turned to look up at him.

"Firecracker,'' he murmured, his eyes narrow and searching. ''Are you like that in bed?''

She jerked her eyes away and concentrated on the eggs. ''Wouldn't you like to get dressed before we eat?''

It was a mistake. A horrible mistake. Because then he knew what she hadn't admitted since he walked into the room. That, stripped to the waist, he bothered her.

The arrogant beast knew it, all right. He moved lazily until he was standing just behind her...so close that she felt him and smelled him and wanted nothing more out of life than to turn around and slide her hands all over that broad chest.

His hands caught her waist, making her jump, and eased her back against him so that she could feel the warm, hard muscles of his chest and stomach against her back. The caftan was paper-thin, and it was like standing naked in his arms.

She felt his fingers move to her hips, caressingly, and her hand trembled as it stirred the eggs to keep them from burning.

"Egan, don't,'' she whispered shakily.

His breath was warm and rough in her hair, because the top of her head only came to his chin. The fingers holding her hips contracted, and she felt the tips of them on her flat stomach like a brand.

"Put down that damned spoon and turn around," he said in a tone she didn't recognize.

She was shaking like a leaf, and God only knew what would have happened. But noisy footsteps sounded outside the kitchen door, and an equally noisy yawn followed it. Egan let go of her and moved away just as Ada walked in.

"There you are!" she said brightly, watching her best friend stir eggs. "I'm starved!"

"It'll be on the table in two shakes," Kati promised, hoping her voice didn't sound as shaky as it felt. Damn Egan!

"I'd better get dressed," Egan commented, winking at Ada as he went past her. "I think I bother somebody like this."

Kati made an unforgivable comment under her breath as he left the room.

"At it again, I see," Ada sighed wearily.

"He started it," Kati said through her teeth. "I didn't ask him to walk in here naked."

"What?" Ada blinked.

Kati looked at her friend with a pained expression. "Oh God, isn't he beautiful?" she whispered with genuine feeling.

Ada chuckled gleefully. "Well, I always thought so, even if he is my brother. But isn't that something of a strange admission for you to make?"

"It slipped out. Just forget it." She dished up the eggs. "I think I'd better put something on too."

"Don't be long," Ada cautioned. "The eggs will congeal."

"I'll hurry."

She ran for her bedroom and closed the door just as Egan opened his. A minute's grace! She got into her jeans, blue T-shirt and shoes, and barely stopped to run a brush through her hair. She hoped it would be a short week. She hadn't expected Egan to have this kind of effect on her. In all the years she'd known him, he'd never even tried to make a pass at her. Now, in less than two days, he'd made more impact on her guarded emotions than any other man had in all her twenty-five years. She was going to have to get a hold on herself. She didn't know what kind of game Egan had in mind, but she wasn't playing.

He was wearing a brown velour pullover when she came back, one that emphasized his dark hair and complexion and the hard muscles she'd already seen.

"We left a little for you," Egan commented as she sat down. He pushed aside his empty plate and poured himself another cup of coffee from the hotplate on the table.

"How kind of you," she said pleasantly. She held up her cup and Egan filled it, studying her far too closely.

"What does your boyfriend do for a living?" he asked unexpectedly.

"Jack isn't my boyfriend," she said. "He's a man I date. And he's a political reporter for the *New York Times.*"

He leaned back in his chair while Ada bit her lower lip and looked apprehensive.

"Is he really?" Egan asked. "He doesn't look like he gets much exercise. A little overweight, wouldn't you say?"

She glared at him. "He works very hard."

He only laughed, and sipped his coffee. "If I took him home with me, I could break him in one day."

"You could break the devil in one day," Kati said, exasperated. "What business is it of yours who I date?"

"Now, that's a good question," he replied. His eyes narrowed, and there was a smile she didn't understand on his chiseled lips. "Maybe I feel sorry for the poor man. He does know what you do for a living, doesn't he? Must be hell on him, having everything he does to you turn up in a book...."

"Egan." Ada groaned, hiding her face in her hands.

"You overbearing, unspeakable, mean tempered..." Kati began in a low tone. She threw her napkin down onto the table and stood up.

"You sure got up on the wrong side of the bed," Egan commented. "Here I am a guest in your apartment—"

"I'd sooner invite a cobra to breakfast!" she burst out.

"You should have," he murmured, glancing at the plate he'd just emptied. "He might have enjoyed burned eggs and half-raw bacon."

She tried to speak, couldn't, and just stormed out of the room.

She left the apartment before Ada could get out of the kitchen, and wandered around the streets shivering in her thin jacket for an hour before she gave up and went back. It was too cold for pride, anyway. All she'd accomplished was to let Egan see how unreasonably she reacted to his prodding. She'd just have to grit her teeth, for Ada's sake.

Egan was nowhere in sight when she got back, and Ada looked apologetic and worn.

"I don't understand him, I just don't," Ada groaned. "Oh Kati, I'm sorry. If I'd realized how bad things were between you, I'd never have invited him."

Kati was generous enough not to remind her friend that she'd tried to warn her. She sat down on the sofa with a hard sigh.

"I'll manage. Where is he?" she added darkly.

"Gone to spend the day with some girl friend of his," Ada said absently. "He said he might not be back until late."

Why that simple statement should make her feel murderous, Kati didn't know. But something gnawed inside her at the thought of Egan with another woman.

"I wonder how much he had to bribe her?" she asked nastily.

"Shame on you," Ada said.

But Kati didn't apologize. And she didn't dwell on her confused emotions, either. She wanted no complications in her life, especially with someone like Egan Winthrop.

She and Ada went shopping later in the day and ate out at a little Italian restaurant just down the street from their apartment. They watched television and eventually went to bed. And Egan didn't come back. Not that night. Not until the next morning.

Kati was sitting on the living room floor with pages littering the area around her. They were galleys of her latest book, which had come that morning by special messenger, and she was going over them. Ada was at auditions for a new play, hoping to be home by lunch if she didn't get held up at the theater during tryouts. That was a laugh. Most of the time, it took hours. Despite the appointments the hopefuls were given, something always went wrong. Ada had never gotten back when she thought she would, and Kati was dreading Egan's arrival. She felt wild when she thought of his not coming in at all, and angry because she didn't understand why. She didn't even *like* the man, for God's sake!

There was a loud knock at the door an hour later, and when she opened it, Egan was standing there looking faintly amused and as immaculate as when he'd left. Still in the same clothes, of course....

She glared at him. "Lose your key?" she asked.

"I thought I'd better not use it, in case you were...entertaining," he said.

She let him in, slammed the door and went back to her comfortable sprawl on the floor.

"Coffee's hot if you want some," she said icily. "I'm busy reading."

"Don't let me interrupt you. I thought I'd have a quick shower and change clothes. I've got a lunch date."

Why oh why did she feel like smashing plates? She frowned and concentrated on what she was doing. Minutes later, he was back, dressed in a navy blue pinstripe suit with a white silk shirt and a blue and burgundy tie. He looked regal. Sexy. Unbelievably handsome for such an ugly man. If he was dressing like that in the middle of the day, he must be on his way to the Waldorf, she thought. And God only knew with whom.

"Ada didn't worry, did she?" he asked, checking his watch.

"Oh, no. She's used to people staying out all night," she lied deliberately, lifting her eyes. It shocked her, the flash of reaction in his face before it was quickly erased.

His eyes ran over her: the gray slacks and burgundy silk blouse she was wearing, her feet hose-clad and without shoes. Her hair was loose, and flowed in waves of reddish gold silk down her shoulders; her face was rosy and full of life.

His scrutiny made her nervous, and she dropped her eyes back to the page she was reading.

He moved closer and suddenly bent to pick up a page. His eyebrows rose as he read, and a slow smile touched his mouth.

"You do put your heart into it, don't you?" he murmured.

She reached up and took the page out of his hands, glancing at it. She blushed and tucked it under what she was reading. Why did he have to pick up *that* page? she groaned inwardly.

"Is that what you like with a man?" he continued maddeningly, his hands in his pockets, his eyes intent. "I've never done it in a bathtub, but I suppose—"

"Will you please go away?" she groaned, letting her hair fall over her eyes. "I don't care where you've done it, or with whom, just please go eat your lunch and leave me to my sordid occupation."

"I suppose I'd better. Stockbrokers sure as hell don't have time to waste."

She looked up as he turned to leave. "Stockbroker?" she murmured incredulously.

He glanced down at her from his formidable height with an expression she couldn't decipher. "I'm a businessman," he reminded her. "I do have the odd investment to look after."

"Yes, I know," she said quickly. "I just thought—"

"That because I was out all night, it was with a woman—and that I was meeting her for a leisurely lunch?" he suggested in a menacing tone.

She turned back to her work, trying to ignore him. It wasn't easy when he loomed over her that way.

"The reasons I stayed away might shock you, city girl," he said after a minute.

"I don't doubt it for a minute," she muttered.

"And that wasn't what I meant. It might have something to do with you."

The careless remark brought her eyes up, and he held them relentlessly for so long that she felt currents singing through her body.

"I didn't expect you to start trembling the minute I put my hands on you," he said in a harsh undertone. "Not after all these years. We've been enemies."

"We still are," she said in what she hoped was a convincing tone, while humiliation stuck like bile in her throat.

"Dead right," he said coldly. "And it's going to stay that way. I don't want complications during this holiday."

"Ditto," she said curtly. "And don't go around flattering your ego too much, Egan," she added. "I was half asleep at the time!"

His darkened eyes searched hers in the stillness that followed, and she was aware of him in a way she'd never been aware of a man before. Of his height and strength, of the devastating effect he had on her senses.

"Saving your pride, Kati?" he asked quietly.

She studied her long fingernails. "I like my life as it is," she said. "I'm on the go too much for relationships of any kind. And what you'd have in mind...!" she began.

"Now who's flattering their ego?" he asked shortly, glaring down at her. "My God, I don't mind experience in my women, but I draw the line at promiscuity!"

She scrambled to her feet and was ready to swing when the dark look on his face worked some kind of witchcraft and left her standing helplessly with her fists clenched.

"You slapped me once and got away with it," he said quietly. "If you do it again now, we'll wind up in bed together."

She felt her body tremble at the words. "No," she bit off.

"Yes." His chest rose and fell heavily, and his eyes cut into hers. "Don't you realize that the way we react to each other is like flint and steel? All it would take is a kiss. Just that. And we'd burn each other alive. I've known that from the very beginning."

She hadn't, and the thought of Egan as a lover made her face burn. She had to smother a gasp as she turned away with her arms folded protectively around her slender body.

"Don't worry. You're safe, city girl," he said in a mocking tone. "I'm not that desperate. Just don't push me too far."

She couldn't even face what he was insinuating. Egan was the enemy. He was going to stay that way too, if she had to bite her tongue in two. She stared blankly out the window.

"And it's Ada that's auditioning for acting jobs," he commented sarcastically. "Playing innocent?"

She didn't have to play, but he'd never believe it. He'd just shocked her to her nylon-clad feet, and she was lost for words. It was a little frightening to be threatened with a man's bed, just for provoking him. She hadn't been aware that she *was* provoking him until now. Which automatically led to her asking why she did it, and that was frightening as well.

"Kati," he called softly.

She stiffened. "Will your stockbroker wait?" she asked quietly.

He frowned at her stiff back. "What the hell's the matter with you?"

"You threaten me with sex and then ask me what's wrong?" she burst out, staring at him nervously over one shoulder.

He blinked, as if she'd shocked him. "It wasn't a threat."

She flushed and walked away.

"Will you stop doing your Lady Innocent act and look at me?" he growled.

She walked into her bedroom and slammed the

door. On an afterthought, she locked it, too. There was a string of unprintable curses from the vicinity of the living room before the front door slammed violently and the room became quiet.

It wasn't going to be possible to stay in the same apartment with Egan after this, she thought miserably. She'd just have to check into a hotel until he left. Having to put up with his incessant verbal aggression was bad enough; but when he started threatening to make it physical, that was the end. The very end.

The conceited beast—to accuse her of being so vulnerable that she'd jump into his bed at the first opportunity. She groaned as she recalled the touch of his hands on her hips, the wild tremors that had run through her untried body. She gritted her teeth. She'd have to get away from him. Because what if he did that again? The real problem was telling Ada she was leaving without spoiling the poor girl's Christmas.

Chapter 4

Kati had half her clothes in her suitcase by the time Ada came home from her tryout. She still hadn't decided what she was going to do, beyond checking into a hotel down the street. She knew for certain that she couldn't take one more night of Egan.

"What are you doing?" Ada asked hesitantly, pausing in the doorway of Kati's room.

"Cleaning out my drawers," came the terse reply.

Ada cleared her throat. "Where are you taking what was in them?"

"To a hotel."

Ada leaned back against the doorjamb wearily. "Egan came home."

"How did you ever guess?" Kati asked pleasantly. She closed the lid of the suitcase.

"You're adults," Ada argued. "Surely you should

be able to get along just during Christmas holidays? Peace on earth?''

"There is no peace where your brother is," Kati said vehemently. She tossed back a strand of hair and glared across the room. "I find it no less than miraculous that he can get people to work for him at all!"

The other woman sighed. "Amazingly enough, most of the hands have been with him for years. He has hardly any turnover." She glanced at Kati. "And he gets along wonderfully with women, as a rule. Polite, courteous, attentive—''

"We are talking about the same man?" Kati had to ask. "The big ugly one who's been staying here for two days and one night?"

Ada shook her head, laughing. "Oh, Kati. Kati." She moved out into the hall. "You win. I'll pack, too. We'll let Egan have the apartment and we'll both go to a hotel."

"Now hold on," Kati protested. "It's Christmas, and he's your brother, and the whole point of asking him here—''

"Was not to ruin your Christmas, believe it or not," Ada said gently. "You're like a sister to me. How can I let you leave alone?"

Kati bit her lower lip and stared helplessly at the suitcase. She didn't know what to do anymore.

"Maybe if you pretend he's not here?" Ada suggested softly.

Kati looked up. "He won't let me. He keeps making horrible remarks; he says..." Her face flushed, and she couldn't meet the curious look in her friend's eyes.

"He has this strange idea about where I get material for my books."

"Suppose I talk to him?"

"That would make it worse." She moved the suitcase aside and sat down heavily. "I'll stay. I can't come between the two of you, not at Christmas."

"You're a doll." Ada grinned.

"I wish I were. Maybe then he'd let me alone," came the muttered reply.

"Just treat him like someone you've never met before," Ada suggested.

"That's an idea."

"Anything's worth trying once."

"Yes. Where do you keep the arsenic?"

"Shame on you! It's Christmas!"

"All right, I'm easy," Kati agreed. "Where's the holly stake?"

Ada threw up her hands and left the room.

It was late that evening when Egan came in, looking disheveled and out of sorts. He glared at Kati as if every ill in the world could be laid at her feet.

"We, uh, saved you some supper, Egan," Ada said.

"I'm not hungry," he returned gruffly, but his eyes still didn't leave Kati.

"I'll bring you some coffee," Kati said pleasantly and with a polite smile.

Egan stared after her blankly. "Concussion?" he asked Ada.

Ada laughed, going to help her friend in the kitchen.

"It's working," she whispered as they filled a tray. "He thinks you're sick."

"When hasn't he?" Kati muttered. She sliced some

pound cake, added some dessert plates, forks and napkins to their coffee service, and carried the loaded tray into the living room.

Egan was sprawled in the big armchair that he'd appropriated since his arrival. He glared up from its depths as Kati put the tray down on the coffee table.

"I said I wasn't hungry," he repeated.

"Oh, the cake isn't for you," Kati said sweetly. "It's for Ada and me."

That seemed to make him worse. He sat up and took the cup of black coffee Kati poured him, sipping it. He seemed to brighten all at once. "Too weak," he said, staring at her.

She ignored the challenge. "Is it?" She tasted hers. "Yes," she lied, "it certainly is. I'll make some more."

"Don't bother," he returned curtly, leaning back with the cup and saucer held on the palm of one large, lean hand. "It'll do."

She nibbled at her cake and idly watched television. The program they had chosen was a romantic comedy about detectives.

"Isn't he dashing?" Ada sighed as the leading man came into view.

"Oh, rather," Kati said theatrically. "So handsome." She glanced at Egan with a lifted eyebrow.

Egan glanced back at her with hard eyes. But he didn't say a word.

"Did you settle that business with our stockbroker?" Ada asked when the commercial came on.

"Yes," Egan replied curtly. He finished his coffee and stood up. "I think I'll get some sleep. It's been a trying day. Good night." He walked out without a word to Kati.

"It's barely nine," Ada murmured, scowling after him. "Egan never goes to bed this early."

"Maybe it's his conscience bothering him," Kati suggested. "About the abominable way he's been treating me?"

"Dream on, my best friend," came the sighing reply.

The phone rang and Ada dragged herself over to answer it, brightening when she heard the caller. "It's Marshal!" she whispered to Kati.

Kati grinned. Ada's boyfriend had been away for several weeks, and the joy of homecoming was in her eyes. She moved the phone into the hall while Kati finished watching television.

"He wants us to double up tomorrow night at the Rainbow Grill. Want to ask Jack?" Ada asked.

"I'd love to, but Jack's still out of town. How about Friday night?"

"Fine! I'll make sure it's okay with Marshal."

"You'll make sure what's okay?" Egan asked, stopping in the doorway with his tie in his hand and his shirt unbuttoned over his broad chest.

"A date, Friday night," Ada volunteered. "Want to come along? I've got a super girl friend—"

"I can get my own women," he said with a tilt of his mouth. "Friday? I'll ask Jennie. What time?"

Kati's heart sank, and it showed in her eyes. Egan happened to look her way; he smiled with pure malice.

"What's the matter, honey, will I cramp your style if I come along?" he asked her.

Kati remembered almost too late the role she'd chosen to play. Polite hostess. No personalities. No hostilities. Christmas. Good cheer.

She gritted her teeth. "You're welcome, of course," she said with a frozen smile.

Egan's heavy eyebrows lifted. "My God, get a doctor," he told Ada.

Kati smiled even brighter. "Now, I think I'll say good night, too. I have this headache…"

"But it's only nine," Ada wailed. "Don't both of you go to bed and leave me alone."

"Don't you want peace and quiet?" Egan asked his sister.

Ada glanced from one to the other of them and sighed. "Well, I think I'll come, too. I need my beauty sleep, I guess."

"Some of us might benefit from it," Kati muttered, glaring up at Egan.

He chuckled softly. "Think I'm ugly?"

She flushed. Her eyes involuntarily ran over the craggy contours, the broken nose, the hard, cruel mouth. For some odd reason, she couldn't quite look away. His eyes caught and held hers, and they stood staring at each other in a silence that blazed with new tensions.

"Excuse me," Ada murmured, trying to hide a grin as she edged past Kati's frozen form and into her own bedroom. "Good night!"

Egan's chest was rising and falling roughly as he stared down at Kati. "Do you?" he asked in an odd tone.

She swallowed. Her throat felt as if it were full of

cactus. Her lips parted, and Egan watched them hungrily. She realized all at once that he hadn't just been making threats earlier in the day. He wanted her!

"I...I'm tired," she managed, starting to move.

One long, hard arm came out, barring her path. "I wasn't threatening you this afternoon," he said tautly. "I was telling you how it would be. You can't be blind enough not to see how we are with each other, Kati," he added half under his breath.

She moved gingerly away from that long arm. "I...have a boyfriend...whom I like very much," she said shakily.

He eased forward, just enough to let her feel the warm strength of his body, the heat of his breath against her reddish gold hair. "Liking isn't enough."

Her eyes came up to meet his. "Isn't it?"

His fingertips touched her throat like a breath, feeling its silky texture, stroking it sensuously. "You smell of roses," he said in a husky whisper.

Her fingers caught his, trembling coldly against their warm strength as she tried to lift them away from her throat.

He caught her hand and moved it to his chest— easing it under the fabric and against thick hair and warm muscle—and her breath jerked in her throat. He felt as solid as a wall, and the wiry pelt of hair tickled her fingers as she flattened them against him. His expensive cologne filled her nostrils, drowning her in its masculine scent.

"Forgotten what to do, Kati?" he murmured roughly. "Shall I refresh your memory?"

She lifted her eyes dazedly to his, and they were wide and curious as they met his glittering gaze.

His head bent so that his hard face filled the world. "'She tore his shirt out of the way,'" he quoted huskily, "'and ran her fingers, trembling, over his hard, male...'!"

"No!" Recognizing the passage, she flushed hotly. Immediately, she dragged her hand away and shrank from him as if he'd burned her.

He laughed, but there was an odd sound to it, and his eyes blazed as she reached behind her for the doorknob to her room.

"Doesn't your reporter friend like having you do that to him?" he asked huskily. "Or does he prefer what comes later?"

She whirled on a sob, pushing open the door. She started to slam it, but he caught it with a powerful hand and she couldn't budge it.

"I hate you," she breathed shakily, frantic that Ada might hear them.

"So you keep telling me," he replied. "You're the one with no scruples, honey, so stop flying at me when I throw them back at you."

"I'm not what you think I am," she cried.

"No kidding?" he murmured insolently, letting his eyes punctuate the insult.

"You go to hell, you ugly cowboy!" she said furiously.

He studied her flushed face and black eyes amusedly. "Ada used to talk about her sweet-tempered, easygoing friend. Before I ever met you, I imagined a retiring little violet. You were a shock, honey."

"What do you think you were?" she returned.

He laughed softly. "No woman's ever pulled the wool over my eyes. It didn't take reading your books to tell me what kind of woman you were. All I had to do was watch you in action."

"The car broke down," she reminded him. "Richard and I had to walk for miles...!"

"Aren't you tired of lying about it? I told you," he added, letting his eyes narrow sensuously, "experienced women turn me on."

"Then why don't you go out and find the friend you spent the night with?" she retorted hotly.

His eyebrows went up and he grinned. "Did that bother you?"

She brought her heel down hard on his instep, without warning; and while he was off balance, she slammed the door and locked it.

"Kati!" he growled furiously.

"Go ahead, break it down!" she dared him. "I'll be screaming out the window until the police come!"

There was a muffled curse; a door opening; Ada's voice, almost hysterical; and Egan's, angry but conciliatory. Minutes later, two doors slammed almost simultaneously. With an angry sigh, Kati started stripping off her clothes and heading toward the shower. She was furious enough not to mind that the water was ice-cold.

Chapter 5

Egan was gone, blessedly, when Kati woke up late the next morning. Jack called to say he was back in town and asked Kati out for dinner. Grateful for the respite, she was waiting for him on pins and needles at six that afternoon.

Ada had been sympathetic about her brother's strange behavior, adding that he had a sore foot and it served him right. It was the first time Kati ever heard Ada say anything against Egan.

"Do you think I'm scandalous?" Kati asked unexpectedly when she and Jack were relaxing over coffee after a satisfying steak.

He stared at her. "You?"

"Because I write what I write," she added. "It's important."

"No, I don't think you're scandalous," he said honestly and smiled. "I think you're extremely talented, and your books are a joy to read."

"You don't think I lead a wild life?"

He only laughed. "No, I don't. What's wrong? Are you getting unpleasant letters again?"

"Oh, no. It's..." She sighed and propped her chin on her hand. "It's Egan."

"Please, don't spoil a perfect evening," he said with a restless movement. "He has a glare that could stop a clock."

"Tell me about it," she muttered. "He's giving me fits about what I write."

"Doesn't he realize the difference between fiction and fact?"

"Not if he doesn't want to," she said with a short laugh. "Egan makes up his rules as he goes along. He's a law unto himself out West."

"I got that idea, all right." He studied her sad face and reached out impulsively to pat her hand. "He'll leave after Christmas," he said bracingly.

"Roll on, New Year," she murmured, and sighed as she sipped her coffee.

They went dancing after dinner, and for a while Kati forgot all her troubles. She drew interested glances in the black dress she was wearing. It had a peasant bodice with a full, swirling skirt, and left her creamy shoulders bare. With her hair in a high coiffure, and a minimum of makeup, she wore the designer gown with a flair.

She felt on top of the world, until she went into the apartment and found Egan waiting in the hall.

"Where's lover boy?" he asked, glaring past her at the closed door. "Doesn't he come in for a nightcap?"

He was wearing a dress shirt rolled up to the elbows and half unbuttoned in front, with his black slacks. Obviously, he hadn't spent the evening at home, either, and his proprietary air irritated Kati even more. She was still fuming from last night.

"He doesn't wear a nightcap," she said with sweet venom, "and I don't lend mine."

His chin lifted at an arrogant angle and he looked at her long and hard, his dark eyes narrowing on her bare shoulders.

Self-conscious with him, she hunched her shoulders so that the elastic top came back into place, demurely covering everything south of her collarbone.

"Shy of me?" he asked quietly, moving forward.

She felt like running. Where was Ada, for heaven's sake? She couldn't get past him to her room to save her life, and she knew it.

"Where's Ada?" she asked quickly.

"In her room, talking to Marshal," he said. "Why? You're a big girl, now; you don't need protecting, do you?"

Oh yes, she did, but obviously she couldn't count on her best friend tonight.

She felt the impact of his rough, warm hands—with a sense of fatalism. Her body jerked under the sensation as he deliberately began to slide the fabric away from her shoulders and down.

"Isn't this how you had it?" he breathed, bending. His chest rose and fell roughly, and she drowned in the warmth of his body.

"Egan…" she began.

"Don't talk. Stand still." His mouth smoothed over her shoulder, leaving a fiery wake. His fingers held her upper arms, digging in as his teeth nipped slowly, tenderly at the silken flesh.

"Don't," she moaned, eyes closed, throat arching as if it invited him—begged him—to do what he pleased.

"You want it," he whispered huskily. "So do I. Desperately…!" She felt his tongue and the edge of his teeth as he moved over the warm expanse of her shoulders and her collarbone in a silence blazing with promise.

His breath sounded oddly jerky as he drew her body against him. "You taste like the sweetest kind of candy," he said under his breath, and his fingers were hurting, but she was too shaken to care. "Baby," he whispered, his mouth growing urgent now as it found her throat, the underside of her chin. His hands moved up to catch in her hair, careless of its neat bun, as he bent her head back and lifted it toward his hard, parted lips. "Baby, you make me ache…!"

His mouth was poised just above hers, and at that moment she'd have given him that and anything else he wanted. But before he could lower his head, the sound of a door being opened shattered the hot silence.

"Oh, damn," Egan ground out. His fingers bruised her, and his eyes were blazing as he pushed her away and turned as if he were blinded by his own passion— a frustrated passion like that which was making her tremble.

"Marshal's sick of the sea, but they won't let him

come home," Ada sighed, oblivious to the wild undercurrents around her. "Why couldn't I find myself a man instead of a sailor? Hi, Kati. Have a good time?"

"Sure," Kati said, smiling through a haze of unsatisfied longing. She glanced toward Egan and saw his eyes, and she flushed wildly. Her eyes went to his mouth and back up; and he muttered something terrible under his breath and slammed into his room without even the pretense of courtesy.

"What's the matter with him?" Ada asked softly.

"Beats me," her friend replied blandly. "Gosh, I'm tired. We went dancing and my feet are killing me!"

"Well, I hope you don't wear them out before Friday night," Ada laughed. "Sleep well."

"I'll do my best," came the muttered reply, and she went into her room and almost collapsed. He hadn't even kissed her, and she was trembling like a leaf. Heaven only knew what would happen if he ever really made a heavy pass. She couldn't bear to think about it! She went to bed and lay awake half the night brooding, only to wake with a splitting headache the next morning.

Egan brooded all day. He moved restlessly around the apartment, like a man aching for the outdoors. Even Kati felt vaguely sorry for him.

"You'll wear ruts in the carpet," she murmured after lunch, while Ada was taking her turn at the dishes.

He turned with his hands rammed deep in his pockets and stared at her. "If I do, I'll buy you a new one."

"That wasn't what I meant," she said, trying hard

to hold on to her temper. She searched his hard face, but she couldn't quite meet his eyes. "You hate being indoors, don't you?"

"With a passion," he agreed shortly. "I couldn't live like this."

"New York is full of things to see," she suggested. "There's Central Park, and the Statue of Liberty, the Empire State Building—"

"I've already seen them once," he said. "And I've walked the streets. What I want, I'm not going to find out there."

She lifted her eyes and had them trapped.

He moved closer so quickly that she hardly saw him coming before he was towering over her. "I want you," he said, his voice like warm velvet in the sudden silence of the room. "I'm through pretending."

"Well, I don't...I don't want you," she said in a breathless little voice. "I have a boyfriend—"

"No competition whatsoever," he returned. "What are you afraid of? I'm not brutal in bed. I wouldn't hurt you."

She flushed deeply, and just stopped herself from slapping him. "I liked it better when you hated me," she said angrily, glaring up at him.

His eyes searched hers. "Was it ever that?"

Her lips parted, but before she could find an answer, Ada was through with the dishes and Kati stuck to her like glue until it was time to leave for dinner that evening.

Jack grinned as he saw Kati in her burgundy velvet dress. "What a dish," he murmured. "And I like your hair down like that."

"Thank you. You aren't bad yourself. Jack, you know Marshal," she said, indicating the tall, dark young man beside Ada.

"Sure." Jack extended his hand. "Good to see you again."

"Same here," Marshal replied. He hugged Ada close. "I still love the sea, but sometimes I get a little hungry for the shore."

"I can imagine. Uh, wasn't your brother supposed to join us?" Jack asked Ada with evident reluctance.

"He's meeting us at the Rainbow Grill," Ada said. "And I made reservations in advance."

"Good girl," Jack said. He took Kati's arm. "Well, let's get it over with," he murmured under his breath.

"It will be all right," she promised as Ada and Marshal fell back. "We can have the waiter pour wine over his head if he starts anything."

"You don't think he would?" Jack asked, horrified.

She patted his arm. He wasn't the type for public scenes, although Kati wouldn't have minded dousing Egan any old where at all. "No, I don't," she promised. "Don't worry. Everything will be fine."

She was to remember those words vividly a little later, when Egan joined them at their table overlooking the colorful lights of the city sixty-five floors down. He had on his arm a windblown little blonde who looked and dressed like a woman who loved money, and her first glance at the other women was like a declaration of war.

"So this is Ada," the blonde gushed, heading straight for Kati.

"Wrong woman," Kati said shortly. "That's Ada."

The blonde shrugged, gave a careless smile and turned to greet a highly amused Ada. "So you're Ada. How nice to meet you at last. I've just heard so much about you from Egan. We've known each other for a long time, you know. He calls me every time he gets to New York. I'm a model."

As if that didn't stick out a mile, Kati thought as the blonde sat down near her and almost choked her with expensive perfume.

"Isn't this the most gorgeous place?" the blonde enthused. "I love the atmosphere. And isn't the combo great?"

Kati couldn't say. She hadn't been able to hear them play, or hear their sultry-voiced vocalist sing, for the newcomer. And just as she was wondering how she'd eat because of the perfume, Egan slid into the seat beside her and ruined her appetite completely.

"Jennie Winn, this is Katriane James and her date," Egan volunteered.

Kati glared at him. "Jack Asher," she supplied.

"Nice to meet you, I'm sure," Jennie murmured. "What do you do, Mr. Asher?" she asked Jack and batted her impossibly long eyelashes at him.

He perked up immediately, the turncoat. "I'm a political columnist, for the *Times,*" he said.

Jennie beamed. "Are you, really? Oh, I just adore intelligent men."

Kati had to muffle a giggle with her napkin. Really, she was behaving impossibly, but that blonde couldn't be for real!

"Something amuses you, Miss James?" Egan asked with ice in his tone.

She got herself under control. "I got strangled, Mr Winthrop," she managed.

"On what? The air?"

"Now, Egan, honey," Jennie crooned, glaring past him at Kati. "You just relax, and later I'll take you back to my place and soothe you."

Kati bit almost through her lip to keep from howling. She didn't dare look at Egan—it would have been the very end.

"Jennie, look at the menu," Egan said curtly.

"Whatever you say, sugar."

"I want the beef Wellington," Ada said. "How about you, Kati?"

"Do they serve goose here?" Egan asked under his breath.

"If they do," Kati replied with a venomous smile, "yours is probably sizzling on the grill right now, sugar."

He glared at her and she glared back at him. Sensing disaster, Jack quickly intervened.

"Kati, didn't you want to try that duckling in orange sauce?"

She tore her eyes away from Egan's and smiled across the table. "Yes, I did."

By then the waiter was back, elegant in his white jacket, to take their order. By and large, Kati loved New York waiters. They had a certain flair and grace of manner that set them apart, and they were unfailingly polite and kind.

"I want prime rib," Jennie said nonchalantly. "Rare, honey."

'A woman after my own heart,'' Egan murmured. ''I'll have the same.''

Kati wanted to mutter something about barbarism, but she kept her mouth shut with an effort. And when the food came, she was far too involved in savoring every morsel to waste time on Egan Winthrop.

But the coffee and dessert came, eventually, and while Kati toyed with her superb English trifle, Egan leaned back and eyed Jack.

"I read your column on the Washington scandal," he told the younger man.

"Did you?" Jack asked with a polite smile.

"Interesting, about the deficit in the agency's budget," he continued. "Apparently your man was allocating funds on paper that never reached the recipients. The audacity of politicians constantly amazes me, and so does the apathy of the public."

Jack perked up. "Yes. What I can't understand is how he expected to get away with it," he said, forgetting his dessert as he went into the subject.

Egan matched him, thought for thought, and the ensuing conversation fascinated Kati. She listened raptly, along with everyone else at the table except Jennie—who looked frankly bored to death.

"You know a hell of a lot about politics for a rancher, Mr. Winthrop," Jack said finally, on a laugh.

"I took my degree in political science," came the cool reply. "Ranching pretty much chose me, rather than the other way around. When my father died, there was Ada and my mother to look after, and no one else to assume control of the property. There was a lot of it." He shrugged. "The challenge is still there," he added with a smile. "Cattle are a lot like politics, Mr. Asher. Unpredictable, hard to manage and sometimes just plain damned frustrating."

Jack laughed. "I imagine so."

"Oh, can't we stop talking about such boring things?" Jennie asked in a long-suffering tone. "I want to go to the theater, and we've got tickets to that hit musical on Broadway. We'll be late if you talk all night."

Egan gave her a look that would have stopped traffic.

Jennie flushed and cleared her throat. "I mean, whenever you're ready, sugar," she said placatingly.

Kati lifted her chin with faint animosity. She'd have told him where to go, instead of pleading with him like that. He knew it, too. Because he glanced at her and caught the belligerent gleam in her eye, and something wild and heady flashed between them when he smiled at her.

Her lips trembled, and she grabbed her coffee cup like a shield.

"See you later," Egan told them, picking up the tabs. "My treat. I enjoyed the discussion," he told Jack.

Before anyone could thank him, he and Jennie were gone and Jack was shaking his head.

"And I thought he hated me. My God, what a mind. He's wasted out West."

Ada beamed. "He was offered an ambassadorship, did you know?" she asked. "He knows everybody in Washington, right to the top. But he turned it down because of mother and me. Since then, he's given everything to the ranch.''

"Not quite everything," Marshal murmured. "His girl was a knockout."

"I'd have liked to knock her out," Kati muttered, flushing at Ada's shocked look. "Well, she must have bathed in perfume; I could hardly breathe," she said defensively.

But Ada only grinned, and Kati hated that knowing look. So she was jealous! She caught her breath. She was jealous? Of Egan? She picked up the untouched wineglass and helped herself.

Egan wasn't home when they finally got back to the apartment, and Kati could just picture him with that sizzling blonde. It made her ache in the oddest way. She took a shower and got ready for bed and then paced and paced around her room.

"Is something bothering you?" Ada asked minutes later, coming in to check on her. It wasn't like Kati to pace. "You're getting to be as bad as Egan about wearing ruts in the carpets."

Kati lifted her shoulders helplessly, grabbing at the ribbon strap that kept sliding off. The green gown was far too big, but she liked its roominess. "I'm just restless."

Ada studied her friend quietly. "He's a man," she said softly.

Kati blushed all the way down her throat and turned away.

"I'm sorry, I shouldn't have said that," Ada said hesitantly. "But, you see, I can't help noticing the way you look at him. And the way he looks back. Normal people don't fight like the two of you do. Anything that explosive has to…well, there has to be something pretty powerful to cause it, don't you see?''

''I hate him,'' Kati said through her teeth. ''That's powerful, all right.''

''But you want him.''

Kati's eyes closed. ''Tomorrow is Christmas,'' she said. ''The day after, he'll go back to Wyoming and I'll go back to my sordid books, and we'll both be better off. There's no future with your brother for any woman, Ada, and you know it.'' She turned around, her face stiff with control. ''He's not the happily-ever-after kind.''

Ada looked worried. ''He says that, but no man really wants to get married, does he? It kind of takes the right woman.''

Kati laughed huskily. ''A woman like Jennie. She suits him just fine, doesn't she?'' she asked venomously.

Ada shook her head. ''She numbs the hurt, that's all. He's a lonely man.''

''He got hurt once and never wants to be again, is that how it goes?'' Kati asked.

''I don't think Egan can be hurt, Kati,'' came the soft reply. ''He doesn't let anyone close enough. I know less than nothing about his private life. But I think he's more involved with you right now than he's ever been before.''

''He's never touched me,'' she bit off.

''Yes, I know. I didn't mean physically,'' Ada said. ''I mean emotionally. Don't you realize that's why he hits at you so hard?''

"He hits at me because he wants me," she told the other woman bluntly. "He said so. He thinks I'm easy."

Ada looked horrified. "Well, did you tell him the truth?"

"Of course not! I don't owe your horrible brother any explanations— Let him just keep his disgusting image of me!"

Ada frowned slightly. "Kati, he isn't a man to let go of something he sets his mind on. I think you'd better tell him."

"Why bother? He'll be gone day after tomorrow," she repeated.

"Kati—"

"Go to bed and stop worrying about me," Kati said gently, and hugged her concerned friend. "Egan and I will go on being enemies, because I won't give in and he'll give up. He makes a nice enemy."

"You wouldn't think so if he'd ever really been yours," Ada replied.

"Anyway, we both need our sleep. It will all work out, somehow. Sleep well."

Ada gave up. She smiled as she went out. "You, too."

But Kati didn't. Not until the wee hours of the morning. And Egan still hadn't come home. He was with that blonde, kissing her with that wide, cruel mouth that had tormented hers so sweetly....

Something woke her. She didn't know what. But she felt the light on her eyelids and the coolness of air on her skin, and her dark, drowsy eyes opened slowly.

He was standing beside the bed, wearing nothing

but a pair of slacks, with his broad chest sensuously bare and a cup of black coffee in one hand. And he was looking at her in a way that brought her instantly alert and wary; his glittering silver eyes were on fire.

She frowned slightly as she realized that he wasn't looking at her face. Her eyes shifted, and she noticed to her embarrassment that the loose gown had shifted in the night, leaving one perfect breast pink and bare.

Her hand went to jerk the bodice back up.

"No, Kati," he said in a husky undertone, and his eyes went back up to hers. "No. Let it happen."

He moved close, setting the coffee on the table. He dropped smoothly down beside her, and she hated the sudden weakness and hunger of her body as she stared up at him. Her hair was spread out on the pillow like a ragged halo of red and gold, her cheeks rosy with sleep, her eyes sultry. And he looked just as disheveled, just as attractive to her, with his hair tousled, his muscular arms and chest bare and tanned.

His hands went under her head, both of them, and he eased down so that his chest rested on her partially bare one.

She gasped at the unfamiliar sensation of skin on skin, and her eyes dilated under the piercing scrutiny of his.

"I'm going to kiss you until you can't stand up," he said roughly, bending. "My God, I want your mouth...!"

He took it, with a hard, hungry pressure that frightened her. Her slender hands lifted quickly to his shoulders and started to push—until they discovered the rough silkiness of his skin, the power in his bunched muscles. She ran her hands slowly down his arms, feeling the tension of the hard muscles, and back up again, to the hard bone of his shoulders.

Meanwhile, his mouth was slowing, gentling. He lifted it so that it was poised just over hers, and he looked at her for a long moment.

"You don't like it hard, do you?" he asked in a gruff undertone. "I do. Hard and hot and deep. But I'll make the effort, at least."

He bent again, coaxing her lips. It was an education in sensual blackmail. She lay tense under the crush of his torso, feeling each brief, soft contact like a brand. Her lips parted because she couldn't stop them, her breath was coming in short gasps and her heartbeat was shaking her. She hadn't known that women felt like this, despite the novels that bore her name. All her research had come from books, from films and television and bits and pieces of gossip. But what Egan was teaching her bore no resemblance to any of that. He was making her catch fire, and she was moving and reacting in ways that embarrassed her.

"That's more like it, baby," he breathed. "Much, much more like it. Now," he whispered, letting his hands slide down the long, bare line of her back, "now, if you want my mouth, come up and get it."

Blind, aching, she arched up and caught his hard mouth with hers, kissing him with enough enthusiasm to make up for her lack of experience at this kind of impassioned caress.

She felt his tongue go into her mouth, and she moaned sharply at the intimacy.

He lifted his dark head as if the sound had shocked

him, and looked down at her rigid, anguished features. His free hand tugged slowly at the other strap of her gown and his eyes followed its movement.

"Do you want me, Kati?" he asked quietly. "Shall I get up and lock the door?"

Her mind cleared instantly with the words as she stared up into his blazing eyes. He was asking her a straightforward question, and the answer would have been an unqualified *yes*. But he was offering a quick, temporary merging of bodies that would shame her when her sanity returned. And what in heaven's name would Ada think?

As if he sensed the indecision, his hand stilled on her arm. "Second thoughts?" he asked softly.

"I...can't," she whispered, searching his narrow eyes.

"I understand," he murmured, glancing toward the door with a wry smile. "We're not likely to be alone much longer."

He thought it was because of Ada, and it didn't really matter, did it? Whatever the reason, the result was going to be the same.

He looked back down at her and shifted so that the thick hair on his chest rubbed against her soft bareness; he smiled at her reaction.

"Like it?" he murmured arrogantly, and his hand came up to tease the softness under her arm, making her gasp.

"You have to stop that," she told him in a halting tone.

"Do I?" He bent and brushed his mouth lightly over hers while his fingers toyed with the silken skin and edged slowly, relentlessly, toward the hardening nub that would tell him graphically how he was affecting her.

"Egan?" she whispered in a voice that sounded nothing like her own. Her fingers lifted, catching in his hair, and her body was no longer part of her. It was his, all his, and every inch of it was telling him so.

His nose rubbed against hers as his mouth brushed and lifted; and his fingers made nonsense of principles and morals and self-respect.

"Kati?" he whispered, sensuously. He nipped at her lower lip. "Kati, take my hand and put it where you want it."

It was the most wildly erotic thing she'd ever heard or dreamed or thought. Helplessly, she reached out for his hand and carried it to the aching peak, and pressed it there.

"Oh God," she ground out, trembling, her face pressing into his hot throat, her body shuddering with the force of her own hunger.

"Silk," he whispered, his own voice rough and unsteady. "You're silk. So soft, so whisper-soft." His mouth found hers and he kissed her so tenderly that tears welled in her eyes, while his hand cupped and his thumb caressed, and it was the sweetest ache in the world that he caused her.

And then, all at once, the bodice was back in place, the sheet was over her and she was lying, shaking, in the bed as he propped up pillows and set her against them like a big doll.

''Ada,'' he ground out, handing her the cup with hands that trembled.

Her own trembled, and between them they just got it steady as Ada opened the door without knocking and came in yawning.

''Morning,'' she murmured, grinning at them. ''I've got breakfast. Bring your coffee with you. Thanks for taking it to her, Egan.''

''My pleasure,'' he murmured, and went out without a backward glance.

''Bad mood again?'' Ada grimaced. ''I thought it might mellow him up if I sent him in with your coffee. I guess I goofed again. Well, hurry up and dress, I've got something special!'' Ada added and went out the door laughing.

Kati sat there with tears suddenly rolling down her cheeks, so shaken and frustrated that she wanted to scream the roof down. She should have listened to Ada, she told herself. Ada had known what she didn't—that Egan was relentless when he wanted something. And what he wanted now was Kati.

Chapter 6

Ada had made fresh croissants—so light and flaky they could almost fly—and she had real butter to go on them. But Kati didn't taste anything she ate. She felt as if she were in the throes of some terrible fever, and every time she glanced at Egan, it got worse.

He was wearing a shirt and his boots now, with his dark slacks, and he was still beautiful. Kati could hardly drag her eyes away.

"You must have been late last night," Ada remarked to her brother. "I didn't hear you come in."

"I let myself be talked into going to a party after the show," he muttered. "Damned bunch of freaks. It was like a drugstore in there."

"You left," Ada said with certainty.

"I left. And took Jennie with me. And she screamed bloody murder all the way back to her apartment." He laughed shortly. "Which got her nowhere at all. She knew how I felt about that from the beginning, I never made any secret of it.''

"Things are different in the city, Egan," Ada said sadly. "Very different."

His head lifted. "Geography doesn't change what's right and what isn't," he said shortly.

"I know that," Ada agreed. "I don't like it any more than you do, but I don't feel I have the right to dictate to the rest of the world. Kati and I just keep to ourselves."

He glanced at Kati then, his eyes sweeping over her pale jersey blouse and slacks possessively. "Are you an old-fashioned girl in that respect, at least?" he asked, but he didn't sound so sarcastic as usual. "Do you drink and pop pills and smoke pot?"

"I drink cola," she replied. "And I do take aspirin when my head hurts." She watched him with wide eyes. "But I don't think I've ever tried to smoke a pot. What kind of pot did you have in mind?"

He burst out laughing. It changed his entire face, erased some of the hard, leathery lines. He looked faintly attractive, despite that cragginess. "My, my, aren't we sharp this morning?"

She lowered her eyes before he could read the embarrassment in them. "Eating improves my mind."

"I know something better," he remarked just as she lifted the coffee cup to her mouth.

"Don't move!" Ada gasped as hot coffee went all over the table and into Kati's lap. "I'll get a towel!"

She disappeared, and Egan mopped at her legs with a napkin.

"That was damned poor timing on my part," he muttered. "I didn't mean to make you hurt yourself."

She looked up into his silver eyes, astonished. "That's a first," she breathed.

He looked back, his gaze intent. The napkin rested on her thigh. "Did I tell you how lovely you are?" he asked under his breath. "Or what it did to me to touch you like that?"

She felt her lips part helplessly. "Egan, about... what happened—"

"I want it again," he breathed, bending so that his mouth threatened hers. "I want you against me so close that I can feel your heart beating."

"You don't understand," she whispered weakly.

"You want me," he returned huskily. "That's all I need to understand."

It was true, but it wasn't that uncomplicated. And before she could tell him how complicated it really was, Ada was back and the moment was lost. And she was trembling again.

She walked around like a zombie, going through the motions of helping Ada in the kitchen. They invited Marshal and Jack over for dinner the next day, since neither of them was going to try to go home for Christmas. And getting everything ready was a job.

Egan watched television and paced. Finally he got his jacket and hat and went out, and Kati almost collapsed with relief. She ached every time she looked at him, until it was torment to be within seeing distance.

He came in just as the annual Christmas Eve specials were beginning on the public broadcasting station, and he tossed his hat onto the hall table and shed his jacket.

"Culture," he murmured, watching the opera company perform.

"Go ahead, Mr. Winthrop, make some snide remark," Kati dared, feeling young and full of life because her heart leaped up just at the sight of him.

He smiled at her, with no malice at all on his dark face. "I like opera."

"You?"

"Well, there was a report awhile back on music and milk production," he told her, dropping easily into his armchair, "and it seems that cows produce more milk when they're listening to classical music."

Kati smiled. "It must cost a lot."

"What?"

"Having the orchestra come all the way out to the ranch."

"You little torment," he accused and reached out to tug a lock of her long hair playfully.

Ada, watching all this, just stared at them.

"Something wrong?" Egan asked her.

Ada shrugged. "Not a thing in this world, big brother."

He grinned at her. "Where's your boyfriend?"

"Begging for liberty on his knees," she told Egan. She laughed. "If he gets it he'll be here any minute."

"I'd bet on him." He glanced at Kati. "How about yours?" he asked tautly.

"Jack's making calls to his family," she said. "He won't be over until tomorrow."

He didn't say anything, but he settled down in the

chair to watch the programs with an oddly satisfied smile.

Marshal came a few minutes later, and Egan even joined in when they sang Christmas carols during the next program. They drank eggnog and ate cake, and Kati thought she'd never been so happy in her life.

Ada led Marshal under the mistletoe on his way out at midnight and kissed him lovingly, winking at Kati as the two of them moved out into the hallway.

"I'm going to walk Marshal to the elevator," she called back. "Don't wait up."

"Don't fall down the elevator shaft!" Kati called after her.

The door closed on a giggle. Which left Kati alone with Egan and trembling with new and frightening emotions.

He stood up, holding out his hand. She put hers into it unhesitatingly and let him lead her to the mistletoe. His lean, strong hands caught her waist and brought her gently against the length of his hard body.

"I've waited all day for this," he whispered, bending.

She stiffened, but his hands smoothed down over her hips and back and he nudged his face against hers gently.

"I know how you like it, baby," he breathed. "I won't hurt you this time, all right?"

She was beyond answering him. Her body throbbed. Throbbed! It was the most incredible physical reaction she'd ever had in her life, and she couldn't control it.

His mouth opened and hers opened to meet it, inviting the new intimacy, and she drowned in the magic of the long, sweet kiss. She breathed him, the tangy fragrance of cologne and, closer, the minty hotness of his mouth.

"I want you," he whispered, his voice shaking.

She drew back a little, trying to catch her breath and regain her sanity. It was impossible, but she couldn't even speak. They were simply torturing each other with this kind of thing. But how could she explain it to him?

He rested his forehead on hers and his eyes closed on ragged breaths. Against her hips, his body was making an embarrassing statement about his feelings, and she withdrew just enough to satisfy her modesty.

"Still playing games, Kati? You don't have to put on any acts for me. That virginal withdrawal—"

"Egan, you have to listen to me," she managed, looking up.

"I've got an apartment two streets over," he said on a harsh breath. "One even Ada doesn't know about. We could be there in fifteen minutes, and she'd never have to know."

Her breath caught in her throat. His eyes were blazing with it, and she knew her own legs were trembling. For one wild second she looked up at him and knew how it would be between them. She could almost feel the length of him without clothes: the silken slide of skin on skin, the aching pleasure of being touched by those lean, expert hands...

"Come with me, Kati," he said unsteadily. "We're just torturing each other. I've got to have you."

"I can't," she ground out. She lowered her chin so that her tormented eyes were on a level with his chest, and her trembling fingers pressed against his warm shirt.

His fingers tautened on her waist, moved to her hips and jerked them into his. "I ache," he whispered. "You know what I'm feeling."

Her eyes closed. She wasn't stupid; she could imagine that it was ten times worse for him than it was for her. But she couldn't undo all the years of conditioning. Flings weren't for her. She had too much conscience.

"I'm sorry," she whispered. "I'm so sorry, Egan, but I can't."

He drew in an angry breath, and she stiffened because she knew he was going to go right through the ceiling. She couldn't even blame him; she should never have let him touch her.

But oddly enough, he didn't say a word. He loosened his grip on her hips, allowing her to move away, and drew her gently into his arms. He held her, his head bending over her, his heartbeat shaking both of them, until his breathing was normal again.

Her hands felt the warm strength of his back even through his shirt, and she loved the protected feeling she got from being close like this. Her eyes closed and, just for a moment, she allowed herself the luxury of giving in completely, of pretending that he loved her.

"I could make you," he whispered at her ear. "I could take the choice away."

"Yes, I know," she agreed softly. Her cheek nuzzled against his chest.

"This kind of passion is a gift," he said quietly. "I

could give you pleasure in ways you've never had it with another man. Not because I'm any damned prize in bed, but because we react to each other like dynamite going up.''

"I can't," she replied softly. "I want to, but I can't."

His hand smoothed her long hair gently. "Because of him?"

She drew in a steadying breath. She was going to have to tell him, and it wasn't going to be easy.

The door opened, thank God, and Ada walked in, stopping dead when she saw the two of them wrapped in each other's arms.

"Wrestling match?" she guessed. "Who's winning?"

"Mistletoe," Egan murmured, nodding upward. "Damned potent stuff. She's got me on my knees."

"That'll be the day," Ada grinned.

Kati pulled away, and he let her go with obvious reluctance. "And I didn't poison you, either," she murmured, trying to keep it light.

"Didn't you?" he returned, but there was a difference in him now, a strangeness.

"No fighting," Ada said. "It's Christmas day."

"So it is," Egan said. "Where's my present?"

"Not until morning," Ada returned.

"Damn." He looked down at Kati. "I like presents. What did you get me?"

"Not until morning," she echoed Ada.

He lifted an eyebrow. "I hate waiting," he murmured, and only Kati knew what he meant.

"All good things come to him who waits, though,"

Ada interrupted; and then wondered why Kati blushed and Egan laughed.

The girls went in to bed, but Kati didn't sleep. She wanted Egan. And there was more to it than that. She was beginning to feel something she'd never expected. She thought ahead to the next day, when he'd leave for Wyoming, and the world went black. She couldn't imagine a day going by without the sight of him. Just the sight of him.

She sat straight up in bed and stared at the wall. She hadn't known that it could happen so quickly. Of course, it could be just physical attraction. She did want him very much, and it was the first time she'd wanted any man. She knew nothing about him really, except bits and pieces. So how, she asked herself, could she be in love with him?

"Love," she whispered out loud. She licked her dry lips and put it into words. "I...love...Egan." The sound of it made tingles all the way to her toes, and when she closed her eyes she could feel his mouth on hers; she could taste the minty warmth of his lips. Shivers went all over her like silvery caresses, and she caught her breath.

You have to forget all that, she told herself. Because what Egan wanted was the limited use of her body, to sate his own hunger. And once he'd had it, he'd be off to new conquests. Like Jennie. Her eyes clouded with bridled fury. Jennie! She'd like to rip the girl's hair out.

She lay back down and closed her eyes. Well, that was his kind of woman, anyway. All she had to do was grit her teeth and bear it until he left. Then she could pull her stupid self together and forget him. Her eyes opened. It was over an hour before she could close them in sleep.

Chapter 7

The thought of the condominium bothered Kati. She couldn't help remembering that Egan had said Ada didn't know about it, which meant he kept it for only one reason. If he was willing to take Kati there, he must have taken other women too. In the cold light of morning, she was glad she'd had the sense to resist him. Egan only wanted her. Someday, with a little luck, there would be a man who'd love her.

But if she was inclined to be cool and collected, Egan wasn't. He watched her covetously when she joined them for breakfast. His silver eyes roamed over the pretty red vest and skirt she was wearing with a long-sleeved white blouse, and he smiled appreciatively.

"Very Christmasy," he murmured.

She smiled as coolly as possible. "Thank you."

She allowed him to seat her, expecting Ada to plop

down beside her as usual. But instead, Egan slid into Ada's usual place, so close that his thigh touched hers when he moved.

"I can help," Kati volunteered quickly.

"No," Ada said as she dished up everything and carried it to the table. "Just sit. We'll both have enough to do later."

So she sat, nervously, hating the close contact because she could feel Egan as well as smell the warm, manly fragrance of his body. He was dressed up, too, in a navy pinstripe suit that made him look suave and sophisticated. And all the time she picked at her bacon and eggs, he watched her. It was as if he were launching a campaign, with her as the objective. And it was getting off to a rousing start.

Ada noticed the tension and smiled. Kati flushed at that smile, because she knew her friend's mind so well.

It didn't help that Ada finished early and announced that she just had to have a shower before she dressed.

"Afraid to be alone with me?" Egan teased gently when the door closed behind his sister.

"Oh yes," she admitted, looking up with fascinated eyes.

His own eyes seemed unusually kind and soft, and he smiled. "Why?" he asked. "Because of last night?"

She lowered her eyes to his smooth chin, his chiseled mouth. She remembered the feel of it with startling clarity.

"Don't hide." He tilted her face back up to his and

studied it quietly. "I can wait. At least, until you've had time to break it off with Asher."

So that was what he thought! That was why he'd been so patient last night. He assumed that she was sleeping with Jack and had to end the affair before...

She caught her breath. "But I can't—"

"Yes, you can," he said. "Just tell him how it is. He doesn't seem to be so unreasonable to me. In fact—" he laughed shortly "—he hardly touches you in public. A man who's committed to a woman usually shows a little more warmth."

"I don't like that kind of thing, around people," she murmured.

"Neither do I, for God's sake," he bit off. "But when people get involved, it happens sometimes. A look, a way of touching, a hand that can't let go of another hand—there are signs. You and Asher don't show them."

"He's...very reserved," she returned.

"So are you. Even alone with me." He leaned closer and brushed his mouth over hers like a breath. "Ada won't be gone that long. And then we'll be surrounded by people. And I won't be able to do this to you...."

His hand contracted behind her head, catching her hair, tangling in its fiery depths to press her mouth to his. As if passion were riding him hard, he bit at her closed lips and shocked them into parting. And then she was his. Totally his, as he explored the soft warmth of her mouth expertly, possessively.

When he stopped, her hands were clenched in his thick hair, and she moaned when he lifted his mouth.

"No more, baby," he whispered huskily. "We don't have the luxury of privacy, and I had a hard enough time sleeping last night as it was. A man can only stand so much."

Her eyes opened slowly and she looked up at him drowning in the silver of his eyes. "I didn't mean to tease," she whispered. "It wasn't like that."

"I know that," he replied quietly. "You were with me every step of the way, from the first second I touched you. Circumstances have been the problem. I need to be alone with you. Completely alone." He drew in a slow breath. "Come back to Wyoming with me, Kati."

Her eyes dilated. "What?"

"You said you had to research that damned book. All right. I'll help you. Fly out with me in the morning, and I'll show you everything you need to know about ranch management."

She studied his hard face. She knew exactly what he was saying: "during the day." His eyes were telling her that he had different plans for the night, and she already knew exactly what *they* were.

"Still afraid?" he asked thoughtfully, watching the expressions change on her young face. "Let's get it out in the open. Why? Do I strike you as a brutal man? Do you think I'd be kinky in bed or something?"

Her face burned and she looked down. "I've never thought about it."

"Liar. You've thought about it every second since yesterday morning, just like I have." He bent his head and kissed her quickly, roughly. "It was just the way I told you it would be. We touched each other and exploded. I wanted you, and it made me rough at first. But it won't be that way anymore. I promise you, Kati. I'll be as tender a lover as you could want."

"You...you never seemed gentle," she said involuntarily. "And you've been so harsh with me...."

He brushed a lock of hair back from her cheek and frowned as he looked down at her. "It's the way you write, damn it," he said. "So...openly."

"Egan, I don't make love with strange men in bathtubs," she said. It was one of the ironies of her life that she could write torrid romances at all. But the writing never embarrassed her. It was as if the characters did what they wanted to, taking over as the words went onto paper. The situations arose from the characterizations, not out of her own personal experience.

He shrugged. "That may be. But no man likes to think he's being used for research."

Her eyes opened wide. Her eyebrows went straight up. "You don't imagine that I...that I'd even consider—" She felt herself puffing up with indignation. "Oh, you monster!"

She jerked up from the table, glaring down at him as she fought tears of pure fury. "What do you think I am, damn you, an exhibitionist? What I write comes out of nowhere! The characters create themselves on paper, and their own motivations produce the love scenes! I do not write from personal experiences with a multitude of lovers!"

"Now, Kati," he began, rising slowly.

"But you just go on thinking whatever you please,

Egan,'' she continued. "You just go right ahead. I don't care. I don't need you at all!''

And she turned, tears in her eyes, and ran from the room, colliding with Ada.

"Hey, what's the matter?" Ada asked gently.

"Ask Dracula!" came the broken reply, and she threw a last accusing glare at Egan before she went into her room and slammed the door.

It was a bad start for the day. And it didn't help that when she got herself together and came back out, Egan had vanished. She'd overreacted, and she was ashamed. But his opinion of her had hurt in unexpected ways and brought home how he considered her widely experienced.

Wouldn't he be shocked, she thought miserably, to know how innocent she was?

In fact, the love scenes in her books were mild compared to those in other genres. They were sensuous, but hardly explicit. That was why she was able to write them. She didn't have to go into a lot of explanations that she'd have to dig out of anatomy books anyway— because she didn't know the first thing about fulfillment, except what she'd learned second-hand.

"Will he be back?" Kati asked miserably when Ada told her that Egan had walked out.

Ada lifted her shoulders helplessly. "I don't know. Things were going so well this morning. What happened?"

"He accused me of doing my own research for the love scenes," she muttered. "In bathtubs with strange men." She hid her face in her hands. "You can't imagine how it hurt to have him think so little of me!"

"Then why not tell him the truth, my dumb friend?" Ada asked. "He doesn't read minds, you know."

"Because…" She clenched her fists and hit the air impotently. "Because," her voice lowered, "the only thing about me that attracts him at all is my 'experience.'"

Ada gaped at her. "You're in love with him," she said half under her breath.

Kati smiled sadly. "Doesn't it show? Hasn't it always shown? Ada, I'd walk over a gas fire just to look at him."

"And I thought you hated him."

"I did. Because he hated me, and I knew it would never be more than that." She smoothed her hair. "And now it's worse, because he's like a bulldozer and I'm terrified of him."

"I warned you," Ada reminded her. "He's utterly relentless."

"He wants me to go home with him," she said.

Ada's face brightened. "He does?"

"Don't be silly, I can't go! If I do, he's bound to find out what an absolute idiot I am, and then where will I be? He'll throw me out on my ear!"

"And then again, he might not."

"I'm no gambler, Ada. Losing matters too much. I'd rather stay here and pull the pieces together. Maybe it's just a physical infatuation and I'll outgrow it," she added hopefully.

"If you'd walk through fire just to look at him, darling," Ada said gently, "it's got to be more than physical. And you know it."

"But what can I do?" Kati wailed. "Ada, I'm not the kind to have affairs. I'm too inhibited."

"Not when you write, you aren't!"

"That's different. When I write, I'm a storyteller, telling a story. In real life, I get too emotionally involved, and then I can't let go. And Egan hates even the idea of involvement."

"He looked pretty involved to me this morning. He could hardly take his eyes off you long enough to eat," Ada remarked.

"You know why, too."

"Men are attracted first; then their emotions get involved. Look at Marshal and me! He liked my legs, so he called me. And now here we are almost engaged!"

"And here it is Christmas and I've ruined it again," Kati moaned.

"No, you haven't. Egan will be back when he cools down. He's mad at himself, I'll bet, not at you." She smiled. "He didn't mean to hurt you."

Tears welled up in her eyes and she turned away. "I never meant to hurt him, either."

"Then cheer up. It will all work out, honest it will."

"So you keep saying. I'll try to listen this time."

They had everything ready just as Marshal and Jack arrived, and the four of them stood around and talked until noon.

"Should we wait for Egan?" Marshal asked.

"Well," Ada said, biting her lower lip. "I don't know when he'll be back."

Even as she said the words, the front door opened

and Egan walked in. He tossed his Stetson onto the hall table.

"Waiting for me? I got held up at Jennie's," he added, glancing toward Kati with pure malice in his eyes.

So much for Ada's helpful optimism, Kati thought as she took off her apron. She didn't even look at him again, and her entire attitude was so cool and controlled that she felt she deserved an Oscar for her performance all the way through the holiday meal. The turkey was perfectly browned, the ham beautifully glazed. Egan, at the head of the table, carved, and Ada passed the plates down. He said grace, and everyone was far too busy to talk for the first few minutes.

Kati was just bursting with fury about Jennie. She could imagine what Egan had been doing and why he'd been held up. She was rigid with the effort not to get up and fling the turkey carcass the length of the table at him.

"The cherry pie is delicious," Jack offered as he finished his last mouthful and followed it with the rich black coffee Ada had made.

"Thank you," Kati said with a smile.

"Kati does all the desserts," Ada told Marshal. "I'm no hand at pastry."

Egan hadn't touched any of the pies or fruitcake. He barely seemed to eat anything, like Kati. Her eyes found his across the room, and it was like lightning striking. She felt the longing she'd been fighting down all day coming to life again. It was incredible that she could look at him and go to pieces like this.

"Well, I hate to eat and run," Jack said, "but I

promised my cousin I'd stop by and see him and his family this afternoon. There are so few of us left these days.''

"Yes, I know what you mean," Ada said quietly, and her face showed the loneliness Kati knew she must feel this first Christmas without her mother.

"I'm sure you do. I'm sorry, I didn't mean to bring up such a sad subject," Jack apologized.

Ada smiled. "Don't be silly. Happy Christmas, Jack. I'm glad you could come."

"Me, too," Kati said, avoiding Egan's eyes as she got up to walk Jack to the door.

"I enjoyed it," Jack said. "Merry Christmas!"

Kati saw him out into the corridor. "I'll see you later, then."

Jack stared down at her quietly. "Do you realize how that big cattleman feels about you?" he asked unexpectedly.

Her face paled. "What?"

"He watched you as if he'd bleed to death looking. And the one time I smiled at you, I thought he was going to come over that table to get me." He laughed self-consciously. "If you get a minute, how about telling him that we haven't got anything serious going? I'd like to keep my insurance premiums where they are."

She laughed too, because they were friends who could ask such things of each other. "I'll do my best. Want to spend New Year's with us?"

"As far as I know, I don't have a thing planned. But," he added with a wink, "you might. So let's leave it alone for now, and I'll call you. All right?"

"All right. Merry Christmas," she added.

"You, too." He bent and kissed her lightly on the cheek. He was just lifting his head when Egan appeared in the doorway with eyes that glittered dangerously.

"You're taking a long time just to say good-bye," he muttered.

"Discussing the weather," Jack said quickly. "Damned cold outside! In here, too. Bye, Kati!" And he took off for the elevator with a grin.

Egan caught Kati's hand in his, holding it warmly, closely, and pulled her just inside the door. They were out of view of the living room, and when he closed the outside door, they might have been alone in the world.

"I can't stand it," he ground out, gripping her arms as if he were afraid she'd fly out of his reach. "You're driving me out of my mind, damn it!"

"You started it," she bit off, keeping her voice down.

"I didn't mean it, though," he returned in a harsh undertone. His hands loosened their grip, became caressing, burning her even through the blouse's long sleeves. "Kati, I'm so used to hitting at you...but this morning I didn't mean to."

Her lower lip trembled as she looked up at him. "You went to her," she said shakily.

Every trace of expression left his face, and only his eyes showed any emotion at all. They glittered at her like silver in sunlight. "I didn't touch her," he said huskily. "How could I? All I want in the world is you!"

Her lips parted, and before she could speak, he bent and caressed them slowly, sensuously, with his own. His breath was suddenly ragged, uneven, and the hands that were on her arms moved up to cup her face and hold it where he wanted it.

"Are you going to fight me every inch of the way?" he asked in a strained tone.

"I'm not," she protested dazedly.

"Then kiss me," he murmured.

She didn't understand what he meant until the pressure of his mouth forced hers open and she felt his tongue in a slow, even penetration that made her blood surge.

She gasped, and he deepened the kiss even more. She felt his body tremble, and he groaned softly— deep in his throat—like a man trying to control the impossible. He whispered her name under his breath and his arms went around her like chains. He crushed her into the taut muscles of his body until she hurt, and she didn't care. She wanted to be closer than this, even closer, with nothing in the way…!

"Kati?" Ada called from the living room.

In a fever of hunger, Kati watched Egan lift his head and take a slow, steadying breath.

"We're talking, all right?" he asked in what sounded like an almost normal tone.

"Oh, excuse me!" Ada called back. "Never mind!"

Egan's eyes burned down into Kati's. "Are you all right?" he whispered, watching the tears shimmer in her eyes.

"Yes. I...just...just feel kind of shaky," she stammered.

He took her hands to his hard chest and held them over the vest. "So do I," he said. "From the neck down. My God, you stir me up!"

Her eyes searched his slowly, curiously. "You're a passionate man," she whispered. "I imagine most women make you feel that way."

He shook his head very slowly. "I'm not promiscuous, Kati. I'm selective. It takes a very special woman."

She felt unreasonably flattered, but then, she wasn't thinking straight. How could she, this close to him, wanting him with a fever that was burning her alive?

"I'm scandalous, remember?" she said. "I seduce men to help me with my research—"

He stopped the words with a touch to her lips. "I'm not a virgin. How can I sit in judgment on you?"

"If you'd listen to me," she said softly, "I'd tell you."

"I don't want to hear it," he said curtly. "The past is over. We'll go from here. Are you coming home with me?"

And there was the question she'd wanted and dreaded, staring her in the face. She looked at him and knew she wasn't going to be strong and sensible. She could feel herself falling apart already.

"You won't...expect too much?" she asked hesitantly.

"Listen," he said, brushing his fingers over her warm cheek, "as far as I'm concerned, you're coming to learn about ranching for a book. You don't have to pay for your keep, Kati. In any way," he emphasized. "I'll let you come to me. I won't ask more than you want to give."

She lowered her eyes to his vest and wondered again, for the hundredth time, what it would be like with him—and knew that it was suicide to think about it.

"Come home with me," he said, tilting her face up to his. "The snow's sitting like a blanket on the Tetons, and the river's running through it like a silver thread. I'll show you where the buffalo used to graze and the mountain men camped."

He made it sound wildly romantic, and his eyes promised much more than a guided tour. It was crazy! She was crazy!

"I'll go home with you, Egan," she whispered.

His breath caught and he studied her eyes for a long moment before he bent to kiss her softly, slowly on her swollen lips. "There's a bear rug in front of the fireplace in my den," he breathed at her lips. "I've wondered…for years…how it would feel on bare skin, Kati."

A tiny, wild sound escaped from her throat, and he lifted her in his arms to kiss her roughly, possessively, until the whole world compressed into Egan's mouth and arms.

"Er-ahmmmm!" came a loud noise from the doorway.

Egan drew away with shaky reluctance and let Kati slide back to her feet just as Ada peeked around the corner.

"Marshal and I wondered if you'd like to go walking and look at the city," Ada asked, trying not to look as pleased as she felt.

"I'd like that," Egan said, smiling down into Kati's rapt face. "Would you?"

"Yes," she said dreamily.

"I hope you don't mind living alone for a couple of weeks, Ada," Egan added as he grabbed his hat and topcoat. "Because I'm taking Kati to Wyoming."

"You are?" Ada burst out, her face delighted.

"To help her with the book," he added, glaring at his sister. "Research, period."

"Oh, of course," Ada said, getting a firm grip on herself. "What else?"

Kati didn't dare look up. It would have blown her cool cover to pieces. Then Egan caught her small hand in his big one as they went to the elevator, and every thought in her head exploded in pleasure. Her fingers clung, locking into his. She walked beside him feeling as if she owned the world, oblivious to the beauty of New York City in holiday dress. Her present was right beside her.

It was almost dark when they came back to the apartment, after looking in store windows and eyeing the decorations around Madison and Fifth Avenues. Then they exchanged presents, and Kati was overwhelmed when she opened Egan's gift. It was a silver bracelet—pure silver with inlaid turquoise, and surely not a trinket. She looked up, pleasure beaming from her dark eyes, to thank him.

"Do you like it?" he said on a smile. "I like mine too."

She'd given him a new spinning reel, something

Ada said he'd appreciate. Although, at the time, pleasing Egan hadn't been on Kati's list of priorities, now she was glad she'd bought it. She saw the real appreciation in his eyes.

All too soon it was bedtime, and Ada was seeing Marshal out in a protracted good night.

"You'll have to get up early," Egan told Kati as they said their own good night at the door of her room. "I want to be out of here by eight."

She smiled. "I'll pack tonight. I have to bring my computer."

"One of those portable ones with a built-in telephone modem?" he asked knowledgeably.

She nodded. "It's my lifeline. I can't manage without it. It even has a printer built in."

"I carry one with me when I travel," he said. "We inventory our herds on computers these days, and use them to print out the production records for sales. I even sell off cattle by videotape. Ranching has moved into the twentieth century."

"I'll feel right at home," she said, laughing.

"I hope so," he said, his face softening as he looked down at her. "No strings, baby. I won't back you into any corners."

She nodded. "Sleep well."

"Without you?" he murmured wistfully. "No chance."

He bent and kissed her lightly. "Night."

And he was gone.

She walked into her room and closed the door, feeling impossibly happy and terrified all at the same time. What was going to happen when, inevitably, Egan dis-

covered that her reason for going wasn't his reason for
inviting her? Because things were bound to come to a
head. And either way, he'd discover for himself that
she wasn't the worldly woman he thought her. What
would he do? She shuddered. He'd probably be furious enough to put her on the first plane to New York.

She reached for the doorknob. She almost went to
tell him that she'd changed her mind. But the prospect
of even a few days alone with him—to glory in his
company—was like the prospect of heaven. And she
was too besotted to give it up. Just a day, she promised
herself. Just one day, and she'd confess everything and
let him do his worst. But she had to have that precious
time with him. It would last her all her life. It would
be all she'd ever have of him.

Chapter 8

Her first sight of the Tetons as she and Egan flew over Jackson Hole made Kati catch her breath.

Seated beside Egan in the ranch's small jet, she stared down at the velvety white tops of the jagged peaks with wonder.

"Oh, it's beautiful," she whispered. "The most beautiful thing I've ever seen!"

"You've never been here in the winter, have you?" he asked, smiling. "I'd forgotten. Honey, if you think this is something, wait until I get you on the Snake."

"Snake?" Her ears perked up and she looked at him apprehensively.

"River," he added. "From the ranch house, we overlook the Snake, and the Tetons look like they're sitting over us."

"I knew it was spectacular in the spring and summer," she sighed, staring back out the window. "But this is magic."

He watched her with quiet, smiling eyes. "I was born here, but it still sets me on my heels when I come home. A lot of battles have been fought over this land. By Shoshone and Arapaho and the white man, by ranchers and sheepmen and rustlers."

She glanced at him. "Are there still rustlers out West?"

"Of course, but now they work with trucks. We have a pretty good security system, though, so we don't lose many. Feeding the cattle during the winters is our biggest problem," he said. "We're pretty fanatical about haying out here, to get enough winter feed. A cow won't paw her way through the snow to get food, Kati. She'll stand there and starve first."

"I didn't know that," she said, fascinated.

"You've got a lot to learn, city lady," he said with a soft laugh. "But I'll teach you."

That, she thought, was what she feared. But she only smiled and watched the familiar lines of the big two-story white frame house come into view as they headed for the landing strip beyond it.

"How old is the house, Egan?" Kati asked after Egan had told the pilot to take the jet to the Jackson airport where it was based.

"Oh, I guess around eighty or ninety years," he said. He led her to a waiting pickup truck. "My grandfather built it."

"And called it White Lodge?" she asked, remembering that the ranch also was called by that name.

"No. That was my grandmother's idea. She was Shoshone," he added with a smile.

She studied him quietly. "And your grandfather? Was he dark?"

He nodded. "The sun burns us brown. Despite all the damned paperwork, I still spend a lot of time on horseback."

"Hi, Boss!" Ramey yelled out the window of the pickup truck.

"Hi, Ramey!" Egan called back. He opened the door and put Kati inside, jerking a thumb at Ramey to get him out from behind the wheel.

"I ain't such a bad driver," Ramey grumbled.

"I don't care what kind of driver you are," Egan reminded him as he got in next to Kati and shut the door. "Nobody drives me except me."

"On account of Larry ran him into a tree," Ramey explained as he shut his own door just before Egan started down the snowy ranch road. The young boy grinned at Egan's thunderous look. "Broke Larry's nose."

"Hitting the tree?" Kati asked innocently.

"Hitting the boss's fist afterward," Ramey chuckled.

Kati glanced at Egan. "And I thought you were the sweetest-tempered man I'd ever met," she said dryly.

Ramey's eyebrows arched. He started to speak, but Egan looked at him and that was all it took.

"Don't reckon you got a Chinook tucked in your bag somewheres?" Ramey asked instead, his blue eyes twinkling.

"A what?" Kati asked blankly.

"Chinook," Egan said. "It's a warm wind we get here in the winter. Melts the snow and gives us some relief." He looked over her head at Ramey. "How's the feed holding out?"

"Just fine. We'll make it, Gig says. Gig is our foreman," Ramey reminded her. "Kind of came with the ranch, if you know what I mean. Nobody knows how old he is, and nobody's keen to ask him."

"The answer might scare us," Egan chuckled. "Damn, this stuff is deep!"

He was running in the ruts Ramey had made coming to the landing strip, but it was still slow, hard going, and powdery snow was beginning to blow again.

"It'd be faster if we walked," Ramey suggested.

"Or rode." He shot a quick glance at Kati, letting his eyes run over her beige dress and high heels and short man-made fur coat. "God, wouldn't you look right at home on horseback in that? I almost made you change before we left Ada's."

She started to object to the wording and then let it go. Why start trouble?

"No comeback?" Egan chided. "No remarks about my tyrannical personality?"

"Why, Mr. Winthrop, I'm the very soul of tact," she said haughtily.

"Especially when you're telling me to go to hell," was the lightning comeback.

She flushed, noticing Ramey's puzzled look.

"We, uh, sometimes have our, uh, little differences," she tried to explain.

"Yes, ma'am, I recall," Ramey murmured, and she

remembered that he'd been nearby when she had walked furiously off the ranch that summer.

She cleared her throat. "Well, you do have the Tetons at your back door, don't you?" she asked Egan, who seemed to be enjoying her discomfort.

He followed her gaze to the high peaks rising behind the house. "Indeed we do. And the river within sight of the front door," he added, indicating the winding silver ribbon of the Snake that cut through the valley far below the house.

"Elk and moose and antelope graze out there during the winter," he told her. "And buffalo used to, in frontier days."

"I've never seen a moose," she said.

"Maybe this time," he told her.

She watched as Egan's elderly housekeeper waddled onto the front porch, shading her eyes against the blinding white of the snow. Egan left the truck idling for Ramey and lifted Kati off the seat and into his hard arms. The sheepskin coat he wore made him seem twice as broad across the chest and shoulders.

"You're hardly equipped for walking in the snow," he murmured, indicating her high heels. "I hope you packed some sensible things."

"Hiking boots, jeans and sweaters," she said smartly.

"Good girl. Hold on."

She clung as he strode easily through the high blanket of snow and up onto the steps, his boots echoing even through the snow against the hard wood. Dessie Teal was watching with a grin, her broad face all smiles under her brown eyes and salt-and-pepper hair.

"I never would have believed it," she muttered as Egan set Kati back on her feet. "And I don't see a bruise on either one of you."

"We don't fight all the time," Egan said coolly.

"Well, neither do them Arabs, Egan," Dessie returned, "but I was just remarking how nice it was that you and Miss James seemed to be in a state of temporary truce, that's all."

"She came to research a book about Wyoming in the old days," Egan told the old woman gruffly, his eyes daring her to make anything else of it.

Dessie shrugged. "Whatever you want to call it. A book about frontier days, huh?" she asked, leading Kati into the house. "Well, you just go talk to Gig, he'll tell you more than any book will. His daddy fought in the Johnson County range war."

Kati asked what that had been about and was treated to fifteen minutes of Wyoming history, including references to the range wars between cattlemen and sheepmen, and the ferocity of Wyoming winters.

"My brother froze to death working cattle one winter," Dessie added later, when Kati had changed into jeans, boots and a sweater and was drinking coffee with the housekeeper in the kitchen. "He fell and broke his leg and couldn't get up again. He was solid ice when one of the men found him." She shivered delicately. "This ain't the place for tenderfeet, I'll tell you." She paused in the act of putting a big roast into the oven. "How come you and Egan ain't fighting?"

"He's trying to get me into bed," Kati returned bluntly and grinned wickedly at the housekeeper's blush.

"I deserved that," Dessie muttered and burst into laughter. "I sure did. Ask a foolish question... Well, I might as well make it worse. Is he going to?"

Kati shook her head slowly. "Not my kind of life," she said. "I'm too old-fashioned."

"Good for you," Dessie said vehemently. "Honest to God, I don't know what's got into girls these days. Why, we used to go two or three dates before we'd hold hands with a boy. Nowadays, it's into bed on the first one. And they wonder why nobody's happy. You gorge yourself on candy and you don't want it no more. At least, that's how I see it."

"You and I should join a missionary society," Kati told her. "We don't belong in the modern world."

Dessie grinned at her. "Well, speaking for myself, I ain't in it. Can't get much more primitive than this, I reckon, despite all the modern gadgets Egan bought me for the kitchen."

"I understand what you mean." She leaned back in the chair and sipped her coffee. "Did Egan really not want to be a rancher?" she asked.

Dessie measured that question before she answered it. "I don't think he knew exactly what he did want. Politics used to fascinate him. But then, so did business. And that's mostly what ranching is these days; it's business. He has Gig to look after the practical side of it while he buys and sells cattle and concentrates on herd improvement and diversification." She grinned sheepishly. "What big words!"

"Is he happy?" Kati asked, because it mattered.

"No," Dessie said quietly. "He's got nobody except Miss Ada."

Kati studied her coffee cup, amazed at how deeply that hurt her. "He's…not handsome, but he has a way with him. And he attracts women," she added, remembering Jennie.

"Not the right kind of women," came the tart reply. "Not ever one he could bring to this ranch. Until now."

Kati blushed to the roots of her hair.

"Now what are you doing?" Egan growled from the doorway, taking in Kati's red face and Dessie's shocked expression at his sudden appearance. "Talking about me behind my back, I guess?"

"Well, who else is there to talk about?" Dessie threw up her hands. "I never see anybody except you. Well, there's Ramey, of course, but he don't do nothing interesting enough to gossip about, does he?"

Egan shook his head on a tired sigh. "I guess not. Damn. You and your logical arguments." He took off his hat and coat. "What's for dinner? I'm half-starved."

"You're always half-starved. There's some sliced turkey in the refrigerator, left over from my solitary Christmas dinner I had all by myself, alone, yesterday."

Egan glanced at the old woman. "Did you have a good time?" he asked.

"I told you I ate by myself!" Dessie growled.

"Well, I guess that means you didn't have any company," Egan said pleasantly.

"Wait," the housekeeper said, "until tonight. And see what I feed you for supper."

"Let me die of starvation, then," he said. "I'll call

up Ada and tell her you won't feed me, and see what you do then!''

Dessie threw down her apron. "Hard case," she accused, her lower lips thrusting out. "Just hit me in my weakest spot, why don't you?"

Egan grinned, winking at Kati, who was seeing a side of him she hadn't dreamed existed. She liked this big, laughing man who seemed so at home in the wilderness.

He even looked different from the man in the pinstripe suit in Ada's apartment. He was wearing denim now, from head to foot, and a pair of disreputable brown boots that had seen better days— along with a hat that was surely obsolete. The only relatively new piece of apparel he had was the sheepskin coat he'd just taken off. But he seemed bigger and tougher and in every way more appealing than the sophisticated executive.

"You look different," Kati remarked absently, watching him.

He cocked an eyebrow as he carried turkey and mayonnaise to the table. "I do?"

"His looks ain't improved," Dessie argued.

"Just mind your own business, thank you," he drawled in her direction and watched her go back to her roast. "And don't burn that thing up like you did the last one!"

"I didn't burn nothing up," she shot back. "That stupid dog of yours got in here and reared up on my stove and changed the heat setting!"

"Durango doesn't get in the house," he told her.

"And he isn't smart enough to work a stove, despite being the best cattle dog I own."

"Well, I wouldn't turn my back on him," she muttered. She put the roast in the oven and closed the door. "Excuse me. I got to go to the cellar and get apples. I thought you might like an apple pie. Not that you deserve one," she added, glaring back as she went out the door.

He only laughed. "Get the bread, honey, and I'll make you one too," he told Kati.

"Where is it?"

"In the breadbox."

She got up and went to the cabinet to get it, but before she could turn around, he was behind her, the length of his body threatening and warm.

"Fell right into the trap, didn't you?" he breathed, turning her so that her back was against the wall. With his hands on the wall beside her, he eased down so that his body pressed wholly on hers, in a contact that made the blood surge into her face.

"God, it's wild like this, isn't it?" he said unsteadily. "I can feel you burning like a brand under every inch of me."

She opened her lips to speak, and he bent and took them. His mouth was cold from the outdoors, but hers warmed it, so that seconds later it was blazing with heat. A moan growled out of his throat into her hungry, wanting mouth.

She felt his tongue, and her eyes opened suddenly, finding his closed, his brows drawn, as he savored the pleasure. But as if he felt her looking at him, the thick lashes moved up and his darkening silver eyes looked straight into hers.

On a caught breath he lifted his lips just fractionally over hers. "Now, that's exciting," he whispered. "I've never watched a woman while I kissed her."

But obviously he was going to, because his eyes stayed open when he bent again, and so did hers. The hunger and need in his kiss inflamed her, and her hands found their way to the top button on his shirt.

She'd never wanted to touch a man's bare skin. She couldn't remember a time in her life when the thought had appealed. But it did now. She could feel the crush of his hips and thighs over hers, and explosive sensations were curling her toes.

Her fingers toyed with his top button while she tried to decide how risky it would be. He was hungry enough without being tempted further, and she wasn't sure she could handle him.

He lifted his head and watched her fingers. "Are you always this unsure of yourself with a man?" he asked under his breath. "Or is it just me? Touch me if you want to, Kati. I won't lose my head and bend you back over the kitchen table."

The wording made it sound cheap, made her sound cheap. The color went out of her face and she eased away from him.

He swore quietly, watching her get the bread and some saucers and start making sandwiches in a strained silence.

"What do you want from me?" he ground out.

She drew in a steadying breath. "I'd settle for a little respect. Not much. Just what you'd give any stranger who came into your house.'' Tears welled in her eyes as she spread mayonnaise. "I'm not a tramp, Egan Winthrop.''

He watched a solitary tear land with a splatter on the clean tabletop, and his hands caught her waist convulsively, jerking her back against him.

"Don't...cry," he bit off, his fingers hurting.

"Don't touch me!" she threw back, twisting away from him.

He held onto the edge of the table, glaring as she wiped the tears away and finished making the sandwiches. She pushed his at him and went to put the knife in the sink.

He poured coffee into her cup and his, put the pot away and sat down. She followed suit, but she ate in silence, not even looking at him. Fool, she told herself. You stupid fool, you had to come with him!

Dessie came back to a grinding silence. She stared at them, apples in her apron, and grimaced. "I leave you alone five minutes and you start a war.''

Egan finished his coffee and got up, not rising to the bait. "I've got work to do.''

He grabbed his coat and hat and stamped out the door. Kati brushed away more tears. Dessie just shook her head and started peeling apples. After a minute, she got another bowl and knife and pushed them at Kati.

"Might as well peel," she told her. "It'll give your hands something to do while your mind works.''

"Mine doesn't work," Kati replied coldly. "If it did, I'd still be in New York.''

"Not many people get under his skin like that,''

Dessie commented with a slow grin. "Good to know he's still human."

"Well, I'd need proof," Kati glowered.

"I think you'll get it," came the laughing reply. "Now, peel, if you want an apple pie."

Kati gave in. And it *was* rather soothing, peeling apples. She had a feeling she was going to make a lot of pies before she got her research done.

Chapter 9

After that little episode, Egan became remote. He was the perfect host, polite and courteous, but about as warm as one of the rocks on his land.

Kati decided that if he could play it cool, so could she. So she was equally polite. And distant. Oddly enough, there were no more violent arguments like the ones they had in the past. Once in a while, she'd notice Egan watching her over the supper table before he disappeared into his study to work, or during a rare minute in the morning before he went to his office down the road. But he kept to himself, and the affectionate, hungry man who'd brought her to the ranch seemed to have vanished into his former, cold counterpart.

But she did accomplish one of her goals. She learned enough about ranching to do a nonfiction work on it.

The logistics of supplies fascinated her. Egan's cows and second-year heifers were bred to drop calves in February and March. So during January, the ranch manager and his men were very much involved in pre-calving planning. That meant buying ear tags, identifying first-calf heifers, checking breeding dates to estimate calving dates and arranging for adequate facilities.

Because of the increased herd, move calving pens had to be added, but those were erected during the fall. The cowboys were closely watching the cows now to make sure there were no problems. One of the older hands told her that he always hated being a cowboy during this time of the year and at roundup in the spring, when the cattle had to be branded, vetted, and moved about fifty miles away to summer pasture.

Listening to the men tell about their adventures took up the better part of her days. She was careful not to interfere with their work, having been cautioned by the boss about that. But she was around during breaks and sometimes after dinner, with her pad and pen in hand, asking questions.

It would have been all right if Ramey hadn't asked her to go to a dance with him. Egan happened to overhear the question, and before Kati could even get her mouth open to say "No, thanks," Egan was on top of them.

"If you're through irritating the men," he told her cuttingly, "they need their rest."

She rose, embarrassed to tears but too proud to show it. "Excuse me, I didn't realize—"

"But, boss," Ramey groaned, "she wasn't bothering us!"

There was a loud tumult as the other cowboys in the bunkhouse agreed with pathetic eagerness.

"All the same, good night," Egan said in his coldest tone. He held the door open; Kati, seeing defeat, shrugged, calling a smiling good night to the men and walked knee-deep in the melting snow back to the truck she'd commandeered for the drive down.

"This way," Egan said curtly, taking her arm. He led her to his pickup truck and put her inside.

"I was just asking questions," she muttered. "You told me not to interfere with their work."

"I didn't say you could sleep with them," he growled.

"You pig!" she burst out. Her eyes blazed; her lips trembled with fury. "How dare you accuse me of such a thing!"

"Ramey asked you out—did you think I didn't hear him?" he asked. He fumbled for a cigarette, surprising her, because she'd seen him smoke only once or twice in the past few days.

"I was going to refuse," she replied. "He's a nice boy, but—"

"But not experienced enough for a woman like you, right?" he asked, smiling insolently.

Her breath stopped. "What exactly do you mean, 'a woman like me'?" she asked deliberately.

"What do you think I mean?"

She clutched the pen and pad in her hand and stared straight ahead.

"No comeback?"

"I won't need one. I'm going home."

"Like hell you are."

"What do you plan to do, Mr. Winthrop, tie me up in a line cabin?"

"Who taught you about line cabins?"

"Gig," she said uncomfortably, remembering the long, amusing talk she'd had with the sly old foreman.

"Gig never talks to anybody, not even me."

"Well, he talks to me," she shot back. "But I guess you'll accuse me of trying to get him into bed too!"

"You'd hate it," he said, lifting the cigarette to his mouth. "He only bathes once a month."

She tried to keep her temper blazing, but she lost and hid the muffled laugh in her hands.

He glanced at her, his eyes sparkling. "If I stop making objectionable remarks to you," he said after a minute, "do you suppose we might try to get along for the duration?"

"I don't think that's possible," she said, glancing at him. "You won't even give me the benefit of a doubt."

"I've read your books," he reminded her.

"How in God's name do you think Edgar Rice Burroughs wrote *Tarzan of the Apes?*" she exploded. "Do you believe that he swung from trees in darkest Africa? When he wrote the first book, he'd never even seen Africa!"

He pulled up at the front door and cut off the engine. "Are you trying to tell me that a woman could write a sexy book without having had sex?" He laughed. "No dice, baby. I'm not stupid."

"That depends on your definitions," she returned hotly. "About me, yes, sir, you are stupid."

"Only when you kiss me in that slow, hot way," he murmured, smiling wickedly, "and try to take off my shirt."

She slammed the pen against the pad impotently and glared at him.

"All right," he said after a minute and crushed out the cigarette. "I'll apologize for the crude remark I made in the kitchen. Will that pacify you?"

"I want to make something crystal-clear," she returned, gripping the pad tightly. "As far as I'm concerned, I'm here to research a book."

His eyes darkened and he studied her closely. "Put it in words, not innuendos."

"I don't want to be mauled around," she replied.

"Tell Ramey. He was the one who wanted to take you off into the woods," he said on a laugh.

"So did you!" she accused.

He shook his head. "No. I wanted to take you into my bed. There's a difference."

"Geographical," she countered.

He sighed and reached out to smooth a long, unruly strand of her hair. "I want you. I haven't made any secret of it. You want me, too. It's just going to take more time than I thought."

"I won't sleep with you," she told him.

"You will," he replied softly, searching her eyes. "Eventually."

"Is that a threat?" she asked, finding her fighting feet.

"No, ma'am," he said, grinning.

She glared at him uncertainly. "I don't understand you."

"You've got a whole lot of company," he told her. He dropped her hair. "Better get some rest. And don't go back to the bunkhouse at night. Keeps the boys awake."

"I have to find out some things about calving," she protested.

"Do you? What do you want to know?" he asked with a wicked smile.

"Oh, stuff your hat...!" she began.

"Now, now, you mustn't shock me," he told her as he got out of the truck. "I'm just an unsophisticated country boy, you know."

"Like hell," she muttered under her breath.

He opened her door and lifted her into his arms. She started to struggle, but he held her implacably and shook his head.

"Don't fight," he said. "We've spent days avoiding each other. I just want to hold you."

She felt a rush of feeling that should have made her run screaming the other way. But instead, she put her arms—pad and pen and all—around his neck and let him carry her. By the time he got to the steps, her face was buried in his warm throat and her heartbeat was shaking her.

"We haven't made love since we were in New York," he whispered as he carried her into his study and deliberately locked the door behind him.

She felt her lips go dry as she looked up at him. He was taking off his hat and coat, and the way he was staring at her made her feel threatened.

"No more games, Katriane," he said softly. He took away the pad and pen, and, bending, took off her warm coat and dropped it beside his on the chair. He lifted her off the floor. "I won't hurt you. But I've gone hungry too long."

There would never be a better time to tell him the truth. But just as she started to, he bent and pressed his open mouth against the peak of her breast. She cried out, shocked speechless at the intimacy of it even through two layers of cloth.

He didn't say a word. She felt him lower her, felt the soft pile of a rug under her back. And then his body was spreading over hers like a heavy blanket, making fires that blazed up and burned in exquisite torment.

His mouth moved up to hers, taking it with a power and masculine possessiveness that she'd never felt before. She wasn't even aware of what his hands were doing until he lifted her and she felt the slight chill of the room and the heat of the blazing fire in the hearth on her bare flesh.

"Egan," she protested shakily as he laid her back down.

"God, you're something!" he breathed, looking down with wild, glittering eyes on what he'd uncovered. His hands went to the buttons on his shirt and unfastened them slowly, methodically. He pulled the shirt free of his jeans and stripped it off, revealing bronzed skin that shimmered smoothly in the light of the fire.

Her eyes fastened on him hungrily, loving every

rugged line of him, wanting the feel of his hard muscles against her own trembling softness.

There was only the crackle of the fire as they looked at each other, only its reddish glow in the room. She knew what he was going to do, but she was powerless to stop him. She loved him. Oh God, she loved him!

He came down slowly, easing his chest over hers by levering himself over her on his arms. His eyes held hers every second as he brushed his chest against her taut breasts and watched the wild, sweet surge of her body upward to make the contact even closer.

"Don't hold anything back with me," he said under his breath. "And I'll please you until you scream with it."

His mouth eased down as his chest did, and she reached up to catch his head in her hands, tangle her fingers in his hair while he kissed the breath from her swollen mouth.

She experienced her own power when she felt the tremor in his long body; and without thinking about consequences, she tugged his head up and shifted to bring his lips down to the bareness of her body.

"Kati!" he burst out as if she'd surprised him, and he dug his hands in under her back. His mouth opened, and she felt his tongue, his teeth at flesh that had never even known a man's eyes.

Her body rippled in his arms, on waves of sweetness, and she moaned as his mouth learned every smooth inch of her above the waist. He rolled suddenly onto his back, bringing her with him, and she felt his hands going under the waistband of her jeans onto the softness of her lower spine.

"Look at me," he said in a husky tone.

She lifted her head just as his clean, strong hands contracted, and he smiled at the hunger he could read in her eyes.

He nipped her earlobe with his teeth and whispered things that excited and shocked, all at once, embarrassing things that she'd only read until that moment.

"Egan," she protested weakly.

"Just relax," he whispered, bringing her hips back against his in a slow, sweet rotation. "Let me show you how much I want you."

He ground her hips into the powerful, taut muscles of his own. She cried out as he freed one hand to bring her shaking mouth down onto his, thrusting his tongue up into it in a rhythm that said more than words.

"My room," he whispered. "Right now."

He rolled her over and handed her the blouse and sweater he had taken off her minutes before. "You'd better put those on," he said in a taut undertone. "In case Dessie's still up."

She clutched the cool things to her, staring at him like someone coming out of a trance.

"Well?" he ground out. "My God, you felt what you've done to me. I need you, damn it!"

She swallowed, trying to find the right words. "I need you too, Egan," she said shakily. "But there's something you'd…you'd better know first."

"What? That you aren't on the pill?" he demanded. "It's all right, I'll take care of it. I won't let you get pregnant."

She blushed and lowered her eyes to the jerky rise

and fall of his chest. Her fingers tightened on the shirt and sweater. "I'm a virgin."

"My God, that's a good one." He laughed coldly. "Try again."

"I don't have to," she said, trying to hold on to her pride and her self-respect, both of which were slipping. "I've told you the truth."

"Sure, I'm a virgin, too," he told her. "Now can we go to bed?"

"Go right ahead," she said with venom in her tone. "But without me! Didn't you hear what I said, damn you, I'm a virgin!"

"At twenty-five?" he asked in a biting tone. "Writing the kind of books you write?"

"I've told you until I'm blue in the face that I don't research those love scenes—most of which are foreplay with a hint of fulfillment!" She flushed, avoiding his eyes. "And some of that is obligatory; I can't get historical fiction published without it. And as for men…" she added, lifting her face to glare at him, "most of them have felt as you do, that a woman's place in the modern world is to be available for sex and then disappear before anyone gets emotional. I can't live like that, so I don't indulge."

"Never?" he burst out.

"Never!" she returned. "Egan, didn't Ada ever tell you about my parents?"

His breathing was steadier now, but he still looked frustrated and full of venom. "That they were old?"

She took another steadying breath of her own. "My father was a Presbyterian minister," she whispered.

"And my mother had been a missionary. Now do you understand?"

He looked as if he'd been slapped. His eyes went over her, right down to the fingers that trembled on her discarded top. "Why didn't you tell me?" he ground out. "My God, the things I said to you…!"

He got to his feet and grabbed up his shirt, shouldering angrily into it. "Get out of here," he said coldly.

She managed to get to her feet gracefully, pausing as she tried to decide between running for it and dressing first.

"Put on your blouse, for heaven's sake!" he snapped, and turned away again to light a cigarette with jerky motions.

She put on the blouse and pulled the sweater on over it without ever fastening a button. She couldn't even look at him as she walked toward the door. Her fingers fumbled with the lock, and when she pulled the door open, he still hadn't turned or said a word. She closed it quietly behind her with trembling fingers and went upstairs as quickly as she could. When she was safely in her room, with her own door locked, she burst into tears.

Chapter 10

It was the most agonizing night Kati remembered spending. Egan had bruised her emotions in ways she hadn't dreamed possible. Rejecting her was enough of a blow. But couldn't he have done it gently? She cringed, thinking of the way he'd been, the things he'd said until she confessed. Ada had warned her. Why hadn't she listened?

Worst of all was the fact that she'd been more than ready to give in to anything he wanted of her. She'd wanted him to know the truth because he was so hungry that she was afraid of being hurt the first time. But her revelation had backfired. Instead of comforting her, he ordered her out of the room and turned his back.

Well, at least she knew how he really felt now, she told herself miserably. She knew that he'd only wanted her, and there was no feeling on his part except desire.

She couldn't remember ever hurting so much. She loved him. What she'd felt in his hard, expert embrace was something she'd never get over. But he'd turned away as if such devastating interludes were just run-of-the-mill. To him, they probably were. With good-time girls like Jennie.

She got up well before daylight. She packed quickly and dressed in her boots and jeans and a burgundy sweater. She decided to go downstairs and have breakfast, and make sure Egan had left the house before she called a cab. It was eight o'clock, and he was usually long gone by then. She didn't know how she could face him if he was still there, not after last night. It made her color, just remembering the things they'd done together.

Her footsteps slowed as she reached the kitchen. She pushed the door open part way and found Dessie puttering around the stove. With a sigh of relief, she pushed it open the rest of the way and came face to face with Egan, who was just behind it picking up his hat from the counter.

She actually jumped aside. He looked down at her with an expression she couldn't read. His eyes were dark silver, cold, angry.

"I want to talk to you for a minute," he said curtly.

He didn't give her a chance to protest. He propelled her through the door and down the hall to the living room. He shut the door behind them and stared hard at her.

"Before you start," she said in a painfully subdued tone, "I realize it was all my fault, and I'm sorry."

He pulled a cigarette from his pocket and lit it, his

fingers steady. "We won't talk about last night," he said. "Stay the week out, finish your research. If you run off this morning, you'll just upset Dessie and Ada."

"What do you mean, if I run off?" she countered defensively.

"Aren't your bags packed already?" he asked, lifting his head at an arrogant angle.

Damn his perception, she thought furiously, turning her eyes to the curtained windows. "Yes," she snapped.

"Then unpack them. You came here, obviously, for a different reason than I brought you," he said with the old, familiar mockery. "Since your work is obviously so important, by all means indulge yourself. Just stay out of the bunkhouse after dark. We've got a couple of new men that I don't know well."

"The only people I really need to talk to are Gig and Ramey," she told him with what dignity she could muster. "Would you mind if I asked them up to the house?"

"Don't be ridiculous," he shot back through a cloud of smoke. "I don't play the master around here; the men are always welcome."

"I didn't mean it that way," she said. She wrapped her arms around her. "Please don't hate me, Egan."

He stood, breathing slowly, deliberately, while his eyes accused. "You knew why I invited you here, Kati," he said after a minute, and his manner was colder than the snow outside. "I didn't make any secret of wanting you. I assumed you felt the same way."

Her eyes lowered to his shirtfront. "I thought I could go through with it," she confessed. "But, last night—" She swallowed. "I was afraid that if I didn't tell you the truth, you'd hurt me."

He made an odd noise deep in his throat and turned away, smoking his cigarette quietly while the clock on the mantel ticked with unnatural loudness.

"I told you once that I like my women experienced. I meant it. I have no taste whatsoever for virgins." He took another harsh draw from the cigarette and moved restlessly around the room, oblivious to her slight flinch. "You're safe for the duration, Miss James," he said finally, glaring at her. "I wouldn't touch you now to save this ranch."

She would have died before she'd let him see how much that hurt. Her face lifted with what pride she had left. "I won't get in your way," she promised quietly.

"Well, that's comforting," he said sarcastically, and with a smile she didn't like.

Her arms tightened where she had them folded over her breasts. "If that's all, I'd like to have some coffee."

"Help yourself."

She left him, her heart around her ankles. It had been better when she hated him, when she didn't have the memory of his hungry ardor to haunt her. But he'd closed all the doors just now, and there wouldn't be any openings again. He'd as much as said so. Virgins didn't interest him.

She laughed miserably to herself. At least he hadn't guessed that she was in love with him. He hadn't understood that she couldn't have given herself without loving, and that was a blessing. She'd finish her research and get out of there. And once she did, she never wanted to see Egan again. It would be too painful.

For the rest of the day, she went through the motions of living without really feeling much of anything. Dessie noticed, but was kind enough not to say anything.

Finally, faced with imminent insanity or work, Kati chose work. She got out the portable computer and began to write, putting all her frustrations and irritations down on paper in a letter to Egan telling him just what she thought of him. She read it over and then erased every word from the screen without ever having fed it to her printer. She felt much better. Then she began work on the book.

Somehow, writing took all the venom out of her. She created without knowing how she did it, watching the characters unfold on paper, feeling the life-force in them even as she put the words down. When she looked at the clock, she realized that she'd been working for hours. She put the information on tape and then ran it off on the printer for hard copy. After a shower, she went downstairs to see if she could help Dessie with supper.

"No need," Dessie told her with a grin. "We've having beef stew and homemade rolls and a salad. Suit you?"

"Oh, yes! I love beef stew!" she enthused.

"You'll like this—it's our own beef. Want to sit down while I dish it up?"

Kati eased into a chair, noticing that only two places were set. "Just us two?" she asked as casually as she could.

"Boss is helping at the calving sheds. Had a handful of first-time heifers calving tonight, and they've already had to pull one. Gets expensive if you lose too many calves," she explained.

"Is the snow still melting?"

"No, worse luck," Dessie grumbled as she put the food on the table. "Weatherman says it's going to come again tonight. I've seen it so that the snow was over the door."

Kati's heart lodged in her throat. "That high?"

"This is Wyoming," came the laughing reply. "Everything's bigger out West, didn't you know? Now, don't you worry. The boys would dig us out if we got snowed in. And we could get another Chinook."

"I remember a painting by Russell," Kati murmured. "A drawing of a cow freezing in the snow, surrounded by wolves, with the legend 'waiting for a Chinook.' I didn't understand it until now."

"See? You're learning." She nibbled at her stew, watching the younger woman curiously. "Uh, you wouldn't care to tell me a little about this new book? I've read all your others."

Kati's face brightened. "You have?"

"Sure. Well, I know you, sort of." She shifted in the chair. "Gave the girls at the bookstore a charge when I told them that." She glanced up. "I like the books, though, or I wouldn't spend good money on them."

"Just for that," Kati said, "I'll tell you the whole plot."

And Dessie sat, rapt, sighing and smiling, while the entire book was outlined.

"What does the hero look like this time?" Dessie asked finally. "Is he blond like your others?"

"No, this one is dark and has silver eyes."

"Like Egan?"

Kati's face flamed red. "His eyes are...gray," she protested.

"Not when he's mad, they ain't. They're silver, and they gleam." She reached over and patted the young woman's hand. "Listen, I don't tell Egan nothing. I won't spill the beans, so don't start clamming up. These eyes of mine may be old, but they don't miss a lot. Besides," she added, sipping coffee, "this morning he ate sausage."

"What does that mean?"

"Egan eats bacon or ham. He hates sausage. I cook it for me." She grinned. "He wouldn't have noticed if I'd fed him raw eggs. In a nasty temper, he was."

And Kati knew why, but she wasn't rising to the bait. "Maybe his tastes have changed."

"Oh, I know that," Dessie said casually. "Yes, I do. Have some more stew."

The snow came all night, but Egan didn't appear. It was late the next morning before Kati got a glimpse of him. He came in cursing, stripping off his jacket as he strode toward his study.

"Damned bull," he muttered. "I should have had his horns cut off... Dessie!" he yelled.

She came running, her apron flapping, while Kati stood frozen on the staircase.

"What?" Dessie asked.

"That big Hereford bull of mine got Al," he grumbled. "Get some bandages and disinfectant and I'll drive you down to the bunkhouse to bandage him until I can get the doctor here. I've sent Ramey to fetch him." He jerked up the phone. "Kati!" he called.

She walked in as he was punching buttons. "What can I do?" she asked hesitantly.

"You can stay with Al's wife and keep her quiet," he told her. He held up his hand and spoke into the phone. "Brad, have the boys tracked that wolf yet? Well, call Harry Two Toes and get him to meet me at the house in twenty minutes. Tell him I'll pay him a thousand dollars for that damned wolf. Right." He hung up the receiver. "Al's wife, Barbara, is pregnant with their first child," he continued, his eyes dark and steady on hers. "I won't let her see him. She gets hysterical at the sight of blood, and she's miscarried twice already. Will you stay with her?"

"Of course," she said without hesitation. "How old is she?"

"Twenty. Just a baby herself. Al was trying to check a sore on that damned bull, and he turned wrong. It's my fault, I should have had him dehorned," he said shortly as he rose from the desk. "Got Al in the stomach. That's a bad place to get gored."

"If he works for you, he must be tough," she said quietly. "He'll be all right, Egan."

His eyes searched hers for a long moment. He turned away. "Get a coat, honey."

She thrilled to the endearment, although she knew that he was worried and probably hadn't realized he was saying it. She ran up the stairs to get her overcoat and knitted hat, and hurried back. Dessie was already wearing a thick corduroy coat of her own, a floppy old hat and hightop boots.

"Let's go," Egan murmured, herding them out into the snow where the truck was parked.

It was slow going. The road was half obscured by the thick, heavy flakes that fell relentlessly. It seemed to take forever to get to the bunkhouse. Egan had Kati wait in the car while he got Dessie inside and checked to see how Al was. He was back minutes later.

"He's stopped bleeding, at least on the outside," he said heavily as he pulled the truck back onto the ruts. "But he's lost color and he's hurting pretty bad. He'll need to go to the hospital, I'm damned sure of that. I told the boys to get him into one of the pickups and put a camper over it and take him into town. I had Ken call Ramey on the radio and have him go on to the hospital instead of to the doctor's and alert the emergency room."

"It's starting out to be a rough day, isn't it?" she asked, thinking of the poor man's wife as well, who still had to be told about the accident.

"Worse." He lit another cigarette. "We had two cows brought down by a wolf and savaged."

"One wolf?" she asked.

"He's old and wily," he told her shortly. "I've lost cows and calves to him for several months now, and

I'm at the end of my patience. I'm going to get an Arapaho tracker I know to help me find him.''

''You must be losing a lot of money if the wolf is bringing down that many cattle.''

''That's not why. I hate killing even a mangy wolf, with the environment in the mess it's in. But you've never seen a cow or a horse that's been attacked by a wolf.'' His jaws set. ''They don't quite kill the animals, you see.''

She did, graphically, and her face paled. ''Oh.''

''We'll trap him and free him in the high country.'' He turned the truck into the driveway of a small house not far below the bunkhouse.

''Will wolves attack people?'' she asked uneasily.

''Not you,'' he said, half amused. ''You won't be walking this ranch alone.''

''That's not what I meant.'' She glanced at him silently.

''Worried about me?'' he asked mockingly.

She turned away. ''Maybe I was worrying about the wolf,'' she grumbled.

He got out and helped her over the high bank of snow. She noticed that he didn't offer to carry her this time, and she was glad. It was torture to be close to him, with all the memories between them.

''Try to make her rest as much as you can,'' Egan said before he knocked on the door. ''I'll have Ramey call here just as soon as the doctor's examined Al.''

''All right. I'll take care of her.''

The door opened, and a pretty young girl with dark hair and eyes opened it. ''Egan!'' she said enthusiastically. ''What brings you here?''

His eyes went from her swollen belly back to her face and he grimaced. He pulled off his hat. "Barbara, my new Hereford bull gored Al," he said softly. "He's all right, but I've had the boys drive him in to see the doctor."

The girl's face went pale, and Kati stepped forward quickly, as Egan did, to help her back inside and onto a chair.

"I'm Kati," she told the girl as she led her to the chair and eased her bulky figure down into it. "I'm going to stay with you. He'll be all right, Barbara. Egan said so."

Egan looked down at her with a faint smile in his eyes. "I'll be out on the ranch with my tracker," he told Kati. "But if Al isn't home by dark, you'll stay in the house with us, Barbara."

"Yes, Egan," Barbara nodded numbly.

Kati left her long enough to walk out onto the front porch with Egan.

"Keep her as quiet as you can," he said. "If you need help, get Dessie."

"I will," she promised. She looked up at him, quietly searching the craggy lines of his face, loving him so deeply that she'd have followed him barefoot through the snow.

He glanced down at her, and the darkness grew in his eyes as they held hers.

"The wolf," she said uneasily. "You won't take chances?"

He moved close, framing her worried face in his hands, and stared down into her eyes for a long moment. "I never take chances, as a rule," he said. "Of course, I blotted my book with you."

"I don't understand."

"What would you call trying to seduce a virgin on a bearskin rug?" he asked dryly.

She flushed and he laughed.

"I lost my head that night," he told her. "I could have broken your young neck when you told me the truth."

"Yes, I know, and your temper hasn't improved since," she said miserably. "I shouldn't have said anything, I guess."

"I'd have blown my brains out afterward if you hadn't," he said. "Kati, I wasn't in any condition for initiation, ceremonies. You had me so worked up, I didn't know my name. That's why it took me so long to get over it."

"Oh," she murmured, studying him. He didn't look so formidable now. He looked...odd.

"I can't get too close to you, baby, don't you know? I don't want you any less right now than I did the first time I kissed you," he breathed, bending to her mouth. "But I could seduce you now without even trying. And that wouldn't be a good thing."

"It wouldn't?" she whispered, watching his mouth brush and probe gently at hers in the cold air.

"Don't they say," he whispered back, "that good girls almost always get pregnant that first time?"

"Egan...!" she moaned as his mouth found hers.

He lifted her against him and kissed her roughly, his mouth cool and hard and sure as it moved over hers. His gloved hand caught at her nape and brought her face closer; and she heard a deep, rumbling sound echoing out of his chest.

"We've got to stop this," he ground out as his mouth slid across her cheek, and he wrapped her up tightly in his arms. "It's just a matter of time before I go off the deep end if we don't. I could eat you!"

"Yes, I know," she whispered achingly. "I feel the same way."

He rocked her slowly in his arms while the wind whistled around the house and snow blew past them. "I have to go, Kati."

Her arms tightened. "Be careful. Please be careful."

He was breathing heavily, and his eyes when he lifted his head were silvery and wild. "I used to be," he said enigmatically. He let her go and tugged at a lock of her hair with rough affection. "See you, city girl."

She nodded with a weak smile. "So long, cowboy."

She turned and went back into the house before he could see the worried tears in her eyes.

"Would you like some coffee?" she asked Barbara with perfect poise. "If you'll show me where you keep everything, I'll even make it."

Barbara dabbed at her eyes and smiled. "Of course. Thank you for staying with me."

"I'm glad to do what I can for you," Kati replied. "Come on. Your man will be all right. You have to believe that."

"I'm trying to," the young girl replied. She glanced at Kati as they went into the kitchen. "Is Egan your man?"

Kati flushed. "No," she managed. "No, he's my best friend's brother. He's helping me with some research on a book I'm writing."

"You write books?"

"Yes. Those big historical things," Kati offered.

"It must be lots of fun." She got down cups. "I wanted to be a singer, but I married Al instead. We've been together two years now." She stared out the window at the thickening snow. "I love him so much. And we've been so excited about this baby."

"What do you want?" Kati asked, seeing an opening. "A boy or a girl?"

"Oh, a boy," Barbara said. "I've been knitting blue booties and hats. He'll be all right, won't he?"

"Egan said he would, didn't he?" Kati hedged.

Barbara smiled wanly. "I guess so. Egan's never lied."

Kati nodded, but her own mind was on that killer wolf and Egan out hunting it. An animal that would savage cattle three or four times its size would think nothing of attacking a man. She closed her eyes to the possibility. She couldn't bear thinking about it.

Two hours went by before the phone rang, and Kati answered it herself.

"Barbara?" came Ramey's voice.

"No, Ramey, it's Kati. How is Al?" she asked quickly.

"Madder than a skinned snake," Ramey chuckled. "He wants Egan to give him that bull for steaks."

"He's all right!" Kati told Barbara, laughing; and Barbara sat down heavily with a tired sigh.

"The boss might do it, too," Ramey laughed, "despite how much he paid for him. They're going to keep Al overnight, but he wants Barbara with him. Pack her a bag, will you? They're going to put a bed in the room for her.''

''I sure will. Are you coming after her?''

''Guess I'll have to. Boss is still out with Charlie.''

That was a worrying thought. ''Will it take them long to find the wolf, do you think?'' she asked hesitantly.

''Anybody's guess, Miss James. See you.''

''Bye.''

She hung up the phone with numb fingers. ''Al wants you to spend the night with him at the hospital. They've even fixed you a bed,'' she said cheerfully. ''He's going to be fine, but Ramey said they want to keep him overnight.''

''Oh, thank God, thank God!'' Barbara whispered. She took a minute to pull herself together before she became practical. ''I'll pack my bag right now. Oh, my poor Al!''

Kati helped her get ready, knowing how she might feel in the same circumstances. And Egan was out tracking that wolf right now. What if something happened to him? How would she manage?

Ramey came and dropped Kati by the house on the way to depositing Barbara at the hospital. Kati waved them off and rushed to find Dessie.

''Is Egan back?'' she asked the housekeeper.

Dessie shook her head. ''It may take all night. Or longer,'' she told the obviously worried younger woman. ''Kati, he's a rancher. This isn't the first time he's had to go tracking a predator; I doubt if it will be the last. It's something you get used to. Back in the old days," she added with a faint smile, "it was rustlers they chased. And they shot back."

"In other words, the wolf is the lesser of a lot of evils." Kati sighed. "Well..." She stuck her hands in the pockets of her jeans. "I guess I'll go work on my book."

"You do that. I'll straighten up the kitchen. Will you be all right by yourself? You won't get scared if I go on to bed?"

"Of course not." She was used to Dessie's early hours by now. "I'll just curl up in a chair and watch TV while I jot down a few notes. Today has been an education."

"I don't doubt it. Sleep well. Barbara doing okay, was she?"

"Yes. Just worried, and that's natural. But she handled it well."

"She's a cowboy's wife," Dessie replied. "Of course she did."

Kati nodded. She was beginning to understand what that meant. She wandered into the living room and watched television until bedtime. Still, Egan hadn't come back.

She paced and watched the clock and listened for the sound of a vehicle. But it didn't come. She thought about going up to bed, but knew she wouldn't sleep. So she curled up on the sofa to watch a late-night talk show. Somewhere in the middle of a starlet's enthusiasm for designer clothes, she fell asleep.

The dreams were delicious. Someone was holding her, very close; she could feel his breath at her ear, whispering words she couldn't quite hear. She smiled and snuggled close, clinging to a hard neck.

"Did you hear me?"

The sound of Egan's voice brought her awake. Her eyes opened heavily, and she blinked as she saw him above her.

"What time is it?" she asked sleepily.

"Six o'clock in the morning," he said, studying her. He was standing and she was locked close in his arms. She looked around and realized that they were in her bedroom. He'd carried her all the way from the living room and she hadn't known....

"I meant to go to bed," she protested.

"Yes, I imagine you did."

Her eyes searched his drawn face: the growth of beard on his cheeks and chin; the weariness that lay on him like a net. "Did you get the wolf?" she asked softly.

"Yes, honey, we got him." He bent to lay her on the bed and looked straight into her eyes. "Were you waiting up for me, Katriane?"

"No, I was watching television," she protested quickly.

He sat down beside her on the bed, still in his sheepskin coat and the wide-brimmed old hat he wore. He put his fingers over her mouth; they were cold from the outdoors, and he smelled of the wind and fir trees.

"I said," he repeated softly, "were you waiting up for me?"

"Well, you said the stupid creature would attack people, didn't you?"

"I didn't think you'd mind too much if he took a

plug out of me,'' he murmured, studying her sleepy face.

''Isn't that the other way around?'' she muttered. ''You're the one with all the grudges, not me.''

''I wanted you, damn it!'' he burst out, glaring at her, and all the controlled anger was spilling out of him. ''Wanted you, you naive little idiot! You write about it with a gift, but do you understand what it's like? Men hurt like hell when they get as hot as you got me that night!''

She dropped her eyes to his chest. ''I wasn't going to say no,'' she managed curtly.

''But you knew I would,'' he returned. ''You knew I'd never take you to bed once I had learned the truth. It's not my way.''

''I wasn't thinking,'' she muttered.

''Neither was I. I brought you home thinking I could have you. You knew it. Then, just when I'm involved to the back teeth and aching like a boy of fourteen, you turn it off. Just like that.''

She couldn't bear the accusation in his deep voice, the anger. Her eyes closed and her fingers clenched by her side.

''And the worst part,'' he continued, with barely leashed fury in his tone, ''is that I think you did it deliberately, despite that lame excuse you gave about not wanting me to hurt you. I think you set me up, Kati, to get even.''

That hurt more than all the other accusations put together. It made tears burn her eyes. ''What an opinion you have of me,'' she whispered shakily, trying to force a smile to her lips. ''First you think I'm a tramp, and then you try to seduce me, and now you think I'm a cheat besides.''

"Don't try to throw it back on my head!" he growled.

"Why not?" She sat up, glaring. "Why not? You were the one who kept putting on the pressure, weren't you? And every time I tried to explain, you shut me up!"

"You knew why I invited you," he shot back. "For God's sake, what did you come out here expecting, a proposal of marriage!"

That was so close to the truth that it took all her control not to let him see it. "Of course not," she replied instead, as coolly as she could. "I expected to be allowed to research my book. And you told me," she added levelly, "that there were no strings attached. Didn't you?"

He sighed angrily but he didn't deny it. His eyes searched over her flushed, angry face, her narrowed eyes. "I guess I did."

Her breasts rose and fell softly, and she looked down at her hands. "As soon as the snow melts a little, I'll leave. I'll need some more data on Wyoming history and a few other related subjects, but I can get that in Cheyenne."

"Writing is all that matters to you, isn't it?" he asked coldly.

She met his eyes. "Egan, what else do I have?"

His heavy brows drew together. "You're young."

"I'll see my twenty-sixth summer this year," she replied. "And all I have to show for my life is a few volumes of historical fiction in the 'J' section of the library. No family. No children. No nothing."

"I'm almost thirty-five and in the same predicament, and I don't give a damn," he told her.

She studied his hard face. "I'm not even surprised. You don't need anyone."

"I do need the occasional woman," he replied.

"I'm sorry, but I don't do occasionals," she told him. "I'm the forever-after type, and if you'd really read any of my books, you'd have known it before you ruined everything."

"I ruined everything?" He glared at her thunderously. "You couldn't get your clothes off fast enough!"

"Oh!" Shamed to the bones, she felt the tears come, and she hated her own weakness. She tried to get up, but he caught her, his hands steely on her upper arms.

"I didn't mean to say that," he ground out. "Damn you, Kati, you bring out everything mean and ornery in my soul!"

"Then it's a good thing I'm leaving before you just rot away, isn't it?" she said, weeping.

He drew in a deep, slow breath. "Oh baby," he breathed, drawing her close against him under the unbuttoned sheepskin coat. "Baby, I don't want to hurt you."

His voice was oddly tender, although she barely heard the words through her sobs. She'd hardly cried in her life until Egan came along.

His arms enclosed her warmly and she felt his cold, rough cheek against hers as he held her. "You've had a hard time of it, haven't you? I wouldn't have asked you to stay with Barbara, but I needed Dessie more to get Al patched.''

''I didn't mind, truly I didn't. She was so brave.''

''She's had to be. Living out here isn't easy on a woman. It's still hard country, and winters can be terrifying. Spring comes and there's flooding. Summer may bring a drought. A man can lose everything overnight out here.'' He stroked her hair absently. ''It was even harder on Barbara. She was a California girl.''

''She loves him, Egan.''

He laughed shortly, the sound echoing heavily in the dark room. ''And love is enough?''

''You make it sound sordid,'' she murmured at his ear, stirring slightly.

''Well, women set great store by it, I suppose,'' he said quietly. ''I never did. What passed for love in my life was bought and paid for.''

She flinched at the cynicism and drew back to look at him. This close, she could see every line in that craggy face. It held her eyes like a magnet, from the kindling silver eyes to the square chin that badly needed a razor.

''Haven't you ever loved anyone?'' she asked gently.

''My mother. Ada.''

''A lover,'' she persisted, searching his eyes.

''No, Katriane,'' he told her somberly. ''The few times I tried, I found out pretty quick that it was the money they wanted, not me. What was it you called me that last time we got into it—a big, ugly cowboy?''

"I meant it, too," she said, not backing down. "But what I was talking about had nothing to do with looks. No, Egan, you aren't at all handsome. But you're all man, so what difference does it make?"

He stared at her, and she flushed, averting her eyes. She hadn't meant to let that slip out.

His fingers toyed with her hair and worked their way under her chin to lift it. He was closer than she'd expected—so close that all she could see was his nose and mouth.

"It's been…a long time since anyone waited up for me. Or worried over me," he said huskily. His breath came heavily. "Kati, you'd better not let me have your mouth."

But she wanted it. Ached for it. And her eyes told him so. He caught his breath at the blatant hunger in them.

"I'll hurt you," he ground out.

"I don't even care…!" She reached up, opening her arms and her heart, and dragged his open, burning mouth down onto hers.

He was rough. Not only in the crushing hold he had on her slender body, but the bristly pressure of his face and the ardent hunger of his mouth. His fingers tangled in her long hair and twirled it around and around, arching her neck.

His lips lifted, poised over hers, and he was breathing as raggedly as she was. "Open your mouth a little more," he said shakily. "Let me show you how I like to be kissed."

Her eyes opened so that she could look into his, and his hands clasped the back of her head as he ground his mouth into hers again, feeling it open and tremble and want his.

"Kati," he breathed as he half lifted her against him, while the kiss became something out of her experience. "God, Kati, it's so sweet...!"

She clung to him, giving back the ardent pressure until he groaned and his rough cheek slid against hers and he held her, breathing in shudders at her ear.

"Stop letting me do that," he ground out, tightening his arms. "It only makes things worse!"

"Yes," she whispered shakily. Her face nuzzled against his, her eyes closed, her body aching for something it had never had.

She began to realize what was happening to him, and it was her fault. She sat perfectly still in his arms and let him hold her until his breathing was steady, until the slight tremor went out of his arms.

"I'm sorry," she whispered.

"Yes, I know, but it doesn't help," he murmured.

"Well, don't put all the blame on me!" she sobbed, trying to push him away.

"I'm not trying to. Stop fighting me."

"Stop making horrible remarks."

He laughed. Laughed! He rubbed his face against hers affectionately; it felt like a pincushion. He lifted his head, and his eyes were blazing with laughter and something much harder to identify. He looked down at her, searching her eyes, her face, and looking so utterly smug that she wanted to hit him.

"You are something else," he said, and she remembered the words from the night he'd made love to her by the fire. She blushed scarlet, and he lifted an eyebrow. "Remembering, are you?" His eyes went down to her blouse and stayed there. "I'll never forget."

Her eyes closed because she couldn't bear the heat of his gaze. "Neither will I. I never meant—"

"Don't," he whispered, bringing her close again. "We made magic that night. I had this opinion of you, you see. For a long time. Kati, I wasn't telling the truth when I said I'd read your books, I'd only read a passage or two. Just enough to support my negative assessment of your character." He lifted his head and looked down at her. "Night before last, I read one. Really read it. There are some pretty noticeable gaps in those love scenes." He searched her eyes. "But some pretty powerful emotions in them, all the same. They were beautiful."

Her eyes burned with tears. "Thank you."

He touched her cheek softly. "I'd like very much to make love with you that way, Kati," he whispered. "I'd like to lie with you on a deserted beach in the moonlight and watch your body move, the way that pirate did in your last book...."

"Don't," she pleaded, burying her face in his shirt. She didn't feel at all like the very cool author who spoke to writers' clubs with such poise. She felt...young.

"So shy with me," he whispered, lifting her across his lap. "And I was the first, wasn't I? The first man to look at you, to touch you, to be intimate with you. My God, I ache just thinking about it, when it never mattered a damn before how many men I'd followed with a woman." His hands smoothed over her back gently while his face nuzzled hers. "I'm like a boy with you, Kati. When we share those deep, hot kisses, I shake all over.''

Her fingers made patterns on his shirt, and she loved the bigness and warmth of his body so close to hers. But he was admitting to nothing except desire. And she wanted much, much more.

"We'd better go and eat, I suppose," he murmured. "And I need a shave and a bath." He lifted his head and studied her pink cheek where his had scraped it, and he smiled slowly. "If we made love and I hadn't shaved, you'd look like that all over," he commented.

It brought to mind pictures that made her ache, and she couldn't get away from him quickly enough.

"There's just one thing," he added, watching her with a lazy smile. "If I ever turn up in one of those damned books, you're in trouble."

"I don't write about real people," she defended, and prayed that he'd never see the first few chapters of her new book before she had time to turn the hero back into a blond.

"You'd better not," he said; and although his voice was pleasant, there was a hard glint in his eyes. "What we do together when we make love is private. For the two of us alone."

She frowned. "You can't believe I'd do that!"

He searched her eyes slowly. "I'm not a writer. Explain it to me."

"It would take hours," she told him.

"I'm not leaving for the rest of the day," he told her. "Let me get my bath and shave. I'll meet you downstairs. You can ask me anything else you need to know about the ranch while we're at it."

The prospect of spending a day alone with him was heady and sweet. "All right," she said.

He winked and went out the door, already a different man. For the rest of the day, they talked as never before. He told her about the early days of the ranch and how his grandfather came by it. He told her about his own plans for it; his dreams; the career he once thought he wanted in politics. In return, she explained to him how she felt her characters come alive on paper and take over the actual writing of the book, right down to the love scenes. She explained how she researched the historical facts and how she'd learned to grit her teeth and smile when people asked where she had learned so much about intimacy when she was unmarried and apparently living alone.

"You see, it's just that you can't write fiction without a little romance." She sighed. "And these days, the more sensuous the better. I won't go the whole hog and write explicit scenes, but the sexiest books are the biggest sellers. I must be pretty accurate, though, because my reader mail is mostly kind."

He shook his head, sitting quietly by the crackling fireplace, watching her. "A virgin. Writing what you write. My God."

"Well, most fiction about scientists isn't written by scientists. Most fiction about lawyers isn't written by lawyers. It's just a matter of research, like anything else," she added.

"You do it very—"

The telephone interrupted him. Expecting news about Al, he sprang to his feet to answer.

"Hello?" His face changed. "Yes, how are you, Jennie?"

Kati felt her body go rigid. That woman! So they did have something going, even after he'd left New York.

"Yes, I know." He toyed with a pen-set on the desk. "Umm-hmm. Yes, we did, didn't we?" He smiled. "Here? No, I don't think that's a good idea, honey. We're snowed in. That's right, about five feet of it. No, we've closed the landing strip. You'd have to fly in to Jackson. Maybe. Tell you what, let's put it off until spring. Yes, I know you don't, but that's how it is, Jennie. No strings, remember? I told you at the very beginning how it was going to be. That's right. Sure. Next time I'm in town. So long." He hung up and turned, watching the expressions cross Kati's face.

"She wanted to stop over for a week or two on her way to California for a screen test," he volunteered. "I said no. Anything else you'd like to know?"

"She...was very pretty," Kati muttered.

"Surely she was. And experienced," he added deliberately. "But she wanted ties and I didn't."

"Freedom is your big problem, isn't it?" she asked on a laugh. "Well, don't look at me as if I had a rope in one hand—I don't want strings any more than you do," she lied, and looked away just in time to miss the expression that froze his face.

"I thought all you women wanted marriage," he said in an odd voice.

"Not now I don't," she returned as casually as she could. "I'm too involved in work."

"Going to remain a virgin for life, I gather?" he asked cuttingly. "Give up a home and children so you can keep writing those damned books?"

She looked up with a deliberate smile, in spite of the glittering anger in his eyes. "I like writing those damned books."

He turned away. "So I noticed. Don't let me hold you up, you probably have a lot of work to get through if you're leaving by the end of the week."

And he walked out of the room, leaving her speechless. Well, what had he expected her to say, she wondered achingly—that she loved him? That she'd lie on the floor and let him walk on her if she could stay with him?

Fat chance! If he could brush Jennie off so easily, when he'd obviously had an affair with her, what chance did she have? Probably he was just biding his time until he could get her into his bed. He knew she'd surrender, she thought miserably, he knew very well that she couldn't resist him. And once she'd given in, he'd be letting her down easily, just the way he'd done Jennie. And he'd be in pursuit of some new woman. With a tiny moan, she went upstairs and opened the case that held her computer. What a miserable end for a wonderful day!

Chapter 11

It wasn't hard to avoid Egan after that. He wasn't home. He worked from dawn until late at night and appeared only briefly to eat. He treated Kati with grudging courtesy, but he didn't come near her.

She packed Friday morning to go back to New York. The snow was melting again, and the skies were sunny and clear. Perhaps, she told herself, it was an omen.

"I sure am going to miss you," Dessie said gruffly as she had breakfast with Kati and Egan. "Been nice, having another woman around the place."

"I'll miss you, too," Kati said genuinely as she finished her eggs and drank her coffee. "I've learned a lot while I was here."

"I reckon Gig's talked more in the past week than he has since I've known him," Egan said mockingly. He leaned back precariously in his cane-bottom chair to study her as he smoked a cigarette. He seemed to smoke all the time these days. "Have you satisfied your curiosity about ranch life, Miss Author?" he added.

"Yes," she said, refusing to let him irritate her. "And about the cattle business. Thank you for letting me come."

"My pleasure. Any time." He swallowed the rest of his coffee and got to his feet. "Ramey's going to drive you to the airport."

"Ramey?" Dessie burst out. "But Egan, you never let Ramey— "

"Just never mind, if you please," he told the old woman, a bite in his voice. He glanced at Kati hard, and his eyes accused.

"I'll clear this stuff away," Dessie murmured quickly and retreated into the kitchen with two empty platters.

"Have a safe trip home," he told Kati quietly. "And give Ada my love."

"I'll do that," she said stiffly.

He started to pass by her, paused, and suddenly jerked her out of the chair by her arms, hurting her as he dragged her against his chest.

"Damn you," he breathed furiously, with silver eyes that glittered dangerously. "Do you think your career is going to keep you warm at night? Will it give you what I did on that bearskin rug by the fireplace?" he demanded.

Her body melted against his and she wished she had the strength to hit him, but she was drowning in his eyes and the feel of his taut, powerful body.

"What are you offering me?" she asked. "A night in your bed?"

His hands tightened on her arms and he looked hunted. "I don't want you to leave," he said gruffly. "We'll work it out somehow."

"How?" she persisted. "Egan, I'm not like Jennie. I can't take an open affair."

"What do you want, then?" he asked under his breath, watching her. "Marriage?"

She searched his angry eyes defeatedly. "You'd hate me for that," she said with quiet perception.

"I don't know," he replied. "We might get used to each other; make a go of it."

She reached up, touching his face softly with her fingertips. "You'd better stick to girls like Jennie," she said softly. "I couldn't settle for what you'd be able to give me. I couldn't live on crumbs."

"I'm a rich man," he said curtly. "You could have anything you wanted, within reason. And in bed, I'd be everything you'd ever need."

"I know that," she agreed. Her fingers traced his hard mouth, feeling its automatic response with wonder. "But it's still not enough."

"Why not, for God's sake?" he growled, catching her wandering fingers roughly in his own.

"Because I'm in love with you, Egan," she said proudly, watching the reaction flare in his eyes, harden his face. "You can't match that with money or sex. I'd wither away and die of neglect and pity. No, I'd rather be totally alone than on my knees at your heart."

His lips parted and he couldn't seem to find the right

words. He touched her hair hesitantly. "You love me?" he whispered huskily, frowning as if he found the words incomprehensible.

"Occupational hazard," she whispered, trying not to cry. "I'll get over it. Good-bye, Egan."

His fingers tightened in her hair. "No, not yet," he said uncertainly. "Not just yet. You don't have to go right now—"

"Yes, I do," she said, on the verge of tears. "I'm running out of pride—" Her voice broke, and she tried to get away, but his arms tightened like a vice and he held her despite her struggles.

"Don't," he whispered, shaken. "Don't fight me. My God, Kati, don't run."

"Egan," she moaned.

"Egan!" Dessie called sharply from the kitchen. "It's the hospital on the phone! Something about Al— Can you come?"

He cursed under his breath, looking down at the tears on Kati's cheeks with eyes that frightened her. "Don't move," he said shortly. "Not one step. You hear me?"

She nodded, but the minute he was out of sight, she grabbed up her bag and made a run for the front door. She couldn't face him again, not after the fool she'd made of herself. If she couldn't have his love, she didn't want his pity. She couldn't bear it!

As luck would have it, Ramey was just getting out of the pickup truck. She dived in on the passenger side.

"Ramey, can you get me to the airport in Jackson

in a hurry?'' she asked quickly. ''There's an emergency—I have to leave!''

''Emergency?'' Ramey jumped back in and started
the truck. ''Why sure, Miss James. Don't you worry,
I'll get you there!''

He turned the truck, and Kati reached down and
very unobtrusively cut off the two-way radio.

''That noise is just awful,'' she murmured, ''and I
have such a headache. Can't we leave it off just until
we get to town?'' she asked with a pitiful smile.

He hesitated, then he grinned. ''Sure. I don't reckon
we'll need it.''

''Good!'' And then she began to talk furiously to
keep his mind occupied. It didn't hurt her, either, to
stop thinking about Egan and the look on his face
when she'd confessed. She didn't know if she'd be
able to hear his name again without going mad.

It seemed to take forever, and despite the four-wheel
drive and snow tires, they almost bogged down a few
times. But Ramey got her to the airport. It wasn't until
she was getting out that she realized she'd left her
computer at the ranch.

''I'll tell the Boss,'' Ramey assured her. ''He'll get
it to you.''

That wasn't a comforting thought; the Boss would
be out for blood. But she smiled anyway. ''Thanks.''
She'd just do those chapters over on her stationary
computer at the apartment, she assured herself; she
could remember most of them.

''Have a good trip!'' Ramey called and was off with
a wave of his hand.

There was a seat on an outgoing plane to Cheyenne.

She'd hole up there for a few days, letting only Ada know where she was. She wasn't strong enough to resist Egan, so she wasn't going to try.

She kept watching the door, although she couldn't help wondering why. Egan wouldn't come after her. Besides, she thought, he'd never make it through the snow anyway.

She checked her bag, went aboard with only her purse, and sat down heavily in her seat. It was over. She was leaving. Now all she had to do was get her mind off Egan and find some way of not thinking about him for the rest of her life. Facing Ada was going to be hard. Living with her would be sheer torture. She knew she'd die every time Ada mentioned her brother.

The plane was running now, and she knew it wouldn't be long until takeoff. She was just starting to fasten her seat belt when she heard a commotion in the back of the plane.

A sheepskin coat came suddenly into view, with a hard, furious face above it.

While she was getting over the shock, Egan reached down, unfastened her seat belt and scooped her up in his hard arms, purse and all.

"You can't do this!" she burst out, oblivious to the amused eyes of the other passengers.

"Like hell I can't," he replied curtly and carried her off the plane.

"Oh Egan, let me go!" she wailed as he walked back toward the terminal, burying her embarrassed face in his warm collar.

"I can't," he whispered huskily, and his arms tightened around her.

Tears rolled down her cheeks. He wanted her, that was all, but she didn't have the strength to walk away again, even if he'd let her. So she lay in his arms, crying softly, and let him carry her all the way to his pickup truck.

He put her in and got in beside her, picking up the radio mike as he started the truck. He gave his call letters and told somebody he was on his way back with Kati and signed off.

"My bag," she began.

"I hope it has a nice trip," he said curtly, glaring at her as he pulled out into the road. "I told you to stay put."

"I couldn't," she muttered miserably, staring into her lap. "I was too embarrassed."

"Best-selling author," he scoffed, glaring toward her. "The sensual mistress of the ages. And you can't tell a man you love him without blushing all over?"

"I've never done it before!" she burst out, glaring back at him.

His silver eyes gleamed. "You're doing a lot of firsts with me, aren't you, city girl? And the biggest and best is still to come."

"I won't sleep with you, Egan," she said angrily.

"Won't you?" He lit a cigarette and smoked it with a smile so arrogant she wanted to hit him.

"I want to go home!"

"You are home, honey," he replied. "Because that's what White Lodge is going to be from now on."

"Do be reasonable," she pleaded, turning toward

him. "You're asking me to give up everything I believe in!"

"That's where you're wrong, Kati. I'm not asking."

"I'll scream," she threatened.

He gave her a wicked smile. "Yes, you probably will," he murmured softly.

"Oh, damn," she wailed.

"Now just calm down, honey," he told her. "When we get back to the ranch, I'll explain it all to you. Right now, you'd better let me keep my mind on the road. I don't want to spend the rest of the day sitting in a ditch."

She sighed. "How's Al?" she asked dully, remembering the phone call.

"On his way home. He called to get one of the boys to drive him. Now hush."

She folded her arms across her chest, feeling miserable and cold and helpless. He was taking the choice away from her, and she didn't know what to do. Didn't he realize what he was forcing on her? She wouldn't be able to go on living afterward, because the memory of him would burn into her like a brand and she'd never be free again. How could he be so cruel?

It seemed to take much less time getting back to White Lodge than it had leaving it. Egan pulled up at the steps and cut off the engine.

"I won't go in," she muttered.

"I figured you were going to be unpleasant about it," he said on a sigh. He got out, lifted her from the cab of the truck and carried her into the house.

"Dessie, take the phone off the hook," he told the

amused housekeeper. "I've got a lot of explaining to do, and I don't want to be interrupted."

"Just keep in mind I'll be out here with my frying pan," Dessie told him, winking at Kati. "And keeping the coffee hot."

He laughed under his breath, carrying Kati into his study. He slammed the door behind him and put her down so that he could lock it.

She retreated to the fireplace, where a fire was crackling merrily, and glanced down at the bearskin rug. She quickly moved away, and Egan watched her as he took off his hat and coat, his eyes sparkling with amusement.

"It wasn't that bad, was it?" he asked, nodding toward the rug. "I thought you enjoyed what I did to you on that."

"Don't you have work to do?" she asked, moving behind his desk.

"Afraid of me, Kati?" he asked softly, moving toward her.

He looked devastating. All lean grace and muscle. His dark hair was mussed, and his eyes were sensual.

"Egan, let me go to New York," she said unsteadily, backing up until the wall stopped her.

He moved toward her relentlessly, until she was trapped between the hard wall and his taut body. He put his hands deliberately beside her head, the way he had in the kitchen that morning, and she trembled with the hunger to feel that hard body crushing down on hers.

"Now we talk," he said softly, watching the emotions play on her face. "You told me you loved me. How? Is it just a physical thing, or is it more?"

Her lips parted on a rush of breath and her body ached for him. He poised there, taunting her; and, involuntarily, she moved against the wall.

"Tell me," he whispered, "and I'll do what you want me to do."

She swallowed, so weak with love that she couldn't even protest that arrogance. "I love you in every way there is," she told him. "Every single way."

"I've got a nasty temper," he reminded her quietly. "I like my own way. And I've lived alone for a long time. It won't be easy. There are going to be times when you'll wish I hadn't carried you off that plane."

Her body felt like jelly as she looked up at him. "I love you," she whispered. "I love you!"

He eased down over her, letting her feel the full, devastating effect the words had on him, and he smiled at the mingled hunger and embarrassment in her face.

"I'll want a son," he murmured, watching the effect of that soft statement. "Maybe three or four of them."

She smiled slowly, wonderingly. "I'd like that, too," she said, trembling as she realized what he was saying.

"No big wedding, though," he added under his breath as his body began to move slowly, sensuously, against hers. "Just the minister and some of the boys and Ada."

"Yes," she whispered, lifting her mouth, pleading for his.

"And if a word of what I'm about to do to you gets

into print," he threatened with his mouth poised just above hers, "I'll chase you to Jackson with the truck."

"Yes, darling," she whispered back, standing on tiptoe to reach his open mouth with hers. "Egan, what are you going to do to me?"

"Come here and I'll tell you," he murmured on a soft laugh.

She felt his fingers taking away the sweater and opening the blouse, but she was too busy unbuttoning his shirt to care. Seconds later, hard, hair-roughened muscle pressed against soft, bare breasts; and she moaned, lifting her arms around his neck as she moved hungrily under him.

"Not here," he groaned. He lifted her and carried her to the rug, easing her down onto it.

"You can't imagine," she managed shakily as he lifted himself over her trembling body, "how many books I've read this scene in."

"You can't imagine," he countered, "how different this is going to be from reading." His hands slid under her, lifting her to the hard pressure of his hips, and he watched her with glittering silver eyes as she cried out. "You see?" he whispered unsteadily. "Kati, I'm drowning in you. Drowning in the feel of you, the taste of you."

He bent, and she gave him her mouth totally, moving instinctively under the weight of his taut body, loving the heaviness and hunger that was crushing her in pleasure.

"Like this," he whispered, guiding, and she felt him in a new and shocking way, and her eyes flew open incredulously.

His face, above hers, was hard with desire, his eyes glittering with triumph as he saw her pleasure in her eyes. "Now," he breathed, and his hands went under her thighs. "Now, just do what I tell you."

She felt his mouth on hers through a fog of incredible hunger, and somewhere in the middle of it, she began to cry. It was the sweetest maelstrom in the world. She felt the rough silk of his skin under her hands, and she touched him in ways she'd never dreamed of touching a man. Her legs tangled with his while he taught her sensations that shocked and burned and stung with pleasure.

"Please, Egan," she whispered into his ear, gasping as he lifted her hips closer. "Please, please!"

"I want you just as much," he whispered back. "But we're not going all the way."

"Egan!" she groaned.

"Trust me, Kati," he whispered. "Give me your mouth, and lie still."

She did, and somewhere in the back of her mind she felt as if she were dying as his body stilled on hers and his mouth began to lose its obsession with hers. He stroked her and whispered to her, and she cried helplessly as the urgency began to recede, to calm into a pleasant exhaustion.

"You and I," he whispered, "are going to burn up when we make love for the first time. I've never felt in my life what I feel when you put your hands on me."

She smoothed his dark hair with fingers that still trembled, and nuzzled against the hair over his hard chest. "Will it be enough?"

His lips brushed over her closed eyelids. "Look at me, little virgin," he whispered. "I want to watch your eyes when I say it."

Her heavy eyelids lifted and she saw his eyes burn like sunlight.

"I love you, Kati," he whispered softly. "I loved you the night you came walking home with my cousin, and I was so eaten up with jealousy that I ate you alive. I've loved you every day since and fought it with everything in me."

Her lips parted but she couldn't speak. Oh God, it was like having every dream of love she'd ever dreamed come true all at once!

"I thought you were having a fling," he said tightly. "Until the night we lay here together and you told me the truth. And I wanted to go through the floor, because I'd misread the whole situation, and I'd said things to you that still make me uneasy." He brushed the hair away from her cheeks and let his gaze drift down to her soft bareness. His jaw clenched and he dragged his eyes back up to hers, while his fingers stroked over skin no man had touched before. "Then you said you didn't want ties, and I realized that I did. I wanted my ring on your finger, for all time. But you were leaving. And I couldn't find the right words." He sighed heavily. "I was trying to, when you told me you loved me."

"I thought I'd embarrassed you," she said softly.

"You'd given me the moon, Kati," he replied, watching her. "The moon, the sun, the stars—I was speechless, just savoring the feel of it, the sound. And then Al called, and you got away. I'd have gone down on my knees to you…!''

"Egan," she breathed, drawing him close with possessive arms, clinging passionately to him. "Egan, it tore me apart to go! But I was afraid you'd pity me."

"I pitied myself for being so damned stupid—for ever letting you out of my sight. It will be the last time, too. As soon as I get a license, we're getting married. Tomorrow, if possible."

"But, I don't have a dress!"

"Get married in blue jeans, for all I care," he told her. "I just want to give you my name. My heart. My life."

Her eyes closed on a wave of pleasure. Tears welled up in them, at the magnificence of loving and being loved in return. She shuddered.

"Cold?" he whispered, concerned. "I'd forgotten how little we have on."

She did blush then, as he handed her her blouse and bra and watched her struggle to rearrange her jeans.

"Don't stare," she pleaded.

"I can't help it. You're so lovely," he said with a grin. He propped himself on an elbow, devastating without his shirt. "I guess we'll have to have at least one daughter to look like you." He caught her hand when she finished buttoning buttons and clasped it warmly to his hard, furry chest. "Can you live here with me and not miss the excitement of the city?"

"My darling," she said softly, "I carry my excitement around in my imagination, and I can work on the roof if I have to. There's a post office in Jackson.

I have you to keep me warm and love me. What else do I need?''

He smiled slowly. ''A good supply of sexy night-gowns,'' he murmured.

''Now, in that last book I wrote,'' she whispered, easing down beside him, ''the heroine had this very modest white gown...''

''Which the hero ripped off on page fifty-six,'' he chuckled softly. ''Yes, I know, but I like that scene in the bathtub. So, suppose tomorrow night you and I try it out?''

''I thought you were afraid of my research turning up in books,'' she laughed.

''Not since I've been reading them,'' he replied. ''Anyway, they're giving me some good ideas.''

She lifted her arms around his neck and pulled him down. ''Suppose we just work on this bearskin-rug scene a little more?'' she whispered at his lips. ''I don't think I've got it the way I want it just yet.''

''After we're married,'' he whispered back, his voice husky with emotion as he stared into her eyes, ''we'll lie here together and go all the way. I'll let you feel this rug under you while I lie over you and—''

''Egan,'' she groaned, trembling, hiding her face.

He laughed softly as he pressed her back into it. ''I can see that having a virgin for a wife is going to be educational,'' he mused.

''It's sort of the other way around right now, though,'' she reminded him. ''You're the one doing the teaching.''

''So I am.'' He rubbed his nose against hers. ''And

I'll tell you a secret, city girl. It's a hell of a lot more fun than fighting.''

She smiled. Indeed it was, she thought as his lips nuzzled against hers. She caressed his back lovingly, and she wondered if Ada was going to be surprised when they called her. Somehow, she didn't think so. She reached up and pulled Egan's head down to hers. Outside, the snow began to fall softly, again.

*   *   *   *   *

Watch for Cord Romero's scintillating story to unfold in July 2002 from MIRA Books

DESPERADO

by
international bestselling author

Diana Palmer

Going deep undercover to crack a merciless international child labor ring teams Maggie Barton up with her childhood-companion-turned-formidable-mercenary, Cord Romero. But the bitter taste of betrayal still hovers between the emotionally scarred couple, both afraid to risk their hearts despite the desire that sizzles when they are together. Now as they travel the globe to solve this treacherous case, they must confront their splintered pasts and walk a precarious tightrope between life...and death.

DESPERADO

Available in a special hardcover edition in July 2002 wherever MIRA books are sold.

Turn the page for a sneak preview....

Chapter One

The ranch outside Houston was big and sprawling. It was surrounded by neat white fences, which concealed electrical ones, to keep in the purebred Santa Gertrudis cattle that Cord Romero owned. There was also a bull, a special bull, which had been spared from a corrida in Spain by Cord's father—Mejias Romero, one of the most famous bullfighters in Spain—just before his untimely death in America. Once Cord grew up and had money of his own, he had traveled to his elderly cousin's ranch in Andalusia to get the bull and have it shipped to Texas. Cord called the old bull Hijito, little boy. The creature was still all muscle, although most of it was in his huge chest. He followed Cord around the ranch like a pet dog.

As Maggie Barton exited the cab with her suitcase, the big bull snorted and tossed his head on the other side of the fence. Maggie barely spared him a glance after she paid the driver. She'd come rushing home from Morocco in a tangle of missed planes, delays, cancellations and other obstacles that had caused her to be three days in transit. Cord, a professional mercenary and her foster brother, had been blinded. Most surprising, he'd asked for her through his friend Eb Scott. Maggie hadn't been able to get home fast enough. The delays had been agony. Perhaps, finally, Cord had realized that he cared for her...!

With her heart pounding, she pressed the doorbell on the spacious front porch with its green swing and glider and rocking chairs. There were pots of ferns and flowers everywhere.

Sharp, quick footsteps sounded on the bare wooden floors in the house and Maggie frowned as she pushed the long, wavy black hair out of her worried green eyes. Those steps didn't sound like Cord's. He had an elegance of movement in his stride that was long and effortless, masculine but gliding. This was a short, staccato step, more like a woman's. Her heart stopped. Did he have a girlfriend she didn't know about? Had she misinterpreted Eb Scott's phone call? Her confidence nose-dived.

The door opened and a slight blond woman with dark eyes looked up at her. "Yes?" she asked politely.

"I came to see Cord," Maggie blurted out. Jet lag was already setting in on her. She didn't even think to give her name.

"I'm sorry, he isn't seeing people just yet. He's been in an accident."

"I know that," Maggie said impatiently. She softened the words with a smile. "Tell him it's Maggie. Please."

The other woman, who must have been all of nineteen, grimaced. "He'll kill me if I let you in! He said he didn't want to see anybody. I'm really sorry...."

Jet lag and irritability combined to break the bonds of Maggie's temper. "Listen, I've just come over a thousand miles.... Oh, the hell with it! Cord?" she yelled past the girl, who grimaced again. "Cord!"

There was a pause, then a cold, short "Let her in, June!"

June stepped aside at once. Maggie was made uneasy by the harsh note in Cord's deep voice. She left her suitcase on the porch. June gave it a curious glance before she closed the door.

Cord was standing at the fireplace in the spacious living room. Just the sight of him fed Maggie's heart. He was tall and lean, powerfully built for all his slimness, a tiger of a man who feared nothing in this world. He made his living as a professional soldier, and he had few peers. His eyes were large, deep set, dark brown. His eyebrows were drawn into a scowl as Maggie walked in, and except for the red wounds around his eyes and cheeks, he actually looked normal. He looked as if he could see her. Ridiculous, of course. A bomb he'd tried to defuse had gone off right in his face. Eb said he was blind.

She stared at him. This man was the love of her life. There had never been anyone but him in her heart. She was amazed that he'd never noticed, in the eighteen years their lives had been connected. Even his brief tragic marriage hadn't altered those feelings.

Like him, she was widowed—but she didn't grieve for her husband the way he'd grieved for Patricia.

Her eyes fell helplessly to his wide, chiseled mouth. She remembered, oh, so well, the feel of it on hers in the darkness. It had been heaven to be held by him, kissed by him, after years of anguished longing. But very quickly the pleasure had become pain. Cord hadn't known she was innocent....

"How are you?" Maggie blurted out, hesitating just beyond the doorway, suddenly tongue-tied.

His square jaw seemed to tighten, but he smiled coldly. "A bomb exploded in my face four days ago. How the hell do you think I am?" he drawled sarcastically.

He was anything but welcoming. So much for fantasies. He didn't need her. He didn't want her around. It was just like old times. And she'd come running. What a joke.

"It amazes me that even a bomb could faze you," she remarked with her old self-possession. She even smiled. "Mr. Cold Steel repels bullets, bombs and especially, me!"

He didn't react. "Nice of you to stop by. And so promptly," he added.

She didn't understand the remark. He seemed to feel she'd procrastinated about visiting. "Eb Scott phoned and said you'd been hurt. He said..." She hesitated, uncertain whether or not to tell him everything Eb had said to her. She went for broke, but she laughed to camouflage her raw emotions. "He said you wanted me to come nurse you. Funny, huh?"

He didn't laugh. "Hilarious."

She felt the familiar whip of his sarcasm with pain she didn't try to hide. After all, he couldn't see it. "That's our Eb," she agreed. "A real kidder. I guess you have—what was her name?—June to take care of you," she added with forced lightness.

"That's right. I have June. She's been here since I got home." He emphasized the pronoun, for reasons of his own. He smiled deliberately. "June is all I need. She's sweet and kindhearted, and she really cares about me."

She forced a smile. "She's pretty, too."

He nodded. "Isn't she, though? Pretty, smart and a good cook. And she's blond," he added in a cold, soft voice that made chills run down her spine.

She didn't have to puzzle out the remark. He was partial to blondes. His late wife, Patricia, had been a blonde. He'd loved Patricia....

She rubbed her fingers over the strap of her shoulder bag and realized with a start how tired she was. Airport after airport, dragging her suitcase, agonizing over Cord's true state of health for three long days, just trying to get home to him—and he acted as if she'd muscled her way in. Perhaps she had. Eb should have told her the truth, that Cord still didn't want her in his life, even when he was injured.

She gave him a long, anguished look and moved one shoulder restlessly. "Well, that puts me in my place," she said pleasantly. "I'm sure not blond. Nice to see you're still on your feet. But I'm sorry about your eyes," she added.

"What about my eyes?" he asked curtly, scowling fiercely.

"Eb said you were blinded," she replied.

"Temporarily blinded," he corrected. "It's not a permanent condition. I can see fairly well now, and the ophthalmologist expects a complete recovery."

Her heart jumped. He could see? She realized then that he was watching her, not just staring into a void. It came as a shock. She hadn't been guarding her expressions. She felt uncomfortable, knowing he'd been able to glimpse the misery and worry on her face.

"No kidding? That's great news!" she said, and forced a convincing smile. She was getting the hang of this. Her face would be permanently gleeful, like a piece of fired sculpture. She could hire it out for celebrations. This wasn't one.

"Isn't it?" he agreed, but his returned smile wasn't pleasant at all.

She shifted the strap of her bag again, feeling weak at the knees and embarrassed by her headlong rush to his side. She'd given up her new job and come running home to take care of Cord. But he didn't need her, or want her here. Now she had no job, no place to live and only her savings to get her through the time until she could find employment. She never learned.

He was barely courteous, and his expression was hostile. "Thanks for coming. I'm sorry you have to leave so soon," he added. "I'll be glad to walk you to the door."

She lifted an eyebrow and gave him a sardonic look. "No need to give me the bum's rush," she said, falling back into her old habit of meeting sarcasm with sarcasm. "I got the message, loud and clear. I'm not welcome. Fine. I'll leave skid marks going out the door. You can have June scrub them later."

"Everything's a joke with you," he accused coldly.

"It beats crying," she replied pleasantly. "I need my head read for coming out here in the first place. I don't know why I bothered!"

"Neither do I," he agreed with soft venom. "A day late and a dollar short, at that."

That was enigmatic, but she was too angry to question his phrasing. "You don't have to belabor the point. I'm going," she assured him. "In fact, it's just a matter of another few interviews and I can arrange things so that you'll never have to see me again."

"That would be a real pleasure," he said with a bite in his deep voice. He was still glaring at her. "I'll give a party."

He was laying it on thick. It was as if he were furious with her, for some reason. Perhaps just her presence was enough to set him off. That was nothing new.

She only laughed. She'd had years to perfect her emotional camouflage. It was dangerous to give Cord an opening. He had no compunction about sticking the knife in. They were old adversaries.

"I won't expect an invitation," she told him complacently. "Ever thought of taking early retirement, while you still have a head that can be blown off?" she added.

He didn't answer. He just glared.

She shrugged and sighed. "I must be in demand somewhere," she told the room at large. "I'll have myself paged at the airport and find out."

She gave him one long, last look, certain that it

would be the last time her eyes would see that handsome face. There was some old saying about divine punishment in the form of showing paradise to a victim and then tossing him back into reality. It was like that with Maggie, having known the utter delight of Cord's lovemaking only once. Despite the pain and embarrassment, and his fury afterward, she'd never been able to forget the wonder of his mouth on her body for the first time. The rejection she felt now was almost palpable, and she had to hide it.

It wasn't easy...

Silhouette Books is proud to present:

Going to the Chapel

**Three brand-new stories
about getting that special man to the altar!**

featuring

USA Today bestselling author

SHARON SALA

*It Happened One Night...*that Georgia society belle
Harley June Beaumont went to Vegas—and woke up married!
How could she explain her hunk of a husband to
her family back home?

Award-winning author

DIXIE BROWNING

*Marrying a Millionaire...*was exactly what Grace McCall was
trying to keep her baby sister from doing. Not that Grace had
anything against the groom—it was the groom's arrogant
millionaire uncle who got Grace all hot and bothered!

National bestselling author

STELLA BAGWELL

*The Bride's Big Adventure...*was escaping her handpicked
fiancé in the arms of a hot-blooded cowboy! And from the
moment Gloria Rhodes said "I do" to her rugged groom, she
dreamed their wedded bliss would never end!

Available in July at your favorite retail outlets!

Where love comes alive™

Visit Silhouette at www.eHarlequin.com

PSGTCC

King Philippe has died, leaving no male heirs to ascend the throne. Until his mother announces that a son *may* exist, embarking everyone on a desperate search for... the missing heir.

Their quest begins March 2002 and continues through June 2002.

On sale March 2002, the emotional
OF ROYAL BLOOD
by Carolyn Zane (SR #1576)

On sale April 2002, the intense
IN PURSUIT OF A PRINCESS
by Donna Clayton (SR #1582)

On sale May 2002, the heartwarming
A PRINCESS IN WAITING
by Carol Grace (SR #1588)

On sale June 2002, the exhilarating
A PRINCE AT LAST!
by Cathie Linz (SR #1594)

Available at your favorite retail outlet.

MONTANA
Bred

From the bestselling series

MONTANA MAVERICKS

Wed in Whitehorn

Two more tales that capture living and loving
beneath the Big Sky.

JUST PRETENDING by Myrna Mackenzie

FBI Agent David Hannon's plans for a quiet vacation
were overturned by a murder investigation—and by
officer Gretchen Neal!

STORMING WHITEHORN by Christine Scott

Native American Storm Hunter's return to Whitehorn
sent tremors through the town—and shock waves of
desire through Jasmine Kincaid Monroe....

Silhouette®
Where love comes alive™

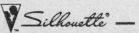